PRAISE FOR *TEN PERFECT GUESTS*

"Devilishly dry, dark, and deadly—this gripping mystery will keep you avidly turning the pages."

—Sophie Hannah

"Smart and amazing. A hallmark of Santlofer's writing is that the reader learns so much. Not to mention the drawings! All of which makes the novel something special."

—Joyce Carol Oates

"A beautiful blend of golden-age charm and modern-day edge—delightful from first word to last."

—Lee Child

PRAISE FOR *THE LOST VAN GOGH*

"A compelling story…a thriller! Fans of Dan Brown and Steve Berry will love it!"

—Harlan Coben, #1 *New York Times* bestselling author

"*The Lost Van Gogh* is a kaleidoscope—a globetrotting thriller, a lesson in art history, a reminder of a crime against humanity that will never be expunged, but most of all, a tremendously entertaining read."

—Joseph Finder, *New York Times* bestselling author of *House on Fire*

"Packed with international artworld intrigue and utterly delicious plot twists, Santlofer keeps readers riveted in this intelligent and wonderfully textured thriller."

—John Searles, *New York Times* bestselling author of *Her Last Affair* and *Help for the Haunted*

"Perfectly paced and plotted, *The Lost Van Gogh* seamlessly weaves together a mystery of unrelenting suspense with a fascinating tale about art and the dangerously criminal culture that surrounds it. A terrific read—one that only Jonathan Santlofer could have written!"

—Alafair Burke, *New York Times* bestselling author of *The Wife*

"*The Lost Van Gogh* is a can't-miss novel of unforgettable suspense. Santlofer masterfully blends his art world expertise with a game of obsessions, razor-sharp characterization, and thrilling prose to create a novel unlike any other—a riveting mystery that explores the weight of family and high-stakes art theft."

—Alex Segura, bestselling author of *Secret Identity*

"Ingeniously plotted, irresistibly readable, brimming with inside information about the high-stakes art world of theft, forgery, and murder, Jonathan Santlofer's *The Lost Van Gogh* tracks the history of a missing self-portrait by Van Gogh against the background of the notorious Nazi campaign against 'degenerate art.' Also included are brilliantly rendered drawings by the author, who is as accomplished an artist as he is a writer of suspense thrillers."

—Joyce Carol Oates, National Book Award and National Humanities Medal award winner

PRAISE FOR *THE LAST MONA LISA*

"Oh, what a web Jonathan Santlofer weaves in this unputdownable book! *The Last Mona Lisa* brings together past and present, and brushes it with plot twists that you don't see coming to create an unstoppable what-happens-next momentum. Santlofer has outdone himself this time."

—Michael Connelly, #1 *New York Times* bestselling author of the Harry Bosch and Lincoln Lawyer series

"Fabulous—instantly immersive, intriguing, and suspenseful, and expert and authentic too… Only a writer who is also an artist—or an artist who is also a writer—could have pulled it off. This feels like the thriller Santlofer was born to write."

—Lee Child, #1 *New York Times* bestselling author of the Jack Reacher series

"From its seductive first pages, *The Last Mona Lisa* carries us along on an utterly irresistible time-jumping, continent-leaping tale of intrigue and family secrets, obsession, and the ineffable power of art itself. I could not put it down."

—Megan Abbott, bestselling and award-winning author of *Dare Me* and *The Turnout*

"This is a terrific read—compelling, intelligent, fascinating, and deeply satisfying. It was a book I did not want to end."

—Peter James, UK #1 bestselling author of the Detective Roy Grace series

"A riveting novel, weaving the real-life 1911 theft of Leonardo's masterpiece into a nail-biting contemporary drama where billionaire collectors, art historians, book collectors, and INTERPOL engage in so many double and triple crosses you're left wondering until the last page whom to trust and whom to fear. *The Last Mona Lisa* is like a master class in how to create a deep understanding of art history while making a seamless thriller."

—Sara Paretsky, *New York Times* bestselling author of the V.I. Warshawski series

"*The Last Mona Lisa* is a pacy, seductive international thriller of the first order. With its seamless blend of action, intriguing maze of family secrets, and the gripping, emotional journal entries of a long-dead art thief, this is a transporting novel, made all the more captivating because of the true story at its heart. Don't miss it!"

—Lisa Unger, *New York Times* bestselling author of *Confessions on the 7:45*

"Astonishingly, Jonathan Santlofer is a brilliant writer of fiction and nonfiction—and a superb visual artist as well. All his skills come together in *The Last Mona Lisa*, and the result is wholly satisfying."

—Lawrence Block, bestselling author of more than fifty novels, including *Eight Million Ways to Die* and *A Walk Among the Tombstones*

"It's hard to imagine another writer who could pull off a feat like *The Last Mona Lisa*, with its combination of thrills, history, and insider knowledge of the art world. A singular achievement by a terrific writer. Really stunning."

—Laura Lippman, *New York Times* bestselling author

"A deliciously tense read that mixes a present-day hunt for the truth with a real-life historical heist to page-turning effect!"

—Ruth Ware, #1 *New York Times* bestselling author of *One by One*

PRAISE FOR *THE DEATH ARTIST*

"A crime novel that is savage and erudite, layered in wit, satire, and psychosis—in short, a chilling read."

—*USA Today*

"Santlofer's insight into the passion at the heart of great art brings this evocative thriller to richly impastoed life."

—Page Turner of the Week, *People* magazine

"A rollercoaster...a sure sense of pace and engaging literary style."

—*Plain Dealer*

"Brisk...inventive...compelling."

—*Washington Post*

PRAISE FOR *COLOR BLIND*

"Smart, lurid, and fascinating, with layered prose and a wealth of detail...vivid and realistic characters who weave their way through the fast-moving plot."

—*Library Journal*

PRAISE FOR *THE KILLING ART*

"Entirely believable… Unsettling… Mr. Santlofer may become even far better known for his writing than for his paintings."

—*New York Times*

PRAISE FOR *ANATOMY OF FEAR*

"A riveting story of a serial killer, a police sketch artist who gets involved in the murders… A tense, psychologically nuanced story that is never less than compelling… The quality of Santlofer's art and the way it becomes a galvanizing force in his prose is stunning."

—*Pittsburgh Tribune*

"Santlofer sure knows how to tell a story! His writing is fluid and vivid, and the illustrations just add this whole other dimension to the suspense, especially toward the end, when things get really manic."

—*San Francisco Chronicle*

PRAISE FOR *THE WIDOWER'S NOTEBOOK*

"Wrenching, heartbreaking, intense, and emotional—but valuable too: we're all approaching the age where this will happen to us—or to others because of us—and understanding that it can be dealt with is consoling. I don't know how Santlofer found the fortitude to write this, but I'm deeply grateful he did. I think the world is a better place with this book in it."

—Lee Child, #1 *New York Times* bestselling author of the Jack Reacher series

"Jonathan Santlofer's stunning *The Widower's Notebook* raises all the blinds on immense and sudden loss, bringing light to all its dark corners. In so doing, he offers a deeply moving, often funny, always big-hearted portrait—not just of grief but of a long and rich marriage brought to vivid life and of a mighty father-and-daughter relationship both tested and enduring. A true gift."

—Megan Abbott, bestselling and award-winning author of *Dare Me* and *The Turnout*

"Deeply moving...beautifully written... It is such an achievement, like running uphill against a strong wind."

—Joyce Carol Oates, National Book Award–winning author

"This chronicle of devastation is devastating, a deeply powerful and unflinching report of how painfully and strangely life continues in the wake of a sudden, tragic death."

—Andrew Solomon, National Book Award winner

ALSO BY JONATHAN SANTLOFER

The Lost Van Gogh
The Last Mona Lisa
The Murder Notebook
Anatomy of Fear
The Killing Art
Color Blind
The Death Artist
The Widower's Notebook: A Memoir

Anthologies as Editor

It Occurs to Me That I Am America
Inherit the Dead
The Dark End of the Street
The Marijuana Chronicles

TEN PERFECT GUESTS

A Novel

JONATHAN SANTLOFER

sourcebooks
landmark

Cover design by Sara Wood
Cover images © Joanna Czogala/Arcangel, Dmitri Korobtsov/Getty Images
Internal design by Laura Boren/Sourcebooks
Title page image © Pakhnyushchyy/Getty Images

Sourcebooks and the colophon are registered trademarks of Sourcebooks.

Published by Sourcebooks Landmark, an imprint of Sourcebooks
1935 Brookdale RD, Naperville, IL 60563-2773
(630) 961-3900
sourcebooks.com

Grateful acknowledgment is made to Carol Ann Duffy and RCW Literary Agency for permission to reprint lines from "Mrs. Faust" from "The World's Wife" Anvil Press Poetry, 1999.

Cataloging-in-Publication Data is on file with the Library of Congress.

Printed and bound in the United States of America.
MA 10 9 8 7 6 5 4 3 2 1

This book is for my grandfather, Sam Brill,
who inspired me with his thrilling stories of murder,
mayhem, humor, and morality, a man who loved me
and whom I loved with all my heart.

Thing is–
I've made a pact
with Mephistopheles,
the Devil's boy.

He's on his way
to take away
what's owed,
reap what I sowed.
For all these years of
gagging for it,
going for it,
rolling in it,
I've sold my soul.

—from "Mrs. Faust,"
Carol Ann Duffy

"It was more than a game. It was a private joke."

—from the 1973 movie
The Last of Sheila

"Show me the money!"

—from the 1996 movie
Jerry Maguire

Prologue

You have to understand, I was going to get caught unless I killed them. I had no choice.

PART I
ARRIVAL

1

You Are Invited
to
Celebrate the Life & Art
of
VICTOR D'ARCANGELO

Alex Bagdasarian stared at the evite on his computer screen. Not exactly what he had been waiting for since the artist's untimely death less than a week ago, but an invitation he could not refuse. According to the details, if he did not show up, he would lose the D'Arcangelo estate.

Sunlight from a wall of river-view windows streamed into the third-floor office of his Chelsea art gallery and across the D'Arcangelo painting that filled an entire wall. It had been thirty years since he had taken on the young Victor D'Arcangelo and built him into an art world phenomenon, a powerful, heady feeling though nowadays it was the artist who supported the dealer.

Bagdasarian leaned back in the ergonomic chair specifically designed to support his weight. He was a big man, but with a year-round tan and bespoke suits made to flatter his extra-large frame, he cut an impressive figure, one few would suspect was drowning in debt from rent on three galleries, overpriced inventory, and a serious gambling habit. The bookies, growing weary of late payments and excuses, were making threats against his life. One in particular called almost every day to say, *"Don't fuck with me!"* If he did not get more money, and fast, he could lose everything. And he was not about to let that happen.

He dabbed the beads of perspiration dotting his forehead. In a month he would be seventy, more than half those years dedicated to art—something most people believed was all about creativity, but he knew better.

He expelled a breath, his life playing back on a sigh: the poor boy from Queens who had studied art history on a full scholarship, who dreamed of becoming a museum curator, the dream discarded when he interned in a trendy Manhattan gallery and saw how much money there was to be made. After that, he climbed the corporate gallery ladder from gofer to assistant to salesman to director to finally owning his own gallery until the part of him that had fallen in love with money murdered the part of him that had fallen in love with art.

Bagdasarian stood, hands gripping the edge of his desk for support. At over 250 pounds, his doctors had been nagging him to lose weight, and he *would*, after this memorial, when he had secured the D'Arcangelo estate, the golden ticket that would sustain him for the rest of his days. But he needed to sell those paintings *now*. With the artist's sudden death, his prices were soaring.

What was the saying: *No artist like a dead artist*?

He lit a cigar, leaned over his computer screen, and reread one of the weekend's annoying details, the date: Memorial Day. Four days if you counted travel time, and he did. Could it be less convenient? He had planned to be in the Hamptons at a big art-world party. Not that he needed to spend any more time with a bunch of ass-kissing artists or money-grubbing dealers, but he hated giving up the prospect of new art collectors, fresh money, fresh blood.

A note at the bottom of his evite:

OTHER IMPORTANT GALLERISTS LIKE YOURSELF WILL BE ATTENDING.

Like who?

But he had a pretty good idea. He was not Victor D'Arcangelo's exclusive dealer, though he intended to be, had to be. Just one more reason to attend: to defend his turf.

He gnawed the end of his cigar, a dozen thoughts competing—money problems, bookies, rival gallerists—then was momentarily distracted by a question: Who had sent the invitation? Clearly not the dead artist. His wife? His ex? His son? It didn't say and there was no name, just a link to RSVP.

The art dealer sagged back into his chair with a huff and reread the travel plans: when and where to meet the plane that would take him to the boat that would deliver him to the island memorial. He let out a sigh, then hit YES.

2

Sabrina Fleming read the invitation thinking, *It's about time!* Until now, there hadn't been a word about a funeral or service or anything. Not that she and her ex-husband spoke that often. When they did, it was usually about their son, Nicky, and his bad habits. Nicky was clean now, or so he said, but what if it happened again? Had Victor left funds to cover another stint in rehab? Had he left Nicky anything? And what about her? He promised he would. But had he kept his promise? She thought back to all his broken promises, starting with *to love, honor and obey*.

Her tiny East Village studio felt cramped, the caustic smell of turpentine permeating the air. A group of painted portraits, commissions she had taken on to make ends meet, filled one wall, but it was the other paintings that grabbed the viewer's attention, a series of meticulously painted plants, some infested with various kinds of insects, the color and detail so vivid and startling they appeared almost too real, pulsating, practically breathing.

Sabrina studied her latest painting, a star-shaped plant in close-up, its flesh-colored petals edged in fuzz descending into a whirling vortex crawling with bloodred flies, all of it depicted fastidiously. She reached for a brush and added a white highlight to one of the flies' wings, then referred to a full-color plate of the plant in the book just beside the easel.

Stapelia gigantea: This carrion flower (or toad flower) releases a rotting-flesh odor to attract flies to pollinate it.

If only I could add the smell! she thought and laughed. Not many collectors were going to want the odor of rotting flesh in their penthouse apartments or Hamptons mansions! This was the tenth painting in her Fatal Flora series. Hanging above were several more jewellike canvases, a white-flowering hemlock dotted with small red spiders beside another of deadly nightshade with a large hawk moth so lifelike you could practically hear its wings batting as it deposited small opalescent eggs on one of the plant's heavily veined leaves.

Sabrina had yet to find a gallery to show the work but was certain the mix of beauty and horror, an age-old artistic theme, would appeal to a certain kind of dealer and collector.

At fifty-four, she was intent upon rekindling her dream of becoming a painter, a dream she had given up too easily but not without resentment when she'd married Victor, who had made it clear from day one that there was room for only one artist in the family.

On the opposite wall, she'd hung one of Victor's paintings, a realistic early work before his abstractions had made him famous. This one, a portrait of Sabrina, had been painted quickly and crudely though he'd caught her unique beauty: the high cheekbones, dark skin, and light-green eyes, an eye-catching blend of her interracial parentage.

She took a minute to study Victor's sketchy brushwork, wondered if he had loved her when he painted it. A part of her had always believed he'd married her to distance himself from his racist working-class parents.

But why had she married him?

Easy. Because he was charismatic and handsome, an *artist,* a *genius,* often mean and withholding. She had always gone for the worst possible men.

Fragments from their ten-year-marriage played in her mind, dinners she'd labored over for *his* curators and collectors, supporting *his* work above her own, always feeding *his* ego. The perfect art wife, even putting up with his numerous infidelities until she no longer could. Then paid him back with one of her own. A decision that had ended in divorce.

Sabrina shook her head, thinking it was a bad idea to dredge up the past. But too late. It was already here, in the form of an evite bringing with it a hefty slice of guilt and all her complicated feelings about Victor.

Damn him.

But she had toughened up since then, constructed an armor-like exterior few could penetrate. She had survived a narcissistic mother and absentee father, their bitter separation, then Victor's cruelty and divorce. That was past. It was time to focus on the future. *Hers.* She deserved more than the pittance he had left her when they split a year before his meteoric rise to art stardom, an allowance he had not corrected when his money started coming in, though he'd assured her he would.

She looked from Victor's painting back to her own, had always known she was the more gifted of the two. Had Victor known that too? Was that why he'd made her quit?

Her fault as much as his, and time to correct it before it was too late. The clock was ticking on her youth and beauty, what she had always been valued for, her parents' little princess, Vincent's gorgeous wife. And now what? She didn't see herself becoming a gaunt Georgia O'Keeffe–like beauty. Gaunt out of the question now that she'd added twenty pounds to her once perfect figure, more zaftig than svelte nowadays though she embraced it, wearing low-cut tank tops and tight jeans, and still turned heads. Either way, she had better get her painting career in gear before it was too late.

A moment to reread the invitation's details—the car, the flight, the boat, the island hotel. So like Victor to have planned a deluxe event for his own passing and spending money that should have been hers! Of course, there was plenty, she was sure of that, though Victor had always been secretive about money, doling out cash when she needed it and no more.

Did he do that with his current wife? According to Nicky, they were separated and planning to divorce. But was it official? She hoped so. If they were no longer married, there would be more for her. Unless Victor had forgotten his promise and cut her off completely. The thought rippled through her with a chill.

She looked back at the invitation, reread the one caveat, her attendance a requirement or she would forfeit any inheritance. As always, Victor had left her no choice, playing games and manipulative even now, from the grave!

Sabrina flung her paintbrush, watched it slam against Victor's portrait of her, a slash of scarlet paint smeared across her throat like blood.

3

Despite the deluxe town car—an ironic and bitter reminder of his former life—Frank D'Arcangelo could not get comfortable. He sat forward, then back, leaned one way, then the other, rolled his head, his neck tight, his mind buzzing. It had been over a decade since he and his brother had spoken, the invitation a surprise.

Attendance required or forfeit your inheritance.

Another surprise, he hadn't expected his brother to leave him anything but bitterness and resentment.

For the past half hour, the town car had crept along La Cienega, then Century Boulevard, now bumper-to-bumper on the freeway, drivers leaning heavily on horns that did nothing but add to his tension. Typical traffic to LAX. Everyone trying to escape. But he was happy to get away. And to some tropical isle, no less. But did it have to be his brother's memorial? And a command performance? What else was expected of him? He had no script, no director telling him what to do, no character to inhabit but himself, a role at which he'd never been very good.

"The traffic is always bad here, sir," the driver said in a thick accent.

"*Sí, sí, lo se*." Frank's Spanish was limited but his pronunciation good. He had used a Spanish accent in an early film where he'd played a drug lord, a supporting role he'd made the most of, snarling at the camera in close-up, dark makeup and a mustache, something that would never fly these days. That was a shame, he thought; it was a part that had gotten him noticed.

"*No se preocupe, señor.*"

"What?" Frank asked. He'd been lost for a moment in those heady early days, the climb up rather than down. "Oh. I'm not worried," he said. The traffic possibly the only thing he *wasn't* worried about.

A moment to check his emails, amazed to find one from his agent. It had been almost six months. Scrolling rapidly, nervously skimming the words... AGENCY IS FORCING ME TO CUT DOWN...OVERWHELMED WITH A-LIST CLIENTS...SPOILED BRATS ALL OF THEM, LOL...BUT NO CHOICE... IT'S COMING FROM ABOVE... SORRY, PAL, YOU KNOW I LOVE YOU, BUT YOU NEED TO FIND NEW REPRESENTATION... I'M SURE YOU UNDERSTAND.

"Fuck!" Frank slammed the phone down so hard it bounced off the seat and onto the floor. No, he did not understand!

"Everything all right, sir?"

Oh sure. Haven't had a decent part in years, bills piling up, can barely pay my mortgage, a massive heart attack less than three months ago, an acute myocardial infarction to be exact, and my agent just dumped me, the topper on this steaming pile of shit called my life. So, yeah, everything was just great! "I'm...fine."

"Do not worry, sir. I will take a shortcut to the airport." The driver steered the car off the freeway and onto a side street.

A part of Frank hoped he would miss the plane; all those memories and expectations waiting for him were too much to deal with. There was only one person he wanted to see though they had not spoken in years, the costar in his ongoing dream. He was certain she'd be there, but would she be happy to see him?

If it weren't for the inheritance, which he needed now more than ever, he would tell the driver to turn around and take him home, where he would get in bed, pour himself a drink against doctor's orders, stream one of his old movies, and feel sorry for himself. He took a deep breath, with it, the muscles in his chest constricting.

Shit. Just what he needed, another heart attack. And the way things were going, he just might have one.

Relax. Breathe.

His yoga teacher's words. He pictured the twentysomething who had not seen any of his movies, who had no idea he'd been a star, a full-fledged fucking movie star, *People*'s Sexiest Man of the Year! So what if it had been fifteen years ago! How the hell was he supposed to relax, to breathe, when all he'd had was gone?

The chest pain worsened. He fumbled the tiny bottle of nitroglycerin out of his carry-on and placed one of the tiny pills under his tongue, leaned back, and glanced out the window at Culver City, the old MGM lot, Sony Studios, places he had not worked for a long time.

The driver drove down one side street, then another. Perhaps they would make the flight, and he would see her again after all these years. He checked his reflection in the rearview mirror, smoothed his hair into place, and noticed it needed a touch-up, a quarter inch of telltale gray roots. Too late now. She would have to take him as he is.

He closed his eyes, their affair starting to play on the small silver screen of his mind. Could the movie have a happy ending this time? The images dissolved in a slow cinematic fade, the tightness is his chest starting to fade along with it, the nitro taking affect, but not the conflict stirred up by the memory. Could he go through it all again: having her and losing her?

He tried to imagine their life together, a second chance, and this time with an inheritance.

A moment to check his phone again, this time for the e-tickets. First class. His brother wasn't cheap; he'd give him that. But did it have to be a red eye? He yawned, already tired.

They'd been close once, Victor, the big brother he'd looked up to, who had watched over him, took care of him, supported him in the early days and through the lean years before his acting career had taken off. And when it did, he'd been proud of him, referring to them as the "famous brothers." Frank pictured Victor at his first big movie premiere, hogging the red-carpet interview, and how they had laughed about it afterward. Not much to laugh about now, those lean years back with a vengeance and no big brother to bail him out. Or so he'd thought until now, until this invitation and its promise of inheritance.

The car jerked forward, then stopped short. They were back on the freeway, the 405, one long parking lot.

"*Idiotas!*" the driver shouted. "Excuse me, sir. But the drivers, they are blind!"

Blind, Frank thought. Like he had been, doing and taking what he wanted no what matter the cost or who he lost. Like his ex-wife, Sarah. He hadn't cared at the time. With his career in orbit, he'd felt untouchable, a barely earthbound star, offers coming in one after another, success going to his head. He'd been brash and overconfident when he'd made his move, seeing the situation and taking advantage of it, knowing she was vulnerable and unhappy.

Not all my fault, he thought. Two to tango and all that. It was possible she had been using him too, both of them using each other, though neither had counted on the consequences, which he regretted: the consequences, not the affair. Her beautiful face shimmering in his mind, he knew he would do it all again.

Was she still beautiful?

He slumped back against the plush seat, chest pain gone but not the fact of it. Since the heart attack, he had become all too aware of his mortality. How long did he really have?

Traffic eased, the driver speeding now, making up for lost time.

Like me, Frank thought.

He wished he had spoken to Victor before he died, had tried to patch things up. He pictured his brother the last time he'd seen him, his face twisted with disappointment and rage.

But the invitation suggested his brother had forgiven him. All he had to do was show up and claim his inheritance. A way to start over, a new lease on life.

4

The seat-belt sign had been on since takeoff, due to nonstop turbulence the pilot kept promising would end but didn't.

Despite the early hour, Jasmin Li was working a Bloody Mary, the glass trembling in her hand. She waved away the first-class flight attendant who offered breakfast, the idea of eating impossible, her stomach doing flip-flops along with the plane. First class, the kind of extravagance she would be forced to relinquish if she didn't act fast.

She bristled at the thought of all she could lose: the museum openings (though she didn't like art), the charity galas (though she did not believe in charity), box seats at the opera (though it put her to sleep), the best restaurants (though she didn't eat). Still, she had married Victor for the lifestyle and no way she was giving that up. Hell, she was still *the wife*. And despite his persistent philandering she'd stuck it out and been faithful. In her way.

For a moment, the one-time, one-named not quite supermodel considered resuming her career, which she had quit when she married Victor. Not so easy at thirty-six (though she only admitted to thirty-one). She'd had a couple of important covers, *Vogue*, *Elle*, but that was a decade ago. Plus, she had never liked the work, standing around for hours, photographers and their assistants hitting on her, the early morning shoots when all she wanted was to sleep. Like now, forced to take this ridiculous predawn flight, just one more way for Victor to annoy her.

The plane did another dip, and she clasped the armrest so hard that one of her perfectly sculpted nail extensions snapped off. "Fuck!"

The man across the aisle looked over. "You can say that again! This damn flight!"

Jasmin ignored him, fussing over her nail, wondering if she would have time to get it fixed before boarding the boat to some godforsaken island. Typical of Victor to make it difficult for everyone, drag them off to a destination memorial on a holiday weekend no less, make them prove their love for him, even now, when he was dead. *It was all so Victor D'Arcangelo!*

The man across the aisle leaned over and tried again. "Buy you a drink?"

"The drinks are *free.*"

"Maybe so, but a beautiful girl like you should not be drinking alone."

Oh, brother. Jasmin appraised him: white, fifties, expensive suit, thick gold wedding band on his finger. A cheater. But weren't they all? She ignored his question and turned back to her broken fingernail, pictured her mother, nails always manicured, hair coiffed, perfectly dressed though they had little money. An uncompromising woman who had pinned all her hopes and dreams on Jasmin. What some Americas insultingly called a tiger mom.

Yǒu zhì zhě, shì jìng chéng.

Translation: *You will be able to achieve your goals as long as you have determination and ambition.* More simply: *Keep your eye on the prize.*

And Jasmin always did.

She thought back to that first night, a MoMA gala, spying Victor D'Arcangelo across the room, knowing exactly who he was. She'd done her homework before the event. Famous artist. Handsome too. Almost thirty years older than she but he looked fit and virile. As it turned out, too virile, constantly bothering her for sex when she'd hoped the age gap would slow him down. She had always figured he would die before her, while she was still young, and he had. Even sooner than expected.

A picture in her mind of Victor the last time she'd seen him, his skin tinged greenish, his blue eyes rheumy. How shocked she had been.

"Darling," she'd said, over and over, taking his damp, clammy hand in hers. "You'll be better in no time, and we will be together."

Thank God she had visited. They were still married but New York was not a community property state, like so many foolish wives believed, but an *equitable distribution* state, meaning the courts decided how to divide the property and marital debt. She hoped Victor had been aware of her visit.

She had no idea how much he'd left her, but the invitation had been clear: Attend the memorial or lose it all. The reason she was here. Plus, the lawyer she'd hired to find a loophole in her prenup had insisted. *You're the grieving widow. No one knows about the state of your marriage. If they do, say it was a trial separation and you reconciled. You're still the wife and that's all anyone needs to know*.

When the plane leveled out, she ordered another drink and raised it in a silent toast. *To you, Victor.*

Dead or alive, she was determined to get something out of him. And frankly, dead was easier.

5

Rachel Ronan gripped her seat. Would this awful turbulence ever end? Would she live to attend the memorial, to see this tropical isle?

The *New Yorker* magazine was jostling in her lap, in it one of her poems, for Rachel a dream come true. She had always been a poet first, an art critic second, though it was through her position as art critic for the *New York Times* that people knew her. If they remembered. When the paper "retired her" almost twenty years ago—all that dreadful man's doing—it had started a chain reaction, her job gone along with her influence and power, no more exhibition previews or private dinners with artists and dealers, the invitations dwindling until they stopped, her social life gone along with Cynthia, her partner at the time, an experiment and a mistake, an artist who had obviously loved Rachel's power and position a lot more than she'd loved Rachel. And the worst part, moving back home after her breakdown.

An exasperated sigh. *Give it up. Rachel. That was then and this is now.* And things were looking up. The unexpected invitation had made it clear she hadn't been overlooked. Victor had not forgotten her or what she had done for him, given him his first review and a good one: *intelligent, sensitive abstractions filled with glowing color, self-assured and mature for such a young artist.* And another good review for his second show. Then another for his third. But when she stopped—rather *was* stopped—and for a reason Victor never knew—she was punished for it. Clearly, the *Times* valued a high-end gallery's full-page ads more than her reviews. What a fool she'd been.

But irony of ironies, the *Times* wanted her back! Only as a freelancer and only one article, but a good one: to interview art collectors whose money had come from questionable sources. The paper had supplied the names, ones whose ancestors had been notorious fur trappers, arms dealers, and the one the paper sought most, a big pharma heiress who, like other members of her family, claimed no knowledge or deception concerning the company's most infamous pain-relieving habit-forming drug.

Clearly, the *Times* wanted a piece on cancel culture and art, something very much in the zeitgeist, and something Rachel could not let on. Only that she was writing about "important families who had collected art for a long time." The line had worked on a few of the subjects, but not the pharmaceutical heiress who had yet to return any of her inquiries and without whom the article was dead.

Her invitation had mentioned a few of the other guests, and more irony or fate, the pharmaceutical heiress was among them! An entire weekend to get what she needed, write an attention-getting article, and with it gain some respect. Not that she could survive on respect or freelance articles, but she wouldn't have to, not with the inheritance coming.

No question her luck was changing.

When the turbulence subsided and the plane settled, she made a dash for the restroom. The pee she had been holding in could no longer wait. She relieved herself, then washed her hands, attempted to fluff her thin, flattened hair, and applied a fresh coat of the same drugstore lipstick she'd been using for years.

In the aisle, she was feeling self-conscious, the boxy shift, just part of the new wardrobe she'd bought on sale at Lane Bryant, clinging to her hips, though it hardly mattered. No one was looking at her.

An opportunity to peruse the first-class passengers: a well-preserved elderly couple and an over-groomed middle-aged man who was downing a cocktail while eyeing a beautiful younger woman across the aisle. The woman swiped her long black hair away from her face, and Rachel caught a glimpse of the diamonds glinting on her earlobes. Rachel smiled at her, but the woman did not return it, busy frowning and fussing over what appeared to be a broken fingernail.

Back in her seat she ordered champagne and, when it arrived, counted her blessings: on her way to a glamorous island memorial, a poem finally published, the promise of an inheritance, and her article in the *New York Times* practically guaranteed, now that she had the pharmaceutical heiress in her sights!

6

Lauren Ziff and Ian Lumley arrived at the Fort Lauderdale pier in their own car, a black Mercedes S-Class. Their driver was a young Dominican whose wife cleaned their Palm Beach home seven days a week. His yearly salary was less than a third of the car's retail price, but they felt good about giving him a job and would have bragged about it to their friends if their friends had not deserted them.

"We can still turn back, love," Ian said, his heavy Mancunian accent, nasal and coarse.

"*You* can," his wife said. "*You* weren't personally invited. But I *was*, the first social event I've been invited to in over a year, and I'm not missing it!" It was true, she had not been invited to any of the events at which her family had been regulars for years: the Met Gala, the Angel Ball at Cipriani, the Imagine Awards at Guastavino's, front-row seats during Fashion Week, all of which the Ziff family had been funding for decades and Lauren would be too if anyone dared take her money and have the Ziff name on their benefactors and funders list or, worse, on the side of their building.

"If you'd grown up with this, you would understand," she went on, practically a cry.

Ian uttered an indecipherable snort. After years of being Lauren's plus-one, he had little sympathy, and he was more than happy to give up the charity balls and galas. But not the money, the reason he was here now by his wife's side. In his mid-forties, his wife somewhat older, how old impossible to tell with all her Botox, fillers, and lifts, he was as surprised as she that they'd been invited. He supposed it was because Lauren had recently bought a large Victor D'Arcangelo painting for their Park Avenue town house.

"My invitation said everything was deluxe, including the guest list, all of them A-listers and influencers."

"Oi, what do you know about *influencers,* love?"

What Lauren knew was that she wasn't one of them, something she had to change.

"It will be fun," she said, not that any of those events had ever been fun, just necessary for her inclusion in New York society, and she was desperate for a way back.

"It's a *funeral*, petal, not a fucking *party*."

"Come or don't come. But I'm going with or without you," she said, her voice colored by a strained affectation.

For a moment, Ian considered it, going back to their Palm Beach home or New York penthouse, a girlfriend waiting in each place, both in studio apartments he paid for with Lauren's money. He squinted at Lauren through his kohl-lined eyes, trying to find some remnant of the pretty young woman he'd met at an Isle of Wight rock concert, now hidden under the mask she called her face. It had been twenty years since they'd married. He could not remember the last good one, but he'd signed a prenup and she owned him. If he left, it would be with the clothes on his back, though in fact she had paid for those too, along with his parents' flat in Manchester and everything else. Lauren's several-billion-dollar fortune had come to her years ago, after her parents' death in a private jet.

The Mercedes pulled to a stop. Ian put on his John Lennon blue-tinted glasses, then slipped out his side of the car while the driver opened Lauren's door.

Florida's bright morning sun illuminated the couple like the harshest police spotlight, everything about them in glaring high definition, her over-bleached blond hair, his dyed too black, her diamonds grossly ostentatious, his silver and onyx skull rings oversized and clunky.

"Can't they do something about this heat?" Lauren said, donning a large straw hat and fumbling her Prada sunglasses into place.

"By *they*, who do you mean, love, *God?*"

She ignored him, already walking ahead, strutting in her formfitting Oscar de la Renta green-striped romper, which gave her the look of an anorexic schoolgirl, her crystal-encrusted mules clip-clopping on the pier's wooden slats and adding a beat to the sound of cooing pigeons and the caw of seagulls. She barked at him over her shoulder, "You coming?"

"Whither thou goest, love," he sneered under his breath. It was a deal he'd made with the devil long ago, their "it" couple status a vague memory, gone once he had given up the rock band and sealed when her family was canceled.

"My God, I hope this place is no indication of the boat or the hotel, which they *promised* was five-star-plus." Lauren may have been frowning as she looked around, though it was impossible to tell as nothing on her face moved. "Where are they?"

"Who?"

"The A-listers!" She lowered her sunglasses and scanned the pier. She was expecting a party of thirty or forty recognizable socialites, all of whom had dropped her. "Oh, wait, isn't that the New York art dealer?" She pointed out Alex Bagdasarian, who had just gotten out of a town car at the far end of the pier. "What's his name?"

Ian was staring in the other direction at two young women in bikinis.

"I *asked* you a question, Ian."

He turned slowly back to her. "If you listen carefully, love, you can hear me not caring."

"I swear, if you existed, I'd divorce you." She sighed loudly then went back to perusing the pier. "And where the hell is this supposed boat captain? I'm not waiting forever. This heat is killing me!"

If only, Ian thought.

7

Under his extra-large seersucker jacket, Alex Bagdasarian's shirt was soaked with sweat. He should have waited in the air-conditioned town car, but the driver had already deposited him on the pier with a suitcase he couldn't abandon but did not want to lug around. He was starting to feel lightheaded, the air hot and thick, all the people and objects, the pier itself, wavering and distorted in the heat. He bought a bottle of water at a small kiosk and drank it down in a few fast gulps. Then asked the vendor if he had any ice.

"Just to keep my drinks cold, pal, not to sell."

"How about twenty bucks for a handful?" Bagdasarian looked down at the soda cans and water bottles jammed into the ice, flecks of dirt and God knows what else dotting the cubes.

The vendor shrugged and Bagdasarian handed him the money, used his handkerchief to scoop up the ice, then wrapped the linen tight and tucked the ad hoc cold pack behind his collar. Almost immediately the ice began to melt, a trickle of cold water snaking its way down the middle of his back along with a shiver of relief.

The invitation had said a boat captain would be meeting him, but he didn't know how long he could wait in this heat. He bought a second bottle of water, took a long pull, and checked out the crowd, a mix of locals and tourists, including a couple of snot-nosed brats chasing each other around the perimeter of the pier. He hoped they would fall in.

The burner phone vibrated in his pocket, and he fished it out. A man's voice distorted and echoey said, "It's done," and clicked off.

Bagdasarian was about to ask, *How did it go?* an absurd question to an anonymous assassin he had hired off the dark web for a tenth of what he owed the bookie.

A sigh. Not quite relief, but at least he could breathe. For the moment. It wasn't a cure-all—there was still a long line of debtors waiting to be paid—but he'd bought himself some time. The biggest and worst of the bloodsuckers was off his back, an old-school bookie who had threatened to break his kneecaps and worse, a real creep who did not deserve to live. He'd done the world a favor, hadn't he?

He glanced up at the sky as if looking for a sign, but there was nothing, everything bleached white-hot. Still, it was the first time he'd had a man killed. Directly. Figuratively he had killed more than his share, dropping artists from his gallery the minute their sales slumped, snuffing out careers without a second thought. One time, he happened upon a *New York Times* obituary, some down-and-out painter who had killed himself, an artist he had booted out of the gallery a few years earlier. He had read the obit feeling nothing, not a scintilla of guilt. Why should he feel responsible for the man's obvious weakness?

He dropped the burner and crushed it under his heel. Then, looking around to see if anyone was watching, he strained to pick it up, found the nearest trash bin, and tossed it in, aware that his hand trembling.

But why?

Shouldn't he be feeling relieved, happy? He told himself he would. After this damn memorial was over and he had the D'Arcangelo estate locked down and securely his.

8

The man who had been sent to meet the guests was a former U.S. Navy captain, his unit having played a crucial role in Operation Desert Storm during the Persian Gulf War, those days long behind him. Now, successfully self-employed and known only as Thomas or Captain, he was a short, muscled man in his mid-forties, though his thinning sun-bleached hair and weather-beaten face made him look older. He was being paid in bitcoin to ferry the guests to and from the island and nothing more. Hired for his discretion (this job, like most, had come via the dark web), his clients knew nothing about his private life, and he knew nothing of theirs, only their names.

As always, he had asked to be put up in one of the many seaside motels, something inexpensive and anonymous, until they set sail on the yacht, a luxury vessel he had navigated before, a basic requirement. Other than that, he knew only the dates, the destination, and the number of guests. So far, there had been only one call, in which his employer, speech distorted and echoey through a voice changer, had stressed that he keep in touch for further instructions, and he would.

He took a minute to scan the pier crowded with marina workers, tourists, and vendors setting up shop. He had received a photo of each guest and spotted a couple of them right away.

So far, it was going smoothly and there was no reason to think it would not. Of course he never expected things to go badly despite the fact that once or twice in the past, they had.

9

Two of the town cars reached the pier at precisely the same moment. Sabrina Fleming stepped out of one. Frank D'Arcangelo the other. Their eyes met for an awkward, expectant moment. Then Frank flashed his full Hollywood smile, capped teeth bared. Sabrina was more tentative, her upper lip lifted, then stopped, a quivering Marilyn smile, undecided, though she felt an ache in her gut and a pang of loss.

She managed to say his name, the bright morning sun lighting up her face, her green eyes shiny and luminous, her auburn curls like a golden halo.

"You haven't changed a day," Frank said, "and still so beautiful."

"Oh please," Sabrina said, but smiled. When she was young, she'd gotten tired of people telling her how beautiful she was. Nowadays she waited for it, and knew how to pose, lifting her chin in just the right way to show off her beauty, which she did now, though she did not move any closer to Frank, the few feet between them charged and weighted with memories—every touch, every hurt, every misstep and mistake.

She noticed his gray roots, the etched worry lines between his eyebrows, the slightly softened jaw, but he was still handsome.

He took a step toward her, arms out for a hug, but she stopped him, a hand on his chest, not sure she was ready for an embrace. She asked him to take off his sunglasses; she wanted to see his eyes, to read him.

He did. With a cinematic flourish.

There were more signs of age, crow's-feet meeting the dimples that had become lines on his cheeks, but his eyes were still the deep cobalt blue she remembered, the same as Victor's but kinder. At least she had thought so. At first.

"Let's find the others and get this weekend over with," she said, not wanting to be alone with him, fighting the attraction she still felt and wished she didn't.

"*Over with?* It hasn't even begun." Frank took her hand, brought it to his chest, and pressed it to his heart as if she could heal him. "It's going to be *fun*."

She wasn't so sure. "Still a dreamer, eh, Frank?"

"What's wrong with dreams?"

Sabrina thought a moment, his heart beating beneath her hand like an alarm. "Well..." she said. "You wake up and realize they're not real." She tugged her hand back and turned away. Then it was *her* heart beating fast as she headed onto the pier, seagulls cawing above, a dark cloud sliding across the sun like a bad omen.

10

Captain Thomas noticed her right away. How could you not? The gorgeous woman strutting across the pier as though she were on a runway.

Jasmin Li had exchanged her designer sweats for a Dolce & Gabbana minidress and Prada platform sandals that added several inches to her already stunning height. From behind her Jackie O sunglasses, she surveyed the pier and her surroundings, finding it all less than appealing. She was used to exclusive country clubs and private beach cabanas.

Thomas checked the photo on his cell phone. "Ms. Li?" he asked, approaching her.

"Who's asking?"

"I'm Thomas, your captain for this trip." He tried hard not to ogle her and failed.

"Uh-huh," Jasmin said. She was accustomed to men staring at her, something she used to her advantage. A memory sputtered behind her eyes, unexpected and disturbing: the bar's dim interior, the man's look of hunger. "Oh," she said, temporarily thrown.

"At your beck and call," the captain said.

"Of course you are," she said, recovering quickly. "Can you get me some water? It's *so* hot."

"There'll be plenty on the boat."

"I'm sure," she said. "But I want it *now*."

The captain nodded. He was used to dealing with spoiled rich people.

"Anything else I can get you?" he asked, sure that one day, maybe sooner than she expected, she would get more than she asked for.

11

Rachel Ronan could feel the sweat on her neck and under her arms. She checked to see if there were stains, and there were. *Darn.* Tired from the early morning flight, she headed across the pier, trying to smooth the badly wrinkled dress that was sticking to her thighs. It brought her mother to mind—beautiful, stylish, and thin. *Really, Rachel, that dress? With your weight?* And worse, the damning statement Rachel had overheard when her mother thought her teenage daughter was out of earshot, or perhaps she didn't care. *It's heartbreaking to have such an unattractive daughter, isn't it?* Something Rachel would never forget and hadn't, not even when her mother was old and sick and dependent, a time Rachel could not bear to think about it, certainly not now.

This is a mistake, she thought. A fancy trip to some tropical isle with glamorous art-world people whom she would have to impress with a freelance job for the paper she had not worked for in years. If it were not for the inheritance and the stipulation of attending, she would turn around and run.

It was then she spotted the woman in the cinched-belted romper—arms and legs bone thin, blond hair lacquered into place—and recognized her, despite the large sunglasses. The other reason she had come. *Be cool,* she told herself, a condition that did not come naturally.

She was somewhat relieved when a sunburned man in jeans and a striped tee signaled to her with a wave. Beside him were the beautiful Asian woman from the flight and another woman she recognized as Victor D'Arcangelo's ex-wife, whom she had met back in day when she was the *Times* full-time art critic. And then, just past the edge of the group, the man who had taken it all away from her.

Rachel sucked in a breath. She could not wave back without lifting her arm and exposing her sweat stains, but it was too late to escape. The man in the striped tee was already closing in, calling her by name.

"Ahoy there, Miss Ronan. I'm Thomas, your boat captain." He smiled, his skin tan and leathery, a cautionary tale of too much time in the sun.

She smiled too, hearing her mother tell her to stand up straight, patted the hopeless wrinkles in her too-tight dress, and tried to act as if she belonged here when clearly she did not. "Oh, *hi*!" she said with too much forced cheer. She glanced past him at the bony blond, then back. She felt the captain's eyes on her, and the beautiful Asian woman's, judging her. "Hello," she said to her. "Nice, um, to see you again."

"*Again?*" the Asian woman asked, her face clouded with doubt.

"I, um, saw you on the plane," Rachel said in her halting, tentative way. "We, um, didn't actually meet," she continued, though the beautiful Asian woman had already turned away, accepting a bottle of water from the captain, who offered Rachel nothing. No doubt, a forecast of what this trip would be like, Rachel thought, little slights here and there.

Though she was wrong: It would be a lot worse.

12

"Stop here," the man said.

"My instructions were to deliver you to the pier, sir." The driver angled a look over his shoulder. "The marina is still a half block away, sir."

"I will walk from here. Open ze door." The man's accent was thick and Germanic, his tone so emphatic the driver did not hesitate, the locks clicking open.

The sun was blazing and hot, a shock after the car's tinted windows and frosty air-conditioning. The man tossed his cigarette away, then slipped on shades with his thick fingers. Somewhere in his early forties, though often mistaken for older, he was a big man, beefy, though muscled. People of a certain age and Bond film aficionados often told him he looked like *Goldfinger,* meaning the German actor who played the character in the movie. He had streamed the film and found the comparison insulting, though it was hard to deny the resemblance, the fleshy freckled face, the sparse ginger hair.

After only a few yards, he was sweating, his linen suit sticking to his broad chest and muscled thighs. But he had been raised to withstand discomfort and knew it was good for him, character building, and so he walked briskly, arms swinging, an image of his father clear in his mind, and the promise he had made to him.

The memorial had been unexpected but timely, coinciding with his family's plan for expansion into the U.S. art market. The invitation had not said specifically who would be there, but he assumed the artist's family and friends, if Victor D'Arcangelo had any. He had always thought of the man as a lone wolf, like himself, and he respected that. Of course, the artist's New York gallerist would attend, and he was counting on it.

He tuned in to the thrum of rippling water and the creaking dock, squawking birds and predatory seagulls, then turned his attention to the slick streamlined yacht that occupied an entire side of the pier, light bouncing off its fiberglass and aluminum like diamonds. A craggy, sunburned man was addressing a small group of people who had gathered to look at the boat, and there among them, though standing apart, was Alex Bagdasarian, just as he had hoped.

Even from a distance he could see the art dealer was grossly overweight and breathing heavily. *Easy prey*, the words that came into his mind.

He pictured the galleries the man had built, extravagant constructions to an insecure ego, galleries he planned to make his own.

A few feet from the art dealer, a woman he recognized from an art opening years ago, Victor D'Arcangelo's wife, or so she had been at the time. He could not remember a word they had exchanged, only her smooth dark skin and light-green eyes and the way her full lips had opened and closed around words he did not listen to as he imagined taking her by force. She was older now, and heavier, but no less beautiful. He could not believe D'Arcangelo had thrown away something so lovely.

He thought, *If I had a woman like that, I would kill to keep her*.

Managing to look away from her to peruse the group, he noticed a middle-aged woman, unfamiliar and of no interest to him, unless she was powerful in some way he could not imagine from her dowdy clothes and slightly disheveled appearance. He focused again on Bagdasarian, whose face was screwed up with worry. He imagined sliding an arm around the man's shoulder and telling him that soon all his worries would be over.

He waited a moment before walking toward him.

Bagdasarian looked up, startled, then composed his face into a strained smile. "Well, well, well, if it isn't Herr Schwegler. What brings *you* here?"

"The same as you, I am sure, Victor D'Arcangelo's memorial."

"*You* were invited?" he said, though he was sure Schwegler would have been and that was the reason he was here.

"As Victor D'Arcangelo's European representation, of course. It is my job to make sure the artist's reputation continues to grow in the coming years, something only a young and healthy gallerist can guarantee." He gave Bagdasarian the once-over, lip raised in a sneer.

"Even you should know there are no guarantees, Herr Schwegler."

"I do, indeed. But we make our own guarantees, do we not?" Something his father always said and exactly what Schwegler intended to do. He was about to say more when a car door slammed behind them, and the group turned to see who it was.

13

A tall young man loped toward the group like a gazelle, his bare feet slapping the wooden slats of the pier, small bells like some Balinese dancer's tinkling from an ankle bracelet.

Lauren Ziff and Ian Lumley, who had joined them, looked up. Lauren, in particular, seemed transfixed. *No A-lister,* she thought, *but that never mattered in bed.*

Rachel Ronan stared too. He reminded her of Johnny Depp in *Pirates of the Caribbean*, but a lot taller, and even more striking in his faded David Bowie tee and artfully torn jeans.

If this were a movie, she thought, *he would be running in slow motion!*

At first, she had taken him for a teenager, but as he got closer, she could see he was older, somewhere in his mid-twenties and even more beautiful than she had first thought, the image of Johnny Depp's pirate replaced by Michelangelo's *David*, lean and muscled with rippling tattooed arms, his wrists festooned with bracelets of raffia, leather, and silver bangles, a puka shell necklace around his neck along with three or four dangling chains, one with what looked like a lion's or tiger's tooth. The diagonal scar across his chin added a note of danger to his otherwise perfect face.

All eyes had turned toward him, and not just the group here for the memorial party, but everyone on the pier, all of them with a kind of lust or envy, his youth and beauty a reminder of what they had lost, though few ever had.

"My fucking plane was delayed!" he said, slightly out of breath as he reached them, dropping a dusty though expensive-looking leather backpack. "Have I missed anything? Burning Man gift giving? Reading of the will?" He threw his head back and laughed as if he'd said the funniest thing in the world, the veins in his neck standing out in relief, his thick sculpted curls bouncing like a shampoo ad, though his hair looked greasy.

Jasmin Li said nothing as he passed, even when his arm grazed hers, but she gave him a sideways glance that Rachel Ronan noticed. Beside her now, the young man gave off an odor of earth and sweat. *Is this what a man smells like?* It had been so long since she'd been with a man, she could hardly remember, though she inhaled deeply and liked it.

Sabrina Fleming had broken out of the group to embrace the young man, her arms around his neck. He lifted her up, everyone watching.

Hans Schwegler wondered if the young man was the ex-wife's lover, a mix of longing and jealousy roiling inside him.

14

Sabrina planted a kiss on the young man's lips. His arms still around her, he set her down gently.

"Nicola," she said, taking him in. "Where on earth are your shoes?"

He kicked a bare foot at his backpack. "In there."

She had to smile. "Well, thank goodness you made it!"

"Are you kidding? I wouldn't miss Father's official departure from the earth for anything!" He laughed, mouth open, exposing perfect white teeth. They kissed again, then Sabrina turned to the group. "This is Nicolo."

"Nicky," he said.

"It's not polite to correct your mother."

"This is your *son*?" Lauren Ziff eyed Nicky as hungrily as a wolf. Or perhaps she was simply starving.

"People 'ave 'em, love," Ian said to his wife. "It's only you who forgot."

"I didn't *forget*," she said. "I already have a baby, *you*." She turned to Nicky, offering him her manicured hand. "Hello, I'm Lauren."

"She expects you to kiss the ring, mate," Ian said. "You know, like the pope."

"Just ignore him," Lauren said. "*Everyone* does."

Schwegler ignored them both, still taking in the mother and son, relieved that he had mistaken them for lovers, their greeting so intimate. But he could see it now, the same green eyes and tawny skin, the resemblance between them so strong he was surprised he had missed it.

Rachel saw it too, their resemblance and beauty. His hands were still around his mother's waist, and she noticed his fingernails were painted black, the polish chipped. She could see the young Victor D'Arcangelo in him as well, though the boy's features were more refined, slightly feminine and feline, while Victor was all man. Or all *dog*, she thought.

"Nicky!" Frank D'Arcangelo got his arms around them both, a way to hug Sabrina at the same time. "You're all grown up!"

"Uncle Frank! Is it really you?" Nicky smiled. As a boy, he had liked his father's playful younger brother a lot more than his father, even if Frank had disappeared for more than a decade. He'd often asked his mother why, but she never said, always shrugging it off. He noticed she looked uncomfortable, quickly sliding out of Frank's grip.

"How's the movie biz treating you?" Nicky asked. "Still *People*'s Sexiest Man?"

"Jesus, how do you even know that?" Frank said, though he repeated it for anyone who might have missed it: "*People*'s *sexiest* man! I mean, *come on*. That was practically before you were born!"

"Before *any* of us were born," Jasmin Li said, moving closer to Nicky.

"Well, before *I* was born," Nicky said to her. "But not before *you*." He grinned.

His mother caught the exchange, not sure what to think about it. Antagonistic or playful? She wasn't sure, but she needed her son to be on *her* side. She insinuated herself beside him, forcing Jasmin out of the way, as Frank moved back in.

Jasmin took in the unholy trinity, wife, son, and brother, annoyed they were here when none of them had been part of Victor's life for so long, their intentions obvious. She gave Nicky another look, but he avoided her gaze.

"Oh—my—God!" Rachel stuttered, looking at Frank as if for the first time, going on before she could stop herself. "You're the movie star, Frank D'Arcangelo! How could I have missed it?" She self-consciously fluffed her hair. "I, um, just loved your films! They don't make movies like that anymore."

They do, Frank thought, *just not with me in them.* "Thanks," he said, flashing what remained of his movie-star smile, teeth not quite so white, one of the front caps slightly chipped.

"I was a *huge* fan," Rachel went on. "I mean, um, I still am." Then added as an afterthought, "I'm sorry about your brother."

"My brother? Oh. Right. Of course." For a moment he'd forgotten he was there because his brother had died.

Lauren recognized Frank too. Still handsome enough, she thought, but surely not one of the A-listers, getting old and no longer a star, so not worth pursuing.

"You make films?" Hans Schwegler asked. He had no interest in actors unless they were rich and collected art.

"Oh, yes. He's, um, a *big* star," Rachel said.

"*Was*," Jasmin said.

"He still *is*," Sabrina said, though she knew Frank hadn't been the star of anything in years and wondered how he was getting by. She hoped he'd saved his money. Then realized that was the reason he was there—for money, for the promise of an inheritance. Had Victor actually left him something? She watched him, the way he was smiling, obviously enjoying the attention. *That's Frank,* she thought, *always the actor. Had he been acting with her too? Was he acting now?*

Captain Thomas leaned against the railing and observed the guests, noting how they kept a careful distance, studying them as he played with the two silver pendants dangling from a chain around his neck, one of Saint Brendan the Navigator, the other Our Lady, Star of the Sea. He was a lapsed Catholic, but a superstitious man.

Gulls were circling overhead, then diving into the water, one emerging with a fish flapping in its beak.

"Oh my!" Rachel gasped.

"So where are we going?" Bagdasarian asked, dabbing his sweaty brow with a handkerchief.

"Yeah, where?" Nicky said as the rest of the group moved in, surrounding the captain, asking similar questions.

"How far is it?"

"What's the island's name?"

The captain backed up and leaned over the railing to point out the glittering yacht. "There she is, folks, your luxury transport, the Pershing 140, top of the line. She will get you there safely and smoothly." Not an answer to their questions, and he went on before they could ask again, his instructions to say as little as possible. "You can sit up on the deck or down in the lounge or take a nap in one of the cabins. There are five upper cabins and four below, meant for the crew, but they've been refitted for your comfort as there is only one other crew member, William."

He nodded at a sinewy man with skin a couple of shades darker and even more parched than his, who scrambled off the boat and onto the pier, moving from one guest to the next, collecting their luggage without speaking. He got a grip on Schwegler's briefcase, but the art dealer stopped him, snatching it back.

"I will keep that," he said, noticing the blurry tattoos on William's arms and the five-dot tattoo between his thumb and index finger.

The man let go and said nothing, but when he looked up, Schwegler was startled by his eyes, which were a light ocher color, almost yellow, like a cat's.

"William is the first mate and only mate," the captain said, adding a laugh. "He will take care of your bags, but he will spend most of the trip in the engine room."

The first mate shot Captain Thomas a side-eyed glance, perhaps a wink, but so fast it could have been a blink or even a tic.

"Just the two of you to handle that whale?" Bagdasarian asked, looking at the boat.

"Sir, I grew up on the water and have navigated every sort of vessel from canoe to motorboat to yachts of all sizes. The Pershing here has four sixteen-cylinder diesel engines designed for speed and comfort, and it practically steers itself."

Rachel was trying hard to stifle the fury tingling through her body. *Let it go, let it go, let it go.* She repeated the words in her head forcing herself to look away from Alex Bagdasarian, the man who inspired them. And she *would* let it go. For now.

Ian Lumley, anxious to put the weekend behind him, asked when they were shoving off.

"Now," Captain Thomas said, then surveyed the group again and realized he'd been wrong, noting that one person was still missing. He would have to amend his text. "I mean, when everyone gets here." He checked the dial of his Panerai Luminor 1950 Regatta, the silver-toned hands indicating 9:43 a.m. on its black face. It was the only expensive item on him, though he wore it with a six-dollar cloth band that made it appear cheap. It was important that he did not appear ostentatious or memorable in any way. A moment later, he looked up, hand shielding his eyes from the sun.

"Ah," he said, relieved. "Our last guest has arrived."

15

The captain waved to a young woman, a girl really, with wild red hair, coming toward the crowd, practically running.

"Captain Thomas," he said as she reached him. "At your service."

"Gee, thanks," she said and saluted. "Am I late? It was *so* early when I started out and I was *so* tired and I couldn't find the car, the *limo*, you know, at the airport, and I must've walked past it like a dozen times and the driver couldn't find me either but he finally did, and then we hit traffic and, like, I thought I'd never get here, but here I am!" She let out a breath and sagged a bit, like a balloon whose air had escaped. Then, she took another breath and laughed, tugging at the drooping neckline of her faded floral peasant blouse. It was obvious she wore no bra.

"Well, you're here now," Captain Thomas said taking in the swell of her breasts, then quickly looking up at her pretty face. "That's what matters."

The girl grinned and rocked back on her heels, her bell bottoms rising, a ragged fringe of hem exposing worn sneakers decorated with hand-drawn flowers.

Rachel smiled. So young and sweet, so pretty, she thought, a genuine throwback to a simpler era, Woodstock or Monterey Pop, not that she herself had been old enough to attend either, or almost any pop concert other than Barry Manilow at the New Jersey Performing Arts Center, which she had loved, *absolutely loved*. She looked around, noticed everyone was watching the girl, all of them with puzzled expressions.

Except for Captain Thomas, who had turned away to slip the burner phone from his pocket to send a quick text to his employer to let him know everyone had arrived, exactly as he had been ordered to do.

"And you are?" Jasmin asked the girl just as the captain returned the phone to his pocket, then clapped his hands.

"Time to get onboard," he said.

"Where are the others?" Lauren asked, looking around at the disappointing group, no well-known socialites, no celebrities other than the one has-been actor.

The captain stared at her blankly. "Others?"

The other A-listers, she thought, but said, "Aren't there more people coming?"

Captain Thomas was about to say *no*, but as he had been told to say very little, he said, "I was hired to pick up *this* group." That was the truth but also an ambiguous statement that led her to believe there was in fact another group coming.

"So, the others are meeting us on the island?" Lauren asked.

The captain smiled, again leading her to believe what she wanted.

For a moment, Lauren held back, thinking perhaps Ian was right, that they shouldn't have come. But of course, Ian was never right. So, when First Mate William took her hand, his as rough as hers was smooth, she let him escort her down the gangway.

16

More like a floating five-star hotel than a boat, the yacht sluiced through the water riding high and proud, leaving a frothy wake like a trail of cumulus clouds behind it.

The captain had gathered the guests for a tour, some more begrudgingly than others. The morning sun was blazing, and the guests eyed each other through sunglasses or from under hats and caps while keeping their distance.

They started at the bridge on the main deck, where the captain pointed out the navigation system.

"Looks complicated," Nicky said.

"Not if you know it, and I do," the captain said. "All from Team Italia."

"Which is *what*?" Frank asked, liking the sound of it, thinking one day he could use it if he played a sea captain.

"One of the best integrated technology systems." The captain showed them a few instruments, then moved them to the sun deck, indicating the pool and a second station command while citing the boat's specs. "One-hundred-and-forty-two feet long, twenty-eight feet wide." His ropy arms swept from stern to bow, from starboard to port side as he spoke. "Her top speed is thirty-eight to forty knots but right now we're cruising at a comfortable twenty-seven." He licked a finger and held it up. "We're moving alee. That's opposite of windward, meaning away from the direction of the wind."

"Alee," Frank repeated, still thinking about playing the role of a sea captain.

"Does any of this really matter?" Lauren Ziff asked, scratching the nicotine patch on her upper arm, then slathering sunscreen below it, more on her chest and into her cleavage. "Is there going to be a test or something?"

"I just thought you'd be interested," the captain said.

"Really?" she said. "What would make you think *that*?"

"*I'm* interested," said the young woman with wild red hair. "Tell us more, Captain."

Who are you? Jasmin was about to ask again, but the captain had resumed talking.

"The Pershing 140 is all aluminum rather than fiberglass, powered by diesel engines and water jets."

"And that's important, *why*?" Bagdasarian interrupted.

Rachel Ronan shot him a sideways look. *Same arrogant bastard as always.*

"It guarantees the boat can navigate in shallow water and with less vibration for a smoother ride. You'll appreciate that if we hit a squall."

"Oh my, do you think we, um, will?" Rachel asked. She was already feeling a bit queasy.

"Unlikely," the captain said. "But if so, the boat can handle it, and you're in good hands." He raised his, all rough skin and thick knuckled fingers, and cupped them like the Allstate symbol. He led the group to the lower deck, through automatic sliding glass doors into a living room as elegant as a Manhattan penthouse, then past the sleek wooden bar and a formal dining area. "There's a lot more to see but that's enough for now."

He told them to make themselves comfortable, pointing out there were all kinds of juice and wine, beer and water in the saloon, chips and snacks, sandwiches and pastries too. "If you're hungry," he said. "I'm going up to the bridge. Catch you in a few."

The guests quickly dispersed, moving forward or back, some to the upper deck, others to the lower, as the boat cruised out to sea, the pier fading behind them like an afterthought. Ahead, the water was deep aquamarine, the sky a bright cerulean.

Rachel stood at the prow and looked out to sea. She was reminded of Marc Rothko's color-drenched canvases, the joyous ones the artist had painted before depression led him to taking his own life, something she had considered in recent years. She gripped the guardrail as the yacht glided over the waves and tried to banish any dark thoughts from her mind, imagining for a moment she was the actress Kate Winslet with Leonardo DiCaprio's arms around her waist.

"*Titanic*," she whispered to the wind and laughed, though a feeling of dread rippled through her.

17

Sabrina and Nicky chose the saloon, where they sat on stools at the shiny wooden bar.

"Is this breakfast or brunch?" Sabrina popped a small pastry into her mouth, washed it down with orange juice, then opened a bottle of champagne to spike the juice.

"Kind of early for that, Mother, no?" Nicky gave her a look.

"Oh please. Nothing like a reformed..." She caught herself, raised her glass, and toasted her son. "I'm proud of you."

"For not drinking?"

"For that and...everything. For turning your life around."

Nicky didn't answer. A bad memory had started to play behind his eyes, one he never wanted to see but one that refused to quit.

Hans Schwegler gave them a clipped nod as he came in and took a seat. He plucked a breakfast roll off the bar and ate it in two bites. "Do you mind passing that down?" he asked, his heavy jaw jutting toward the pitchers.

"Which one?" Sabrina asked. There were several of juice, as well as open bottles of wine and the champagne.

"Whatever you are drinking, my dear," he said, and smiled at her.

She noticed his teeth were small and discolored as she slid the bottle of champagne toward him. "Here, before it goes flat," she said and returned his smile. There was a kind of sophisticated brutality about him that made her think he would like her Fatal Flora paintings. "You know, we met years ago."

"Ya, of course I remember," he said and held her gaze.

His eyes were small and amber-colored, and they made her uneasy, a hunger in them as if he were digesting her.

He poured the champagne into his juice and asked if it was okay to smoke a cigarette.

"Ok-ay," Sabrina said, a singsong tease in her voice. "But only because the bar is open to the sea on both sides."

Schwegler shook a long, thin cigarette out of a sleek package. "Would you like one?" He offered the open pack of Davidoffs to Sabrina and Nicky. "They are quite special, vanilla flavored."

"Vanilla-flavored cigarettes?" Nicky's face wrinkled with disgust.

"I'll try one," Sabrina said.

The narrow elegant cigarette looked a lot better in her hand than Schwegler's, which was thick, the nails blunt and slightly chewed. He flicked open a gold lighter and Sabrina leaned in, cupping her hands around his.

Nicky watched, his look of disgust ratcheting up another notch.

Schwegler exhaled a long stream of smoke.

Nicky thought he looked like a cartoon dragon stuffed into an expensive suit.

"You were Victor's art dealer in Europe," Sabrina said. "You're German, right?"

"*Swiss* German."

"Ah, Switzerland!" Alex Bagdasarian blustered his way into the bar, a cigar clamped between his teeth. "The art-dealing, art-looting center of the Western world, conduit for the Nazis during and *after* the war. Wouldn't you agree, Herr Schwegler?"

"I would *not*," Schwegler said, biting off the word and turning his back to Bagdasarian.

Sabrina looked from one man to the other, wondering how best to play the two art dealers. *Against each other*, she decided, though she wanted them both on *her* side.

"Mr. Bagdasarian," she said. "My husband, *ex*-husband, always spoke so highly of you. He said you were the best art dealer in New York." From the beginning, even when Victor was desperate for an art dealer, he had referred to Bagdasarian as the best *scoundrel* art dealer in the world, *which is why I want him on my side.*

Schwegler scoffed and Bagdasarian gave him a look.

"You have a problem, Herr Schwegler?" Bagdasarian puffed heavily on his cigar.

"Not at all." *It is you who have the problem.* He downed his drink and stood up. "But you will excuse me," he said to Sabrina and Nicky, his back still to Bagdasarian, "I am a little tired. I have had a long trip and little sleep." *Feigling! Coward! Stay and fight.* His father's words.

But he *was* tired, and he *would* act. Later. He did not want to give his hand away, not yet. He did a half bow and headed out.

"Terrible man," Bagdasarian said, once he was gone. "Victor never trusted him, I can tell you that."

"Well, he had *you*," Sabrina said, mustering as much sincerity as she possibly could. "What more could he want?"

It was Nicky's turn to scoff.

"What?" Sabrina said to him.

"Nothing, Mother, just something stuck in my craw. How about yours?" He slid a bottle of coconut water toward her. "Here, your favorite. It might help you swallow it."

18

Jasmin Li found a chaise on the upper deck, untied her sandals, and lay back. She spent time smoothing heavy sunscreen on her arms and legs and over her chest, a lighter cream on her face. Still, she couldn't relax, and it was not the thought of age spots or skin cancers that was bothering her. She had watched Sabrina and Nicky head downstairs, the two of them arm in arm, and it infuriated her.

What are they doing down there? Talking about me? And saying what? Oh, the things *she* could say!

A flash of Victor's face purple with rage, a vein in his temple pulsing, spitting his words at her, *You fucking whore!* Like *he* didn't deserve it, like *he* hadn't pushed her into it.

Propped on an elbow, Jasmin stared at the staircase that led down to the lower deck, waiting for the mother and son to emerge. After another minute she gave up and forced herself to look away, taking in the deck, the shiny wood and chrome, the party pit and raised pool, her anger swelling again, this time at Victor for the amount of money he had spent on all this—the boat, the town cars, the first-class plane tickets—all money that should be *hers*!

She took a deep breath, then another. She had to remember why she was here: to get what she wanted, what she deserved.

Yǒu zhì zhě, shì jìng chéng.

Eye on the prize.

A shadow slid across her face.

"Hi, I'm Rachel. We, um, met briefly on the pier and we were on the same plane, remember, both of us in, um, first class, but I wanted to introduce myself and, uh, say hello," the words fumbling out of her mouth.

"You're blocking my sun," Jasmin said, squinting up at her. Then, realizing she needed to know who this woman was and why she was here, she softened. "I'm sorry. Were you a friend of my husband's?"

"Oh, well, no, not a friend." Rachel's hands fluttered around her hair, trying to keep it in place, though the sea breezes made it impossible. She knew she must look awful, and next to this beautiful, perfect woman. "I'm an art critic. Well, I...was full time at the *New York Times*." She laid emphasis heavily on the newspaper's name. "Now, well, I'm just freelance." She laughed uncomfortably, then looked around, hoping to see Lauren Ziff, but there was no sign of her. "I wrote about Victor's work for the paper, the *Times*. I was an early advocate of his work and, um, a serious fan and supporter." She stood there fluffing her hair and smiling awkwardly.

"How nice," Jasmin said flatly, then considered the information: *an early advocate of Victor's art*. Had he left her any money? "Have a seat, Rachel, dear." She patted the chaise beside hers. "And tell me *all* about *you*."

19

The captain gathered the group again. "I'm sure you folks are tired and would like to get to your rooms to rest or freshen up." He read off each of their names along with their cabin number. "All alphabetical," he said. "No favoritism."

"So that means I get penalized with the worst room?" Lauren Ziff said.

"There are no bad rooms," the captain said. "Just above or below deck."

"I cannot possibly be housed *below* deck," she said, scratching at her nicotine patch.

"I'll switch with you," Rachel said, attempting to get into Lauren's good graces.

Lauren raised her sunglasses and gave her a surprised look, though it was her normal look after two eyelid surgeries.

"You're below deck too," the captain said to Rachel.

No one else volunteered to switch rooms.

"Echo Ojai?" Jasmin said, repeating what the captain had said when he assigned a cabin to the girl with the wild red hair. "That can't possibly be your real name."

"Like *Jasmin Li* is *yours?*" the girl said. "I thought it was some kind of herbal tea!"

Sabrina laughed.

Jasmin did not.

And neither did Nicky. He was studying the young woman, detected something cunning beneath the hippie clothes and innocent presentation. She caught him looking and flashed a smile. He returned it, his smile guarded, then turned away and asked the captain how long the trip was going to take.

"About five hours, four if the tide is with us." The captain stared out to sea as if looking for something specific.

"*That* long?" Lauren Ziff said, fanning herself.

"That's no time at all, love," Ian said. "Just pop another Dramamine and Klonopin and you can sleep through the whole bloody trip, the way you do through your life." And he hoped she would, his eyes flicking between Jasmin and Sabrina.

"*Anyone* living with you would want to sleep through their life!" she said. "What's my *below*-deck room number again?" she asked the captain, then headed off.

Rachel followed, stopping her midway to the lower deck. "Hi! We haven't, um, been formally introduced, I'm Rachel Ronan."

Lauren lowered her sunglasses a fraction of an inch and peered over them. "Yes," she said, neither question nor comment.

"I, well, you're Lauren Ziff. I, uh, recognize you."

"You mean you just heard the captain say my name."

"Well, yes, I did, but I *do* recognize you." She was starting to feel queasy, not sure if it was nerves or seasickness.

"*Oh?*" Lauren squinted at her.

"Yes, because, uh, you see, I'm writing a piece, for the, um, *Times*, and I have been trying to—"

"Oh, so that was *you* behind those endless emails!"

"I think only, well, only two emails." She laughed nervously but kept talking, afraid to lose Lauren. "It's going to be an exceptional piece, very, um, serious, about families that have collected art for a long time. There's a Rockefeller nephew and his wife who are, um, carrying on Nelson Rockefeller's tradition of collecting African art and—"

"My *parents* were the serious collectors," Lauren said cutting her off. "I only…"

"Dabble?" Ian offered. "Me wife here is the ultimate dabbler, aren't you, love?"

Lauren ignored him.

"Well yes, your parents *were* famous art collectors," Rachel went on. "Was it your father or grandfather who, um, started Ziff Pharmaceuticals?"

Lauren shot her a look so poisonous it was surprising Rachel remained standing.

"So," she said, "the interview has begun, has it, and *all* about Ziff Pharma?" She took a step closer to Rachel, arm raised as if she might strike her, and she wanted to… These goddamn reporters who had so publicly shamed her family. If this woman dared ask her one more question about Ziff Pharmaceuticals… "It was my *grandfather*," she said, spitting the words. "*There!* You got your answer. The interview is *over*!"

"But I haven't…"

"Did you *hear* me? *Over!*" Lauren's hand was in a fist now, twitching in front of Rachel's face.

"I didn't m-mean to…" Rachel stuttered. She hadn't meant to say anything about the pharmaceutical company, certainly not yet. *Don't you ever know when to shut up?* Her mother's voice, always in her head. "I'm sorry, I only…"

Too late. Lauren had already grabbed hold of Ian's arm and was leading him away.

Watching them from across the deck, Nicky could see from their faces and body language that something unpleasant had transpired, though he hadn't heard what. He took a step away from the small group and whispered to Jasmin, "Looks like someone just got reamed."

"Who cares?" she said, exaggerating a yawn.

"That guy, Ian, looks so familiar. I think I know him from somewhere."

"Must be from your crack-house days," she said under her breath but loud enough. "He looks it."

Nicky ignored her and turned back to the captain. "So, where are we going, *exactly?*"

"To a beautiful island."

"Does it have a name?"

"All I have are the coordinates, twenty-two north by seventy-two east, that's latitude and longitude. That mean anything to you?" He figured it would not. He had been told to hold back information and had not questioned his employer. Once he accepted a job, he never did.

"Not a damn thing," Nicky said.

"I haven't been there myself," the captain said, and that much was true.

"Then how do you know it's beautiful?" Nicky asked.

"Is this a mystery cruise?" Jasmin asked.

Echo Ojai, said, "Oh, I love a mystery!"

"Well, I *hate* them," Jasmin said, and she meant it. She liked to know everything that could possibly happen at all times, so she was prepared. She stared out at the sea, a never-ending stretch of blue, no other boats, no markers, nothing but water.

20

Alex Bagdasarian found himself in the master suite by the good fortune of his last name. The room, more like an apartment, had a lounge area, a separate bedroom, walk-in closets, an enormous bathroom, and light streaming through shark's-gill windows painting everything with stripes.

He tugged off his shoes and sagged onto the bed. *My luck is changing!* he thought. After the weekend he'd have the D'Arcangelo estate, and his money problems would be a thing of the past. And of course he *would* get the estate. Who else had the knowledge or the expertise?

Only one other person. He sat up, an image of Hans Schwegler filling his mind like poison gas.

Was it possible that Victor would turn his estate over to that Eurotrash Nazi? *No, no way. It couldn't be.* But why else would the man be here? Clearly, he'd been invited for a reason. Had Victor found out about the cash sales and unpaid commissions?

Up now, Bagdasarian rooted around in his bag, found a Montecristo, and lit up despite the NO SMOKING sign in his cabin. He took a drag and thought it through. Suppose Schwegler *did* get the estate. *What then?*

He exhaled, the answer coming to him as if written on the long plume of smoke: the man from the dark web, the assassin.

Of course.

21

Frank D'Arcangelo could not believe he had snagged the VIP cabin.

An omen, he thought, *of good things to come.*

The room was spacious, the bed king-size, the bathroom luxurious with double sinks, a large shower, even a Jacuzzi, everything about it so much better than his apartment back home. He'd sold the Beverly Hills mansion years ago, and the profits, which he'd been living off, were nearly gone.

There was a time when he had spent without thinking, running up debt, never suspecting his career would dry up—and so fast. It wasn't fair, the taste of success, of fame, so delicious, gone.

He drew a sharp breath, felt some tightness in his chest. Though nothing like the pain he had ignored until he couldn't. The stents had saved his life. *You're lucky*, his doctor had said more than once. *Twenty years ago, you would have been dead.* Though he'd also said Frank might need another stent and that the residual damage from the heart attack had been serious. *We can't fix everything.*

The old Bee Gees song played in his head: *How can you mend a broken heart?* Frank laughed, though it wasn't funny. Heartache, heartbreak, came in so many forms.

He sat heavily on the edge of the bed and ran his hands over the silky sheet, thinking of Sabrina, the shame and excitement of making love to his brother's wife. Was it possible she was even more beautiful now? They hadn't talked about their past or their future, but he had seen something behind her eyes, a longing he hoped he had not invented.

Even if I have, I will make her fall in love with me again.

He knew the right things to say, the script writing itself in his head, knew the moves too, could see the camera moving in for a close-up as they kissed.

Some sort of seabird, a gull or a tern, at his cabin window broke the spell, and the idea of inheritance was back in his mind. What exactly had his brother left him? *Money? A few paintings?* He knew the good ones went for millions at auction.

Was Sabrina thinking the same thing? He was sure she didn't retain much feeling for Victor other than payback. She had said as much during their long-ago pillow talk.

He imagined them together, pooling their resources. And in love. Something he wanted badly. Though if he were honest, the love part not nearly as much as the money.

22

Hans Schwegler did a slow three-sixty, his boxlike below-deck cabin an insult with its narrow double-decker bunk and cramped bathroom. If this boat trip were any longer, he would put up a fuss at being treated like this, an insult. He chewed his thumbnail, told himself to relax, that he would not be spending much time in the room except to send texts and make calls, like the call he had to make now.

There were several long beeps before his father picked up.

"*Vater*," Schwegler said, whispering into the phone. "He is here. And he is not well. It will be easy. *Es wird einfach sein.*"

"*Enttäuschen Sie mich nicht—ausnahmsweise einmal!*" *Do not disappoint me—for once!*

Schwegler promised he would not.

"*Gut*," his father said. "*Komm nicht nach Hause, wenn du es tust!*" *Do not come home if you do!*

23

"Can you believe this fucking room, so tiny and *below* ground?" Lauren Ziff said with disgust, shaking her head.

"Below *deck*," Ian corrected. "And it's a *cabin*, love, not a *room*."

Lauren gave him a look, "Well, aren't we the sophisticated little Cockney git."

Ian wished they were above deck only so he could push her overboard. "There's no reason to spend time here, love, except to take a shite."

"Now that's more like the classy guy I know," Lauren said, changing into a Dolce & Gabbana gold-threaded bikini that barely covered the scars of her tummy tuck. She admired herself in the narrow mirror, turning this way and that, waiting for Ian to say something until he finally caught on.

"You look good," he said.

"You're not looking at me."

He tried not to sigh as he gave her an exaggerated once-over. "You're looking peng, baby." He used the Mancunian word for *looking great,* which Lauren knew, and almost smiled. Then she ruined it.

"Did it kill you to say that?"

Almost, he thought, pulling on a black Speedo that accentuated his soft belly, his thin arms and legs dotted with tattoos, all from his rock-and-roll days. He put on a Morrissey T-shirt, then unearthed his stash and lit a joint.

"Must you? There's no air in here as it is. And I'm trying to quit, you know that!"

"You quitting the fags doesn't mean I'm quitting the weed, love." But he did what she said, nipped the joint out and stuck it in the waistband of his Speedo.

"Do you believe that woman, Rachel What's-her-name, the dowdy one with the bad hair? She's a *reporter*, for Christ's sake! Here on the boat! My God, they're like roaches, *everywhere!*"

"Oi, let it be, love. You put her in her place, didn't you?"

"I damn well did and she'd better stay there! One more word out of her about Ziff Pharma, and I swear..." Her hands balled into fists again, her nail extensions digging into her palms.

"Chill, love. She's easy enough to ignore."

"*How?* We're going to be trapped on an island with her!"

Ian was about to say, *You're the one who wanted to come*, but thought better of it. Over the years he'd watched the pretty girl he'd met and married turn into a shrew, firing workmen and assistants one after another, telling people off, recently slapping a former friend who'd had the bad sense to say something about the scandal. *Come now, Lauren dear, you must have known something.* A slap that sent the woman reeling, the assault and battery charges still pending, a lawsuit Lauren would have to settle out of court, and not the first.

"And *you*," she said, turning on him. "You forgot our anniversary."

"No, love, I didn't." He rummaged through his bag and came up with a small box, the bright yellow-gold ribbon crushed.

Lauren recognized the white box with its matching yellow-gold writing, knew their personal shopper had bought the Monica Rich Kosann eighteen-karat gold-and-diamond locket necklace because she had told her to, had even supplied the small photograph inside the box. She opened it, acting surprised, a game they played on birthdays and anniversaries, though she was genuinely touched looking at the photo of them twenty years ago.

"The Isle of Wight," she said. "Remember?"

"Aye, love." He peered through the cabin's small window at what he could see of the ocean and the tiniest sliver of sky, the memory washing over him: the Isle of Wight concert, his band, the Bleedin' Drunks, opening for the Verve, their first important gig, Lauren, the girlfriend of the Verve's drummer and just about the prettiest bloody thing he'd ever seen.

He watched her loop the chain around her neck, caught another glimpse of the photo of them in the locket, a different girl entirely.

"Help me with this," she said, lifting her hair.

Ian got hold of the chain, noted the lines at the nape of her neck that had escaped the surgeon's scalpel. Back then, it didn't matter that she was a few years older (it turned out to be a decade), but he didn't care. He'd never met anyone like her, the super-confident New York girl, funny and smart, life of the party, picking up the tab for drinks, supplying pot and coke and everything else.

He secured the clasp, his mind on full playback mode, the poor boy from Manchester, undereducated, unworldly, only twenty-two at the time, and in love. Back then, everyone was in love with Lauren—the band members, the roadies and sound engineers, the lighting guys and stage managers, even the merch staff hawking band T-shirts and posters, all of them hitting on her too, but Ian hadn't dared: She was so clearly out of his league.

"There," he said, securing the clasp, still lost in the past, thinking how it had been Lauren who broke the ice, commenting on his "cute" Mancunian accent, his punk black hair and big blue eyes, which she made up one night before the show, lining them with the blackest kohl, her face inches from his, hands gently on his cheeks. They'd slept together that night and the next and she ditched the

Verve drummer, and when the concert ended, she laid out money for the Bleedin' Drunks' first American tour, even helped get them a recording contract where they made two middling albums and had a couple of indie hits before they broke up.

Lauren held the locket toward him, opening it again, and Ian got a last look at the old photo before she snapped it closed, taking the twenty-year memory with it.

He told her he was going for a swim and asked if she'd join him, though he hoped she would say no.

"You *know* I don't swim," she barked, something to do with a childhood accident, almost drowning in a pool, her nanny distracted. "But I'll sunbathe at the beach club. Meet me *there*, *not* the pool."

"Aye, love," he said, and would have saluted if he dared.

Ian climbed the staircase to the upper deck, body sluggish with regret, that old photo having made it all too clear that twenty years had passed, taking his youth along with them, and here he was, shackled to Lauren by money and no way out.

The view from the yacht's deck was spectacular, sparkling ocean and bright blue sky, a few powder-puff clouds, the boat moving at a clip, the sun and salt in Ian's face as he made his way toward the rear of the boat and the beach club.

He flopped onto a lounge chair and lit a joint, then looked up to see Lauren heading toward him. He noted the beach club's side panels were open to the sea, just a foot above the water and the fast-moving waves, no guardrail at all.

"Oi!" he shouted. "Over here, love," already picturing the accidentally on-purpose shove that would send her into the water.

24

Rachel was lost, not unusual. In Manhattan, a grid and easy for most people, she often found herself heading uptown when she wanted to go down, her sense of direction nonexistent. *You would get lost in your own bedroom!* Her mother, always loitering in her head ready to criticize. And here she was, lost below deck, her bearings off even more than usual, that confrontation with Lauren Ziff having thrown her.

Why on earth had she said anything about Ziff Pharmaceuticals?

She walked down one short stairwell, then another in search of her room, was trying to remember the number—*Was it six or seven?*—when she took yet another stairwell and spotted the first mate down at the end of the narrow corridor.

He was turned away, leaning against a wall beside an open door to what she supposed was the engine room. She could see a bit of machinery, glittering silver, and hear the loud purr of the turbines. He had a cigarette in one hand and an old-fashioned flip phone in the other, pressed against his ear, and she could just make out what he was saying.

"I don't know, and I'm not gonna ask."

It was the first time she'd heard him speak, and she was surprised. She'd had no idea the man could even talk, his voice rough and hoarse sounding.

She was about to call out and say hello, but stopped. Something about the way the man was standing, slightly bent over and shielding the phone, made her feel as if she had come upon a private moment. She took a step back, but too late.

He looked up, caught her eye, and snapped his phone closed, a leering smile spreading over his gaunt, leathery face. A second later, he disappeared into the engine room, leaving behind only a puff of smoke.

25

"So," Nicky asked. "What do you make of this little posse Father has put together?"

He and Sabrina were up on the upper deck, in what the captain had referred to as the "party pit," a sunken area with table and chairs, a stereo system, and a hot tub. Sabrina sipping a second bottle of coconut water she had swiped from the saloon. Both had changed into bathing suits, Sabrina poised on the edge in a one-piece, deep scarlet with a plunging neckline and cut high on the thighs. It was a size too small, but she wore it well, like a '50s pinup, ripe and voluptuous.

Nicky did a quick scan of his arms, something he did automatically and unconsciously, checking for track marks that were gone, thanks to multiple laser treatments. He lay back on the sun pad face up, hands behind his head and legs spread. His suit, no more than a thong, exposed the small skull and crossbones tattoo on his lower abdomen, a memento of pre-rehab days and something he could not remember getting.

"Your suit is indecent," Sabrina said.

"You should talk." He stretched, causing his bathing suit to become even more revealing. "I would have gone naked, but I was afraid I'd freak the others out."

She rolled her eyes, then dared a question: "What's with you and the dragon lady?"

"*Excuse me?* That's racist, Mommy dearest."

"Oh, please. She's clearly a monster, so why not a dragon? And don't call me *that*."

"A racist or Mommy dearest?"

"Seriously, what do you think of her? You never say."

Nicky rolled onto his stomach slightly away from her and mumbled, "I dunno."

"They were getting a divorce, she and your father, right?"

"That's not my business."

"Are you *kidding*? It totally *is* your business—your future is at stake!"

Nicky didn't answer. Through half-closed eyes he was watching Jasmin as she emerged from below deck. She paused a moment to look at him, then struck a pose, head back, chest out, her bathing suit cut quite like his mother's, but dark iridescent blue, like a layer of paint over her perfect body. She was heading directly toward them, and he braced himself, but she stepped over him without a word. She gave Sabrina a frosty hello, then kept going.

"Quite the performance," Sabrina said once Jasmin was out of earshot.

Again, Nicky said nothing.

"Are you sleeping or ignoring me?"

"Ignoring you," he mumbled.

"*Nicolo!*" She used his name like a lance.

He raised his beautiful head and half turned toward her. "What?"

"Is there something you're not telling me?"

He lifted a hand as if to shield his eyes from the sun, though it had temporarily slid behind a cloud. "Like what?"

Sabrina knew her son well, knew he could be intentionally evasive. Nicky, the boy with the high IQ and terrible grades, the classic underachiever who, already in his young life, had drifted from one creative field to another. But smart, always smart, she knew that too. Even as a kid he always *got* everything, knew exactly what was going on, knew how to hide his understanding, his intelligence and his feelings too. *He keeps a lot inside.* What so many teachers had told her, therapists too.

Victor's fault, she thought. The guilty absentee father always bailing him out.

But was she any better, going along with it? She blamed them both, their combative marriage, a war zone. What child could survive that?

Clouds raced across the sun, shadows sliding over her son's beautiful face, the scar on his chin, a memento of the "incident," the way she always thought of it. She'd let Victor sweep that under the table too; what mother wouldn't? She hated to think about it, that her son was capable of such a thing.

Maybe we are all capable of such things, she thought. Frank being here, a reminder of her own transgressions.

"You're doing okay now, right?" She took a sip of coconut water, pausing before she asked, "Still going to meetings and talking with your sponsor?"

"That's not your business, that's why they use the word *anonymous*, remember? But yes, I am."

"Good. I'm simply concerned," she said, and it was true. If there was one thing, one person in the world she loved, it was her son, whom she had tried to keep safe but had not always succeeded. She reached over and touched his arm. "Is it so bad that I worry about you?"

For a moment he felt bad. She had always been there for him, and he loved her despite her boundary issues.

"We're in this together, right?" she said.

"You mean being here at the memorial?"

"*Yes*. And stop playing dumb," she said, annoyed now. "You know *exactly* what I mean."

He did. They were here at this absurd memorial to find out what his father had deigned to leave them and to be able to claim it. "The inheritance."

"Yes." She dropped her voice to a whisper, "And whatever it is, we will divide it, fifty-fifty, like we do everything, right?"

"Sure," he said, still watching Jasmin, who had stopped halfway across the deck and was glaring back at him over her shoulder.

26

Hans Schwegler was sorry he had bought the matching cabana set online, the terry cloth jacket too short for his arms and, worse, impossible to button over his belly, which he tried to hold in as he made his way toward the party pit, his eyes on Victor's beautiful ex-wife, her red bathing suit outlining her nudity more than hiding it. A quick look down to make sure his erection was undetectable in his baggy swim trunks.

"*Guten Tag!*" he said, all smiles, then looked at Nicky, his tone becoming serious as he lowered himself onto a deck chair. "I have been meaning to say I am sorry for your loss. Your father was a great artist."

Nicky looked up, the sun in his eyes. "Rich and famous doesn't mean you're great, just rich and famous." He yawned. "I'm curious, did my father invite you to this?"

Schwegler pulled back, chin tucking into his thick neck. "But of course. I received an invitation like everyone else. My family gallery has represented your father's artwork in Europe for several years."

"And doing a great job, I can tell you that!" Sabrina said, trying to make up for her son's rudeness, which was difficult as Nicky scoffed.

Schwegler gave Sabrina a big smile exposing those tiny discolored teeth. "You must come to Zurich to see my gallery. It is one of the biggest and best, but we have small rooms as well, perfect for jewellike paintings."

"Really?" Sabrina tried to keep her excitement in check, always better not to seem too needy, though she gave him her best smile, sexy and full of promise, a carrot dangled until he she got what she wanted: her paintings on his gallery's walls. Why not have European as well as American representation?

"Ya," he said. "Perfect," smiling at her, drawing his tongue drawn across his thin lips.

She smiled back, though she worried she might have to deliver more than a smile. She focused on a spot above his ear so she did not have to see his face or imagine his fleshy body under that ridiculous terry cloth outfit. What she would do if she had to go further to seal the deal? Nothing new. She had stared past more than one man's ear while going through the motions, and for a lot less.

Schwegler watched her, openly staring at her breasts.

"I'd love to see your gallery and those small jewellike rooms," Sabrina said, exactly how she had described her paintings to him earlier, and he had not forgotten. She saw he was ogling her breasts, and her first instinct to fold her arms across her chest. Instead, she sat up and inhaled. "But it's so far away."

"Only a plane trip, my dear," he said, and then unable to control himself though it was not yet public information, he said, "You know, my family is expanding into the U.S. art market."

"Oh, how exciting," she said, then thought for a moment. "Will you be working with Mr. Bagdasarian?"

Schwegler made a kind of snorting noise through his nose, sorry now he'd said anything, but unable to stop. "Mr. Bagdasarian does not control the D'Arcangelo market and..." He waved a hand. "Never mind. It does not matter."

"Why not?" Nicky asked, raising his head.

"Nothing. Only that he is getting old, no? And he does not look well. I do not imagine he will be able to work much longer." *Stop talking!*

"Has he mentioned retirement?" Sabrina asked, genuinely interested, a question she would put to the New York art dealer herself when she had a chance. If he was retiring, she did not want to waste her time with him.

"No. But…" *Shut up! Den Mund halten!* His father in his head. Schwegler cleared his throat, then changed the subject. "Is that Man Ray?" he asked Nicky, indicating the tattoo of a woman's eye with diamond tears inked over Nicky's heart.

"Pretty dope, right?" Nicky said, his finger circling the tattoo.

Just plain dope, Sabrina had always thought but didn't say.

"You know his real name was Emmanuel Radnitzky," Schwegler said. "A Jew from New Jersey."

"*Philadelphia*," Nicky corrected. He pretty much knew everything about Man Ray. "A great artist, and yeah, I know he was Jewish. You have a problem with that?"

"Not at all. I was just mentioning it, in case you did not know."

"Like the way some people *mention* my mixed race or are super careful *not* to mention it. Is that what you mean?"

"Nicky enjoys being confrontational," Sabrina said, adding a faux laugh while glaring at her son. "Don't you, dear?"

"Not really," Nicky said.

"I did not mean anything by it," Schwegler said. "It was just… information."

"*Information*," Nicky repeated, making the word sound damning.

"There he goes again," Sabrina said, forcing another laugh.

"It is so hot," Schwegler said, tugging the terry cloth cabana top away from his chest, already sweating.

"Is it?" Nicky said. "I hadn't noticed."

"I think I will get something from the bar." Schwegler stood. "May I bring anyone a drink?"

"No, thank you," Sabrina said sweetly. "I have this." She waved her bottle of coconut water.

"No thanks…" Nicky said, waiting until Schwegler was only a few feet away before adding, "douchebag."

"Be quiet!" Sabrina hissed. "He'll hear you."

"I hope so. Fucking antisemitic asshole." He sat up and faced her. "You think he's not calling *you* names—even if he does have the hots for you?" He made a face. "I guess you're like forbidden fruit or something." He sang, "Brown Sugar, how come you taste *sooo* good?"

"*Please*, Nicola. Stop being so vulgar."

"I'm not the one sucking someone off for a gallery exhibit."

"So, what if I *am*?" Sabrina snapped.

"Just sayin'." Nicky stood and stretched. "I'm going to hit the pool." He took a few steps, then turned back to her. "You know, underneath all that flirting and lust, I think that guy looks mean as fuck. If I were you, Mother, I'd watch my step."

27

Rachel had finally found her below-deck cabin but could not sit still. Pent up after that confrontation with Lauren Ziff, she needed air. Now she paced along one of the covered side decks, their conversation, if you could call it that, on replay.

This interview is over!

And that look on her face. If looks could kill!

One more time Rachel chastised herself: Why had she said anything about the pharmaceutical company? She knew better, had even practiced the questions, ones about art and art collecting, charity work, and then, only then, after softening the woman up, a hint at the pharmaceutical fortune that had made the art collecting possible. But no, the first words out of her mouth had to be about Ziff Pharma!

Oh, Rachel. She sighed heavily just as the yacht swerved, her stomach along with it.

The question now, could she fix it? Or had she blown it before she'd even begun? Without Lauren Ziff, the article would be killed along with any hope of jump-starting her freelance career.

But article or no article, she had an inheritance coming. *Thank God.*

She sucked in a breath, a taste of brine on her lips, refreshing, then nauseating. She swallowed hard, looked around, glad she was under the covered side deck and no one was nearby. The last thing she needed was to throw up in front of these people!

Stomach feeling worse, she tried to find something to focus on, but all she could see was a never-ending expanse of blue.

The yacht swerved again, not much but enough to make her stomach do another flip. She took a deep breath and leaned over the aisle wall just in case, telling herself she'd be fine.

But then another swerve, the horizon going off-kilter a moment, her head starting to spin, and were those voices? They sounded nearby but she was too busy trying not to be sick to look.

Sweating, her breath coming rapidly, she leaned further over the railing.

Seconds later the world turned upside down and she was falling, the sea rising up to meet her. She heard the splash like a crack of thunder, then everything was dark, muted, the gurgling sound of air bubbles as if they were far away. Everything still. Then, panic. Rachel floundering. The weight of her dress dragging her down, she paddled frantically, furiously, managed to get her head above the surface, spitting out water, waving her arms and screaming, "*Help!*" The side of the boat was silvery and reflective, blinding. Rachel tried to grab it, but there was nothing to hold on to, her hands sliding off the smooth surface, the boat's engines roaring in her ears as the waves dragged her backward into the wake, swallowing water every time she tried to take a breath. Rising, falling, knocked one way, then the other, she was going down again, a burning sensation in her lungs, panic and pain giving way to a sense of calm as the ocean closed in, a dark tunnel, her mother at the end of it, calling her name, "Rachel, *Rachel*!"

Then the water inside her was exploding out of her and there was a smudge of something flesh-colored in her vision, a face taking shape, details filling in: Frank D'Arcangelo.

Am I dead? Is this a movie?

She reached out and touched Frank's face.

"Oh—" All she could say before coughing, more water spewing out of her mouth, one arm still hooked through a life preserver though she had no memory of it before now.

"Lucky I saw you," Frank said, Nicky beside him, both breathing heavily. "Took both of us to haul you out of the water onto that life preserver!"

Even now, disoriented and trying to breathe, she was mortified by the statement.

"Are you okay?" It was Sabrina this time. Then the others. All of them staring down at her while she struggled for breath, feeling cold, teeth chattering, confused and ashamed.

"I'm…okay." She managed to sit up, felt the sopping dress cling to her, outlining her body, and tugged at it. "I don't know how I…" She was trying to patch her thoughts together. Behind the faces, the sky was so blue, the sun blinding, her body shaking, her mind still juddering while a recollection made its way up through the confusion: the moment before she fell, feeling something…*a nudge, a shove?* Had that really happened? She wasn't sure. She'd always been clumsy, just ask her mother. And yet…

"Here you go." The captain draped a blanket over her shoulders.

Thank goodness, she thought, and not just because she was cold, once again taking in the faces surrounding her, the looks of concern.

"You weren't in the water very long," the captain said. "Not long enough for hypothermia. You'll be okay." *Just get them all to the island,* his employer had stressed, and he had almost lost one.

"I'm—okay," Rachel said, still coughing. She tried to get up, unsteady. Her legs felt loose, unhinged.

"Easy now." Nicky, the young god, sweat glittering on his bare chest, helping her to her feet.

She was still shivering, even now with the blanket half covering her as she awkwardly attempted to hide her body.

"Get some rest before lunch," the captain said, wondering if he would have to report this to his employer, and if so, what he should say.

Rachel managed a nod, noted Echo practically glued to the captain's side, red hair whipping around her face like flames, but when she pushed it away, Rachel thought the girl was grinning. *About what?*

Nicky and Frank were on either side of her, helping her up, everyone uttering words of encouragement.

But no, not everyone. She saw that now.

From across the deck, Alex Bagdasarian watched the action, a plume of cigar smoke issuing out of his mouth. And just a few feet from him, Lauren Ziff gazed out to sea as if her life depended on it.

28

The captain checked his phone. Still no answer to the text he'd sent his employer about the incident. A good sign, he was sure. Until he wasn't. He thought about sending a second, then decided to leave it alone. The less said, the better. Perhaps he shouldn't have reported it in the first place. Too late now and he had to stop second-guessing himself, which was neither his nature nor a good thing, though the thought continued to play in his head while he set out lunch in the main saloon, First Mate William by his side. Croissants and rolls, cheeses and prosciutto, little quiches, fruit and berries, bottles of a wine and prosecco and S.Pellegrino until the long wooden bar resembled a Flemish still-life painting of a cornucopia.

The room opposite was spacious and elegant. Two large sofas, matching love seat, club chairs, everything upholstered in a high-end white synthetic that looked better than leather and obviously was made to withstand the elements, accents of burnt orange and black from throw pillows arranged perfectly here and there. The wooden wide-planked floor was smooth and shiny, the ceilings high with recessed lighting and a modernist chandelier hung over a coffee table cube that looked like a minimalist sculpture by Donald Judd. Just beyond the open sliding glass doors was a private dining area with a table that could easily seat a dozen, hidden yet open to the sea, balmy ocean breezes wafting into the room.

Soon filled by the guests, everyone except Rachel, all of them rehashing what had happened.

"Do you think she's okay?"

"How on earth did she fall in?"

"Should we see if she's all right?"

The captain reassured them it was a freak accident, that he'd never had a passenger fall overboard or ever lost one. "Not once in all my years at sea!" he said, then tapped William, the two of them exchanging a look before they took off.

Diving into the food and drink, the guests soon forgot about Rachel.

Nicky was the first to fill his plate, his mother behind him.

"Couldn't you have put some clothes on?" she said.

"I *did,*" he said. He was wearing a gauzy white shirt unbuttoned, his chest exposed, and still in his thong.

"Oh, it's a naked lunch," Jasmin said to him, joining the buffet line. "I didn't get the memo."

"It looks like you *did,*" he said, eyeing her up and down. She'd changed into scanty hot pants and what looked like a bra.

Lauren Ziff filled a glass with prosecco, drank half and refilled it. Still in her gold bikini, though she'd topped it with a sheer swimming jacket that hid nothing. She had reapplied her makeup, lips outlined in dark red, blue eyeshadow, hair brushed out and down around her shoulders, the new gold locket bobbing above her breasts. "Guess it's okay that I'm still in my suit," she said.

"Sure," Sabrina said. "We're all friends."

"Are we?" Jasmin said. "Guess I missed *that* memo too."

Nicky and Sabrina arranged themselves on the couch. Jasmin squeezed in between them, nudging Nicky over and gave Sabrina a thin smile. "I understand you're the president of the first wives' club."

"And once your divorce is final, you can be secretary," Sabrina said. "Though I'm guessing *you* would rather be *treasurer*."

"Oh, I *like* you," Jasmin said, and almost meant it. "But I was *not* getting divorced. I don't know how that nasty rumor got started. Victor and I are, *were*, mad for each other."

"Really?" Sabrina said. "I only heard about the *mad* part."

Frank hovered above them, balancing his plate and a glass of prosecco, despite doctor's orders to stop drinking. It was easy enough to rationalize one drink, and he would stop after the weekend. "Can I join this little tête-à-tête?"

"That term implies *two*," Jasmin said. "Or didn't they teach that at Hollywood High?"

He couldn't come up with a retort, so he ignored her and chose a seat bedside Sabrina, the couch getting more crowded. He raised his glass. "Here's to new friends, old ones, and family!" He clinked Sabrina's glass and leaned in close, his face inches from hers, her breath warm on his cheek.

Sabrina pulled back, but not before a cluster of memories had jostled her mind.

Lauren balanced on the arm of the couch beside Nicky. "You must be an artist like your father."

An image from his first and only exhibition flared, then sizzled like a piece of film caught in an old projector. "No. I was never interested in art."

"Don't believe him," Sabrina said. "He's *very* talented."

Jasmin leaned across Nicky and aimed a finger at Lauren's locket. "Monica Rich Kosann, am I right?"

Lauren used it as an excuse to bend over, her breasts inches above Nicky's face as she flicked the locket open.

"Who are the people in the picture?" Sabrina asked.

"Me, of course," Lauren said, and looked up as Ian entered. "And *him*."

"Wow," Sabrina said. "You guys were beautiful!" After an awkward moment, she added, "Of course, you still *are*!" She looked from the locket to Lauren, watched as she smoothed her hair back, exposing telltale scars at her ears. "You look great, you really do," she said, thinking about her own beauty and if she would one day succumb to the knife. She had considered it but could never afford it. Though now, with an inheritance coming, she could and maybe would.

She studied Lauren's too-taut face a moment longer, could see she had once been pretty, her eyes still a luminous aquamarine, though they looked hard. *No, not hard,* she thought, *sad.* She wondered what *her* eyes gave away. She knew she had become harder after her marriage and divorce from Victor but hoped something remained of the softer young woman she'd once been, even if she rarely exposed that part of herself to the world.

"Thanks," Lauren said to her. "But at my age, it's all work!"

Sabrina figured she and Lauren were the same age, Lauren possibly younger, though the surgery made her appear older, the mere fact of it declaring, *I am old but refuse to admit it!* "Well, I think you look wonderful!" she said. "In fact, I'd like to paint you." The idea came to her spontaneously if not innocently: Her commissioned portraits of rich people paid the rent. Something she hoped would be a thing of the past, but for now, insurance. And having a well-known art collector as a friend never hurt.

"I thought you only painted poisonous plants," Lauren said. "Is *that* how you see me?"

Sabrina laughed. "Not at all! There's something...regal about you that I'd like to capture."

"*Regal?*" Lauren scoffed, but raised her chin, posing, queenlike.

"I'm serious."

"I'd be honored," Lauren said.

Nicky watched, impressed though ambivalent about the way his mother treated everything and everyone like an opportunity. She was like his father in that way, probably why they ended up hating each other.

"We can figure out a time for you to model once we get home," Sabrina said.

Lauren looked Sabrina over, taking her seriously for the first time. "Yes," she said, still posing, head up, breasts out.

Ian snorted and Lauren glanced over, taking him in with a look of disgust. He'd put on a pair of gray sweatpants that draped over his bare feet and showed off the fact that he was not wearing underwear. He was about to sit on the love seat opposite when she held out her glass. "Top me off," she demanded.

He put his plate down, took her glass, and refilled it. "You shouldn't drink so much, love."

"There are the people you want to drink with and people who make you want to drink," she said with an eye roll in Ian's direction, then turned to the group. "You know, he tried to drown me at the beach club!"

"That's not true, love. Me beautiful wife here was drinking and almost fell in. Lucky I was there to rescue her." Not quite true. It was only after he had accidentally on purpose jostled her, that he'd had a change of heart and caught her before she went overboard.

"As if," Lauren said.

"Two people overboard in one morning," Jasmin said. "What is this, a lifeguard training school?"

"Well, I didn't go over," Lauren said, casting a look around the room. "Where's what's-her-name? Has she decided to jump off the boat again?"

"Maybe we should check on her," Sabrina said.

"Leave her be," Jasmin said. "She's a big girl. And I swear I only mean that chronologically."

Such a bitch, Sabrina thought, hoping she had made Victor's life miserable.

Alex Bagdasarian came in shirtless, a towel around his shoulders, swim trunks sagging below his gut.

"Oh my God," Jasmin said. Fingers half splayed over her eyes, she watched Bagdasarian settled his bulk onto a stool at the bar. "Is it okay to look yet?"

"We really should be BFFs," Sabrina whispered to her conspiratorially, still hoping to get the true status of Jasmin and Victor's marriage, something she needed to know. "I'm serious. I mean, we have so much in common."

"Like bad taste in husbands," Nicky said.

Hans Schwegler, still in his too-tight cabana set, overfilled his plate and looked around as if he were hunting. He wanted nothing more than to sit beside Victor's beautiful ex-wife, to feel the heat of her body, but she was surrounded. Resigned, he arranged himself on a club chair with a view of everyone, though he felt isolated, alone, the way he had felt much of his life. He gobbled a quiche and drained his wineglass, then lit one of his long, thin cigarettes, his eyes still on the ex-wife and the artist's brother crushed beside her.

In his mind, he saw Frank D'Arcangelo keel over and die.

29

Rachel had changed into one of the two Diane Von Furstenberg wrap dresses she'd been talked into buying for the trip, this one a floral-print crepe that the saleswoman had assured her was "slimming," though after turning this way and that in the full-length mirror, she had her doubts. Even on sale it was more than she could afford. She had bought all the clothes for the trip on a credit card, an investment in her future to be paid back when she got her inheritance.

Now she hovered just outside the entrance to the living room, still not over the shock and embarrassment of the fall, trying to decide if she would appear at all. She observed the others eating and drinking, Lauren Ziff squeezed beside Nicky D'Arcangelo, her clearly augmented breasts practically bursting out of her bathing suit. She watched as the woman caressed a gold locket with perfectly manicured nails. Had those nails been on her back just moments before she went overboard? A slight shift of vision to catch Alex Bagdasarian at the bar, towel over his fleshy shoulders barely concealing his gut. *Disgusting.* Had *he* pushed her? But why? He appeared to have no idea who she was. If anything, she should have pushed *him*!

That was it. Enough, she couldn't face them. She started to sneak away when she heard her name called and saw Sabrina heading her way.

"Rachel, dear, how are you?"

"Fine. Really. Thanks." Rachel forced a smile.

"What a lovely dress," Sabrina said.

"DVF, right?" Jasmin was up too, showing more interest in the dress than Rachel, pinching the fabric between her fingers. "Is this crepe or silk? I have a dozen of these, in silk, of course."

"Gosh, I–I don't know," Rachel said, though she remembered the saleswoman saying crepe.

"That's the beauty of the wrap dress," Jasmin said, giving Rachel the once-over. "It fits *every* possible size and shape."

"Just ignore her," Sabrina said. "You look great."

Jasmin frowned. "When did I say she didn't?"

"Are you sure you're feeling okay?" Sabrina asked Rachel again, Frank beside her now, asking the same thing.

"Yes, *yes*." She just wanted them to stop asking. "I can't imagine how I slipped."

Frank and Sabrina were both trying to imagine it, slipping *over* a railing. It seemed nearly impossible. "Are you sure?" Frank asked, meaning the slip, not how she was feeling.

"I'm *fine*," Rachel said, underlining the word.

Nicky offered to get her a drink and she watched him pour it at the bar, noting Alex Bagdasarian looking at her, glowering.

Was he assessing her? Did he recognize her?

Nicky handed her the small glass. "Brandy," he said, "for strength."

"I'm *fine*!" she said again, too loud, then embarrassed, mumbling an apology and downing the brandy. "I slipped is all," she said again to Nicky, who was wondering if she had tried to drown herself and, if so, why.

"Let's, uh, just forget it ever happened, *okay*?" she said, a plea.

For a moment everyone was quiet; then they began to refill plates and glasses and were back in their seats and talking as if a switch had been flipped.

"This is all *so* Victor, isn't it?" Jasmin said. "Dragging us all to a deluxe destination *memorial*, all to honor *him*." Then she remembered she was the grieving widow and quickly changed her tone. "I still can't get over it, such a terrible shock." She raised the back of her hand to her eyes as if wiping away a tear.

Nicky snorted.

"Something funny?" Jasmin glared at him.

"Everything," he said.

"I'm really sorry for your loss," Frank said to Jasmin, recalling a funeral scene he'd played in an acting class. "This must be hard for you."

"You can't imagine *how* hard. Victor and I had just celebrated our third wedding anniversary. It was like we were still on our honeymoon." Another swipe at her eyes. "I'm sorry for you too, losing your brother," though she had never heard Victor mention Frank's name, not once in their years together.

"Yes. It's tough to lose a brother," Frank said.

One you hadn't spoken to in years, Sabrina thought and knew the reason why.

Rachel said little, happy that people had stopped asking how she was. She kept an eye on Lauren, trying to think of a way to bring up the interview again and ignoring the fact that Lauren may have just tried to kill her.

Lunch dragged on and positions changed. Sabrina had moved to a barstool beside Bagdasarian. "I hope you're never going to retire," she said after only a minute, digging for information she needed to know.

"Absolutely not!" he practically bellowed.

Exactly what Sabrina wanted to hear. She pulled her barstool closer.

Frank and Schwegler watched them from a distance, both unhappy.

"Tell me," Lauren said to Jasmin, a little drunk and slurring her words. "Do you think the other people meeting us on the island will be"—she looked around then leaned in and whispered—"of higher quality?"

"What other people? Who do you mean?" Jasmin asked.

"The others...the better crowd...the A-listers," Lauren said, practically leaning against her.

"*Excuse me?* I happen to be an A-list model *and* an A-list person!" Jasmin stood up so abruptly that Lauren tumbled forward face-first into the sofa and stayed there.

Ian snorted, then turned to Nicky and asked if he would help carry her back to their cabin.

Jasmin was left standing with Rachel, unable to keep herself from being disappointed the woman hadn't drowned, one less heir to worry about.

"Sure," Nicky said as the two men tried to get a grip on Lauren, Nicky her arms, Ian her legs.

"You're a musician, right?" Nicky asked what had been on his mind since first spotting the Englishman. "Guitarist from... Wait, don't tell me."

"The Bleedin' Drunks," Ian said. "And that's *lead* guitarist, mate."

"Fuck, yeah! So sick. You know, I've got every one of your tracks on my phone." He let go of Lauren's arms to get his cell phone, scrolled through his music, and held it up for Ian to see. "Look: 'Killer Love,' 'My Dead Girlfriend.'"

"*Sick* is right, mate," Ian said, letting go of Lauren's ankles and grinning.

Rachel watched the two men, *little boys*, she thought.

"You still play?" Nicky asked.

An innocent question that stung: Ian hadn't performed in years, not since he and Lauren had married and moved into her Park Avenue town house. That's when everything changed.

She'd convinced him to give up his music and take a job with her big pharma family, which didn't work out, the Isle of Wight dream already dying or dead, Ian miserable about giving up his rock star ambitions, and Lauren losing respect for him even while she tried to mold and change him.

"'Fraid I hung up me guitar a while back, mate."

"That sucks, man. You know, I DJ part-time at a Tribeca club, and I'm always playing your tracks."

"Flamin' Nora! No way, mate!"

"Yeah. I kind of know your life story too. Born and raised in Manchester, like Morrissey and Oasis, Mick Hucknall, Johnny Marr, even fucking Herman's Hermits!" Nicky was showing off, setting the stage.

"Bloody hell! This lad's a fucking genius." Ian laughed and cuffed Nicky playfully on the arm.

"Hey!" Lauren raised her head, blond hair crushed to one side. "Are you guys helping me back to that shitty little cabin, or what?"

Nicky got a grip on Lauren's wrists. "There's more I want to ask about your music, something I've been thinking about that might interest you."

"Yeah? What's that, mate?" Ian asked, flattered and interested. It had been a long time since anyone cared about his music.

Nicky looked around. "I'll tell you later."

They were just lifting Lauren off the couch when Echo Ojai burst into the room like the White Rabbit late for the tea party.

"Gosh!" she said. "I fell asleep."

"And you were terribly missed," Jasmin said. She got hold of the girl's arm. "So, who the hell *are* you?"

"I'm Echo," she said, swiping a wedge of cheese off the bar.

"I know *that*, if it's your real name. But why are you *here*?"

Echo put the whole chunk of cheese into her mouth and chewed slowly, giving everyone time to stop what they were doing and watch. "Oh, didn't you know?" she said, finally swallowing the cheese. "I'm Victor D'Arcangelo's daughter."

30

"*Daughter!*" Jasmin took a step back, her mouth dropped open.

"That's me," Echo said.

Nicky stopped in his tracks, passing Lauren off to Ian. "*Daughter?*" he repeated, staring at the girl along with his mother and everyone else.

"*How?* How are you Victor's daughter?" Sabrina asked, though she could imagine Victor had more than one unknown child out in the world.

"That's not your business," Echo said.

"Actually, it very much *is* our business," Jasmin said.

The boat swerved and everyone with it, providing a few seconds' break.

Nicky continued to study the girl, taking in her taunting sneer and cunning eyes, not just the fact of her being here but her very existence and what he might have to share with her.

"Who exactly is your mother?" Sabrina asked.

"My mother..." Echo started and stopped, images like a quick-cut movie juddering across her brain, the man in her mother's bed, the rainy night, the trunk of the car slamming shut. "She's...out of the picture," Echo said, taking a breath, her fingers fretting the edge of her peasant blouse.

"As in *dead*?" Jasmin asked and hoped she was.

"To me she is," Echo said.

Sabrina and Jasmin moved in closer, Frank too, all of them surrounding her. Only Nicky stood back, watching, still registering the shock.

"And you can prove this?" Jasmin asked, already calculating what percentage of the inheritance she might lose.

"Yeah. I have papers and a DNA test."

"I want to see them!" Jasmin demanded.

"I can dig them out of my knapsack later."

"So, Victor *invited* you?" Sabrina asked.

"Same as you. I can show you the evite on my laptop." She gave them all a mean grin. "So, here we are, one big happy family."

Frank and Sabrina exchanged a look, clearly *un*happy that this girl, this upstart, was here to lay claim to their money.

Nicky finally snapped to, and when he did, he laughed.

"What's so funny?" Echo asked, glaring at him.

"You are," he said, processing the fact that his father's cheating had spawned another offspring. He wondered if others would start appearing, one by one, to claim their due.

"Well...I don't know about you," Echo said, moving away from her interrogators and filling her plate. "But I'm starved."

Sabrina and Jasmin watched her a moment, then huddled together, whispering like teenagers.

Ironic, Nicky thought, his father's wives bonding over this latest threat to their inheritance. And to his.

31

The others had left but Nicky hung back, watching Echo stuff her face with hunks of cheese and slices of prosciutto, her fingers greasy. He'd lost his appetite, a combination of watching Echo eat and the realization of who she was and what she was after taking root and no longer funny.

"*Hungry?*" he asked, the word loaded.

"*Starved*," she said.

"I'll bet."

She stopped, a piece of prosciutto in her fingers and poised at her lips, then popped it into her mouth and chewed aggressively.

"Yeah, I get it, you're tough. But so am I."

"Not half as tough as me," she said with a smile, but meant it.

"Don't underestimate me," he said, a flash of that other girl's face in his mind, her trust turning to fear. He blinked, drew a quick breath. "So," he said, coming back to the moment. "Tell me about you."

Echo paused, still chewing. "Like *what*?"

"Like, anything. I'm interested."

"You mean, *threatened*."

"I just like to know what I'm up against."

"Cards on the table, huh?" she said, dropping the innocent game she'd been playing since she had arrived.

"Did you even know him, my father?"

"You mean *our* father. No, I never met the bastard, if that's what you're asking."

"Well, you're right about that. He was a bastard."

"So I've heard."

"From your mother?"

Echo took a moment, deciding if she wanted to have this conversation, sizing Nicky up the way he was sizing her up. "That's right," she said. "Okay, my turn."

"For what?"

"A question. Are you with her?"

"Who?"

"That stuck-up Asian bitch. Your father's *wife*."

"Whoa! That's not nice."

"I wasn't trying to be nice."

"You succeeded," he said, taking her in more carefully, the full lips and wild red hair, the broken-heart tattoo peeking out of her peasant blouse above her left breast. Sexy, in a trashy sort of way, something he liked. "Are you for real or is this all an act?"

"You mean am I really Victor's daughter? Yes, and I'm not going away, so you'd better get used to me."

They eyed each other, acknowledging they were adversaries, but Nicky saw something under Echo's defiance, a longing and need, a sadness not unlike his own. Maybe it was true they had the same father.

She laid a hand on his arm, drew her fingers back and forth lightly. "As long as we understand each other."

He stared at her blue-painted nails. Was she flirting, trying to seduce him? "Did you forget I might be your brother?"

"Not *might*. And *half* brother, so..." She moved her hand to his chest, felt his heart pumping under her palm. But only for a second.

Then he grabbed her wrist and gripped it so tightly she thought he might break it.

"You're hurting me," she said.

He held on a second longer, then eased up and let go. "I was only playing."

"Don't play with me, rich boy. You'll lose."

"We'll see about that."

"Yeah, we will." She flicked her fingernails across his chest, leaving a scratch.

"Something to remember me by," she said, then turned and hurried away.

32

Echo headed up to the bridge. She wanted to be near the captain in case she needed his help, though she wasn't worried. She could take care of herself, always had. It was true what she'd told the spoiled son, that she had never met Victor D'Arcangelo. According to her mother, *a one-week stand and a month later, I'm knocked up*. But she told Echo his name and that, plus the fact that he was an artist, had been enough to find him.

The sea air felt good on her face, like nothing she had ever experienced—liberating, soothing. She thought about the search that had brought her here, what she'd learned about Victor D'Arcangelo, how much he was worth, and how she was going to get her piece of it. She pictured his photo online, the dark hair and swarthy completion, nothing at all like her pale skin and red hair. She had wondered if he really was her father, though her mother had sworn to it. And she looked like her mother, Charlene, who, in between clients, cleaned rooms at the nearby Ojai spa, which is how she had chosen her name, and where her mother had met the famous artist who doled out fifty-dollar tips to the pretty redheaded cleaning woman. And more than that once they had started sleeping together.

A goddamn love story, a fairy tale, isn't it? her mother had said.

Echo worried he wouldn't remember, but tracked him down using Intelius and the internet's Whitepages, got his address, and sent him a handwritten letter threatening him with exposure if he didn't pay up, though she hadn't named a price. Then, she waited.

It was a full month later that his letter arrived, just three sentences:

Go ahead. Expose me. I don't care.

But he'd enclosed a check. For ten thousand dollars. More money than she'd expected or ever seen. But rather than buying her off, it only whetted her appetite. If he could toss off 10K, she figured she could get more.

"Hey," she said, sidling up to the captain. "You mind if I hang with you?"

"Sure," he said, more than happy to have the young woman's attention and beckoning her closer. He pointed out a string of green islands in the distance like an emerald necklace in a sapphire sea. "Beautiful, eh?"

"You bet," Echo said. She snapped a cell phone picture and made it her screen saver. *For inspiration*, she thought, the kind of paradise she never imagined she would see, but now that she had a taste of it, she intended to get more.

"Try this." The captain took her hand and put it on the control panel's joystick. "Now, slowly ease the throttle forward. There you go. You feel all that power right there in your palm?" He kept his sea-roughened hand on top of hers, but she didn't mind. If her mother had taught her anything, it was how to manipulate men.

"Oh, I *feel* it," she said.

33

From his lounge chair on the port side aisle, Frank D'Arcangelo watched the captain hitting on Echo. Or was the little conniver hitting on him? *People were so predictable*, he thought. He'd had his share of underage girls back in the day. And before #MeToo. *Thank God*. He'd been lucky, though there were stories to be told. He wondered about Echo's story too. *Victor's daughter.* Was she really? Maybe. He knew his brother got around. They had that in common.

The boat cut through the waves, and he watched a speck of an island slide by and disappear. Had it been an illusion? Like his idea of reuniting with Sabrina, of sharing their inheritance and living happily ever after? But why not? There was something between them, more than just an old spark. He'd felt it, and there was plenty of time to fuel it, the weekend just beginning.

A flash of something in his peripheral vision, Jasmin coming up from below deck, adjusting the straps of her bathing suit. She couldn't see him, but he watched her as she looked both ways, then glanced up at the captain and Echo, a look of disgust spoiling her pretty face.

A minute later, Nicky emerged from the same staircase, his body shiny with suntan oil. Or was it sweat? He was bare-chested, wearing pants made of some thin, loose fabric, and he was tugging on the drawstring waist, as if he had he just put them on. He looked both ways as if getting his bearings. Or was he making sure no one was watching? There was something furtive in the way he surveyed the deck.

Frank shifted his gaze from Nicky to Jasmin, who was halfway to the front of the boat but had stopped, looking back at Nicky, who seemed to nod, though the movement was so slight Frank couldn't be certain. Then each of them turned and headed in the opposite direction, Frank unsure of who to follow, who to watch.

34

A half hour later, Nicky found Ian alone, slumped on a chaise in the beach club at the back of the boat, sucking on a joint. “There you are,” he said. He’d been avoiding everyone else, especially his brand-new half sister, wondering what, if anything, he could do about her. “I was looking for you.”

“Oi, well, you found me, mate.”

Nicky sat on the edge of the chaise and Ian offered him a hit off the blunt.

“No can do, man. I’m in the program.”

“So am I.” Ian laughed.

Nicky laughed too. He didn’t take the weed, though he wanted to.

The boat was moving fast, a foamy wake on either side of the beach club, a breeze whipping Ian’s hair across his face like streaks of black ink.

“So, like I was saying earlier, I DJ, a part-time gig at my friend’s club, Wilson’s, in the East Village.” He was talking fast, like an excited kid, explaining what he’d been thinking about since he first laid eyes on the Bleedin’ Drunks’ lead guitarist. “You know it?”

“Know it? It’s bloody sick, mate, the new CBGB.” Ian blinked as if finally waking up.

“CBGB was the fucking model!” Nicky nodded up and down, thinking his next sentence through though he knew it well. “Only problem, my friend is afraid the club might go under.”

"Oh fuck, mate, sorry." Ian took another toke.

"Right. But here's the thing, he's looking for a house band, something to bring the heads back in." Nicky was talking as fast as the ship was moving and the clouds zipping by. He knew what he was suggesting and watched it take hold, something starting to percolate behind Ian's stoned eyes. "I know this might sound a little out there, but any chance of you getting the band back together?"

Ian's past glory sparked in his brain, the band he'd created, broken up now almost twenty years, the best years of his life. *Could he do it?* Except for Teddy—gang mate turned bandmate who had died in prison—most of the old band members were still in Manchester, working as mechanics or hospital aides, and he knew they would jump at the chance, though he would have to stake them. "I dunno, mate. I mean…"

"Think about it, the Bleedin' Drunks back together! That's fucking news!"

"You reckon?"

"You kidding? *Big* news!" Nicky took a breath. Now came the hard part. "Problem is my pal needs some cash to keep the club afloat. If he doesn't find it soon, the place is dead."

Ian caught on, but didn't mind, the idea of a comeback already getting him hard. Maybe he could light a fire under Lauren, remind her of her groupie days, convince her to be the sugar mommy. She had more money than she knew what to do with. "Look, mate," he said. "I ain't got a quid of me own."

"No, no, I didn't mean that. I was just…"

"Sure you did, mate." Ian winked a kohl-lined eye. "But don't you worry. Let me think on asking me wife. You never know," he said, though he could not imagine Lauren going for it, not these days. A picture of them, young and happy, flickered in his mind, then died.

"Look, it's not just you. I'd be kicking in too," Nicky said, thinking about his inheritance, the idea spreading out in front of him: the two of them in business, club owners, pals, a back room of celebs. "It could be high-key, man, that's all I'm saying. Think about it: you, me, the Bleedin' Drunks, the Wilson."

The Pershing's engines were louder back here, a reverberating roar that had Nicky's blood beating faster.

Ian nodded. Nicky's excitement infectious. "Yeah, mate, could be mint."

"*Yes!*" Nicky's hand shot up for a high five and Ian slapped it. Not exactly a deal but something.

35

Captain Thomas had invited the guests to join him on the upper bridge "for the view," which was spectacular. The blue sea dotted with small green islands.

Lauren settled on the sun pad. Ian, on a chaise beside her. Jasmin was in one of the two plush padded seats behind the captain's controls, Rachel in the other. Sabrina and Frank were in deck chairs exchanging furtive looks. Echo stayed glued to the captain's side. Bagdasarian was beside her, puffing on a cigar. He asked if they were going to be anywhere near Cuba.

"I could use more of these." He raised his cigar.

"Sorry," the captain said. "Cuba is to the west a good five hundred, six hundred miles away." He thought back to a job that had taken him to Havana, the group of six men he had brought there, only five on the way back to Miami, drunk, removing a bloodied hand from a box, tossing it around, and laughing.

"Too bad," Bagdasarian said, trying hard to avoid eye contact with Schwegler, only a yard away, but thinking only of him.

Nicky was perched at the railing, dividing his attention between Echo and Ian, wondering what she might try and impatient to know if Ian had asked his wife for the money.

Schwegler shifted his vision between Sabrina and Frank, then Bagdasarian.

Rachel smiled at Lauren but got no reaction.

Everyone's not-too-hidden agendas were made clear in their glances.

The captain pointed out a low, elongated island in the distance, a cluster of tall buildings around a harbor and a long line of pink beach and lush greenery, all of it as if floating on the ocean. "That's Nassau," he said.

"I made a movie there once," Frank said, the boat moving fast, Nassau slipping away as fast as his career.

They passed other small islands, straight, curved, several encircling bright coves of startling turquoise water. "All part of the Bahamas," the captain said.

"It's an archipelago, isn't it?" Bagdasarian said, knowing it was and showing off.

Obnoxious braggart, Rachel thought, giving him a sour look.

"That's right," the captain said. "Made up of seven hundred islands, only thirty or so inhabited."

"Are we going to see any swimming pigs?" Echo asked. "I've read about them, and they sound so cute." She was doing her innocent child act again, Nicky watching her and not buying it.

"Sorry, that's not on our itinerary," the captain said.

"Which is *what*?" Jasmin asked, furiously swabbing her arms and legs with sunscreen.

"Getting you folks to the island, safe and sound." His primary order. He was still waiting for his employer's answer to the text about the overboard incident and concerned that there had been no answer. "The swimming pigs are in Big Major Cay, not that far, but out of our way." He checked his coordinates, the numbers similar to a past naval maneuver that had gone bad, one that would have gotten him a dishonorable discharge, possibly prison, but there'd been no survivors to challenge his version of the story.

Sabrina took in the turquoise water and emerald-green islands and thought she just might come back, once she got her inheritance. She smiled and Frank smiled back, thinking the smile was meant for him.

"How about Thunderball Grotto?" Echo asked. "Like in the James Bond movie."

"Sorry again," the captain said. "That's in the Exuma Cays."

"I don't think anyone would mind if you made a detour and dropped Echo off," Jasmin said.

Echo ignored her, as she had the looks from Sabrina and Nicky.

"So, where *are* we going?" Lauren asked. "Are you *ever* going to tell us?"

"It's beyond the Out Islands."

"That means nothing to me," she said.

"Or me," Sabrina said.

"Or me," Frank said.

"There are hundreds of Out Islands," the captain explained. "Some sparsely populated. Some not populated at all. They're like a frontier dividing the Atlantic from the waters of the Caribbean."

"I didn't ask for a travelogue," Jasmin said. "Just a location."

"A frontier?" Echo said. "Like the final frontier in Star Trek?"

Nicky scoffed, Echo's little kid act too much to bear now that they had seen her true colors.

"Aren't you going to tell us where we're heading?" Jasmin asked.

"We'll be there soon enough," the captain said.

"Why the fucking mystery?" Nicky asked. "It's not like we can jump ship and swim back home."

The captain laughed. "I don't have the name, just the coordinates," he said again. A lie. He had been told not to say anything specific about the island, which he did not fully understand, but no matter, he was following orders.

An hour later, he let them know they were crossing through the Out Islands and pointed to a good-sized island in the near distance.

"That's Mayaguana, one of the last stops in the Bahamas." He steered the boat in a half circle, an arc-like wake foaming beside them. "We're going against the trade winds," he said. "Some sailors refer to this as the 'thorny path' because of all the reefs and sandbars. It can get a little rough."

"How rough?" Rachel clutched her armrests, sensing an image from her recent near-death experience of water closing in, the echo of her labored breathing, air bubbles, and her lungs aching.

"Don't worry," the captain said. "This baby is built for calm or rough seas. You'll hardly feel a thing. But maybe *you* should stay in your seat."

"I wish we could get stranded like in *Lost*," Echo said. "But shipwrecked."

"How about just *you*?" Jasmin said, getting ahold of her seat as the boat turned and cut across the wake like a skipping stone.

"No chance of anything like that," the captain said, but he crossed himself out of habit.

"There's always a *chance,*" Echo said. "I mean they thought the *Titanic* would never sink, and it *did*, like, on its matron voyage!"

"*Maiden*," Jasmin said, rolling her eyes, though no one heard her over the waves and the loud purr of the yacht's accelerating engines. She could not imagine Victor would have left anything to this idiot girl. But if he did, she was ready to fight—and fight hard.

"We won't really sink, will we?" Rachel asked the captain, her knuckles going white on the armrests, thinking God might finally punish her for what she had done.

"No way." He straightened the wheel, and the yacht surged ahead, a couple of larger islands coming into view. "That's Acklins Island and beside it, Crooked Island."

"But never *our* island, is it?" Jasmin said.

Nicky joined her, half sitting on the edge of her seat, Sabrina watching them and unsure of what to make of it.

"Our destination is past them," the captain said. "On the other side of the Mayaguana Passage."

"Finally," Jasmin said. "I'm getting burned." She stretched her long legs and made a show of smearing them with more sunscreen.

"It's an hour away," the captain said. "But we'll get there with plenty of time for you to see the island." He checked his watch. "It's not even three and it stays light till nine or ten."

"No way I'm staying up that late!" Sabrina said. "I'm already fading."

"You and me both," Frank said, stroking her arm.

"What sort of island is it?" Schwegler asked. He had pulled a deck chair beside the sun pad, and was eyeing Lauren, who appeared to have fallen asleep.

"It's part of an atoll," the captain said. "A ring-shaped island that encircles a lagoon." He referred to his control panel, checking coordinates again. "But totally self-contained and totally isolated."

36

An hour later, from his perch on the upper bridge, the captain cried, "Land ho!" something he only said as a joke and for tourists.

The sun and wind in her face, Rachel thought she had never seen anything so beautiful, the island an oasis of greenery rising out of water so blue and varied it was almost impossible to describe. *Paradise*, she thought.

They were still some distance away, all of them on deck watching as the captain slowed the boat. He directed them to move to the back, to the area beneath the cockpit where First Mate William was handing out life jackets and ushering them into motorized rafts, the water around the island too shallow for the Pershing, rocky too, making it dangerous.

Captain Thomas got in to pilot the first, Echo immediately beside him. Bagdasarian followed, the raft tilting precariously as he stepped in, then took up two seats.

Jasmin and Nicky waited until Bagdasarian had settled and the raft no longer looked as if would sink, then got in when the captain signaled them.

William steered the second raft, Rachel beside him in the copilot seat, Hans Schwegler behind her, Ian and Lauren behind them. Frank offered his lap to Sabrina, and she had no choice. It was Frank's lap or wait for a second trip. He slid his arms around her waist.

Below the rafts, the crystal-clear water put on a show: silver fish, jellyfish, coral, and golden kelp. But there were rocks and cracks and sandbars too, the rafts just able to navigate around them.

Halfway to shore, Nicky, anxious and excited to swim, shed his life jacket and looped his leg over the side of the raft.

"*No!*" the captain shouted over the roar of raft's motor. "All sorts of unfriendly species in this water—lionfish, possibly shark."

Nicky hauled himself back and fell into the seat against Jasmin, who laughed as the raft bounced and Bagdasarian let out a yelp.

Both rafts tilted in the waves, creating a skewed view, everything a little off-kilter as the island loomed closer, the strip of white beach elongating, shrubs and tall palms coming into focus, and there on the shore, a blur that became a man who was waving.

PART II
THE ISLAND

37

For a moment everyone was quiet, overwhelmed by beauty: the clear blue water, the sparkling ivory sand, the leafy palms shivering in the breeze, a tall cliff of lavalike stone, all of it framed by a cobalt sky and lit by the afternoon sun.

The man who had been waving said, "I've been waiting for you." Somewhere in his thirties with a medium build though his cutoff work shirt exposed gym-rat arms. "I'm Marcus." He spoke softly, his words almost lost beneath the sound of waves lapping at the shore and the rustling palms. "Some of you know me."

Nicky looked him over. "You're one of my father's assistants, right?"

"Not to brag," he said, looking down, shy. "But number *one* assistant."

"Like Charlie Chan, number one son," Bagdasarian said, using an insulting cartoonlike accent.

"And you're here, *why*?" Nicky asked.

"Your father asked me to carry out his last wish, this memorial."

"When did he do *that*?" Jasmin squinted at him from beneath the brim of her straw hat. She remembered seeing him a couple times on her rare studio visits but could not remember if they had ever exchanged a word. But why would they?

"Months ago," he said. "Didn't you know?"

"*Of course* I knew," she said, though she hadn't, then softened her tone. "It's been…a difficult time."

"Yes. For all of us." The assistant nodded sympathetically.

"For you too?" Nicky couldn't help but ask, feeling immediately competitive.

"Well, sure. I worked for your father for almost five years," the assistant said. "I did everything for him—ran the studio, took care of art supplies, travel plans, expenses, hiring and firing of other studio assistants, liaised with the galleries and museums. As you well know, Mr. Bagdasarian." He nodded at the gallerist, who had been struggling to get out of the raft until the captain helped him, and he stumbled as he found his footing in the sand.

Already sweating, he squinted at the assistant. He could not remember dealing with him, but then he didn't deal with any of his artists' assistants. *His* assistants did that.

Lauren had her sandals off, pedicured toes digging into the warm white sand. She wanted to ask if he knew why Victor D'Arcangelo had invited her, but the answer no longer mattered. She was here, and it was beautiful, birds singing, a soft breeze on her face. If it were not for that damn reporter, she would almost he happy in a way she hadn't been since the scandal had broken.

First Mate William was depositing bags on the beach, making trips back to the yacht for more.

"I liaised with Mr. D'Arcangelo's international management too," the assistant said, this time nodding at Hans Schwegler, who acknowledged him with a clipped half bow. The Swiss German art dealer remembered speaking with him though they had never met, and it didn't matter. He was sweating again, the sun low in the sky, a vibrating orange ball.

Bagdasarian gave him a narrow-eyed glance, then looked away.

"*Liaised?*" Nicky sneered. "Is that even a word?"

Sabrina gently touched her son's arm and said, "Be nice, dear."

"It's all just part of my job," the assistant said softly, then locked eyes with Nicky and asked, "You're a painter or *were* a painter, right?"

The question registered like a slap. *Better to give up painting now before you waste your life and not get anywhere*, his father had said to him at his first and last art exhibition. The words replayed when Nicky attempted anything new. "No, not anymore," Nicky said, trying hard for nonchalance. The truth: He'd only wanted to be an artist to please his father, to get his attention, which was impossible. Even now, that was the reason he was here: to please his father, his *dead* father. "I mean, why *bother*? Everyone knows painting is dead."

"Not *everyone*," Bagdasarian said.

"And *not* your father's paintings!" the assistant added as if Nicky's words had been sacrilege.

"Is that a fact?" Nicky tried to control the unexpected anger and humiliation battling inside him.

Always intuitive when it came to her son, Sabrina slid her arm around his waist, but Nicky pulled away, wanting to disappear. He knelt to pick up a large conch shell, held it in his hand, and ran his finger along the smooth pink slit.

Rachel, fussing with her too-tight shift, watched, then looked away, her face going as pink as the shell.

The first mate deposited a few more bags, then took the raft back for another run. He seemed to be taking forever. In any other situation, the guests would have been squawking even louder than the seabirds, but they were calmed by the idyllic setting, the gentle breezes and the lapping waves.

Jasmin studied the assistant more closely. She recalled hearing Victor mention his name—*Marcus is taking care of this, Marcus is taking care of that*—though she had not paid much attention. Now her mind was spinning with questions: *How much did he know about*

Victor's plans? Had he been privy to Victor's will? She looked him over again, his hair in a careless top knot, scraggly beard not quite hiding old acne scars, though he wasn't bad looking, his eyes a cool blue. She could do what was necessary to get information out of him, if she had to.

"I was surprised to hear that Victor had planned his memorial," Bagdasarian said. "Unless he knew he was going to die, and that wasn't the case. Or was it?"

Hans Schwegler said, "We are all going to die."

"Such a German thing to say," Bagdasarian said. "And so inappropriate."

Was it? Schwegler had no idea. *Must you always say the wrong thing?* His father again, constantly scolding.

"I don't think Mr. D knew how serious it was. It just seemed"—the assistant choked up—"like a flu. That's all."

Jasmin started to say something but stopped, her words tangled, a picture of Victor the last time she'd seen him, the strong, confident man she had married pale and weak. "I—" She stopped again, unexpectedly overcome with emotion, her eyes welling up with tears.

Sabrina touched her arm, a reflex, then Frank touched Sabrina's.

A quiet moment filled with birdsong and palm trees flapping overhead, waves crashing against the sandy shore.

"I'm...okay," Jasmin said, though the image of a weakened Victor had momentarily rocked her normally impervious foundation, bringing with it a rush of memories: the mother who never hugged her, the father who hugged her too much.

The assistant turned to Frank. "You're Mr. D's brother. I recognize you. I've streamed a few of your movies."

"Have you? Thanks." Frank beamed.

"He didn't say he *liked* them," Jasmin said, turning her emotion into aggression. "Only that he *streamed* them."

"Mr. *D*?" Nicky raised an eyebrow.

"Yes, that's what I called him." The assistant looked down again, possibly blushing.

Sabrina found it endearing, Nicky, infuriating.

"Do actors make any money from streaming?" Bagdasarian asked. He had rolled his seersucker pants up, exposing his pale, dimpled calves. "Artists make nothing from auctions or resales." *And a good thing.* He would be putting the best D'Arcangelo paintings up for sale at Sotheby's as soon as he controlled the estate. He got his phone out, held it up, then moved it side to side. "I can't get a signal."

"Oh, sorry. But you won't," the assistant said. "There's no reception on the island."

"Damn," Bagdasarian grumbled. "I guess I can wait till we're at the hotel."

"I'm afraid you'll have to wait longer than that. The entire island is off the grid."

Now everyone had their phones out, shifting them here and there, searching for a signal that didn't exist.

"Are you *kidding*?" Bagdasarian said, still waving his phone around.

"Some people like it," the assistant said. "Being free from calls and social media, completely cut off."

"Completely?" Schwegler asked. He was shaking his cell as if that might help.

"It could be refreshing," Sabrina said. "Why spoil all this beauty with technology?"

"You're right," Frank smiled at her. "It will be a relief to get away from all those annoying business calls and emails." His agent's kiss-off email replayed like salt in a wound.

Lauren felt some relief as well, a break from social media and op-ed pieces condemning her family. If only that awful reporter had drowned! She cleared her throat. "So, what's it like, the hotel? You've seen it, haven't you?"

"I slept there last night," the assistant said. "It's an old hotel, built in the sixties, but revamped at a later date."

"The *sixties*?" Jasmin said. "Is it a Motel 6?"

"Oh no," the assistant said very seriously. "It's beautiful. You'll see. In fact, we should get going."

"What about our bags?" Lauren noted only one of her Louis Vuitton suitcases was on the beach, already dusty with sand.

"William and I will follow you," the captain said. "He's getting the rest of the suitcases and the luggage trolleys. You all go ahead."

"I hope it isn't far," Rachel said, tugging at her dress, then fanning herself with her hat.

"Just a short walk—through there." He indicated a break in the tall palms and low vegetation where the beach ended. "It's a little overgrown, but it's either the path or over the bluff." He pointed up at the stone cliff.

"Can't we drive?" Bagdasarian asked, exhausted before he'd begun. "There must be a hotel jeep, or something?"

"I'm afraid there are no cars on the island," the assistant said. "And even if there were, the path isn't wide enough."

"No cars, no phones," Bagdasarian said. "This place is goddamn prehistoric!"

A break from real life sounded okay to Ian, not that he did much of anything. He was smoking weed again and mellowing out.

"See, it *is* like *Lost*!" Echo said and started to slip off her sneakers.

"Don't do that!" the assistant said. "There could be snakes and... let's just say, barefoot is not a good idea." He looked from Echo to Lauren.

"*Snakes?*" Rachel jerked back.

"Don't worry. They pretty much keep to themselves."

Jasmin raised a foot to display one of her platform sandals. "Will these do?"

"Not exactly hiking gear but they should be okay." The assistant turned to Sabrina. "But flip-flops are no good at all."

"Jesus, what is this place?" Bagdasarian asked.

"The tropics," the assistant said with a smile.

Half the guests started going through their luggage, taking out sneakers or walking shoes.

The assistant handed Echo an aerosol can of bug spray. "Cutter Backwoods, twenty-five percent DEET. Use it on your legs, arms, and neck, and dab it on your face and ears too, any skin that's exposed. The insects here can be pretty fierce."

"This just gets better and better," Bagdasarian said, swiping the aerosol can from Echo's hand.

"I have my own," Jasmin said when Nicky tried handing her the spray. She dug around in her bag and came up with a small bottle. "Lemongrass and geranium, organic and holistic," she said, spraying her arms and legs, gently patting more on her neck and face.

"Smells good," the assistant said. "But DEET is a lot better, trust me."

"It's *poison*!" Jasmin dropped her organic spray back into her bag without offering it around.

"William and I will bring your bags to the hotel," the captain said, watching the first mate stack suitcases on the luggage cart. "We're not staying, but I'll be back for you after the weekend." He shielded his eyes for a look at the sky, the tiniest knot of dark clouds loitering in the distance, and felt a slight chill though it was hot, his hand fondling the Saint Brendan and Our Lady, Star of the Sea, pendants at his neck.

"Be careful with *that*!" Jasmin shouted as the first mate slammed a large suitcase on top of her Prada tote bag.

"Well, the hotel staff had better be decent," Bagdasarian said with a huff.

"There is no staff," the assistant said. "But the house is fully stocked."

"Are you *kidding*?" Bagdasarian said for the second time.

"You mean no one will be serving us?" Lauren Ziff said.

"I'm afraid after I leave, it will be self-serve," the assistant said.

"Self-serve sounds like fun," Echo said.

"Because you're used to cafeterias!" Jasmin said.

"What about you?" Lauren asked the assistant. "Won't *you* be serving us?"

"I would," he said. "But I'm not staying."

"You're leaving?" Jasmin asked, peering at him over her sunglasses.

"I'm just here to get you settled."

Nicky tugged at his neck bandanna, already soaked with sweat, and looked around at the group. "So, it's just us?"

"Yes," the assistant said, handing out bottles of water as he led them toward the path.

38

The path was narrow, bordered by low shrubs, the sun hovering above, the air so hot and thick you could taste it.

The assistant led the way, Echo beside him. She had quickly shifted her allegiance to him from the boat captain.

Others fell in step, but Bagdasarian was soon lagging behind and breathing hard.

Frank too, his face wet with perspiration, that familiar ping in his chest starting up.

"You okay?" Sabrina asked, a hand on his arm.

"I'm... *fine*!" he said, flashing a made-for-television version of his movie star smile. "How are *you*?"

"Losing weight!" she said. "Who knew this would be Outward Bound!" They both laughed, Frank with a slight wheeze.

Just a few yards in, the vegetation and brush grew fuller and the path deepened as if scooped out, littered with fallen branches bleached white like bones.

Nicky could see his uncle was straining and looped an arm around his waist to help him, though he made sure it looked like an affectionate gesture.

"What about *me*?" Jasmin whined.

"You? You're made for the jungle!" Nicky whispered, then laughed.

"Sorry about the rut," the assistant said. "It must be caused by the rain and the tide coming in."

"Sounds like you've been here a while," Sabrina said.

"No. I just got here yesterday to prepare for you folks."

Echo swiped the sweat off her face with the back of her hand. When she did, Sabrina noticed the freckles on her cheeks had smudged.

"I thought you said it was just a short walk." Rachel was huffing, trying to keep up, her thighs chafing under her too-tight shift.

"Just ten minutes or so," the assistant said.

"Who the hell builds a hotel so far from the beach?" Bagdasarian asked, breathing hard.

"Someone who wants privacy," the assistant said.

And just like Victor to find it and foist it on us, Jasmin thought.

The assistant plucked a thick branch off the ground and handed it to Bagdasarian. "Here you go, instant walking stick."

The art dealer took it not knowing if he should be insulted or thankful, but he used it.

"Thank God for my personal trainer!" Lauren Ziff said, high stepping and swinging her arms.

Ian gave her a look. He was short of breath from too many cigarettes and too much weed.

"The ground gets a little wet up ahead," the assistant said, and it did.

In only a few yards, the path became damp and muddy, marshlike, a totally different landscape, enclosed by treetops that blocked the sun. There was a narrow stream bordered by gnarly trees with thick knotted roots half exposed above algae-coated green water, frogs croaking, yet all of it eerily beautiful. It was darker too, and cool. A relief, and they paused to take it in.

"Can we take a break here?" Bagdasarian asked, trying to catch his breath.

"Sure," the assistant said. "But just for a minute."

Jasmin complained about her ruined sandals. Lauren asked for more DEET. Rachel, happy to stop, admired a plant with small green leaves and open pods with clusters of bright-red berries, which she plucked off the branch.

"*Don't!*" Sabrina said and smacked them out of her hand. "That's rosary pea, and poisonous! It causes vomiting, convulsions, liver failure, and even *death*!"

"Oh my God!" Rachel rubbed her fingers against her dress over and over.

"Jesus Christ!" Lauren said.

"It's okay," Sabrina said. "You would have to *eat* the berries and their seeds to get the poison. Oh, and right next to it, that plant that looks like Queen Anne's lace? That's hemlock, very poisonous. It causes paralysis and death."

"How do you know that, love?" Ian asked, looking from the poisonous plants surreptitiously, at his wife.

"From my paintings," Sabrina said.

"You paint?" Bagdasarian asked, distracted for a moment and his interest piqued, something to think about other than the heat and humidity, the muck of wet, clotted leaves under his feet.

"My mother is the unsung artist of the family," Nicky said. "Her new series of paintings is amazing! The art dealers are lining up to show them." He enjoyed touting his mother's art over his father's. "Tell them, Mother," he said to Sabrina, who didn't miss a beat in describing her series of deadly plants.

"Sounds interesting," Bagdasarian said.

Schwegler leaned in, metal briefcase he would not give up hot against his side.

"The collectors are lining up too," Nicky said.

"Really?" Bagdasarian said. "I should come by to see them when we get back to civilization." The idea of having another D'Arcangelo artist to sell interested him, one that was new and naive. He would insist she use her former husband's last name for cachet.

"I will be in New York for a few days after the weekend," Schwegler said, "and would like to see them as well."

Sabrina looked from one art dealer to the other, savoring the moment.

Rachel could not believe Sabrina was bragging about her paintings here, in this heat, in the middle of a jungle. Though she saw what Sabrina was doing, playing the two dealers. She understood the art world, a world that had been cruelly taken away from her. She eyed Bagdasarian leaning against a tree, breathing heavily. Perhaps, she thought, he will die all by himself before the weekend is over. "Thank goodness you recognized those berries," she said to Sabrina. "I owe you my life!"

"Sabrina has always been a lifesaver," Frank said, smiling at her.

"Well," Sabrina said, "one day when *I* need rescuing, you can pay me back." She liked being appreciated and having an audience, pointing at another plant, this one with pink and purple trumpetlike flowers. "Foxglove," she said. "Pretty, isn't? Otherwise known as digitalis."

"The old standby heart med?" A medicine Frank knew.

"Apparently good in pill form, but don't eat the flower!" Sabrina laughed.

"Ready to get going?" the assistant asked.

They started moving again with assorted huffs and groans, the air heavy, buzzing and electric with cicadas, frogs, and beetles hopping and crawling over the fallen branches cluttering the path.

"This is *disgusting*," Jasmin said, kicking a frog out of the way with her sandal.

"It's just a little further," the assistant said.

"You said that before," Bagdasarian said, his walking stick sinking into muck and mud.

Echo and the assistant were in the lead again. Lauren was still going strong, Ian beside her huffing as he lit up a joint. Nicky, his arm around Frank, was just behind them. Sabrina had slowed down to walk with Bagdasarian, talking to him about her paintings as if he were already her art dealer.

No one noticed Schwegler had dropped back and tugged a handkerchief from his pocket. When he was sure no one was looking, he set his briefcase down, plucked a pod of the rosary pea berries off the branch, wrapped the handkerchief around them, and slipped them into his pocket.

39

The path became more overgrown, clotted, a jungle hothouse. Sabrina continued playing the expert, identifying more poisonous plants, then explaining to Bagdasarian exactly how she painted them.

"Careful." The assistant pointed out small animal carcasses in various stages of decomposition that littered the path, the air a mix of loamy earth tinged with decay.

"My goodness, this place," Rachel said, self-conscious about the sweat stains ruining her dress and rethinking her idea of paradise.

Just then Jasmin started shrieking, slapping her neck and arms and legs. "I'm being eaten alive!"

The assistant came to her rescue with the can of Cutter's. "Just mosquitoes," he said.

"I hope they don't carry malaria or West Nile?" Rachel said.

"Oh, that's fucking helpful!" Jasmin said, frantically spraying her arms and legs.

"Not in this part of the world," Sabrina said, another fact she knew from her paintings. "Here, the worry is Zika virus. But it's rare. Even rarer that people *die* from it. Don't worry, sweetie," she said, taking more than a little pleasure in it.

Lauren sprayed herself with Cutter's again and so did the others.

"Are you okay?" Nicky asked Jasmin.

"Do I *look* okay?" Dozens of tiny red marks dotted her arms and legs.

"There are first aid kits back at the hotel, even EpiPens," the assistant said.

"My God, do you think I *need* one?" Jasmin was trying not to scratch.

"Is it okay if we take another break?" Bagdasarian asked again, already lowering himself onto a toppled tree.

"Not there!" the assistant cried.

Bagdasarian looked down. The tree trunk appeared to be moving, a quivering mass of ants. He bolted up, batting at ants crawling up his pant legs.

"Bullet ants," Sabrina said, helping him swat them off. "They sting but they're not poisonous. You'll be okay." She turned to Bagdasarian and then Schwegler. "I've used them in two of my paintings. Their reddish-black color is just gorgeous to paint."

"You're like a walking *National Geographic*," Echo said to Sabrina, and made it sound bad.

The assistant helped steady Bagdasarian, the two of them knocking off the last of the ants. "We're almost there. You can all take showers and baths, and the AC is on full blast."

"Thank God!" Bagdasarian said.

Frank felt the pain in his chest sharpen. He could use a nitroglycerin pill, but they were in his bag, somewhere behind them on a luggage cart with that mute first mate. Even so, he would not have gotten the pills out in front of the others, especially not Sabrina. He would take one when they got to the hotel. "Clearly, there will be no strolls in *these* woods!" he said, a hand inadvertently held to his chest. Sabrina asked if he was okay and he said, "Totally. It's just an itch, seeing all those ants!" He made an actorish show of scratching his chest.

"You will all be safe and sound once we're inside the house," the assistant said. "Just another minute."

Hans Schwegler kept his eyes on Bagdasarian, watching him huff along and struggle to breathe. He thought perhaps the swamp and heat and ants might kill the big man and save him the trouble, his fingers fretting the edge of the handkerchief in his pocket.

40

The path finally ended, the trees and brush parted, and there it stood, the hotel, tall and grand, a three-story mansion with white fluted columns and loggia-like balconies built over a lagoon in a way that made it seem to float, all of it spotlit in the afternoon sun and backlit by an indigo sky.

"Goodness, it's…the most beautiful place I've ever seen," Rachel said. "Like Tara, in *Gone with the Wind*!"

"More like an architectural hodgepodge!" Bagdasarian said. "Greek Revival meets Neoclassical meets Italianate with some Beaux Arts thrown in!" Not an expert but he had shown a few architects in his galleries and had picked up the basics along with the lingo. "Doric *and* Ionic columns?" he went on, showing off. "A portico entranceway *and* wraparound verandas? Somebody went to town."

"I *like* that it's eclectic," Sabrina said. "Why stick to the rules?"

Bagdasarian pointed up at the large triangular structure above the entranceway. "The pediment is Greco-Roman."

"Are those, like, letters?" Echo referred to the triangle, which was decorated with mosaics. "Does it say something?"

"It does," the assistant said. "*Cursum Perficio*. It's Latin."

"Which I'm *sure* you can read," Nicky said.

"A little," the assistant said shyly. "It means *My journey ends here*."

Lauren repeated the phrase, feeling a slight chill.

"I don't like that the sound of that!" Frank said, a hand to his chest, though he forced a laugh.

"Just think of it as coming home after a long, tiring day," the assistant said.

"Well, it's surely been that!" Rachel said, wiping perspiration from her forehead and laughing.

They stopped to look at the koi pond that spanned half the length of the hotel's facade, a few of the guests stepping back with shock when they got a look at the fish, many over two feet long, spotted orange, red, and black.

"Jumbo Japanese koi and totally safe," the assistant said.

"They look like Jackson Pollock painted them," Sabrina said.

"More like spray-painted by a graffiti artist!" Bagdasarian said.

"The pond's got its own filter system like a pool but for fish, not humans," the assistant said. "The human pool is out back, behind the hotel. Let's do a two-minute tour of the grounds so you'll have the lay of the land."

"I've had enough lay of the fucking land," Jasmin said, scratching at her bug bites.

"It'll only be a minute."

"I thought you said *two*," Nicky said.

The assistant laughed, though no one else did, all of them sagging a bit after the trek to get there. Bagdasarian wasn't sure he had two minutes left in him but refused to admit it after his display of fatigue on the path, and certainly not in front of Herr Schwegler, who looked as eager as an obedient soldier.

"It'll be fast," the assistant said. "Everything is right here surrounding the hotel, like its own little island within the island." He gestured up at the grand white building, two-thirds of it ringed by towering palms with bony brown trunks notched with circular scars, their tops dense clusters of fan-shaped fronds batting against the hotel or draped over it like giant claws.

"Do you know what that is?" Sabrina pointed to a dense vine with dangling cucumber-like gourds that covered an entire side of the hotel. She was hoping it was poisonous, something she could use in a painting.

"That's *Momordica charantia*," the assistant said, "commonly called bitter melon, the cucumber-like things are its fruit and edible."

"Too bad," Sabrina said.

"How do you know all this?" Nicky asked.

"I did my homework, that's all."

"I'll bet you did." Nicky was liking him less and less, the know-it-all assistant who appeared to have been more of a son to his father than he ever was.

"Does any of this matter?" Lauren asked, using her straw hat like a fan. "I'm ready for a drink."

"Amen to that," Jasmin said.

"I just want to familiarize you with the setting and point out a couple of things to avoid." Though it had given the impression of being under the hotel, the lagoon was just past it.

"This is the one big *don't*," the assistant said, leading them just close enough to see into the clear turquoise water, where schools of small iridescent fish were trailed by a gray-blue mass, undulating just below the surface. "Tiger shark," he said, just as its top fin broke the water's surface.

"Jesus!" Bagdasarian stumbled back.

"*Ach du meine Güte!*" Schwegler exclaimed among the multiple gasps and curses. He dropped his briefcase, then quickly scooped it up.

"It's okay," the assistant said. "It's not like they can walk out of the water." He laughed but no one else did. "The lagoon is fed by the sea. Apparently, the warm shallow water attracts sharks."

"Fuck all!" Ian said. "Are they dangerous?"

"Afraid so." the assistant said. "Tiger sharks are one of the big three known for their unprovoked attacks on humans, alongside great whites and bull sharks." The groups watched in awe as the shark's jaw opened wide, then snapped shut, ingesting dozens of the small fish. "Did you get a look at its teeth?" the assistant asked. "They're serrated and notched, designed for shearing and causing significant damage."

"No swimming in the lagoon," Frank joked. "Got it." He put his arm around Sabrina as if to protect her.

"I wasn't planning to go in," she said.

Echo took a step forward. "Look, I see another one," she said, pointing. "And there's a third!"

The assistant laid his hands on her shoulders and gently moved her back from the edge.

"What next?" Jasmin asked. "Fucking King Kong?"

"Just monkeys," the assistant said. "But they'll leave you alone."

"Christ," Bagdasarian said. "Why on earth did Victor choose this place?"

Sabrina and Jasmin exchanged a knowing look: It was just like Victor to put them through some sort of test.

"So, what is beyond the lagoon?" Schwegler asked.

"The sea," the assistant said.

"So, what you're saying is we're isolated here," Bagdasarian said. "Totally cut off? No internet, no phones, no way in or out but that damn path?"

Nicky did a slow rotation taking in the hotel's paradise-like setting, the lagoon and pond, the lush green shrubbery and tall palms. *More like paradise lost*, he thought.

A zigzag of lighting stuttered across the sky, followed by distant thunder.

"And now it's going to rain? Just perfect," Jasmin said.

"It's the tropics. Storms come and go, but they're quick," the assistant said. "Except in the rainy season."

"Which is when?" Bagdasarian asked, a hand over his head as a few drops began to fall. He was trying to keep up with the others, who were hurrying to get inside as thunder rumbled again.

"June," the assistant said.

"June?" Nicky repeated. The last one inside, he closed the hotel doors behind him. "But that's only a few days away."

41

Inside, the foyer was cool and bright, an anteroom as large as most living rooms with a high ceiling and a hanging multitiered chandelier of glass and steel, the walls veneered with brushed nickel so the entire space glowed. The room stretched several yards before it opened into a marble-columned living room with soaring ceilings, tall potted palms, and white orchids, a few shedding their petals as if the visitors had arrived just in time to watch them die. Just beyond, a grand staircase swept up three flights with a curving banister of gleaming white marble flecked with gold.

"Wow..." Rachel said.

"Beautiful," Bagdasarian said, surprised and relieved, for the moment forgetting his exhaustion.

"Where on earth did they get all the marble?" Sabrina asked, caressing one of the smooth fluted columns.

"From what I read, it was imported from Carrara, Italy," the assistant said.

"Where else?" Lauren said, scratching at her nicotine patch that was itching even more since their trek along the path. "It's what I used for our Park Avenue kitchen counters, beautiful but let me tell you, hard to clean. The dirt just wedges itself into the marble."

"Oi, love, and you know this *how*?" Ian peered at his wife over blue John Lennon glasses. "One of the maids tell you?"

The living room was large and open, with several private,

half-hidden niches that could easily hide a dozen people, the furniture a mix of elegant Queen Anne chairs and sofas upholstered in heavy damask and pale-gray wicker chaises with overstuffed pillows in floral prints. Sliding glass doors and picture windows offered views of the pool, lagoon, and grounds. The huge paned windows and skylights cast late-day sunlight on walls, picking out dozens of African masks, helmets, and headdresses, some wood, others of metal and terra cotta with beards of straw or animal hair and painted shell eyes that seemed to follow you as you moved.

"The bedrooms are up there." The assistant indicated the tiered interior balconies that wrapped around the upper half of the space. "I've assigned rooms in alphabetical order."

"Oh, great." Lauren Ziff groaned. "Meaning I will get the worst room *again*!"

The assistant assured her that all the rooms were equally good, and all with balconies.

"Are there enough, I mean, aren't there others joining us?" Lauren asked, still hoping for those A-listers.

"No, you're it," the assistant said. "Lots of rooms, ones that won't even be used."

Lauren let a sigh of disappointment, but clearly, it was too late to go back.

"Can I lock my balcony doors?" Echo asked. "I tend to sleepwalk. My mother did too. I guess it's, like, inborn."

"Don't you mean in*bred?*" Jasmin said.

"I wonder how no one's killed you yet?" Echo said to her with a mean grin.

"There's still time," Sabrina joked, though she did not want to be on Echo's side.

The assistant found the calamine lotion. "I don't think either of you need the EpiPen," he said to Jasmin and Bagdasarian.

"I am so glad that you will be fine," Schwegler said to Bagdasarian.

"And you as well," Bagdasarian said, thinking he would contact the dark web assassin as soon as he got home. Schwegler was lucky there was no cell service on the island.

First Mate William, his leathery skin shiny with sweat, appeared with a luggage cart and began to unload the bags. Just behind him, Captain Thomas, equally sweaty, with a second cart, did the same thing.

"I supposed we have to haul our own bags upstairs," Bagdasarian said.

"No, there's an elevator," the assistant said.

"You missed the point," Bagdasarian said, getting a grip on his bag.

The captain used his bandanna to wipe his face, then wished them all a good stay. "See you in three days," he said. "On Memorial Day."

"Three days." Jasmin moaned.

"Just don't forget us!" Lauren tugged her tote off the floor and began rummaging through it. "I imagine a tip is in order."

"Oh no," the captain said. "None at all." He had been strictly forbidden to take any money from the guests, a large tip forthcoming from his anonymous employer for completing the job.

Schwegler hugged the briefcase to his chest as he reached for his carry-on bag.

"What have you got in there that's so damn important?" Nicky asked.

"*Meine Effekten*."

"Yeah, that explains it." Nicky scoffed.

"Personal effects," Schwegler said.

Nicky gave him a look; he didn't like or trust the man.

Jasmin, spreading calamine lotion on her arms and legs, was silently cursing Victor for bringing them here, wishing he were alive so she could kill him.

Backpack slipped over his shoulders, Nicky got a hand on his mother's bag, then Frank's. He did not want his uncle, still a bit red-faced from the walk, to carry it.

Hoisting her own heavy Prada tote, Jasmin gave Nicky a dirty look.

The elevator was beautiful but old-fashioned, a gilded cage with an ornate metal gate that needed to be closed by hand before the elevator would move.

"Settle in," the assistant said. "Rest, relax, wash up. But let's have drinks and dinner early, say five?"

"That's less than an hour away," Jasmin said.

"Fine with me," Lauren said. "I'm ready for a drink."

"Great." The assistant smiled shyly. "I'll meet you all down here for drinks in a half hour."

"No doubt you'll be taking attendance," Nicky said.

"Why would I do that?" The assistant looked genuinely baffled. "I'm sure you will all be here. Where else could you go?"

42

Door closed firmly behind him, hand deep in his pocket, Hans Schwegler carefully extracted the handkerchief, stained red, the berries squashed. *Mein Gott!* He dropped the handkerchief, the squashed berries scattering across the shiny parquet floor. Belt opened, he pushed his pants down fast, seeing more red stains like a rash on his thigh. Pants bunched at his knees, he stumbled to the bathroom, soaked a towel with soap and water and scrubbed his thigh. *Was it too late? Had the poison already permeated his skin?*

Then he remembered what Victor's beautiful ex-wife had said, that you had to ingest the berries or eat the seeds to get the poison.

He let out a deep breath, and pants off, crab-walked across the floor, collecting the berries. But what to do with them? Save them? Extract a few seeds to slip into Bagdasarian's drink? How many would be enough? And could he get away with it?

Dummer Junge! Stupid boy! He thought of the many times his father had called him that, then sent him to his room without dinner. Or worse, locked him in a closet where he cried though no one heard him. For a moment his eyes filled with tears, the forty-two-year-old man a little boy swiping at the tears so violently it hurt.

Genug! Enough!

He tossed the berries into the toilet and flushed them away. Told himself it had been a good idea, just badly executed. He could not be blamed for that. How was he to know the berries would get squashed?

Suddenly exhausted, he lay back on the king-size bed and took in the room for the first time. Large and ornate, crowded with an overstuffed love seat and too many pillows, a tall potted palm in the corner, two tall narrow windows spattered with raindrops, more of those native masks on the walls. He looked up, the ceiling painted with clouds, beautiful but faded in places, the plaster cracked. He closed his eyes, thought he could sleep forever.

Fauler Junge, steh auf! Lazy boy, get up! His father again, always right.

He pulled himself out of bed and took a shower, thinking about the plan and which route he would take. Through diligent research and connections, he had had acquired a list of Bagdasarian's debts and the individuals who held the markers, most with a piece of the man's galleries as collateral. Some he would pay off in exchange for ownership. Others, he would urge to keep up the pressure, hoping Bagdasarian would crack. Then, he would swoop in and buy him out. A good plan. Though his father was impatient.

Mach es einfach zu Ende! his father said. *Just finish it!*

43

The king-size bed was inviting, the room beautiful but frigid, air-conditioning up too high. But that didn't matter. What mattered to Frank was that he needed a pill and could finally take one.

Suitcase open on the bed, he found his Dopp kit and brought it into the bathroom, which had pink and white tile, a gold-framed mirror above a large basin sink, and a shower as well as an old-fashioned claw-foot tub.

Toiletry bag beside the sink, he searched for the tiny nitroglycerin bottle but couldn't find it. Then remembered he'd taken a pill in the car, so the bottle must be in his jacket pocket. But when he looked, it wasn't there. Had it fallen out? *Damn.* But he had his other pills, his real medication.

He found the blue plastic pill case and opened the first of seven small compartments, surprised to find it empty. So was the next. And the next and the next, every compartment, the entire week's supply, gone. *How was that possible?* He was certain he'd filled it before he left home. Or had he? He been so distracted these days, even more so before he'd left.

He told himself to take a breath. *It's not a catastrophe.* He had backup medication, remembered tossing it into the bag, which he rummaged through again, finally turning it upside down, travel-size toothpaste, disposable razors, Q-tips all spilling onto the counter. But no pills. Not even his baby aspirin.

Back in the bedroom, he went through his carry-on. Again, no pills.

What the…

He stood back, recalling his cardiologist warning him about the danger of missing his medication. *You had a serious heart attack… significant heart damage…lucky to be alive… Take your medication every day… You don't want a stent thrombosis, do you?*

Fuck, no, he did not!

But what could he do? And right now he felt okay, no chest pain at all. *Thank God.* He'd be home in a few days, would take his meds and be just fine.

44

Rachel felt overwhelmed by it all: the hotel, her room—three times larger than her entire apartment—the flat-out beauty of her surroundings. She'd never seen such foliage or flowers, so much color, so much light. True, the junglelike path had been rough, but she'd managed it, which felt good. But then she shivered, recalling those poison berries and, even worse, her fall from the yacht. *If that's what it was.* She tried to shake it off, the idea that someone had pushed her. *It wasn't possible, was it?* At least she hadn't eaten the berries, thanks to Victor's ex-wife—who hadn't recognized her.

Had she changed that much? A full-length mirror confirmed that she had. My God, she looked a mess. She closed her eyes, did not want to think about the fall or the berries or anything unpleasant, not here, not in paradise, and not when she was about to collect an inheritance.

She unpacked quickly; she did not have much. But who was she trying to impress? Was there anyone among the guests she even liked? Not Victor's new wife, Jasmin, who had *acted* nice to her but was clearly after something, a devious woman, she could see that. Maybe Victor's brother, Frank, though she knew she was a little starstruck where he was concerned. Another time in her life she might have flirted with him, but not now. Plus, he only had eyes for Victor's ex, that much was clear. Who was she kidding? A man like that wouldn't give her a second look, even now with his career on the skids. And Victor's son? He'd been kind to her after her near-drowning, but she could tell he was self-centered and spoiled. They all were. The worst of the lot, Lauren Ziff, her prey so to speak, wasn't speaking to her.

She sighed, not sure she even cared anymore.

There was only one person who mattered, a man she detested, a grudge she could not give up.

I should have saved those poison berries for him! She pictured him doubled over, his fat face contorted with pain. But too late for that.

A moment to peruse the fancy amenities in the bathroom—soaps and shampoos, samples of perfume—then laid out a few of her own toiletries—sunscreen and cold cream, toothbrush and floss. Then, with the sharp metal nail file clasped in her hand, she thought, *I will find another way to pay him back.*

45

Ian lay on the oversized bed blowing smoke rings toward the ceiling. He was feeling good, still somewhat buoyed from his conversation with Nicky and then the one with Lauren, where she had shocked him by saying *maybe*. The idea of reuniting the band and owning a club a possibility, a way to jump-start his dream and lost youth. Perhaps she had dreams too, something he had not been privy to for a long time. He tuned in to the sounds of her taking a shower, could not help the image that slid into his mind: Lauren slipping and cracking her skull on the hard marble floor. Then he would not have to ask her for anything, the one loophole in the prenup and the only way he'd inherit anything: if she were dead.

There now, lad, don't think such thoughts, not now when she is being nice.

He glanced at the window and thought about his lame attempt at the beach club, how *he* had almost fallen overboard trying to push Lauren. Typical and ironic. So much irony in both their lives. The fact that Lauren, of all people, was addicted to pain pills, which she blamed on her surgeries, all elective, and the fact that she could get all the oxy she wanted. Not like the poor slobs who got addicted to her family's wonder drug, then resorted to heroin and cheaper drugs that ultimately killed them.

Could he swap her twenty-milligram oxy for a much higher dose? Would she notice the eighty-milligram pill was a different color? Did she even look when she popped her pills? God, how the press would go mad for that: big pharma heiress ODs on her own company's drug!

He had to laugh. And had to stop thinking these terrible thoughts now that Lauren had agreed to the club's bailout money, *maybe*.

"Ian! Get in here!" His beloved calling from the bathroom.

"Oi, what is it?" Ian dragged himself out of bed and into the bathroom, where Lauren was squeezed into a corner of the shower stall, naked and shaking, pointing at the floor.

"Kill it!" she screamed.

He crouched down for a closer look. Vision blurry from too much weed, it took him a few seconds to make out the inch-long spider, black and shiny. When he did, he jumped back.

"Fucking hell!"

Then the shower spray hit it, and it rolled over, legs twitching, a red hourglass on its belly.

Bloody hell, a black widow?

He could ask Victor D'Arcangelo's ex-wife, the poison expert, to have a look, but clearly there wasn't time.

"What are you doing down there?" Lauren had flattened her body against the tiled wall. "Kill it, for Christ's sake! *Just kill it!*"

"Hold on, love. I'll get me a magazine."

"*Hurry!*"

Ian tried out one magazine then another, *Vanity Fair*, *Rolling Stone*, the *New York Times*, the whole time Lauren screaming in the bathroom, "What the hell are you doing? Get *in* here!"

"Coming, love!" He rolled the Lifestyle section of the *New York Times* into a tube and was just heading back to the bathroom when Lauren shouted, "Get in here you do-nothing worthless piece of Cockney shit!"

Ian stopped and slumped back onto the bed. *Do nothing, eh? Worthless piece of shite? Okay, love, but you can't have it both ways!* He unrolled the newspaper, started to skim an article about the dangers of camping in the wilds while listening to Lauren scream and scream. Then she stopped.

Has she been bitten? Has she collapsed? Is she dead? Would it happen that quickly?

A moment later she was standing at the foot of the bed, naked, dripping wet, and glaring at him. "You motherfucking piece of shit! You were waiting for it to bite me!"

"No, love, no, I was getting ready. Look." He rerolled the newspaper quickly.

"Too late, you bastard! I crushed it with a bar of soap. It's dead!" She slipped on a robe, her body still shaking. "I should have saved it and dropped it into your crotch, except that part of you is already dead! Like that money for your club!" She turned away, tugging the sash of her robe.

"No, wait, love, wait."

"You think you can get rid of me that easily?" She barked a laugh. "Try it again. Try anything and..." She spun back, her face hard. "The minute we get back to New York I'm calling my lawyer, getting that long-overdue divorce, and cutting you *off*! It's back to fish and chips for you, my friend!"

"Lauren, love, Petal." Ian was plaintive, his club dream dying and, worse, the idea of being poor again, starting over at forty-two with no skills other than his boyish charms, which even he knew were on the wane. "C'mon, love, did you think a little bug would kill you? It was nothin'."

Lauren lanced him with a look. "You'd better hope something kills me before this weekend is over. Because once we're home, we're *finished*, and you're *out*!" She stopped, considering something. "Oh, and maybe it's time the Manchester police got an anonymous call, you know, about that unsolved gang crime."

"You wouldn't." A split-second image of the pimple-faced kid, falling.

"Oh, wouldn't I?" Lauren smirked. "What was the name of your gang, the Mad Dog something or other?"

Ian bit his lip. "C'mon, Petal, you know I love you."

"*Ha!* That why you tried to push me into the ocean and feed me to a spider?"

"Oi, love, we was just havin' some fun, weren't we? Exercising, like we do."

"Well, from what I hear, you will have plenty of time to *exercise* in prison!"

46

What a room! Echo moved from the king-size bed to the love seat, then admired herself in the full-length gold-framed mirror. It was like something out of her mother's all-time favorite movie, *Pretty Woman*, the one where the hooker picks up the millionaire who takes her away from her life on the street. *As if*, her mother said every time she watched it, but always cried.

The bathroom was even better, a separate shower and enormous tub, all with gold fixtures, though looking more closely, one was a little rusty. Still, like nothing she'd ever seen.

Echo rinsed her face, then took her time penciling a few new freckles across the bridge of her nose and over her cheeks. They made her look younger, not eighteen as she claimed, closer to sixteen, though in fact she was twenty-two. Not that it mattered to this group of losers. All they cared about was their fucking money and the fact that she was here to claim her share of it.

She finished the last freckle, assessed her work, then gathered up the bathroom freebies—the Costa Brazil hand soap, the Marula oil and perfume samples, the lavender bath crystals, the shampoos and conditioners—and jammed them all into her backpack, even the gold soap dish. Though the weekend would be over soon and she would be rich. Like her mother always said, *Get it while you can, kid*. And she intended to.

47

They were seated at the long dining room table, white linen table-cloth, baroque silverware, crystal wineglasses, many of the guests on their second drink, though Nicky thought about acceptance and surrender, and stuck to Pellegrino. Half a dozen decorative candles cast flickering shadows across the table, the walls, the guests' faces and several fierce-looking primitive masks, all of it reflected in a huge floor-to-ceiling mirror in fractured overlapping images like a fun house.

They had started dinner early, late-day sunlight still creeping through the windows and skylights as they passed around platters of exotic fruits—mango, papaya, sugar apples, all peeled, sliced, and arranged artfully on a platter. Another of fish, large white slabs sprinkled with fresh thyme.

"Love that we're doing an early bird special," Sabrina said. She had changed into tight white pants and a white spandex top that showed off her breasts. "I'm starved and it looks great!" She scooped a spoonful of salad, varicolored chunks of white, red, green, and yellow. "What is this?"

"Conch salad," the assistant said, at the head of the table wearing a shirt with a Mexican tribal pattern. "It's been marinating in lime juice all day."

"Well, it ain't bloody fish and chips," Ian said, wolfing down a mouthful. His eyeliner looked refreshed, but he had not changed out of his rumpled clothes, and he was drinking heavily, worrying about his future.

"I'm guessing a lot better than prison food, right, darling?" Lauren said to him.

"It's all lovely," Rachel said. Still shaky from her near-drowning, she had applied bright-red lipstick to offset her pallor and changed into her other DVF wrap dress. This one was a multicolored snake-skin pattern, which she'd thought would be appropriate and witty for island attire, though now she wasn't so sure, and the print stretched too tightly across her bust.

"This is actually good," Jasmin said, making no attempt to hide her surprise. Nor did her floor-length caftan hide the calamine-dotted bug bites on her wrists and hands, a few on her cheeks. "I didn't think there was any help."

"There isn't," the assistant said.

"Then who made all this?" Bagdasarian asked, washing down a bite of fish with white wine. He was sporting a double-breasted linen jacket too tight to button. "You got the locals to cook for us, eh?"

"There aren't any locals," the assistant said. "Not since Hurricane Dorian in 2019."

"You mean we're it?" Frank looked around the table.

"Yes." The assistant shook his head, his topknot wobbling. "You have the entire island to yourselves. Isn't that great?"

The looks exchanged between the guests suggested otherwise.

"So who made the food?" Nicky asked.

"I did," the assistant said, looking proud and shy at the same time.

"By yourself?" Lauren said.

"Not everyone keeps slaves," Ian said to her, refilling his drink. He figured it no longer mattered what he said.

"Like in prison," Lauren said. "Where you become someone's slave, *bitch* rather. Isn't that what happens to the weaker, prettier men?"

Several guests looked at the couple, wondering what they were talking about.

"I was used to cooking for Mr. D," the assistant said.

"And did you cut up his food and feed him too?" Nicky said, mocking.

"Only at the end," the assistant said softly, a pained look spreading across his face that made the group go uncomfortably quiet.

"Yes, I *know* it was bad at the end!" Nicky snapped. "I was *there*!" Though he had only visited once, not realizing his father was going to die. He wondered if he would have visited more had he known; he wasn't sure.

Hans Schwegler had snagged the seat between Frank and Sabrina, so that Frank had to lean forward or back to catch Sabrina's eye, impossible as she was deep in conversation with the Swiss German art dealer, once again talking about her deadly plant paintings, clearly working both art dealers.

"Do you think those are…real bones?" Rachel pointed out a mask with a skull and teeth and braided straw for hair.

"It's a shaman's mask," Bagdasarian said.

"You mean like a witch doctor?" Echo asked.

"Exactly," Bagdasarian said.

"Of course *you* would know," Rachel said, though she had not meant to say it aloud.

"In fact, I *do*," he said, taken aback by her hostility. "I happen to collect African art, or I did." He had recently sold off his collection for much-needed cash. "I was going to say shamans can be healers or priests, and that mask with the skull symbolizes the spirits of the dead."

"Well, it gives me the creeps," Lauren said. She was wearing a low-cut designer jumpsuit with a long string of pearls that dangled between her breasts, the effect somewhat marred by the large nicotine patch on her upper arm. "But not as much as *spiders* do." She glared at her husband.

Sabrina interrupted her conversation with Schwegler to say, "Spiders are *very* important. They eat ants and flies and all sorts of mosquitoes."

"Clearly not *all* the mosquitoes!" Jasmin said, scratching a bite on her hand.

"Gosh," Sabrina said in a saccharine voice. "I hope those bug bites aren't as *awful* as they look!"

"I'm considering a lawsuit," Jasmin said.

"Against who?" Nicky said. "The mosquitoes?" He had changed his T-shirt, this one vintage with Jane Fonda's old mug shot, the young actress with her fist raised.

Schwegler said, "The bigger spiders eat lizards and frogs, some even birds. It is always the way, no? Survival of the fittest." He cast an eye at the New York art dealer but looked away when Bagdasarian returned the look.

Nicky leaned closer to Ian and quietly asked if he'd had spoken to Lauren about money for the club.

"Oi, there's a story there, mate," Ian whispered. "But not now."

"What story?" Lauren said, pulling a linen shawl over her bare shoulders. "It's freezing in here."

"The air-conditioning is on automatic," the assistant said. "But perhaps I can lower it."

"Don't touch it!" Bagdasarian said, tugging at his sweat-stained shirt collar.

"I've been wondering," Nicky said, turning his attention back to the assistant. "Was it you who sent the evite?"

"All I did was hit Send," he said. "The invitation was figured out and written months ago, predated and set to go."

"By Victor?" Sabrina asked.

"Who else?" the assistant said.

"When did Victor do all this?" Jasmin asked. "Rent this island, hire the cars, the yacht, get the plane tickets?"

"Didn't he share that with you?" the assistant asked.

"Well, sure," she lied, not wanting to seem like he hadn't. "I mean, he talked about planning his funeral, but he wasn't…specific. I guess he wanted to surprise me."

"Surprise you *how*?" Echo asked with a grin. "By dying?"

"So, he planned the memorial *before* he got sick?" Sabrina asked.

The assistant nodded.

"I still don't understand why Victor did all this if he *didn't* know he was going to die," Jasmin said, thinking aloud and trying hard not to sound pissed that Victor had spent so much money and never told her. Though they had been separated, and truthfully, he told her very little.

"Perhaps he had a feeling," Rachel said. "You know, um, a premonition." Until the invitation had arrived, she'd had more than a premonition that her life was over, had even contemplated ending it herself.

"Maybe my brother thought it was time to deal with the fact that he was getting older," Frank said, a reality he had trouble accepting himself despite his own recent brush with death.

"Victor thought he was invincible," Sabrina said, shaking her head. "I always thought *he* thought he would live forever."

"No one lives forever," Schwegler said.

Thunder rumbled in the distance as if underscoring the remark.

"Thanks for reminding us," Frank said and laughed, though he needed no reminder.

"God, this weather," Jasmin said. "Is it going to rain all weekend?"

"Why don't you check with God," Nicky said. "While you're discussing your mosquito lawsuit."

Echo laughed, her mouth open, filled with food.

"Funny," Jasmin said to Nicky, her eyes narrowed.

"Don't worry," the assistant said, "there are plenty of umbrellas and all of your rooms have hurricane lamps."

"You're expecting a *hurricane*?" Jasmin said.

"It's just a precaution," he said.

"What next?" Bagdasarian sighed. "Frogs? Locusts?"

"We already had frogs on that awful path," Jasmin said with a shiver.

"Does this place have a name?" Sabrina asked.

"I believe the island was originally named Parataiso Mulimuli by a movie star who bought it," the assistant said. "That's means *the Last Paradise* in Samoan."

"So now you speak Samoan?" Nicky scoffed.

Before the assistant could answer, Rachel said, "Oh, I know all about the movie star. I'm a fan." She blushed but went on. "He, um, bought the island after filming a movie here in the sixties. He wanted to escape the craziness of his Hollywood life but sadly, it followed him." She thought about a piece of her past that would always follow her.

"Oh, I know that story," Frank said, thinking about his own escape from Hollywood, not by choice. "But I thought it was just old movie folklore."

"I think it's true," the assistant said. "After the actor's death, the place fell into disrepair until some fancy hotel chain bought it. They fixed it up and named it…" He thought a moment. "Paraíso Puerto de la Cruz."

"Wait a minute," Bagdasarian said. "Paraíso Puerto de la Cruz? Isn't that the name of the place where all those tourists died?"

"I don't know," the assistant said.

"Really?" Nicky said. "I thought you knew everything."

"No," the assistant said, keeping his cool. "It's news to me."

"Well, it *was* news," Bagdasarian said. "A long time ago, maybe forty years."

Drink poised at her lips, Lauren leaned forward and asked, "How did they die?"

"I can't remember," Bagdasarian said. "I'd google it if I *could*. All I know is they got marooned here and died."

48

Talk of the dead tourists was tabled as there was no way to find out more or check on the story's veracity, though the idea of it had seeped into everyone's subconscious.

"I'll never forget those dinner parties you and Victor had in your loft," Rachel said to Sabrina, making a stab at small talk.

"Oh?" Sabrina said, a memory of that time washing over her with all her conflicted feelings.

"I was at two, no *three* of those dinners. I wrote about Victor's work," she said quietly. "But, um, you don't remember me." It wasn't a question. Of course, the woman did not remember her; she already knew that. It had been foolish of her to bring it up again.

And it was true, Sabrina had forgotten Rachel, but not the dinners or the work involved, the days of planning the menu, the shopping and cooking, the seating arrangement—the right curator beside the right art dealer beside the right art collector—everything orchestrated, the perfect art wife to her genius husband who thanked her by sleeping with other women. "Of course I remember you," she said and, feeling bad, added, "You should come visit when we get home. I can't promise handwritten place cards, but I can throw lunch together."

"*Really?* I would love that—and may I see your paintings?"

"Of course. But that's not why I asked," Sabrina said, and it was true, though she liked the idea of someone who had written about Victor's art coming to see *hers*. "I'd love you to see the paintings, lend me some of your expertise."

"Oh, I *will*!" Rachel said, genuinely touched. It had been a long time since anyone asked her opinion about art, about anything.

The assistant clinked a fork against his wineglass to get everyone's attention, then stood and slid a folded piece of paper from his pocket. "Sorry to interrupt but I have something to read from Mr. D."

"*Mr. D*," Nicky could not help but scoff again, though he sat up, curious.

"Is it the will?" Jasmin asked, excited but trying to keep her cool.

"No, I have nothing to do with that. You'll have to consult the lawyers after the weekend."

"*After* the weekend," Sabrina repeated, thinking it was so like Victor to keep them in suspense, to play them like puppets.

The assistant unfolded the piece of paper slowly, almost ceremoniously and began to read. "*Welcome. I am so happy you could all interrupt your busy lives to be here. You have each been invited because you played a crucial role at a moment in my life.*"

Everyone was quiet now, leaning forward, straining to hear the assistant's soft purring voice.

He went on. "*I trust your travels were pleasant, the cars and flights and boat ride. I did my best to make you as comfortable as possible and hope you will enjoy the weekend. But first, a question.*" The assistant paused, then: "*Please tell the group how you have helped me or hurt me. That is your assignment for the weekend, to answer that question.*" He looked up, eyeing the group. "That's Mr. D asking, not me."

There was a moment of silence punctuated by a few deep breaths and sighs, utensils lifted and put down, the gulping of wine.

Then Lauren said, "Well, I never met Victor, so I couldn't possibly have hurt him. I guess I *helped* him by buying one of his paintings just a few months ago."

"Lots of people have purchased Victor's paintings," Bagdasarian said. "It can't be *that*."

"Maybe it has somethin' to so with all those D'Arcangelo paintings you inherited from your mum and dad," Ian said. "You know, love, the ones you sold at auction."

"I—" Lauren gave her husband a venomous look before her head jerked back like a turtle pulling into its shell.

Bagdasarian studied her a moment, trying to place her revamped face. "Paintings you inherited from your parents?" He tapped his chin. "Of course! Harold and Lily Ziff were your parents!"

Lauren said nothing, a picture of her sweet Jamaican nanny in her mind, the one she had believed was her mother until she was old enough to realize it could not possibly be true, that her mother was that *other* woman, the cold one she rarely saw, the one who cared more for jewels and paintings than she did her little girl.

"Your parents were *very* serious art collectors," Bagdasarian said, bringing Lauren back to the moment. "And they often bought from me. I remember now. I tried to buy those D'Arcangelo paintings back."

"At a *discount*," Lauren said. "I preferred to take my chances at auction."

"Yes, you did," Bagdasarian said. "Despite what I told you, that putting so many paintings by one artist on the market at the same time could be a disaster. It ruined his auction prices for years!" He turned to the group. "The same thing happened to the Italian artist Sandro Chia when his biggest collector, Charles Saachi, put half a dozen of his paintings up for auction at the same time. It just about killed his career. It always amazes me that collectors don't care about devaluing an artist's work once *they've* sold it."

"Oh man, that really sucks," Echo said.

Lauren played with her long string of pearls, wrapping them around her fingers. "I didn't realize it would do that."

"I'm sure you didn't," Sabrina said, hoping to hold on to Lauren's commission portrait. "How could you know?"

"But you *did* know," Bagdasarian said. "Because I *explained* it to you."

"Oi, love, he *did*," Ian said, his multiringed hand wrapped around his drink. If his wife was going to sell him to the coppers and toss him out on the street, he would go out with style. "Don't you remember, love? You came home and told me *all* about it. You said, *Fuck that art dealer! They are me own paintings and I'll do what I want! That art dealer bloke, he just wants to sell the bloody paintings himself!*"

"And you, you agreed with me," Lauren stuttered. "Even urged me on."

"It wasn't up to me though, was it, love? I mean they weren't me paintings to sell. I was just supportin' you, wasn't I, like I always do?"

Lauren glared at him, then back at the table, the pearl necklace wrapped tightly in her fingers. "My parents had just died," she said, a throb in her voice. "I was upset. I had a lot to, to deal with."

"That's the bleedin' truth," Ian said. "I swear down she *did*. Dealin' with a ten-billion-dollar inheritance can be bloody hell."

Lauren stared at Ian as if she wanted to kill him, while everyone else stared at her like she was the devil.

Bagdasarian said, "Well, clearly, *you* are in the *hurt* category!"

"But I didn't mean to..." Lauren said, then her necklace snapped, pearls scattering everywhere.

49

The candles were melting, guests pushing food around on their plates or refilling wineglasses, Lauren trying to collect her scattered pearls from the floor when Rachel turned to Bagdasarian.

"And what about *you*?" she asked. "How did *you* help or hurt Victor?"

"*Me?* Are you *kidding*? All I ever did was help. I found him as a young artist, promoted him, packaged him, made him an art world superstar!"

"And you did that all by yourself, did you? Tell us exactly how you supported Victor D'Arcangelo and all your artists. *Please.*"

"I already said." Bagdasarian looked at her, trying to figure out what she was hinting at. Could she possibly know something about his illegal activities, his under-the-table art sales with no percentage to the artists and nothing to the IRS? No, it wasn't possible. They were all cash sales to foreign collectors who wanted discretion as much as he did. "I have no idea what you're getting at," he said, as cooly as possible.

"Well, you did not create Victor D'Arcangelo by *yourself*! It wasn't just *you*!" Her face twisted in anger. "*I* was the first one who wrote about his work for the *New York Times*! *I* was the one who made him known to the public, to the world! Not *you*!"

The table had quieted, everyone watching her.

"You don't remember me?" Rachel said, waiting, heart beating fast.

Bagdasarian looked her over. "Oh. Wait. You're that little art writer. I remember now. But clearly, my dear, you are overrating your contribution. And you only wrote about him, what, once? And then you abandoned him, stopped writing about him as if he had contributed nothing important for the rest of his career."

"That's not true!" Her normally timid voice nearing a shout. "I wrote about his work *three* times! And it was *your* fault I stopped writing about him, stopped writing entirely!"

"*My* fault?"

"Yes, *yours*!"

"But *how*?"

The group watched them like a tennis match, back and forth.

"You tried to blackmail me into writing about *all* your gallery artists, but I wouldn't do it. That's why I stopped reviewing Victor, because of *you,* because of your threats! And for that you got me fired, ruined my career—ruined my *life*!" Rachel shouted at him while another image tore across her mind: a dinner tray knocked from her hands, tomato soup spilling on her dress, her shoes.

Bagdasarian looked nonplussed, though he did remember calling the *New York Times* publisher and threatening to withdraw all advertising for his galleries unless a certain critic was let go. "Oh, please," he said. "Let's not get melodramatic."

"You—" Rachel's lips were twitching, words trapped in her throat. Then she was up, out of her chair, leaning over Bagdasarian, her fists pummeling his chest.

All the guests sat silent, stunned, except for Echo, who cheered, "Get him!"

Then Nicky was up, his arms around Rachel, gently tugging her away from the art dealer. "Okay," he said, softly. "That's enough."

"You don't understand! My job—everything—gone—because of *him*!" Rachel wrenched herself free and pointed a finger at

Bagdasarian. "You'll be sorry!" she said, her body vibrating with anger.

"I don't think I'm the one who should be sorry," Bagdasarian snipped, smoothing his jacket, then changed his tone. "Look, it's such old news. Let's say we bury the hatchet, eh?"

Rachel sniffed back tears, suddenly aware of everyone watching her. The only place she could imagine burying a hatchet was in the art dealer's chest, but she bit off the words, "Yes—of—course. Sorry. I–I don't know what came over me." Voice shaky, she just wanted to disappear.

"Atta girl," Bagdasarian said.

His condescending words only inflamed her, but she dared not show it, having already made a spectacle of herself, more than once. *My God, Rachel, get a grip!* Her mother again. "Yes," she said. "I...I'm not myself, jet-lagged and...the fall." She felt like she was drowning all over again, this man always there dragging her down.

"Quite all right." Bagdasarian waved a dismissive hand. "Let's pretend it never happened, shall we? It's all forgotten."

No, Rachel thought, *not forgotten—and never forgiven!*

50

It was still light out, but the wind had kicked up, palm leaves batting against the windows. Inside, the room felt hermetically sealed, a brittle electricity in the air ready to spark from all the arguing.

Wanting to scream, to lash out, Rachel managed to contain her rage. She got up carefully, excused herself, and walked slowly but purposely to the bathroom.

"That was intense!" Jasmin said the moment she was out of earshot.

"What on earth is *her* problem?" Lauren said, fueling the fire, happy to have the focus on someone else, especially the reporter.

"If you ask me, she seems kinda unstable," Echo said. "Like, first she throws herself into the ocean, now this."

"No one asked you," Jasmin said, though she had to agree.

"The poor woman clearly has problems," Bagdasarian said, trying to sound magnanimous when he didn't care one bit about Rachel or her pathetic accusations.

"You don't think she actually threw herself into the ocean, do you?" Sabrina whispered, an eye on the dining room entrance, watching for Rachel.

"It's more likely than *slipping* over the railing," Frank said.

"Maybe she was trying to swim home," Jasmin said. "I know I'm ready."

There were a few awkward laughs that stopped short when Rachel reappeared.

She avoided everyone's eyes as she resumed her seat. She had not wanted to come back to the table but no way she would let the art dealer win.

Sabrina broke the uncomfortable silence by holding up her place card. "Who made these?"

"I did," the assistant said. "I took a calligraphy course in school."

"Pre-K or kindergarten?" Nicky asked.

A few people laughed but not the assistant who answered seriously. "*Art* school. All of Mr. D's studio assistants went to art school, and most of them were working artists."

"I'm going to art school too," Echo added. A lie. At her mother's insistence, she had dropped out of high school at sixteen and worked menial jobs, sweeping up hair in the local beauty salon, cleaning rooms in a third-rate motel, the smell of Lysol and cigarettes clinging to her for days after. The kind of work she had no intention of going back to, not with Victor's money on the horizon.

"So, you and the other assistants helped Victor make his paintings?" Sabrina asked the assistant.

"Some," he said. "Mixing colors, making Mr. D's special medium, his secret blend of sun-thickened linseed oil, damar varnish, and just few drops of cobalt dryer."

"Not a secret anymore," Nicky sneered.

Sabrina said, "What I was asking was if you and the other assistants ever painted *on* Victor's paintings."

"Well...sometimes." The assistant fidgeted with the elastic around his topknot. "I mean, when things got busy."

"Like *how*?" Nicky leaned forward.

"Ya, please do tell us," Schwegler said. "I too am interested."

"Just the normal stuff," the assistant said softly. "Like laying out an image on the canvas—according to Mr. D's sketch of course—and then, sometimes, working on the initial layer and sometimes on the final coat."

"I see," Nicky said. "So essentially, you and the other studio assistants *painted* my father's paintings."

"Oh no, I wouldn't say *that*."

"You just *did*." Nicky stared at the assistant, waiting.

"It's not an unusual practice," he said. "All the great Renaissance artists—Leonardo, Raphael, Titian—had workshops where the assistants worked on the master's art."

"The Renaissance *masters*?" Nicky scoffed a laugh. "You forgot Michelangelo, or did my father take his place?"

Several guests laughed too, but not the assistant, nor the two art dealers.

"Did you ever feel jealous making Victor's paintings for him?" Jasmin asked.

"First of all, let me repeat, we did *not* make his paintings," the assistant said.

"You just said you *did*," Nicky said, wanting to see the guy squirm.

"No, I didn't," he said. "And why would I feel jealous?" He was not squirming at all.

"Well, Victor got paid a fortune," Jasmin said. "While you and the other assistants..."

"We were paid for our work."

"Like how much?" Nicky demanded. "Twenty, thirty bucks an hour? While my father sold the paintings for...what?" He looked to Bagdasarian for an answer. "Hey, art dealer, how much? Ballpark?"

"Yeah, like how much?" Echo echoed.

"Well, there are many factors that determine a price..." Bagdasarian took a long, stalling sip of wine. "The size of a painting, its complexity, provenance. But really it is in bad taste to discuss money."

"*Bad taste?*" Jasmin snorted. "You must be the only art dealer in history to ever utter those words *out loud*."

"That's exactly why I bought our recent D'Arcangelo at auction," Lauren said. "So, it was *public*, no art-dealer funny business involved."

"I resent that," Bagdasarian said. "And for the record, auction prices are always higher than what one pays at a gallery. I suspect you overpaid, Ms. Ziff."

"I resent it as well," Schwegler said to Lauren.

Bagdasarian gave him a look like: *Don't agree with me*.

"So, let me get this straight..." Nicky sat forward, a finger tapping his lip. "You and the other assistants laid the paintings out and worked on the first and final layers. So, you knew *exactly* how to paint my father's paintings, and could—hypothetically, of course—continue to create them *after* his death."

"Oh no. We would *never* do that!" The assistant was indignant, losing his cool for the first time, his soft voice cracking.

"No, of course not," Nicky said, his sarcasm thick. "Also, just wondering, did my father leave behind any sketches for future paintings?"

"I guess," the assistant said.

"You know everything about my father's artwork, but now you only *guess*?"

"Yes," the assistant said more definitively. "Mr. D often did preparatory sketches so there must be some around."

"Preparatory sketches just *waiting* to become new paintings," Nicky said. "Signed and predated."

"I already said that would *never* happen!" the assistant said. "If there are preparatory sketches, I will make sure they are *destroyed*."

"You will do no such thing!" Bagdasarian bellowed, then collected himself and said calmly, "*I* will take care of any preparatory sketches as they are part of the artist's estate."

"When did Victor assign his art estate to *you*?" Jasmin said, folding her mosquito-bitten arms across her chest.

"I *am* his art dealer," Bagdasarian said.

"In New York," Schwegler said, managing to stop himself from saying, *for now*.

Bagdasarian saw a way to turn the tables. "So, Herr Schwegler, you never answered the question, how did *you* help or hurt Victor?"

"I have only *helped* by expanding his market in Europe, and my family business has plans for further expansion." *Vorsichtig. Careful*, Schwegler's father hissed in his ear.

"Ah, yes, your family's *business*..." Bagdasarian nodded. "Which manages certain European art that has, shall we say, *dubious* provenance. Remind us, *Herr* Schwegler, how your grandfather bought—sorry, *stole*—art for Hitler."

Schwegler stood so abruptly that he upset his place setting, a wineglass tumbling. "That is a lie! A vicious rumor!"

"*What?*" Lauren's eyes narrowed in his direction. "Your family worked for the Nazis?"

"Oh, *yesss*," Bagdasarian dragged out the word. "Herr Schwegler's grandfather was a Nazi VIP, one of Hitler's *appointed* art dealers. It's well documented. I would google it if my phone had service."

"My family lost art in the Holocaust, and many of them..."—Lauren's voice was suddenly trembling—"lost their *lives*!"

"Whoa, intense," Echo said.

"There, there, Petal." Ian leaned over to pat Lauren's arm, a lame attempt to make nice, but she pulled away.

"I am sorry to hear that," Schwegler said. "But it has nothing to do with me or—"

Bagdasarian cut him off. "Could be your family has some of Lauren's family's looted art hidden in some Swiss vault, like so much Nazi-looted art?"

Schwegler's face was red, his thin lips quivering. *Do not answer such a question.* His father, whispering in his ear again. *Think, boy. You have other weapons to use.*

He sat down slowly and, recalling his careful research, responded coolly. "If I am not mistaken, Mr. Bagdasarian, three of your major artists left you for other galleries this year."

"That's not true," Bagdasarian said. "I *asked* them to leave. They were losing money."

"Is that so? Because I represent two of those artists in Europe and they are enormously successful, and they have informed me that you sold their work without their knowledge and without paying them."

"That's a *lie*!" Bagdasarian banged his wineglass down so hard it splattered drops like bloodstains across the tablecloth. "And libelous!"

Rachel sat quietly, but she was smiling.

"I imagine you did the same with Victor's art," Schwegler went on. "Which would put *you* in the harm category."

Bagdasarian stood so fast he upended his chair, which crashed to the floor. "I've had enough of these lies and character assassinations! I'm going to bed!"

"Gentlemen, *please*," the assistant said, a plea in his voice, looking from one man to the other. "The last thing Mr. D would want is to have his art dealers fighting."

"Right," Bagdasarian said, and still fuming, he sat. He had made his plans for the Swiss German dealer, no reason to let the man get to him.

51

Sabrina leaned in to Nicky. "I'm proud of you," she said quietly.

"For what?"

"How you handled the situation with..." A quick look at Rachel, then away.

"Aww, that's touching," Echo said, eavesdropping. "Real mother love." She stuck a finger into her mouth and mimed a gag.

"No one was talking to you," Sabrina said. "And speaking of mothers, is yours really dead, or just dead to *you* or maybe *you're* dead to *her*?" Sabrina was wondering if the appearance of the illegitimate daughter meant the girl's mother would soon be making a claim on Victor's estate as well.

"That's not your business," Echo sniped.

"No?" Jasmin said. "Why not tell us about your mother? Or does she not exist?"

"Oh, she exists all right," Echo said.

"So then..." Jasmin leaned back in her chair, arms folded. "Tell us all about her."

"Fuck you," Echo said.

"Hey, let's be civil," Frank said.

"Yes," Lauren said to the girl. "*Try*." She was reminded of dinners in her parents' palatial apartment, the long dining room table, where she at a far end sitting silently, hands clenched in her lap, afraid to speak for fear of being sent to her room.

"Fuck you too, bitch!" Echo said.

Lauren smacked Ian's arm. "Say something! Defend me!"

Ian stoned and drunk, raised his head. "Oi. What's 'appenin'?"

"Oh, shut up," Lauren said.

"I don't need any of you!" Echo hissed.

The assistant looked from one to another, about to intervene, then stopped.

"No?" Nicky said. "Then why are you here? Oh, right. To claim your *illegitimate* inheritance. But first, answer the question. How did *you* help or harm my father? And blackmail doesn't count as *help*."

"Forget *me*," she said. "How did *you* help or harm him?"

"I'm his son. Helping was not my job; it was *his*."

"Such an entitled little brat," she said, visions of herself on hands and knees scrubbing filth off a motel's cracked linoleum floor, sweeping up snarled hair at that crummy beauty salon, of strange men in her bed. She winced.

"*Me?*" Nicky was unable to control his outrage at Victor's bastard child, who had no idea what he had endured—his father's constant belittling, his parent's hideous marriage and divorce, his battle with drugs. "You have no idea what I've been through."

"It's *you* who has no idea what *I've* been through, what *I* had to do to . . ." Another vision: a blurred face, blood, an open-mouthed scream. *His mouth? Her mouth?* The image morphed then broke apart, Echo blinking.

"You're the brat!" Sabrina said, coming to her son's defense. "Acting all innocent with those ridiculous painted freckles on your cheeks, but you can't disguise the dollar signs in your eyes!"

"So says the bitter *old ex*-wife!" Echo shouted, practically bouncing in her seat, then seeing it again and trying to blink it away: *the scream, the blood, the thump of the car's trunk*.

"Watch your mouth," Frank said to her, up now, fists balled at his sides.

Echo, back to the moment, turned toward him. "You know what Victor called *you*? His pathetic has-been brother! And there was more..." She made a show of tapping her chin as if trying to remember something, though she recalled every word her mother had told her about Victor D'Arcangelo and how he had talked incessantly about his family's betrayals. "Oh, right, now I remember. He said you fucked his wife."

Sabrina gasped, her eyes shifting from Echo to Frank to Nicky, and all of them staring at her.

Frank stiffened but only for a second. Then he slapped Echo across the face. It was the first time he had ever hit anyone outside of a movie and he was shocked by it, his hand stinging. "I'm sorry," he said, though in fact, he wasn't. He wanted to hit her again.

Hand to her cheek, Echo stood, her face red and body trembling, "Oh, you *will* be sorry."

"Everyone, please, be cool," the assistant said. "I know Mr. D would not like you folks to be fighting."

Nicky scoffed. He thought it was exactly the kind of thing his manipulative father *would* like, and probably the reason he had brought them all here.

52

For a moment the guests were quiet, playing with their food or gulping drinks. Nicky, the only one not drinking, was staring at his mother, aware of the fact that neither she nor Frank had denied Echo's statement.

"Now what?" Lauren said. "A round of pin the tail on the donkey, or do we have a piñata to smash?"

"No piñata," the assistant said seriously. "But there are games." He indicated the bookcase and a stack of board games.

"I was *kidding*," Lauren said.

"Why not?" Echo said, totally composed, as if nothing had happened.

"I'm not playing a game," Jasmin said. Her whole life seemed like a game, this weekend just one more.

"I think we've had enough games," Bagdasarian said.

"But we haven't had *any*," Echo said.

"It might not be a bad idea," the assistant said. "A way for you all to get to know each other."

"I think we know each other well enough," Lauren said.

"I'd do a round of charades," Frank said, always ready to show off his acting skills.

That was all it took to get Echo up, perusing the stack of games. "There's Monopoly and Clue..."

"Clue? Now there's a good idea," Jasmin said. "Mr. Bagdasarian in the library with a candlestick. And the victim is…" She looked from one art dealer to the other.

Echo said, "There's also Truth or Dare and Never Have I Ever! Oh, wait," She tugged out a squarish black box and brought it to the table. "Bad People. The best game ever!"

"What the hell is that?" Bagdasarian read the subtitle, "*Find out what your friends really think of you.* You must be kidding!"

"What exactly *is* a bad person?" Schwegler asked, considering the question for himself.

Other than the wind and patter of rain, it was quiet a moment as the others considered the same question and if they fit the description.

Frank broke the ice with, "Liars?"

"*Everyone* lies," Jasmin said.

"Speak for yourself," Sabrina said.

"Okay, then how about stealing?" Frank said. "I haven't, never even shoplifted as a kid."

Lauren looked at her husband, "*You* did," she said, and threw him a sly grin.

Ian laughed, then saw himself running, the untraceable gun in his hand and Teddy's hand squeezing his.

"Bully for you," Jasmin said. "I wonder if bad acting makes someone a bad person."

"That's not very nice," Rachel said.

"And *you're* nice?" Lauren said. "Writing nasty exposés of other people's business?"

The group looked from Lauren to Rachel, no idea what had transpired between them.

"I'd say it's about the way you conduct yourself in the world," Sabrina said. "How you treat other people."

"Oh, so high-minded," Jasmin said.

"Some of us are," Sabrina said.

"How about when no one is looking?" Jasmin asked her.

"It is your *thoughts* that make you who you are," Schwegler said, still thinking about himself, his own thoughts, ones he never said aloud.

"No one wants to see inside *your* head," Nicky said to him, picturing the man leering at his mother and making antisemitic remarks about the artist Man Ray.

"That's a fact," Bagdasarian said, then worried, just for a moment, that people could see inside *his* head.

"But we *all* have terrible thoughts," Sabrina said. "You're only bad if you *act* on them."

The assistant who had been quiet, spoke up "Nietzsche said *bad* was a social construct."

"*Nietzsche?*" Nicky scoffed.

"He was a German philosopher."

"I *know* who Nietzsche was," Nicky said, though he had no idea what the man had said or stood for or anything else about him.

"So what does that imply?" Sabrina asked. "That we're all good or all bad?"

"Does any of this matter?" Jasmin said, the image of a man and blurred headlights cutting across her brain. "Who—who cares?" she said, trying to end the conversation.

But Rachel, who had not said a word, kept it going. "What about murder?" she said quietly, almost to herself. "Surely that makes you bad."

A clap of thunder shook the hotel, and everyone started.

"I would say it depends," Schwegler said. "If the murder was accidental or intentional, no?"

Rachel emitted an almost imperceptible sob.

"I doubt anyone here has killed anyone," Frank said, then added, "*intentionally*," and laughed.

A few guests laughed too loudly. Others raised wineglasses to their lips or fidgeted with napkins or silverware.

"Let's play already," Echo said, opening the box and reading from the instructions. "Up to ten people can play. Like, how perfect is that?"

"How do we play?" Frank asked.

Echo explained that one person "called the *dictator*" was supposed to read the questions. "But my friends play it like everyone just draws a card and we all answer the question and the rest of us say if they think that's true or not."

"There's no way I'm doing that," Lauren said.

"Oh, come on," Frank said, always up for a game. "It could be fun."

53

"I'll do one round and that's it!" Lauren said, refilling her drink.

"I'll start!" Echo drew a card off the deck and read: "*Most likely to have a naked picture of themselves on the internet?* That's a good one."

There were several groans, though half the table looked at Nicky.

"Why me?" he said. "Because I have the best body?" He flexed a muscle to make a joke of it.

"I agree," Lauren said.

"Agree that young Nick here has the best bod?" Ian said. "Or that you'd post a nude selfie? Oh, wait, you already did that?"

"I did *not*," she said. "But I have nothing to be ashamed of." She sat up, chest out.

"So did you?" Echo prodded Nicky.

"What? Post a naked selfie? No," he said. "Though I've sent a few privately."

"That counts." Echo pushed the stack of cards toward him. "You draw next."

Nicky sighed but swiped a card. "*If we were all on* Survivor*, who would be the first person voted off the island?* Oh, that's easy." He looked at Echo. "*You.*"

"I agree," Sabrina said.

"Me too," said Frank.

"Clearly, it's unanimous," Jasmin said as thunder clapped again and the lights flickered. "Oh my God, we *are* on *Survivor*."

"We're not going to lose the electricity, are we?" Lauren asked.

"Don't worry," the assistant said. "There's a backup generator."

Echo read the next card. "*Most likely to marry for money?*"

Half the table looked at Jasmin, the other half at Ian.

"Don't look at me, mates. I bloody well married for love," he said, and meant it.

Lauren cackled, then looked sad enough to cry.

"You next," Echo said to him.

Ian plucked a card off the deck with a shaky hand. He had lost count of his drinks. "*Most likely to murder their spouse for the insurance money and get away with it*?"

The group continued to look at him, laughing.

"He'd never get away with it," Lauren said, sounding deadly serious.

"Okay, you choose," Echo said to Lauren.

"Fine," Lauren said with a sigh, then read the card. "*Who has secretly done something very illegal and gotten away with it?*"

Several guests said, "Not me!" simultaneously, then laughed uncomfortably.

"I'll bet *you* have," Echo said to Nicky, her tone challenging.

"And *you,*" he shot back. "But maybe you won't get away with it this time."

They stared at each until Frank broke the moment by drawing a card and reading: "*Who has done the most walks of shame?*"

Lauren felt the group's eyes on her, though this time no one said a word.

Then Bagdasarian said, "How about you, Herr Schwegler? Or do you not feel shame?" He was still wondering if the man really knew about his under-the-table dealings or was just bluffing. Either way, he couldn't take the chance.

Schwegler shuddered, feeling his father's slaps and the terrors of a dark closet.

"You next," Echo said to him before he could answer, choosing a card and handing it to him.

Hand shaking slightly, he read, "*Who would be the most successful serial killer?*"

"Oh, that's easy," Lauren said. "*You!* If history has anything to say about it."

"I have no idea what you mean," Schwegler said, though he knew exactly.

"This game must be rigged," Jasmin said.

"Maybe that's enough," the assistant said. "I need to get going."

"One more," Echo said, swiping a card off the deck and reading it before anyone could stop her. "*Who would sell their soul for the least amount of money?*"

"That's too easy," Jasmin said. "You."

"Or *you*!" Echo shot back. "But I'm guessing you sold your soul a long time ago."

There were a few laughs, then everyone was quiet, the droning hum of the air conditioner suddenly louder, as if the volume had been turned up, each guest considering the question and remembering why they were here.

54

"I need to get going while it's still light out," the assistant said, already up, slipping on his backpack and adjusting the straps.

"Lucky you!" Jasmin said.

"You're really going to abandon us?" Lauren said.

"Sorry," the assistant said. "But I was not invited to spend the weekend, only to get you settled."

"You've had enough of us, that it?" Nicky said and meant it.

"No," the assistant said softly. "My work is done, that's all. This memorial was my last official duty. I promised Mr. D I would make sure his wishes were carried out, and that was it." He looked at Nicky. "Why don't you take over? After all, you are Mr. D's son."

"Me? Take over?" Nicky wasn't sure if he was flattered or annoyed. "How?"

"Just see that everything runs smoothly till the boat returns to get you all. Nothing to it." He leaned closer and whispered conspiratorially, "I couldn't help but notice you're the only one not drinking, a clear head to keep the peace, right?" He patted Nicky on the shoulder but didn't wait for his response. "I've got to go. There's a small boat waiting for me."

"Take me with you," Jasmin said, her hands in prayer, only half kidding and annoyed she hadn't had time to get any information out of him, though she wasn't sure he had any.

"You're really going to leave us alone?" Sabrina asked.

"You're not alone," he said. "You have each other."

The guests eyed each other with unease.

"What are we supposed to do?" Frank asked. "Play more *games*?"

"I think we've had enough of *those*," Lauren said.

The assistant looked back at the paper he had read. "I think Mr. D would want you to contemplate his question: how you helped or hurt him, what it meant to him, and to you."

So that was it, Sabrina thought, why Victor had brought them here, to think about what they had done to him. Victor, who always had to win every argument, who never saw or heard anyone's else's side.

"All weekend?" Jasmin said.

"Well, I'm sure he would want you to enjoy yourselves too." The assistant folded the paper back into his pocket. "I mean, he went to a lot of trouble and expense to bring you here."

Too much expense, Jasmin thought, *spending money that should be mine!*

"You sure I can't go with you?" Lauren asked.

"You're forgetting the rules," Sabrina said. "*We* have to stay."

"She's right," the assistant said. "You do. But I'm sure it's going to be a very memorable weekend for you all."

55

Lauren stopped Sabrina on her way out of the dining room, a hand on her arm. "Thanks," she said. "I appreciate what you said back there, trying to defend me."

"Oh, it was nothing. You had just lost your parents. You weren't thinking about Victor's auction market. I get it."

"Well, that's only half true but thanks."

Lighting flashed, bleaching Lauren's face for a moment and Sabrina thought it looked like one of the masks on the wall, smooth ivory with blue shell eyes.

"We've all made mistakes," she said.

"*Yes*," Lauren said, the word loaded with sadness. "You know, I admire you. Your dedication to your artwork is…inspiring."

"It's just what I need to do." Sabrina shrugged but she was flattered. "Isn't there something you want to do?"

"There was…" she said, the Isle of Wight back on her mind, her work with the Bleedin' Drunks, helping to promote them and produce their records, an exciting time. "But it's gone, and I can't get it back." She shrugged but sounded wistful. "You have to careful with your dreams. They're fragile. They should be stamped, *Handle with care!*" She laughed but there was such sadness in the laugh that it made Sabrina want to cry.

"I haven't been particularly careful with my dreams," Sabrina said. "But I will be from now on."

"That's good," Lauren said.

Frank, who had loitered with intent, called to Sabrina from the elevator and she reluctantly joined him, still thinking about her dreams.

56

On the way to their rooms, Frank and Sabrina were more than a little tipsy when they stopped, inches apart, awkward, as if meeting as for the first time.

"I'm sorry about what that brat Echo said." Frank touched her arm.

"Well, I guess it's out now," Sabrina said, thinking she should talk to Nicky, try to explain it to him, though it wasn't really his business, and she wasn't sure if it mattered anymore. "I'm going to bed," she said and tried to get around Frank, but he blocked her.

"Come on, Sabrina, let's…"

She put her hand on his chest. "Please, Frank, stop."

"You don't even know what I'm going to say."

"I have a pretty good idea."

"Do you?" He smiled a little sadly. "Am I alone out here, the only one who feels it?"

Sabrina sighed but she did feel something, a tug, an ache, though probably just some ancient scar tissue. "Let's not start this, not again."

"So, you *do* feel it. I'm not crazy."

"You *are* crazy," she said, but smiled. "I've got to get some sleep, I'm exhausted. You should too."

"I don't want to sleep. Not…alone." A flash of his once-famous smile.

"That sounds like a line from a movie."

"Everything's a movie!" he said and laughed.

"To you, Frank." She gave him a serious look. "But this movie ended a long time ago, and badly, remember?"

"I hear the sequel is going to have a happy ending."

"Oh, brother, you have an answer for everything." She shook her head but had to smile.

"I do," he said.

Thunder clapped, closer this time, and lightning flashed in the windows.

"Very dramatic, very cinematic," she said. "Did you plan that?"

"If only I could." He laughed, then got serious. "Can't we try?"

"Why?" she asked, a dozen memories stinging like bees.

"Because we may not get this chance again—because it's worth trying—because I've never stopped thinking about you, caring about you—because I never wanted anything, *anyone*, so badly." Maybe it was a movie, the lines coming so fast, so easily, but he meant what he said—or thought he did. One thing he knew for sure: He was aching for her. The sister-in-law he had lusted after from the first day his big brother had brought her around. And later, aware of and shocked by how carelessly Victor was treating her, he'd made his move, their first embrace like no other, with a soundtrack and the camera moving in for a close-up, *love*, or as close to love as Frank ever felt.

Sabrina looked into his eyes, trying to see if he was on the level or just playing a part. Had he said all this the last time? It sounded too familiar. But she saw something else, the beginning of their affair when it was exciting and dangerous, and they were young and beautiful. So when he put his arms around her, she let him, and when he kissed her, she kissed him back, and still not sure she wanted it to happen, she let him lead her into his bedroom.

57

Nicky's mind was buzzing—Rachel's accusations, the art dealers fighting, the studio assistants replicating his father's work, his mother and Frank—when someone gripped his arm and pulled him into a dark room. Next thing, he was in bed, lips against his, hands lifting his T-shirt.

"Finally…" he said, before he was silenced by a tongue in his mouth. He tried to move but was pressed back against the sheets, the smell of black cherry liqueur and bitter almonds, sweet and tart, the familiar perfume intoxicating, the sound of palms batting against the windows to match his fast-beating heart. His lips on hers now, her neck, her breasts, he slowly worked himself inside her until she met his thrusts, her breath in his ear.

He finished, not sure if she had climaxed or faked it, not sure if she even liked sex, always something a bit stagy and mechanical about her performance, though he never asked.

After a minute, he said, "Do you think anyone knows about us?" Then supplied the answer, "Probably. You haven't been subtle."

"*Me?*"

"Please." He scoffed. "I thought you needed to keep us on the DL to play the heartbroken widow and all."

"I *am* heartbroken." She said it like a joke, but Nicky thought she was, always had been, though not by Victor's death. "At least that's what the lawyer advised but does it really matter here, among this crew?" Propped up on an elbow, her dark hair spilling over her shoulder, she ran a finger over the scar on Nicky's chin. "You never said what this was from."

"I did. You don't listen, that's all. I fell when I was like...twelve." A picture in his mind, cupping his chin, blood running through his fingers, but he wasn't twelve.

"Who are you worried about finding out about us, your *mommy*?"

"I'd just rather she didn't know."

She singsonged, "Mama's boy."

"Better a mama's boy then someone who fucks their underage stepson."

"You were *never* underage!" she snapped, her features sharpening in the dim light, a few dabs of chalky calamine lotion on her cheek coming into focus. "Not even when we started."

"But close," he said, thinking back to their forbidden first kiss, an act she had initiated, though he hadn't fought it; she was *so* beautiful. But that wasn't it. He'd been with plenty of beautiful women, beautiful men too. It was a combination of passion and payback, a way to get even with his father.

"So, report me to the authorities."

"I might," he said, running his hand over her breasts. He was still attracted to her, and if he was honest, her bitchiness was a turn-on. Most of his lovers were too thankful. "Still, it's best if my mother didn't know."

"Why? She's fucking your *uncle*, for Christ's sake!"

"You don't know that for sure."

"Oh, *please*. And trust me she already knows about us and she's going to find out for sure when we divide the estate."

"Uh-huh," he said, thinking about his mother and his uncle.

"Are you listening?"

"Yes."

Rain pummeled the windows, along with the night sound of insects buzzing, high-pitched and shrill.

"What is that awful noise?" she asked.

"Cicadas. I think."

"This place is like some hideous camp for inner-city kids." She took a breath. "So, you heard what I said about dividing the inheritance."

Yes, he'd heard. He just wasn't sure what he wanted to say. It had been her idea to pool their inheritance no matter who got more, or less, a guarantee of getting *something*, which she worried about more than he did.

"Yeah, I heard you. But I'm going to give her something."

"Who? Sabrina?"

"Yes. She's my mother and I love her, you know that."

"Do I ever." She wrapped the sheets around her naked body and faced him. "What about *me*?"

"You're asking if I love you, or if I love you more than I love my mother?"

"I know the answer to *that*."

"Hey, she got me into rehab," he said, more to himself, thinking how she had been there for him, the long days and nights when he had tried to quit drugs, holding his hand, and more.

"I thought it was Victor who got you into rehab. That's what *he* said."

"He *paid* for it, that's all." It was true. His father had paid for rehab. And hired lawyers and investigators to make sure none of Nicky's mess followed him, not that he'd wanted to. *Why should I help a son who doesn't know how to help himself?* One more statement Nicky could never shake.

"Sweetie," she said, her hand on his cheek. "Who knows better than me that Victor was a louse?"

"But you chose to marry him."

She shrugged, her motives for marrying Victor D'Arcangelo so obvious they needed no explaining or apologizing. "Well, it's over," was all she said.

"Because he *died*."

"No. It was already over, and you know that. And stop being so mean to me all the time. Or is that just an act so your mommy won't suspect?"

"No. I like being mean to you. Same as you do, to me."

She dropped the blanket and leaned her bare breasts against him. "Stay the night."

"That's not a good idea."

"Why not? Scared of what Mommy will say?"

"Fuck off."

"*Fine*," she said. "And give your mommy all you want—from *your* half. Though I wouldn't give her a dime, and I doubt Victor left her even *that*!"

Nicky said nothing, though he guessed his father cared more about his ex-wife than his current one.

"You know, as the wife I am entitled to *everything*."

"That kind of depends on the courts, doesn't it? Unless Victor has stipulated otherwise."

"Are you *trying* to upset me?"

"Just stating the obvious, babe. You wouldn't have come to this memorial if you *knew* what Victor had left you. And in case you forgot, he knew about us, so it's possible he's going to punish you and leave you a big fat nothing."

"Or punish *you*!" she snarled, then softened. "That's why we need this arrangement as insurance. For both of us."

You mean for you. He still had his college fund, mostly untouched as he'd been kicked out of school for using drugs after his first semester. It wasn't that much money but something. And one thing he knew for sure, whatever he or Jasmin inherited they would not be splitting. It was a game they were playing, like the way they pretended they cared about each other. But he knew she'd hired a lawyer, a fact she had not shared with him. She was using him, a way to pay Victor back for his philandering. It was Jasmin, after all, who had made sure Victor caught them. He knew that too. Funny, he thought, how they both had wanted to hurt Victor. It was clear which category they were in. "Yeah, insurance, for both of us. Sure."

"Good." She stared at his profile in the dim light, the aquiline nose and sculpted jaw, his beauty his best quality, possibly his only good quality. He wasn't even a great lay, or was it that she didn't like sex? Either way, whatever she inherited, was *hers*. "Love you," she said.

"Love you too," he said.

58

Alex Bagdasarian couldn't sleep, sweating, though his room was frigid, his head spinning from a mix of alcohol and anxiety.

Had those damn artists told Schwegler? But how did they find out? How did they know?

He'd been so careful, all those transactions conducted out of the country, in cash, no paper trail, anonymous. Or so he'd thought. Either way, they were over. Way too risky now. One more money stream dried up.

Will I be ruined?

Who was he kidding? He was already ruined. Debts on top of debts. Bookies waiting to be paid. And he couldn't have them *all* killed.

He almost laughed, the absurdity of it, of his life and what it had come to. But no, it wasn't over. Not if he got the D'Arcangelo estate.

But what if Victor had found out about the illegal sales?

Then he *was* finished.

Up now, out of bed, he unwrapped a cigar, hands shaking, three tries to get the damn thing lit. A puff of smoke exhaled and with it a sentence coming back to him: *So, you know exactly how to paint my father's paintings and could continue to create them after his death.*

An idea and a damn good one. He would make a deal with a few of the former studio assistants—no doubt hard up for cash now that Victor was dead—to create new paintings—ones never seen before or recorded—instant inventory, ready to sell.

Yes!

A deep drag on the cigar, and he raised the window to let out the smoke, sultry air seeping in. The rain had stopped but everything was wet, palm trees slouching, their huge fronds batting the window. He was closing it when something slithered over the sill and dropped at his feet, some kind of centipede but almost a foot long, on its back, legs wagging in the air. He jumped back, dropped his cigar, grabbed a print off the wall and brought it down hard, the frame cracking, glass shattering.

A moment to catch his breath. *Now what?* With no chambermaids to clean it up, he would have to do it himself. He pushed the mess toward the wall with his foot.

This goddamn place.

He plucked his cigar off the rug where it had fallen and burned a hole. *Who cares?* He just had to make it through the rest of the weekend and pay his due diligence so he could lock in the D'Arcangelo estate. Then all would be well.

He shivered, due to a chill from the frigid air-conditioning and an afterimage of that hideous centipede. He threw a newspaper over the crime scene.

A bath, that's what he needed. That, and a Xanax. He fished one out of his bag and tossed it back. Then he turned on the taps in the large oval tub.

59

Rachel Ronan fluffed her pillows, then punched them, turned one way, then the other, her mind replaying the fight with Bagdasarian over and over and over. Seeing him again had brought it all back, triggered her anger and resentment, the need to punish him almost overwhelming.

How long had she been in bed? An hour, two, the blankets, sheets rumpled and damp. She pulled herself up, stared at the lacy pattern of raindrops on the window, so pretty until she looked closer and saw it was insects, hundreds of them, could practically hear them buzzing and chattering. She shuddered and stepped back quickly.

In the bathroom, she studied her reflection: a nondescript woman of middle age, hard to describe, impossible to remember.

What happened to that young woman filled with so much promise?

But she knew exactly what happened, how she had lost her job and her confidence, then Cynthia, the final blow. Months and months alone in her apartment, unable to go out, to face people, to face the world. Finally, her "nervous collapse," time spent in a *facility*, meds and therapy. By the time she was better and ready to reclaim her so-called career, it was too late. People had forgotten who she was, or if they remembered, word was out that she was unstable. She was finally forced to move back home with her mother, the worst decision and biggest mistake of her life.

The memory was immediately playing in her mind, delivering

dinner on that last night, her mother confined to bed, had been for months, body feeble but her mind sharp, as demanding and cruel as ever.

"What is *that*?" she asked, eyeing the tray in Rachel's hands.

"Tomato soup. What you asked for."

"I asked for *chicken* soup! Stupid girl, can't you get *anything* right?" Knocking the tray from Rachel's hands, soup all over her skirt, her shoes, the rug, Rachel on hands and knees trying to clean it up, tears of fury burning behind her eyes.

Still furious hours later when her mother called out, Rachel listening to Jay Leno's monologue and thinking, *Let her wait for once!* She continued to ignore the grating demands that became whimpered pleas, even taking some pleasure in it, until she had finally relented and gone into her mother's bedroom and found her on the floor, unconscious. And an hour later, despite the medics attempts to revive her, she was dead. "If only we had gotten here a few hours ago, we might have saved her," one of the medics had said to Rachel with a mix of sympathy and suspicion, noting in his report that the body appeared to have been on the floor for some time indicated by signs of blood pooling, his words rippling through Rachel like someone had opened her heart and filled it with hot molten guilt, something she would never get over: letting her mother die.

Her deep sigh fogged the mirror and her reflection, a good thing. The past was the past. Over, and no way to change it. She had to look forward, to the future, and thanks to Victor—who had remembered her, *God bless him*—she had one. And no way Bagdasarian was going to ruin that too.

She rummaged through her cosmetic bag, finally dumped the contents on the counter, deodorant, Q-tips, lipstick, hair spray, nail file, and there it was, what she needed to sleep, the Ambien prescribed by her doctor. She uncapped the vial and popped a pill.

Back in bed she waited for it take effect, but an hour later she was still awake, Bagdasarian's smug face blinking like a neon sign she could not turn off. Another Ambien, blankets on, off, pitching one way then the other, still unable to sleep.

Up again, though not quite sure if she was awake or asleep, she plucked the metal nail file off the bathroom counter and slipped it into her bathrobe pocket.

In the hallway, the walls seemed to expand and contract, shadows crisscrossing the floor like a German Expressionist film. Those chattering insects, deafening.

Are they inside the house or inside my head?

Rachel stopped, stood in front of the door trying to remember how she had gotten there, trying to read the room number but it kept changing, six, then nine, her mind a kaleidoscope of fractured images: her editor's face and his words echoing in her brain—*pack up your desk*—then the art dealer's words—*little art writer... overrated... finished.* A moment of clarity before she reached for the doorknob, thinking of all he had done to her.

60

Back in his room, Hans Schwegler was close to exploding. How dare that man say such things about his family?

Es ist Zeit, dass Sie dem ein Ende setzen! Time you put a stop to it! His father's voice in his head, as always.

He popped the lock on his briefcase and removed two pieces of paper. One, a formal contract written on his gallery stationery, something he had drawn up that would give him full title to all three of Bagdasarian's galleries, New York, Palm Beach, and LA. The terms and conditions all typed out. How they would pay off his debts, plus give him some cash for his property, a good deal for Bagdasarian; he would convince him of that. And threaten that if he did not sign, the banks and bookies would descend, his signature would be forged, and he would not be paid a cent. An offer he could not refuse. His family's way of doing business. Everything on paper, proof, legal. Almost. Though it would take time and his father was impatient.

Werde ihn einfach los! Just get rid of him! Wenn du dazu in der Lage bist. If you are capable of it. His father always skeptical, always putting him down.

The reason for the second paper: Bagdasarian's suicide note. One sentence about his overwhelming debt and depression. All Schwegler needed to do was place it beside the body.

But could he do it? Knees suddenly weak, he sat, tried to be calm, to breathe.

Feigling! Coward! His father again.

"No, *Vater*! I am not a coward!"

He lifted a flap in the main pocket of the briefcase and removed a small lead box, its black shadow on a TSA screen passed over, at two and a half inches seen as too small to hold anything dangerous. Inside, a World War I Kolibri—the German word for *hummingbird*—and the fitting name for the world's smallest gun. At just twenty-two kilometers, less than half a pound, it looked like a toy.

Schwegler held the pistol between his meaty forefinger and thumb to study the Austrian watchmaker's clever design. He snapped in the seven-round magazine, remembering that his father had warned him to load only five of the tiny cartridges because it tended to jam at six, something he had discovered when his father forced him to shoot the neighbor's dog. He winced at the thought, remembered how he had thrown up and secretly cried for days.

He tested the pistol's coil-spring pullback, closed his eyes, and imagined holding the gun against Bagdasarian's temple, firing all five rounds to make sure the tiny bullets did their damage.

When he opened his eyes, the miniature gun was shaking so badly in his hand that he had to put it down or he would drop it. Perhaps his father was right; he was a coward.

He sighed, almost a sob, then stripped off his clothes and did push-ups and sit-ups until his muscles burned. His body ached, but he felt better, stronger. Skin wet with perspiration, he opened the glass doors to his balcony and stood naked in the heat and humidity. A good feeling until the mosquitoes started biting but he endured them, keeping images of his father and grandfather in mind. His grandfather, it was true, one of Hitler's appointed art dealers.

When it was finally too much, he slapped the mosquitoes, one after another, over and over, then licked the blood off his hand.

After he showered, a spritz of vetiver cologne; then he slicked back his ginger hair and put on his suit, attempting to smooth out the wrinkles. His father always said it was important to look your best when conducting business.

He checked the time. It had been almost three hours since dinner. He knew Bagdasarian had been drinking and would be asleep. *Easy prey.*

The suicide note in one pocket, pistol in the other, Schwegler opened his bedroom door and stepped into the hallway.

61

Bagdasarian leaned back, the large claw-footed bathtub just big enough to contain his bulk, warm water up to his chin, skirting the tub's edge and threatening to spill. He inhaled the bergamot-infused bathwater with a satisfied sigh, peaceful for the first time in months, banishing thoughts of bookies and debt, even the Swiss German art dealer. He could handle him. He could handle them all.

A soapy sea sponge drawn over his shoulders, then along each fleshy arm, an image of his mother bathing him, cooing to her little boy. *Im p'vok'rik ark'ayazn. My little prince.* A gentle woman he had not seen in almost a year, now in her nineties, installed in the Queens condo he had bought for her after his father's death almost a decade ago, an apartment he had never seen. He thought of the story she had often told of him of his grandparents and how they had fled the Armenian genocide, managing to get out with nothing but their children, the clothes on their backs, and a constant fear for survival. Something they had passed onto their son, though for him it was more than a need to survive. It was a need to conquer.

I should see my mother, he thought, bring her a box of kourabia, the shortbread cookies she liked so much from the Armenian bakery, sit and talk and hold her hand the way she'd held his as a child. He missed her, missed himself too, or who he had once been. He told himself he would call her once he got home.

Outside, the wind was howling, insects chirping so loud, he did not hear the turn of the doorknob or the creaking floorboard.

Not until someone was in the room.

"What the—" Bagdasarian tried to sit up, his slippery arms sliding off the bath's rim, water splashing. "What the hell are you doing here! *Get out!*"

A second later he was pushed back, arms flailing, soapy hands unable to get a grip but trying to fight as he was shoved down and held under, splashing violently. A moment to right himself and gasp a breath before he was forced under again, water flooding his nose and mouth. Body thrashing, arching, he felt the hands on his shoulders, his head underwater. Unable to hold his breath, his mouth opened and flooded as he tried to scream, but his vocal cords were in spasm and there was a burning sensation in his chest as water filled his lungs, along with fear and panic and confusion. *Where am I, what's happening?*

A flicker of recognition, the distorted face and features seen through the bathwater, mind fracturing, a scattershot of images and sounds, a cell phone ringing, a disembodied voice rasping, *It's done*, his mother's sweet cooing, his own gagging. Then everything became an abstraction, and overwhelmed by exhaustion, his muscles gave out, his heart stopped, his breath extinguished, and he was floating not toward light but into a never-ending sea of darkness.

62

A gray drizzly morning, only their second day on the island but it felt a lot longer, half the guests with hangovers pouring cups of black coffee and moving slowly.

Lauren took her coffee and sat by a window watching the rain. Ian was beside her, but there was an invisible wall between them.

Wearing the same Jane Fonda tee, Nicky came in looking like a *Playgirl* model after a long, arduous shoot, more stubble on his cheeks, eyelids at half-mast, his dark Caravaggio curls shiny with grease. He got a coffee, then signaled for Ian to join him in a quiet corner of the living room. "So?" he asked, expectant and excited like a child.

Ian shook his head. "It's no good, mate. The ol' ball and chain weren't having it." He looked up, the smudged remnants of his eye makeup making him look like a sad panda.

"Just like that?" Nicky asked.

"Sorry for the mither, lad, but I tried."

Nicky didn't bother to ask for a translation; he'd gotten the gist, was already seeing his club dream break apart and disintegrate like so many other dreams. Still, he asked, "You sure?"

Ian nodded, sighed deeply. "But who knows, mate. I mean, something could..." He didn't finish the sentence, could not think of anything that would change Lauren's mind. "But I hope we can be pals." He tossed off the words, not realizing that underneath the club plan, friendship was something Nicky craved.

"Yeah. We can grab a beer back in town. For sure!" Nicky added cheerfully, wanting to offset the signs of his disappointment.

But Ian caught it. "Look, mate, you got your whole life ahead of you. Not like me, who's made a right mess of things, blew it all, I did, wasted me whole fuckin' life, didn't I?"

"No, no way. You know how many people love your fucking music?"

"Let's see…" Ian counted them off on his fingers. "There's you, me sister—I think—and Ollie, one of me old bandmates, who's too stoned to know we ever stopped playin', and me mum. No, I take that back. She hates it, calls it bangin' on a trash bin!" He laughed but the sound was cynical and caustic.

"She's wrong and you're wrong! You *did* something, man, made songs that fucking touched people—that they'll remember." The words made Nicky think about all the things he had tried and failed. "You know, I'm going to find a way to keep that club afloat and bring the Bleedin' Drunks in as house band, no matter what!" He meant what he said, though he didn't know how he would do it. His college fund would only go so far, and he didn't know how much money his father had left him, but probably not enough.

Jasmin joined them, interrupting their moment. Nicky, immediately stood up, painting on a smile, rapping Ian on the shoulder, telling him it was okay, and trying hard to believe it as he moved away.

"What's okay?" Jasmin asked.

"Nothing," Nicky said, switching his attention to his mother and Frank, the way they were keeping a studied distance between themselves.

He looked up when Rachel came in, saw her taking in the room as if trying to get her bearings.

"Good morning," Frank said, looking her over. "Are you okay?"

Rachel felt woozy, confused. When had she awakened and how had she gotten downstairs? An image flickered and spun at the edge of her memory like an old-fashioned zoetrope, standing in a hallway, doors opening and closing, the metal nail file in her hand. She checked her hand to see if she was still holding it.

She nodded at Frank, or thought she did, still trying to remember last night and trying to speak. When she did, her words were slurred. She reached for a mug but could not coordinate it with the coffee urn.

Frank filled her cup, asked if she wanted milk or sugar, and she said, "Yes," though she could not remember how she took her coffee, or if she even drank it.

Sabrina leaned in, a hand on Rachel's back, "You okay, hon?"

Why are they all asking me that? Rachel managed to form the word *fine*, then looked down and saw she was wearing her bathrobe. "Oh!" She tugged the robe tighter, one hand holding the mug, almost spilling the coffee.

Frank and Sabrina shared a look, trying to figure out what was going on with her. But not for long. They were too caught up in the afterglow of the night they had just shared, conscious of speaking in formalities, *please* and *excuse me* and *thank you*.

Jasmin took a bite of a muffin and spit it into her napkin. "This is disgusting! It's been nuked."

Sabrina avoided the muffins, taking a small box of cereal. She asked Nicky—who was about to sit with Jasmin—to sit beside her. He hesitated, then did.

Jasmin gave him a look, then mouthed the words, *Mama's boy*.

They were all at the long table when Echo burst in, chatting and cheery, as if she hadn't told them all to go fuck themselves last night or spilled the beans about Frank and Sabrina. She poured an herbal tea and took two muffins. "How'd everybody sleep?" she asked, all chipper, and took a seat beside Jasmin, who eyed her like the plague. "Me, I slept like a rock." She exaggerated a stretch, then slathered a muffin with jam and ate it with gusto.

"Somehow I knew you'd like Styrofoam," Jasmin said, watching her eat.

Nicky saw Ian light up a joint. His way of coping and avoidance. Something Nicky had done for a long time, wanted to again, but didn't dare. Once again, he shifted his gaze between Frank and his mother, Echo's statement droning in the back of his mind. He knew it was true, finally understanding the rift between his father and uncle.

Sabrina felt her son's gaze and shifted uncomfortably. "Did you sleep well, darling?"

Nicky nodded offhandedly.

"*Really?*" Jasmin said with a sly grin. "You *did*?" Despite a couple of calamine dots, her face was fully made up, lipstick, false lashes. "Someone—or something—kept me up half the night. Unless I was dreaming...a sex dream too!"

Nicky threw her a look.

Sabrina watched them, the thought she kept trying to deny becoming impossible.

Schwegler's suit was so wrinkled it looked as if he'd slept in it. He greeted no one as he poured himself a cup of black coffee. Anyone nearby would have seen his hands were shaking. He headed toward the far side of the room to a pair of glass doors, cracked one open, and lit one of his long, thin cigarettes, blowing the smoke outside.

Thunder clapped so loud the chandeliers swayed, the silverware and dishes trembled on the table, and Rachel spilled her coffee.

Nicky watched her frantically mopping it up; then he surveyed the group, counting heads. Without thinking, he was doing what the assistant had asked, taking over, a way to keep himself busy and distracted. He counted again, trying to figure out who was missing. "Where's Bagdasarian?"

"Probably sleeping late and licking his wounds," Jasmin said.

"That was quite a scene those two had last night." She indicated Schwegler in the doorway, puffing hard on his cigarette.

"Maybe the German killed him," Lauren said, and laughed.

Rachel gasped, blotting the coffee stain so hard the table rocked.

"Wait till he hears about the *fabulous* breakfast he missed," Jasmin said.

"Has anyone seen him?" Nicky asked.

"Not since last night," Frank said. "When he was fighting with..." He stopped talking, nodded toward Schwegler, then at Rachel, who was still frantically wiping up her spilled coffee.

"You think he's all right?" Sabrina asked, worried her prospective gallerist could be ill.

"Hungover is all, I'm sure," Lauren said, washing down a couple of aspirin, more than a little hungover herself.

"I'll see how he's doing," Nicky said, taking his job seriously, determined to do one thing right.

Frank followed. He wanted to make sure his nephew was okay after last night's announcement about him and Sabrina.

"God, it's great to see you," he said as they got into the elevator.

Nicky said nothing, thinking, *So, you fucked my mother before, and you're doing it again*.

"This place, what a shit show, huh?" Frank strained for conversation that Nicky refused to pick up. Right now, with his club dream in tatters, he wanted everyone to suffer. He stepped out of the elevator and pulled the gate closed behind him without a word. Frank followed.

Bagdasarian's door was half-open.

Nicky knocked, then called his name. When there was no answer, he called again then pushed the door open.

63

Nicky did not remember letting out a cry or calling for help, Frank beside him, the two of them staring at Bagdasarian in the tub, head tilted back, mouth twisted in a grimace, a heavy arm hanging limply over the side, the flesh wrinkled and bloated, the air already tinged with a smell of something sweet and cloying.

Without speaking, they moved to opposite sides of the tub. Frank almost slipped, the floor soaked. He did not want to touch the body but took a breath as they got Bagdasarian by the arms and struggled to lift him.

Nicky tried not to stare at the man's face, the protruding eyes, lips swollen and blue, but could not look away.

"It's like *Diabolique*," Frank said.

"What are you talking about?"

"It's a movie, a French movie. I was slated to star in an American remake, but the financing fell through."

Nicky just shook his head. *That's* what his uncle was thinking about *now*? He wondered what his mother saw in the man.

They had lifted Bagdasarian up a foot when Frank lost his grip and the body slid back into the tub, water sloshing over the sides.

"*Fuck!* Let's try again," Nicky said. "We need to get him out of the tub."

"Why?" Frank asked, though he tried to get hold of the body. "I mean, he's obviously dead. It's a job for the police."

"There are no police, Frank, remember?"

"What do you think happened?" Frank asked as they tried to get a tighter grip—not easy, the flesh bloated and waxy. "Heart attack? Stroke?"

The body slipped back again. Nicky got a towel and dried Bagdasarian's arms, grimacing the whole time they strained to lift the body. Bagdasarian was well over two hundred pounds and literally deadweight. They dropped him again, more water splashing over the sides onto Frank's sandals and Nicky's bare feet.

Frank jumped back. "Jeez! Do you think we can catch something?"

"Like what? *Death?*"

Once more they tried. This time, getting a grip higher up on the fleshy arms, lifting the big man up and out of the tub before Frank lost his grip and the body fell to the floor with a thud, arms and legs making thwacking sounds, rolls of belly fat undulating. The overhead light illuminated blotches of green discoloration on the flesh that looked like bruised fruit.

Both men were winded, Frank gasping, a hand to his chest.

"You okay?" Nicky had to ask.

"Yeah," Frank said, trying to catch his breath and hold it at the same time, the body already giving off an odor. "Shouldn't we cover him?"

"Why?"

"I don't know, decency? Isn't that the thing to do?" He thought about a small role he'd played as a detective in a murder mystery where they had covered the dead body, but maybe that was more for the censors. He looked down at Bagdasarian's penis, swollen under a layer of fat.

"What's going on in there?" Sabrina called from the bedroom.

"Don't come in!" Frank shouted, but too late.

"Oh my God!" Sabrina said and clutched Frank's arm. "What happened?"

"I'm guessing a heart attack," he said.

"We have no idea," Nicky said.

Jasmin, just behind Sabrina, asked the same thing, then raised one foot after the other, her sandals soaked and sticky. "Shit!"

Lauren and Ian peered in from the doorway, Ian leaning forward for a better view. "Oi, the bloke looks bloody awful."

"Yeah," Jasmin said. "Because he's dead."

"Dead?" Lauren said. "My God, what happened?"

"Heart attack," Frank said, this time with even more authority.

"Whoa!" Echo said, joining the group. "What the fuck happened in here? Is he dead?"

They were all crowding into the tight space, elbowing each other for a better look, the bathroom's yellow light giving them all a slightly jaundiced aura.

"Shouldn't we *do* something?" Sabrina said.

"Like what?" Nicky asked.

"I don't know, call the coast guard?"

"With *what*?" he said. "We'll just have to wait till the boat comes back."

Rachel pushed her way past Lauren and Ian. She looked pale and unsteady. "Oh, is he...? Has he been stabbed?"

"*Stabbed?*" Nicky gave her a look. "Not that I can see."

"You think someone stabbed him? Why?" Sabrina asked.

"Let's turn him over and look," Echo said, excited.

"Good idea," Jasmin said to her. "You try."

"No one *stabbed* him," Nicky said and pointed at the water. "Look, there's no blood. He was drunk and drowned."

"Or had a heart attack," Frank repeated, recalling his own theory.

"It sort of smells in here." Jasmin waved a hand in front of her face.

Emitting a whimper, Rachel sagged back against the door, gripping the knob.

"Don't touch that!" Frank snapped. "Fingerprints!" One of his lines in the murder mystery. "You're contaminating the crime scene." Another.

"What crime scene?" Nicky noticed that Rachel looked faint, her face gone white. "You should lie down," he said, offering her a hand.

"If it *is* a crime..." Sabrina said, lifting her hand from the towel rack she'd been leaning on. "Then we've all touched *something*."

"Yeah!" Echo said. "Which would make all of us suspects!"

64

"No one is a *suspect*!" Nicky said. "The man drowned."

The guests, minus the dead man, were back in the dining room, rain streaking the windows.

Ian, a cigarette dangling from his lip, had assumed the unofficial position of bartender, breaking out booze and boxed orange juice to make mimosas.

Lauren looked at him, surprised; at home he did nothing. She scratched at her nicotine patch, tempted to grub a cigarette, but held on. Nicky, Sabrina, and Frank did not, all of them shaken, bumming cigarettes from Ian; the room soon filled with smoke.

"Should you be smoking?" Sabrina asked Frank.

"No," he said. "But I'll stop when I get out of here."

"God, I feel so bad," Sabrina said. "I mean, he's dead. It's…such a shock."

And there goes your gallery dream, Nicky thought but didn't say.

"We can't just leave him on the bathroom tiles, can we?" Sabrina asked.

"Why not?" Jasmin said, sipping her mimosa.

Nicky was finding it was more difficult than ever being the only sober one. "The authorities will deal with it after the boat gets here."

Echo brought up all the water on the floor, and Nicky explained it happened when they were getting the body out of the tub.

"Well, we added to it," Frank said. "The floor was already wet. I almost slipped, remember?"

"So, like, the guy struggled or something?" Echo asked.

"No one said that," Nicky said.

"So, we just leave him there on the floor?" Lauren said. "That's awful and I hate to say it, but won't he start to stink?"

"He already does," Jasmin said.

"We closed the bathroom door and opened a window," Nicky said.

"That will not help," Schwegler said. "The smell can't be..." He stopped speaking and closed his eyes, a picture of his mother's body discovered after two days, the color of her skin, the dried blood on her wrists, the nearby razor blades, the odor, all things he would never forget.

"Where were you?" Nicky asked Schwegler, the only one who had not joined them upstairs.

Schwegler took a moment to answer, waiting for the picture of his mother's body to fade. "I was down here, smoking a cigarette."

"And you weren't curious to know what was going on?" Lauren asked, probing. She didn't like the man.

"I heard *das Aufheben, the fuss*, followed the clamor, saw what was going on, and left."

"And that was it?" Frank asked.

"What was I to do about it? I could see the man was dead." Schwegler was trying hard to keep his voice and emotions under control while a different image played in his mind—himself at Bagdasarian's door, the tiny pistol in his hand. He scanned the room for Rachel, who was not there.

"It's, like, kind of an embarrassing way to die," Echo said. "I mean, like, you know, naked in the bathtub."

"I'm sure you bathe fully dressed," Jasmin said. "That is, if you bathe at all."

"So how would *you* like to die?" Sabrina asked the girl.

"Me? I never think about it," she said, a picture of her mother, hennaed hair and dime store jewelry, the blood on her hands as she slammed the trunk shut.

Lauren, already working a second mimosa, said, "I'd like to die in my sleep or making love."

"Sort of the same thing for you, ain't it, love?" Ian snorted.

She gave him a nasty look, but Jasmin laughed. If there was one thing she understood after three years of marriage to Victor D'Arcangelo, it was marital loathing.

"I always thought it would be great to die at the height of my career," Frank said.

"Too late for *that*!" Jasmin said.

"Don't be mean," Sabrina said, rubbing Frank's arm. "Frank was a big star in his time."

The phrase *in his time* rippled through Frank with waves of disappointment and rejection, all the parts he could no longer get.

"How would you like to die?" Sabrina asked Jasmin.

"Rich."

Echo said, "That's all any of you care about."

"Oh? And you're here for *what*?" Jasmin said. "The food and company, the games?"

"Money does not make you happy," Lauren said, something she never said aloud or even to herself, the words for her too true.

"I'll vouch for that," Ian said, topping off people's mimosas. "If you want to know what God thinks of money, just look at the people he gives it to." He cast an eye in his wife's direction.

"Yes," Lauren said, returning his look. "Life is full of disappointments."

Jasmin thought, *Rich is enough for me*. "Happy is overrated," she said, trying to remember a time when she had been happy, fighting a memory at the edges of her subconscious, the shadow of a man looming over her, the smell of him, her fear. "Uh, what about *you*, Sabrina? How does the VP of the first wives' club want to die?"

"At my easel, paintbrush in hand."

"How *romantic*." Jasmin sneered but felt envious; there was nothing she was willing to die for. "Did you read that somewhere, an artist's handbook of corny things to say?"

"I mean it," Sabrina said.

"Well," Frank said, touching her hand. "Not till you're a hundred and twenty and as famous as Grandma Moses."

Jasmin turned to Nicky. "And how about you, number one loving son? Or do you think you'll live forever, like your father, and look how *that* turned out!"

Having come close to overdosing more than once, Nicky was fully aware of his mortality. But he wasn't thinking about his own death, only those he might have caused.

"Well? *How?*" She poked him, playful but annoying.

"Fighting for something I believe in. No. *Doing* something I believe in," he said, thinking about one too many failed dreams.

"Oh, so altruistic," Jasmin said.

The wind howled and rattled the windows, a few of the primitive masks shaking and threatening to topple off the walls.

"I'm writing a Yelp review," Jasmin said. "Bad weather, bad food, and a dead body." She and Echo were the only ones who laughed.

"And what about you, Ian?" Nicky asked. "How do you want to die? I'd say, back on a stage playing lead guitar, but many years from now."

"From your lips to God's you-know-what, lad." Ian closed his eyes to fight a picture in his head: the pimple-faced kid falling. He rephrased the question. "Suppose you killed someone and were condemned to death. How would you choose to die? Which method?" He was asking himself but looked at Lauren.

"Are you planning to kill me?" she asked.

"It was only a question, love." He wondered, worried about Lauren turning him in, and if he would get to choose how to die.

"You know," Frank said. "Some states leave it up to the prisoner to choose the way he wants to die."

"How do you know *that*?" Jasmin asked.

"I played a convict on death row, my second Golden Globe nomination for best actor in a drama."

"Which of course you lost," Jasmin said.

"He should have won," Sabrina said, though she hadn't seen the film, hadn't seen any of Frank's movies in years.

"Did you *ever* win an acting award?" Jasmin asked.

"Sure," he said, though he never had. He asked Ian for another cigarette and Ian gave him the pack, told him to keep them.

"So, like, you're saying a death row prisoner can choose between the electric chair or what's it called, lethal injection?" Echo asked, for once serious, as if she were considering the options.

"That's right. Or the gas chamber, if it is on that state's menu," Frank said, though he figured he would not be given a choice about his death, that his heart would simply give out.

Lightning lit up the windows offering a split-second view of the pond and lagoon, the heavy rain.

"Another rotten day," Jasmin said, wondering if Victor had paid off God for the bad weather. The thought touched something she had been trying to get at but couldn't. "What about you?" she asked Nicky.

Maybe it had something to do with the lightning, he wasn't sure, but he said, "The electric chair."

Sabrina looked at her son, then away, let out a sigh.

Schwegler, who had been quiet, said, "I would choose lethal injection. I like the idea of simply closing my eyes and going to sleep." He shut his, but no soothing image came, only one he saw too often, the boy on the ground with a pool of blood spreading around his head.

"*Really?*" Lauren said. "I was certain *you* would choose the gas chamber."

"Please, can we drop this terrible topic?" Sabrina said.

But it was too late. They were all thinking about death, and how they might die.

65

A few hours later, the group was still at the table, trapped inside by the nonstop rain, some drunker and more morose than others. The mimosas were finished, the table a mess. King-size bags of pretzels and chips had been ripped open and passed around, crumbs everywhere.

"So now what?" Lauren asked. "Tiddlywinks?"

"I know," Echo said. "Let's play another game!"

"With a dead man upstairs?" Sabrina said.

"What's that got to do with it?" Echo said.

"Can someone teach this *child* the difference between right and wrong?" Lauren said.

"You mean someone like *you*, the big pharma heiress whose family killed how many people, like a million?"

The room got quiet, the sound of rain like a nervous tic, everyone's eyes on Lauren, who said nothing, only sighed, a sour look on her face; she'd heard it all before. She glanced over at Ian. He was puffing on a joint, his eyes half closed.

"That's enough," Frank said.

"Why? Because you said so?" Echo taunted. "Okay, forget the game. Aren't we supposed to be contemplating how we hurt or helped my father?"

"Your *fath*—" The word stuck in Jasmin's craw.

Nicky's too, though he wouldn't give Echo the satisfaction of seeing she had gotten to him. He had other plans for her.

"What if he was murdered?" Echo said.

"Who? *Victor?*" Sabrina sat up and exchanged a look with Jasmin, who twitched.

"No," Echo said. "Bagda-what's-his-name? Upstairs. That would mean one of us is the killer." She looked around the table at each of them.

"Oh, please," Lauren said.

"Well, don't look at me," Jasmin said.

"Or *me*," Sabrina said. "I mean, the man offered me a show in his gallery, one of the best in New York. Why would I kill an opportunity like that?"

Nicky gave her a look. "You've got to be kidding, Mother."

"No, darling. You were there when he said it. You heard him."

"That's not what I meant." At times his mother's narcissism could be glaringly unattractive, something he had been accused of more than once.

"Oh." She pictured the art dealer's dead body on the bathroom floor, realized what she had said, and felt embarrassed.

"I would suggest that he killed himself," Schwegler said.

"You're saying he held *himself* underwater?" Nicky scoffed.

"It is possible. The man had serious problems. He was in debt and close to bankruptcy." Schwegler thought about the suicide note he had not used or destroyed. He put a handful of pretzels into his mouth to keep from saying more.

"How do you know *that*?" Sabrina demanded, then softened, "If you don't mind me asking." She needed to be nice and concentrate her attention on Schwegler's gallery now.

"I have my sources," he said, a few flecks of pretzel flying from his mouth.

"I'll bet you do." Nicky eyed him, thinking it was true.

"So where were you when this happened?" Frank asked.

Schwegler wiped his lips. "I have already said I was down here, having a cigarette."

"I meant last night?"

"In bed, of course."

"Can you *prove* it?" Frank said, playing the detective again.

"I do not have to prove anything." Schwegler was thinking about the contract in his briefcase, how it might look and if he should destroy it. Though by then he would be long gone. "I did nothing." A flash of himself in the hallway, in front of Bagdasarian's door. *Gib niemals etwas zu. Never admit anything*, his father's and grandfather's motto.

"Well..." Frank relighted his cigarette with a flourish, as if for the camera. "We may *all* have to prove where we were and what we were doing when the time comes."

"Let's everybody just cool it, okay?" Nicky said, recalling the assistant's words about keeping the peace. "It was an accident. The man had too much to drink, and he *drowned*, period."

"I dunno..." Echo said, twirling a strand of hair around her finger. "He had fights with lots of people last night." She glanced at Lauren, then at Schwegler, and was looking for Rachel when she realized she wasn't there. "How do we know what really happened? I mean, like you two"—she stared accusingly at Schwegler—"were really at each other's throats. We *all* saw that!"

Lass es Ihr nicht durchgehen. Do not let her get away it. "I would advise you to be very careful, miss. Or else..."

"Or else *what*? You all heard that, right? The way he threatened me?"

"Everyone just *stop*!" Nicky slammed his hands onto the table.

"But we haven't gotten his answer," Lauren said, glaring at Schwegler.

"I do not have to answer or listen to these insults!" Schwegler stood and headed toward the archway.

"Where do you think you're going?" Lauren called after him.

"To my room!" he said.

"Oi, let him be," Ian said, weary of his wife, of all of them. "The bloke has nowhere to go."

"That's true," Jasmin said. "He's trapped here like the rest of us."

66

Back in her room, Rachel was pacing. She was trying to reconstruct the events of last night but after taking the Ambien, her mind was a blank. The last thing she remembered was standing in front of Bagdasarian's room, could still see herself staring at the number painted on the door and wondering how she had gotten there.

Did I go in? She tried to remember but could not. And you would remember such a thing, wouldn't you? Fingers trembling, she found the vial of Ambien and read the label:

> CAN CAUSE COMPLEX SLEEP BEHAVIORS, INCLUDING SLEEPWALKING, SLEEP DRIVING, AND ENGAGING IN OTHER ACTIVITIES WHILE NOT FULLY AWAKE. THESE COMPLEX SLEEP BEHAVIORS HAVE RESULTED IN SERIOUS INJURIES AND DEATH.

They meant injury to the Ambien *user*, right? That *she* had been at risk, not others. No way she could have gone into someone's room and held them underwater without remembering. No. She could not possibly have done such a thing, even to a man she detested, and not remember doing it.

She checked the Ambien vial again, saw there had been thirty, opened the vial and spilled the contents into her palm. She tried counting the pills but lost count, her mind still cloudy from the drug, a growing panic adding to her confusion. She thought a moment, remembered taking a second pill. But had she taken another? She tried counting the pills again, but her hand was shaking too badly, and she gave up.

Then, another thought: *What have I done with the nail file?*

But Bagdasarian had not been stabbed.

No blood in the water.

Hadn't someone said that?

But even if there was blood, wouldn't it have washed away?

She was driving herself mad, had to stop but couldn't.

Shivering with dread, she searched through her toiletries for the nail file, scattering items across the counter, onto the floor: her lipstick, a compact. But no nail file.

Once again, she saw herself at Bagdasarian's door. Her hand on the doorknob, she remembered the knob turning in her palm. *But then what?*

How was it possible she remembered that much but no more?

A quick glance at the Ambien warning label: CAN CAUSE COMPLEX SLEEP BEHAVIORS.

A shiver of panic. Were her fingerprints still on the doorknob? But others had touched it. It meant nothing.

But what if her fingerprints were elsewhere—on the sink or the rim of the tub? Or worse, on his body? Did human flesh retain fingerprints? She had no idea. And again, they had all been in the bathroom this morning *contaminating the scene*. Someone had said that too. But would there be more of *her* fingerprints?

Her mind was spinning out of control.

Should I tell them what I did? What I might *have done?*

No. Impossible. Her future, her *life*, was at stake.

And he was a bad man who deserved to die.

Wipe the room clean! That was it, the only answer, erase any evidence. She was ashamed to be thinking like a criminal, like a murderer.

But too late, she was already moving, clean washcloth in her hand, tiptoeing down the hall. She stopped a moment to listen, could hear the hum of chatter from downstairs.

It was now or never.

Washcloth gripped like a glove, she opened Bagdasarian's door, closed it quietly behind her and stood there a minute, her thoughts ping-ponging: *Stay—Go—Get out of here—Are you insane?*

Yes, she was.

But she was here, moving on automatic, opening the bathroom door, hit by the smell, reeling back, then pressing forward, catching fractured glimpses of the body—a flaccid arm, a blackened toenail, the enormous belly dotted with bluish-purple bruises—as she wiped down the edges of the tub, hand shaking so badly she dropped the cloth close to the body, her fingers brushing against a mottled thigh. She felt sickness rising in her throat but kept going, wiping anything and everything she might have touched—if in fact she had done this ungodly act—something she might never know.

But it is possible.

Holding her breath against the stench, she wiped and wiped, a mad Lady Macbeth, the sink, the counter, a third, fourth swipe along the bathtub's rim, unable to stop, her mind a split screen flipping between the past and present, on her knees mopping up tomato soup beside her mother's dead body, the cloth in her hand now wiping away fingerprints, real or imaginary.

Was it enough? She had no idea, but she stopped, started to back out, then tripped over an uneven tile and went down, landing just beside him, and trying to break her fall, accidentally swiped the towel from his face, on the floor eye to eye with the dead man, his eyes glazed over with a translucent film like a blind man.

Stifling a scream, she managed to right herself, trembling, stomach heaving. She tore out of the bathroom, then stopped, caught her breath, and collected her thoughts enough to go back for the washcloth she had left behind.

Back in her room, she could not stop shaking, first chilled, then flushed with heat, a fever of guilt.

I did it, she thought. Then, *Did what, exactly?* Killed him or covered up a crime she might not have committed?

Too late to be rational. It didn't matter. It was done. Whatever *it* was.

But how to live with it? The way she lived with her mother's death, in denial.

Hands trembling, she tugged a window open, stood there shaking, and thought about jumping. But would she land in the pool or hit the ground? And would either kill her? It was only three flights.

She pictured the others finding her with a broken arm or leg, her dress up, cellulite thighs exposed along with her guilt.

No, she would have to live with this—the possibility and the doubt. Either way he deserved to die, and she wasn't sorry.

Then, another thought—she had an inheritance coming, a chance to start over, a new life—and so, taking the washcloth she had just used to clean up the possible crime scene, she hurled it out the window, then slammed it shut.

67

The remaining guests lingered at the table drinking, still debating Bagdasarian's demise, a growing cabal convinced of Schwegler's guilt, Echo leading the charge with Lauren close behind.

"We should search his room!" Echo said.

"We're not searching anyone's room," Nicky said, taking his keep-the-peace role seriously.

"I don't know," Sabrina said.

"He could be hiding something. Don't you agree?" Lauren elbowed Ian, who looked asleep.

"Oi, what's that, love?"

Lauren gave him a disgusted look.

"I'm with her," Echo said, which got another disgusted look; no one wanted to be with Echo.

"For the record, where were *you*?" Jasmin asked.

"*Me*?" Echo said, outraged. "Where the hell were *you*?"

Jasmin didn't bother to answer. She was picking at her broken fingernail, making a mental note to call the salon the minute she got home.

Nicky, the only one still not drinking and tired of their talk, had been scribbling one of the twelve steps on a paper napkin. *List all persons I have harmed and am willing to make amends to*. So far, he had written only one name. *Emily*. The name of his girlfriend at seventeen, when he'd been using heavily. Had he ever known her last name? Though it didn't matter; there was no way to make amends to a dead girl. He scrawled a line through her name and looked up at the others, sick of their conversation, sick of them. "That's enough," he said.

"Since when are you calling shots?" Echo said. "You know…" She tapped her cheek, smudging a few freckles. "Maybe it was *you*."

Nicky refused to be baited, least of all by Echo. Just one more offense committed by his father.

"Fine," Lauren said. "I'm going to my room. I need to change for dinner."

"Oi, me too, love," Ian said, trying to stand up.

"It's too late for you to change *anything*!" Lauren said.

"We should go too," Frank said, nudging Sabrina.

"Another meal with all of you." Jasmin offered them a tight-lipped smile. "I can't wait."

"So what about Rachel?" Echo said.

"What about her?" Nicky said.

"Well…" She wanted to keep it going, keep them at odds with each other. "We all heard her accuse Bagdasarian of ruining her life, right? It could have been her."

"Her *what*? The man drowned. Just stop. We've all had enough."

"You can't tell me what to do," Echo said. "And, like, *have* we had enough?" She looked around, trying to gauge whose button to push. "I still say we need to search Schwegler's room. I mean, with his history, right?" She glanced at Lauren. "And maybe search Rachel's too, after all she said last night and with the 'accident' on the yacht, we all know she's pretty unstable, right?"

Nicky could see Echo's motive was to divide and conquer.

"Not *search*, but maybe we should *talk* to Rachel," Sabrina said. "Just to see how she's doing. She *was* very upset."

"You think talking to her is going to make her *less* upset?" Nicky was starting to feel like the only grown-up in the room, a surprising role for him.

"I'm with you, Sabrina." Latching onto the friction between mother and son, Echo seized the opportunity to separate them even more. "We really should talk to Rachel. I mean, to make sure she's okay."

"Fine," Jasmin said, not wanting to miss anything that might affect her inheritance. "I'm coming with you."

"You're just asking for trouble," Nicky said.

68

Rachel cried as she retold the saga of Bagdasarian getting her fired and how it had ruined her life, though she omitted the nervous breakdown and her stay in a mental facility.

Sabrina played mother, soothing and consoling, Jasmin her impatient self. Echo just watched, enjoying someone else's pain.

After a while, Rachel stopped crying. The women were ready to leave when a piece of the puzzle that had been missing came to Rachel, and she said it. "I saw him!"

"*Who?*" the women said in unison.

"Schwegler."

That was all they needed to resume their positions, Sabrina and Jasmin on either side, Echo pacing, watching and waiting, happy for more drama.

"What do you mean?" Sabrina asked.

"A picture of him, of Schwegler and…somehow connected to last night." Rachel closed her eyes, and the inchoate image began to develop like an old-fashioned photograph, the details and surroundings filling in, and as it did, she described them. "It was late, I'd just left my room… I couldn't sleep, I was upset…and I went into the hall and…" She paused, losing the image for a moment.

"*What?* What is it?" Echo had stopped pacing, leaning over her.

Sabrina raised a hand to keep her away, keep her quiet, then stroked Rachel's arm and softly repeated her words back to her, "You went into the hall *and*..."

"I couldn't sleep. I needed to...to confront him...to say my piece." She paused again, a part of her confused, yet another part conscious enough to edit herself, to not let them know what her intentions had been or, worse, that she had cleaned up the crime scene! But she went on because she needed to remember what happened as much as they did. "I was turning the knob when I heard him close his door."

"Wait," Echo said. "Close which door? What do you mean?"

Jasmin told her to be quiet. "Let her speak," she said, arranging herself beside Rachel, whispering, coaxing. "Go on, honey. Let it out. I'm here for you."

Sabrina gave her a look though she was just as anxious to hear what Rachel had to say.

"I can see it, my hand on the doorknob and it's turning, and that's when I heard *the other* door close." Rachel's brow was furrowed, her eyes closed. "I looked up and I saw..."

"Go on, honey," Jasmin whispered, "You're safe with me."

"*Him!* I saw *him*—at the end of the hall. He was coming out of his room so I quickly let go of the doorknob and retraced my steps, walking fast, practically running back to my room!" She could see it now, even feel it, how quickly she was moving, on tiptoes, bathrobe swishing against her bare legs, turning the hallway corner that led to her room where she stopped to hide, then peeked out and saw him, Schwegler, coming down the hall and stopping just where she had stopped—at Bagdasarian's door! "He's reaching for the doorknob," she said, eyes pressed tightly shut. "And he has something in his hand." She saw it, what she had first thought was a toy. "It's small, like a child's cap gun..."

Sabrina and Jasmin leaned in, both whispering assurances. "Okay, honey, go on. He's got a cap gun in his hand and…?"

"A cap gun?" Echo said.

Jasmin put a finger to her lips. "Shhh!"

"I'm not sure," Rachel said, trying to see it all again, how Schwegler had looked in her direction and how she tried to hide, but possibly too late. *Had he seen her?* "I'm back in my room and I'm…taking another pill."

"Wait. *Wait!*" Echo was shouting. "What happened *before* that? Before you got back to your room, with Schwegler and the cap gun?"

Rachel shook her head, no longer sure if any of it was real or if she had invented it, her mind playing tricks on her. "I can't remember… The pills, they… But…" She let out a sigh of relief. "It wasn't *me*! I see that now. I *didn't* kill him!" She stopped, her face screwed up. "At least I don't think so." Confused again, the chemical fog drifting back over her mind like a snowdrift.

"Did you see if Schwegler went into Bagdasarian's room?" Sabrina asked, gently probing.

Rachel tried to see it again. *Had she seen him go in? Or had he been coming out?* But the image was gone. "I don't know. Maybe I'm wrong. I took too many pills and…maybe it was just another effect of the drug, an Ambien dream! Maybe I *did* do it! How can I be sure?" She covered her eyes and started to cry again.

"*Think!*" Echo said, shouting, while Sabrina and Jasmin gently coaxed. But it was no good. Rachel was inconsolable, sobbing into her pillow.

"What do you think?" Echo asked once they'd left Rachel's room. "Did she kill him?"

"I can't imagine she could," Sabrina said, shaking her head. "Look at her. She's incapable of hurting anyone. The poor woman is a wreck."

"Maybe wrecked with *guilt*!" Echo said.

"Oh, just shut up!" Jasmin said to her.

"We just don't know," Sabrina said. "Not for sure."

And it was true, they didn't know for sure, but they'd heard enough to pass it on to the others, which they did.

69

Back in the dining room, Rachel's comments caused a stir among the guests.

"She said *what*?"

"You're *kidding*!"

"I *knew* it was Schwegler!"

If there was a murderer in their midst, they had to know.

70

Schwegler's bedroom was warm, a window open, moist air wafting in.

Frank and Nicky stood facing him.

"So, you went to Bagdasarian's room last night," Frank said, not a question.

"I did not," Schwegler said. *Leugnen, leugnen, leugnen. Deny, deny, deny*, words his father had drummed into him.

"Then why would Rachel say she saw you there?" Nicky asked. "At Bagdasarian's door?"

"I have no idea. She must have been dreaming."

Perhaps she was, Nicky thought. "She said you had a gun."

"A *gun*?" Schwegler scoffed. "Why? Was Mr. Bagdasarian shot? I did not think so."

"That's not the question!" Frank fired back, employing a sense-memory acting technique, drawing upon one of the many arguments he'd had with his late wife, Sarah.

Of course it *was* the question, Nicky thought, or a part of it. If Schwegler had shot Bagdasarian, there would have been a wound, blood in the water. He pictured the art dealer's waterlogged body on the bathroom floor. They had not inspected it carefully, had not turned him over to look for bullet holes or stab wounds. The idea of doing it now, with the body in a further state of decay, not something he wanted to do. Still, they should have done it before accusing anyone.

"Rachel described it as looking like a toy," Frank said. "Like a cap gun."

"A *cap* gun? And you think she was *not* dreaming?" Schwegler laughed, exposing his small discolored teeth while the event played out in his mind: slipping into Bagdasarian's room, the tiny hummingbird gun clenched in his hand, opening the bathroom door and finding the man in his tub. So, what if Rachel Ronan had seen him? She was an unreliable witness. "Perhaps..." he said, choosing his words carefully, "you should be asking her what *she* was doing at Mr. Bagdasarian's door? After all, she detested the man, something she made all too clear last night."

"We're not here to talk about Rachel!" Frank growled, leaning over him, still method acting.

"But that is *exactly* why you are here," Schwegler said. "Because of Miss Ronan's accusations. It all seems rather convenient, does it not? This unstable woman who despised Bagdasarian, throwing suspicion on someone else, on *me*. And yet, through her own admission, we know that it was *she* who went to his room in the middle of the night."

Sehr gut. Very good. His father's words again, approving for once. But when he reached for his cigarettes, his hands were shaking.

"If we are finished, I would like to get ready for dinner."

Nicky didn't know what to say. They had acted without thinking, had accused the man based on the word of a possibly unstable woman. And yet, observing Schwegler now, his one eye slightly twitching, the cigarette shaking in his hand, Nicky wondered if Rachel was right.

"Not so fast!" Frank said. "There's still the question of the gun."

"You mean the *cap* gun." Schwegler managed a grin. "I thought we agreed that Mr. Bagdasarian drowned." He looked at Nicky. "Did you not say so yourself, and quite emphatically? It was a tragic accident, *unless* Miss Ronan had something to do with it." He underlined what he had already suggested, then walked them to the door and closed it behind them.

A moment of listening to their footsteps retreat, then Schwegler knelt and tugged the briefcase out from under the bed.

The small pistol was exactly where he had put it after returning from Bagdasarian's room last night. He took it out again and raised it to the light. *Cap gun, indeed.* It was a work of art! He checked the chamber, then slid the gun under his pillow. No reason to hide it now. Better, he thought, to keep it close and easily accessible.

71

The guests rummaged through the pantry for dinner, finding boxes of instant foods, chow mein, powdered potatoes, Cup-a-Soup, tins of tuna and salmon, jars of pickles, and the freezer stocked with frozen dinner rolls, bags of peas, carrots, string beans, and sausages.

Jasmin proclaimed it all "disgusting."

"Completely inedible," Lauren agreed, pouring more wine into her glass.

"Isn't there anything fresh to eat?" Sabrina asked. "What happened to the fruit and vegetables from the first night?"

"I don't see any," Frank said.

"So, this is it?" Jasmin pushed aside jars of pickled vegetables.

"Can't we go fishing?" Frank asked.

"Where do you suggest, mate?" Ian asked. "The shark-infested lagoon?"

"Let's make the best of it," Nicky said, still playing the peacekeeper.

"It all makes me want to puke," Jasmin said.

"I'm sure that's like part of your normal eating and purging ritual," Echo said.

Frank rummaged through shelf after shelf of boxed and canned food. "It looks like someone expected us to be here for a long time."

"It already feels long," Sabrina said, "but it's only our second day!"

"That makes me want to scream," Jasmin said.

"Have another drink," Nicky said to her, while the others dug in best they could. Lauren heating rolls, Ian pouring drinks, Frank zapping frozen veggies, Echo opening the canned tuna and salmon.

"This is fun," Echo said. "Like a picnic."

Jasmin gave her a sour look.

They ate and drank at the long dining room table, Jasmin swearing again she would complain about the food and lack of service the minute she got home.

"Complain to who?" Nicky asked, thinking, *My dead father, your dead husband?*

Schwegler joined them late as if nothing had happened, as if he had not been interrogated.

"Where were you while we all *slaved* over dinner?" Jasmin, the only who had not helped, asked.

"Cleaning up," he said.

She looked him up and down, his wrinkled suit, the stubble on his cheeks. "Doesn't look it."

Schwegler avoided Frank and Nicky and planted himself beside Sabrina, where he chugged wine and scarfed dinner rolls, butter smeared across his thin lips as he complimented her on her baking skills.

"Thanks," she said. "But it wasn't me."

"It was *me*," Lauren said, smiling.

"You *defrosted* them, love," Ian said. "You didn't bake them!"

"And you poured liquid out of bottle!" she said.

Sabrina tossed back a glass of wine, still upset by Bagdasarian's death. She was embarrassed that she had made it about herself, but the idea of finding a gallery at this point in her life felt daunting and exhausting. She painted on a smile for Schwegler, the idea of a European exhibition a solid second choice. She asked how long he would be in New York.

"Long enough to visit your studio, my dear." He laid his meaty hand over hers.

Sabrina fought the urge to pull her hand away while keeping her smile in place. "Let's set a date," she said.

Nicky saw what his mother was doing, but this time he did not help her. He was watching Schwegler, thinking about Rachel's accusations and wondering if they were true.

Frank watched Schwegler too, but for a different reason, surprised at the intensity of his jealousy. He wanted to tear the man's hand off Sabrina's, knock him from his chair, punch him in the face, only managing to control his anger because he knew Sabrina would not appreciate it.

Bottles were passed around, wineglasses were refilled, everyone but Nicky drinking heavily.

"Here's to our last supper!" Sabrina said.

"Here! Here!" Frank said, leaning in to clink her glass while he groped her thigh beneath the table.

"Thank the Lord!" Jasmin said.

"*He* was smart enough to skip *our* last supper," Sabrina said and laughed.

"He, who?" Echo asked.

"No one special," Jasmin said. "Only Jesus."

"You think his last supper was any better than ours?" Frank said.

"It *had* to be," Jasmin said, pushing her plate aside.

"Maybe," Ian said. "But the poor bloke died after *his* supper."

"Who's to say this supper won't be *our* last?" Sabrina said joking, then was immediately sorry, though everyone laughed, then got quiet.

Nicky raised his glass of Perrier to break the silence. "Well, amen," he said.

"Fuck, yeah," Ian said, and everyone toasted.

Frank said there should be a movie about the weekend, and he would play himself.

"You'd never get the part," Jasmin said.

Sabrina resumed talking to Schwegler about her poisonous plant paintings and figuring out a date for him to see them, Echo eavesdropping.

"I don't know if your paintings are any good," she said. "But knowing that stuff saved Rachel's life."

"Yes," Sabrina said. "And they *are* good."

"They *are*," Frank said, though he'd never seen them.

"I am sure they are excellent," Schwegler said, smiling at Sabrina.

"My point was, like, Sabrina saved Rachel's life," Echo said. "But no one cares about that."

"*I* do," Sabrina said.

"Me too," Jasmin said without much conviction.

"Yeah, right," Echo said.

"I *do*," Sabrina said and scanned the table looking for Rachel to make sure she'd heard her. "Where *is* Rachel?" she asked.

72

Rain was pounding on the skylights, the wall sconces producing a maze of shadows as Sabrina headed down the hallway. She knocked on Rachel's door and, when there was no answer, tried the knob, which turned easily in her hand.

The room was dim, and it took a minute for her eyes to adjust, to see Rachel in bed, asleep.

Poor thing must be exhausted from all the drama and crying, best to let her sleep.

Sabrina was tiptoeing away when she noticed the vase on the floor and the large wet stain on the rug and the spilled flowers. And was that an empty pill vial? She took a few steps in, saw she was right, plucked the vial off the floor, and read the label.

AMBIEN 10MG TABLETS TAKE 1 TABLET BY MOUTH AT BEDTIME DO NOT TAKE WITH ALCOHOL QTY 30

She's taken a pill, Sabrina thought, backing up again to let her sleep. It was then she realized the vial was empty.

"Rachel?" she said quietly, coming closer, tapping her shoulder, tapping her again, then laying her hand against Rachel's check. It was cold. A hand on the woman's chest, the dress wet and strewn with flowers, more flowers clenched in her hands. Then she looked closer and saw Rachel's eyes were slightly open and fixed.

Oh my God. "Rachel, wake up!" Shaking her now, repeating her name, checking for a pulse in her neck, her wrist, shouting: "*Rachel! Rachel!*"

Then she was tearing down the hall, hitting the elevator button, her mind spinning as she turned and took the stairs two at a time.

Stumbling breathless into the dining room, she raised the plastic vial in her hand.

"It's empty!" she said. "She must have taken them!"

73

Nicky lifted Rachel's body from the bed and tried to make her stand. No stranger to overdose, he shouted her name and slapped her face, then dragged her into the bathroom and held her under the shower, cold water soaking them both. Finally, inserting his fingers into her mouth, he tried to make her gag, the other guests crowding into the room, speaking over each other, "What happened?" "How is she?" "What's going on?"

Nicky laid her back on the bed, her wet hair soaking the pillow, body limp. "We need to pump her stomach. *Now!*" He shouted to the others, "See what you can find!"

Sabrina and Jasmin stayed behind, patting Rachel's hands and cheeks, still trying to revive her, while Frank and Schwegler raced downstairs and searched through drawers and closets for a tube, anything they could use.

74

An hour later, the guests were gathered in the living room, Rachel's body upstairs, under a sheet.

Rain beat heavy against the skylights, thunder clapped. Lightning flashed in the windows, highlighting the masks on the walls, their beads and bone and shards of teeth.

"My God!" Jasmin said. "Two suicides."

"Like, what are the odds?" Echo said. "But she tried it before, on the boat."

"That was an accident," Nicky said.

His mother looked at him, thinking he'd always had trouble with reality, too often escaping it with drugs. "Is it our fault?" she asked, looking around, a glass of whiskey trembling in her hand.

Frank was beside her, arm over her shoulder, consoling. "You never know what someone is going to do." Thinking how he had considered doing the same thing after the collapse of his career and his life went to hell.

"How could we know?" Jasmin said. "We listened to her, let her cry it out. What else could we do?" For a moment she felt bad, sorry for the woman, then a note of reality: one less person to cut into her inheritance. "There is no reason for us to feel guilty."

"Rachel was the one feeling guilty," Echo said.

"Guilty of *what*?" Lauren asked, working her second glass of vodka and feeling awful she had treated the woman so badly.

"Duh, like drowning Bagdasarian in his tub," Echo said. "What else?"

"I believe she may be right," Schwegler said, lighting a cigarette.

"And convenient," Nicky said. "Would sort of let *you* off the hook."

Schwegler gave him a piercing look. "I thought you believed it was an accidental drowning."

And it was true, Nicky did think that, or he had. Now, he was not so sure.

"I am just stating the obvious," Schwegler said. "What we all think."

"Don't speak for me," Lauren said.

"Or me," Ian said, lighting up another joint.

Frank stroked Sabrina's arm. "I guess seeing Bagdasarian after all these years, she just snapped."

"So, you're all agreeing with him?" Jasmin shot a look at Schwegler. "You think Rachel killed Bagdasarian?"

"I can't imagine it," Lauren said. "He was a very big man. It seems impossible."

"Rachel was no lightweight," Echo said.

"Don't you ever shut up?" Lauren said to her.

"Poor Rachel," Sabrina said, feeling guilty, thinking of the woman who had been at her dinner parties years ago, a woman she had totally forgotten. "Does Ambien work that fast?" she asked, trying to take it in. "Is it even deadly?"

"In larger doses," Nicky said. He knew about drugs.

"It's all...too much," Lauren said, feeling shaky. She hadn't eaten, and the alcohol had gone to her head.

"It is," Sabrina said. "Just awful. Horrible."

There was another clap of thunder, the lights blinking on and off, the walls quaking so badly a mask fell to the floor and splintered.

"It's this fucking *place*!" Jasmin said. "It could make anyone go crazy!"

Nicky was quiet a moment, considering the two deaths—Bagdasarian drowned in his tub and the convenience of Rachel taking her own life. "It's too damn neat."

"What are you suggesting?" Sabrina asked.

Nicky shrugged. He didn't know, but he wasn't buying it, two suicides in a row.

"Well, you gotta look on the bright side," Echo said. "At least Rachel wasn't murdered, right?"

"Of course she wasn't murdered," Jasmin said. "Unless someone stuffed her mouth with pills!"

"Bollocks!" Ian said. "She looked totally at peace."

Sabrina saw the scene again, Rachel in bed, the flowers on her chest and in her hands, the broken vase on the floor. "Did she knock the vase over?" she said, more to herself. "And what about the flowers? Half of them were on her, some on the floor, the rest in her hands. It doesn't make sense."

"Why not?" Echo said. "She knocks the vase over and, like, the flowers scatter."

"Into her *hands*?" Sabrina shook her head. "Why would anyone care about saving a few flowers if they had just taken pills—if they were dying?"

"Oh God, does it matter?" Lauren felt a rush of guilt, Rachel suddenly standing in for the thousands who had died from her family's drug. "The poor woman is *dead*. I don't see how a few flowers make a difference."

Sabrina could not come up with an answer, though she saw something at the edge of her consciousness. She shook her head, then raised her glass. "Here's to Rachel," she said softly, unexpected tears filling her eyes.

"Amen," Lauren said.

Frank tapped his glass against Sabrina's and kissed her cheek. "To the living," he said. "And to the future."

Sabrina met his eyes for a moment, then turned away, but not before Echo caught it.

"So, like, what's the deal? Are you guys fucking again?"

Sabrina gasped.

"That's enough out of you!" Frank said.

"Yes!" Lauren said. "Be quiet for once!"

"Ya, *genug*! Enough!" Schwegler said, coming to Sabrina's defense. He found it hard to believe she would be involved with such a weak man as Frank and hoped to win her away. "That will be all from you!"

Echo laughed in his face. "Like you are so thirsty for her, it's pathetic! You think she'd ever go for *you*! That's a laugh. She's using you, dude, for your gallery."

"*Halt den Mund!* Shut your mouth!" he said, feeling the heat rise in his face, the muscles in his jaw clenching.

"You don't scare me," Echo said.

Schwegler took a deep breath, measuring his words. "I was... not trying to scare you. But I could if I wanted to..." His words trailed off and darkness closed in around him, the chastened little boy locked in a closet, no one coming to his rescue.

"As if!" Echo spit. "I've dealt with a lot scarier dudes than you!" Her laugh cut through Schwegler's flashback but trigged her own: Her mother's john crawling into her bed, and he was not the first, but this one had to be carried out with a knife in his chest, the scene blazing across her brain—the man reeling back, blood spurting, her mother, already strung out, screaming. But Echo had taken charge, stripped the guy of his clothes, his ID, his cash. Then, the two of them stuffed his body into the trunk of the car and drove, neither speaking, not even when they dumped his body into a polluted lake miles away. They just watched him sink. It wasn't until they were back home cleaning blood off the floor that her mother said, "Girl, you got ice in your veins." And it was true. Echo hadn't felt much of anything; she had learned how to deaden her emotions early in life.

"We will see," Schwegler said.

"See?" Echo said, momentarily confused, then back to the moment. "Oh…fuck you, Nazi!"

Do not let her get away with saying such a thing, Schwegler's father always in his head. "Do not make me prove it!" he said.

"*Enough!*" Nicky said.

"He's right," Frank said. "It's late, and we're all under a strain."

"Maybe you are," Echo said. "You and your new, *old* girlfriend. You know, I been thinking I'm going to write up this whole fucking weekend and publish it online."

"You can't do that!" Jasmin said. "I have a right to my privacy. I'm a celebrity!"

Echo laughed. "Oh, right, the aged-out, *un*-supermodel!"

Jasmin did not hesitate, her drink thrown in Echo's face.

And Echo, her features screwed up with rage, charged.

Nicky managed to get between them and hold them apart.

Echo broke free but gave up the fight. "Whatever," she said, as if bored. "I'm going to bed."

It seemed like the only thing to do and the perfect end to the evening.

75

Back in her room, Jasmin was still railing. "Can you believe that little bitch? I wish it had been *her* in the tub or overdosed on pills! *Aged out? Me?*" Hands shaking, she checked her nails to make sure another had not broken during their skirmish.

Nicky was sick of all the fighting and accusations, and worse he was jonesing for a drink. He watched rain streak the window of Jasmin's room. It felt like his DJ dreams, like so many others, being washed away.

"You have to stay with me tonight," Jasmin said. "I'm scared." She had gotten out her feng shui charm, red tassels and gold coins, a gift from her superstitious grandmother. "Please." She leaned against him, her hand on his thigh. "You know why we're here. It's important, necessary."

The words too familiar, like his mother's. He moved her hand away. "I thought you were scared?"

"I am, but we're talking about money, the inheritance. We have to think about our future."

He knew she meant *her* future.

Jasmin nuzzled his neck, his skin salty and sharp. He could use a bath. As usual. But she kept going, lifting his T-shirt and kissing his chest. It was possible Victor had left her nothing, but she was pretty sure that Nicky, the only son, would inherit, and if so, she needed to secure their fifty-fifty deal.

"You're a mercenary little bitch, aren't you?" Nicky said, his hand in her hair, tugging her head away.

"Of course. That's why you like me. Because we're alike."

I'm better than that, Nicky thought, but he knew it wasn't true, just that money was not his main concern.

"So?" she said, leering at him.

"So, shut up," he said, drew her toward him and kissed her, his tongue in her mouth before she could say another word.

76

Frank waited in the hallway until the last guests had gone into their rooms before he knocked.

Sabrina opened the door a few inches, a sliver of her beautiful face in the darkness.

“Come in,” she said, an unexpected urgency in her voice. Not because she wanted Frank so badly, but after two unexpected deaths, she did not want to be alone.

Frank pulled the door closed behind him and embraced her as if everything depended on it, and for him maybe it did.

Sabrina’s emotions were in conflict, his touch unlocking her inhibitions but along with that, the past. She pulled back, their ancient affair sounding an alarm, the bad ending, the unintended tragedy.

“Are we making a mistake, Frank?”

“Of course not.” He kissed her as if holding on for dear life. No way he was going back to the scraps of his former existence, the bit parts and dwindling one-night stands with wannabe starlets who held a vague memory of who he had once been. He had a future now. *They* had a future. One with money and security. All thanks to Victor!

The thought of it, the irony, almost made him laugh, but he kept kissing her, touching her, trying to insure his future.

77

Hans Schwegler studied his hands, surprised at how steady they were, how calm.

Guter Junge, his father said. *Good boy.*

He tugged the briefcase out from under the bed. The contract that would give him title to Bagdasarian's galleries was still inside. If discovered, it would look suspicious, and with two deaths there would surely be questions, and there was no reason to keep it, not now.

In the bathroom, he lit a match to the corner, watched as it sparked and flamed, the paper going red, then black. He held it until it singed his fingers and even a moment longer, the pain a test. Then he dropped it into the toilet and flushed it away.

78

Frank sat up in bed with a start.

Was that a scream? He rubbed his eyes as they adjusted to the dark and saw Sabrina asleep beside him. He touched her shoulder to make sure she was real, that he wasn't dreaming.

Sabrina mumbled, "What is it?" pushing the curls out of her face.

"I thought I heard something. Maybe just the rain or… I don't know. Sorry, darling, go back to sleep."

"What time is it?" she asked, half awake, propped on an elbow.

Frank checked his watch. "Almost four."

"It's the middle of the night," she moaned, and fell back against the pillows just as someone knocked at their door.

"Mother, it's me. Everything okay?"

"Jesus," Sabrina whispered, "it's Nicky," motioning for Frank to hide. She slipped into her robe and went to the door, cracked it open a couple of inches. "What is it?"

"There were noises, screams, I think. Just checking to make sure you're okay."

"Yes, yes," she said, holding the door in place. "I'm fine. I was asleep."

"I'm going to check on the others."

"I'll come with you," Sabrina said, slinking out the half-open door, casting a glance back at Frank, waving her hand for him to stay where he was.

In the hallway, she was surprised to find Jasmin just behind her son. Had Nicky awakened her, or were they sleeping together and no longer bothering to hide it? She didn't ask. And what could she say with Frank in her bedroom? She followed the two of them down the hall, Nicky in the lead, with a knife.

"Just in case," he said, holding it up.

Pattering rain on the skylights followed them like another set of footsteps.

Schwegler was standing in his doorway, pajama pants drooping below his belly, a tiny revolver in his hand. "What is going on?"

"So, you *do* have a gun!" Nicky said. "Rachel was right!"

"I never said I did not have a gun, only that Bagdasarian was not shot."

"The cap gun!" Jasmin said.

"I can assure you it is quite real." Schwegler noted the knife in Nicky's hand. "And what about *that*?"

"Swiss Army Champ XXL," Nicky said, a knife he'd had for years, one he had used in the past for cutting cocaine and heroin.

From behind the group, Frank slipped out of Sabrina's room and joined them. "What's, uh, all the fuss?" He exaggerated a yawn and rubbed his eyes, a master class in bad acting.

"Isn't your room at the other end of the hall?" Nicky asked, taunting; he knew where his uncle had been. He gave his mother a look, an eyebrow raised.

"Let's wake the others," Frank said, talking fast.

Lauren had undereye patches and a compression strap around her neck, her face slick with night cream. Ian, eyeliner smudged, inky hair flattened, yawned, his breath reeking of weed and booze. "What's the beat?" he asked.

"There were screams, I think," Nicky said. "Did you hear them?"

"Not me, mate, I was zoning, zonked, and Lauren took a pill—or three."

"*One*," she said, her eyes narrowed at him above the anti-wrinkle patches. "And I did hear it, but I thought it was some kind of bird or something outside."

"Well, everyone is here," Frank said. "So, I guess it's okay, a false alarm."

"No," Nicky said, looking around, counting. "Not everyone."

79

Echo's door was ajar, the room empty. Her backpack was on a chair, open, underwear strewn on the floor along with her hand-painted sneakers. The bed empty, the blankets rumpled. They checked the closet, also empty.

Sabrina came out of the bathroom holding a brown eyebrow pencil. "Her freckle maker is still here."

"And everything else," Lauren said. "Her toothbrush, toothpaste, a hairbrush, all in there."

"She uses a toothbrush and comb?" Jasmin exaggerated her surprise, but no one laughed. Not now, after two people had died and one was missing, the anxiety in the room sucking up the air.

"She must be around." Frank said, his specialty: stating the obvious.

"Wait," Lauren said. "She said she sleepwalks, remember?" She was fighting her own sense of sleepwalking, the pills she had taken a few hours ago, not yet worn off.

They headed down the hallway, wall sconces scooping out arcs of light and dark, the guests' reflections fleeting and distorted in rain-splattered windows as they went in and out of empty bedrooms and baths.

Downstairs, they split up and searched. First, the living room, into its curved, half-hidden window seats and its tucked-away niches. Then, the library with its floor-to-ceiling bookcases, the top shelves lost in shadow, the small private nooks for reading dark and empty. In the dining room, the long rectangular table was a mess no one had bothered to clear or clean. Frank peered beneath it, made a face when he saw ants crawling over crumbs and bits of food.

The kitchen, even larger than the dining area, had hanging pots and pans, two restaurant-style ovens, a work counter that ran the length of the room, cabinets filled with dishes and glassware, but otherwise empty. The pantry, half the size but still big, was stocked with those familiar tins and jars of packaged food, but no sign of Echo anywhere.

"Out here!" Schwegler called from the foyer.

He was just closing the front door, but not before the wind and rain had blown in leaves, the area hot and buzzing with bugs. In seconds, they were all swatting and cursing.

"Not again!" Jasmin said, smacking mosquitoes on her arms and neck.

No one thought Echo could possibly be outside in the rain and with these bugs, but Nicky insisted they have a look, and Schwegler offered to go with him. Not Nicky's first choice of a companion, but he didn't say no.

Sabrina volunteered, but they told her stay inside.

"That's ridiculous," she said. "That the men are going but not the women."

"Speak for yourself," Jasmin said.

Lauren said, "Ian will go with you," her hand on his back nudging him forward.

They found slickers in the front closets and large industrial-looking flashlights, along with flares and cans of DEET and several first aid kits, the hotel clearly ready for hurricanes and disasters.

"You really think she'd go out in *this*?" Sabrina asked. "Wouldn't the rain wake her?"

"*Nein*," Schwegler said, and he knew: he'd been a sleepwalker as a child and was punished for it as if he had committed a crime, often awakened with a slap by his father, the worst possible way to wake a sleepwalker. "When one sleepwalks, they are unaware of what they are doing or their surroundings."

Slickers on and sprayed with repellent, the three men headed out.

The hotel's dim outdoor lights did little to illuminate the night, the moon shrouded by clouds, the rain light now but steady. A mist cloaked everything in fog, the air electrified by crickets and cicadas. Under their slickers, the men were already soaked with sweat. Despite the rain, it was sweltering, the air so oppressive it felt viscous and tangible, like you could grab hold of it and take a bite.

With their flashlights shuddering thin streams of light into the darkness, and moths and bugs doing frenetic dances in the beams, the men moved forward.

There was nothing in the pond but koi flitting under the water, flashes of their glittery spotted skins captured in fragmented seconds of light.

"We need to check out back, the pool," Nicky said, half his words carried off by the wind.

Ian was ready to turn back but nodded. Nicky gave him a brotherly clap on the shoulder. He was feeling somewhat heroic, a new sensation for him, and it felt good, a way to make up for his sins, though he knew that was impossible.

Even with the flashlights, it was hard to see, the ground wet and muddy, the grass tall in places, and the bugs were bad, the sound of slapping flesh and mumbled curses adding to the nighttime symphony of frogs and rain and rustling palms.

They were at the far edge of the hotel, about to head toward the back, when Schwegler stopped, his flashlight aimed in the other direction, picking out fractured pieces of the landscape like an old-time movie.

"There!" he said. "What is that?"

Nicky and Ian swung their flashlights in the same direction, the beams of light skittering over the lagoon's dark surface and stopping on something tall and standing upright, several feet out of the water.

"I do not remember there being a tree in the lagoon," Schwegler said.

Nicky didn't either.

They headed toward it, their flashlights trained on the ground so they would not fall into the lagoon, and stopped at the edge, the surface relatively calm, broken only by the ripples created by raindrops.

Nicky and Schwegler aimed their flashlights at the tree, which they could now see was a stalk of bamboo, seven or eight feet long, embedded in a large slick mound, a sort of island in the lagoon. Which seconds later, was moving. It was a moment before they realized it was a shark, a dead one, moving only because it was being attacked by other sharks, who took turns tearing at the dead one, feasting.

"Jesus!" Nicky sucked in a breath, then spat out the small bugs that had flown into his mouth.

"Let's go, mates!" Ian said.

"Wait," Schwegler said. His flashlight had picked out something else, something white and bunched floating on the water near the sharks, a piece of cloth, torn, ragged. Then another object broke the water's surface, and it was only a few seconds before their eyes and minds could make sense of it and believe what they were seeing. When they did, they leapt back, gasping and crying out, Ian practically falling.

"Holy shite!"

It was part of a leg, knee to foot, bouncing as if it were alive as the sharks fought over it until one of them, jaws wide open, then snapping shut, dragged it under into the dark water.

Then there was another shark and another, their short blunt snouts breaking the water's surface, jaws snapping at other floating objects. *A hand? A foot? A torso?* Flashlights jerking in their hands catching the action in quick juddering frames of horror. Then a head bobbed up, hair soaked dark red, almost black, covering the face, but there was no question who it was, as the sharks fought over it and the men watched, stunned, Ian doubled over, retching.

"Let's go!" Nicky finally said. He got an arm around Ian and tugged him from the scene, Schwegler beside them breathing hard, all of them trying not to fall as they broke into a run.

80

Inside, they told the others what they had seen in fits and starts and half sentences, Ian and Schwegler chugging brandy. Nicky wasn't sure he could make it without a drink, but he held on, dragging on one of Ian's cigarettes, hand shaking as he inhaled puff after puff.

They were back in the dining room, the tablecloth stained, dirty dishes shoved to the side, everyone asking questions and wanting to hear the details but cringing when they did.

"Oh my God!" Sabrina tossed back a drink, trying, impossibly, to steady her nerves. "She must have sleepwalked into the lagoon!"

"Awful, just awful," Jasmin said, imagining it had been her, the images in her mind horrifying.

"At least it wasn't another suicide," Frank said.

"What difference does *that* make!" Lauren barked at him. She had taken off the neck sling, removed the eye patches, and looked terrible, as if she had aged a decade in the past hour.

"A *big* difference," he said, trying to defend his remark.

"No, there's no difference!" Jasmin said, practically shouting. "Everyone is *dying*!"

Nicky got an arm around her though he was still trembling, trying to wrap his head around it, the idea of it someone sleepwalking into a shark-infested lagoon. *Was it possible?*

"What the hell is going on here?" Lauren asked, her voice cracking, hand shaking as she poured herself another drink.

"This place is cursed!" Jasmin said. "We've got to get out of here! We've *got to*!"

"We will," Nicky said, trying hard to sound calm, but thinking the same thing: *What is going on here?*

Schwegler poured himself more brandy and chugged it down, his nerves and mind finally beginning to quiet and with that, a question: "Who harpooned the shark?"

"What are you talking about?" Lauren asked, disgusted, angry, scared.

"There was a dead shark," he said, then turned to Ian and Nicky. "You saw it, ya? With a spear stuck into it."

"So *what*?" Jasmin said. "Who cares about the *fucking* shark!"

"Well," he said, slowly, trying to make sense of it. "I do not think it is possible that it was harpooned by another shark."

"What are you suggesting?" Sabrina said, the answer coming to her as she asked. "That there's someone else on the island?"

Wind swept large palm fronds across the skylights, the rain coming down harder now, hitting the windows like pebbles.

"You mean...other than us?" Lauren asked, her eyes darting from one person to another.

Schwegler lit one of his long, thin cigarettes, his hands unsteady. "All I am saying is that someone harpooned that shark."

81

It was four thirty in the morning but impossible to go back to sleep, everyone jittery, adrenaline pumping.

Ian had broken out more bottles of brandy.

Nicky raised a glass, inhaled the sweet, heady aroma, then put it down, his hand shaking. "There has to be an explanation," he said, though he could not come up with one. He eyed Schwegler. Did the man have a motive for pushing the idea of someone else being on the island? *Didn't they all?*

"Like what, mate?" Ian said. "Like the bloody shark banged into the harpoon *accidentally*?"

"It had to be Echo. She must have done it," Frank said.

"While she was being attacked? But how?" Nicky was trying to see it. "She somehow makes it back to shore, breaks off a six-, seven-foot shoot of bamboo, goes back and stabs the shark? No way. If she'd made it out of the water, she'd have run!"

"It's the only explanation," Frank said.

"You didn't see it, mate," Ian said to him, pictures of the horrific scene back in his mind. He shook his head trying to dislodge them.

"Maybe the shark was depressed and tried to commit suicide!" Jasmin said and laughed but it was high-pitched, tinged with hysteria.

"Three people are *dead*!" Lauren said to her. "Don't you *care*?"

"Of course I do!" Jasmin said, but the only emotion she could locate was her own fear.

"A harpooned shark?" Sabrina said. The image struck something in the back of her mind, but she couldn't say what, couldn't think straight.

"What about it?" Frank asked.

"Never mind," she said.

"No, tell us," Lauren said. "*Please*. Anything to distract us from this horror show."

Sabrina exhaled a deep breath before she spoke. "I was just thinking about Rachel, how I found her in bed with the water and the flowers. It reminded me of a Pre-Raphaelite painting, of a woman drowned with flowers strewn around her."

"Honey," Frank said, stroking her arm. "This isn't the time for an art history lesson."

"You're right." Sabrina said, though she resented him for saying it. "But...there was something about the way Bagdasarian died too." The image of a dead man in his bath like another famous painting, *The Death of Marat*, one she knew well but she did not want to say, it felt crazy making these art associations. *Who would do such a thing?* "Forget it," she said.

"But what if there *is* someone else on the island?" Lauren asked, feeling a chill.

"Like *who*?" Nicky asked, trying to imagine it, someone here, his paranoia impossibly ratcheting up another notch.

The guests eyed one another. A few took inventory of their enemies: Lauren wondered if it was someone who had lost a loved one to Ziff's opioid, but if so, wouldn't they have killed her first? Schwegler figured there were many people who might want him dead, camp survivors and their heirs who had it in for his family. Sabrina couldn't think of anyone she had hurt or offended enough to make them want to kill her. *Except for Victor,* she thought. *But he's dead.*

"If there *is* someone here..." Frank said, "where are they hiding?"

Then they were all talking at once: "In a vacant room?" "A closet?" "Is there a basement?" "An attic?"

"But we just searched the place," Ian said, seeing a flash of Echo's severed leg floating in the lagoon, and he crossed himself.

"We didn't check all the rooms," Nicky said.

"You mean *our* rooms?" Schwegler said. "I do not see the point."

"That's *exactly* the point," Nicky said. "Unless you have something to hide."

"We should check the other rooms too," Frank said, "Bagdasarian's and Rachel's."

"Would anyone actually hide with a dead body?" Jasmin shuddered.

"What if we actually *find* someone?" Lauren said.

Nicky took a deep breath, once again assuming the leadership role. "If we stick together," he said, "we can handle whatever we find."

"You mean as well as we have so far?" Jasmin said.

Nicky turned to Schwegler. "Get your little gun," he said. "I'll get my knife."

82

They searched the rooms, starting with those of the dead.

Bagdasarian's body had become even more bloated and was emitting a noxious odor that made it impossible to stay in his room for very long, just a quick search of the closet and a peek under the bed was all anyone could stand.

Rachel was covered by a sheet, but an odor had begun to permeate her room as well. Again, a quick check of the bathroom, the closet, and under the bed produced nothing. The strewn flowers Sabrina had pointed out were wilted and dying.

Together, they checked their own bedrooms, which produced a few awkward moments—the dildo on Lauren's bedside table, the huge stash of weed on Ian's, the condoms and lube in Schwegler's. They also found the briefcase under his bed, but it was empty.

"What about outside?" Frank asked.

"We were just there," Ian said. "And I ain't going back out till we leave this bloody island."

They all agreed that going outside seemed redundant and no one wanted to do it.

"Well, that's that," Frank said. "No hint of an intruder or telltale sign of a psychopath's lair."

"That's a relief," Sabrina said.

"Is it?" Nicky asked.

It only took a moment for the group to understand what he was implying: that if there was no one else on the island, one of them was the killer.

83

Night gave way to a gray dawn, their third morning on the island.

Too anxious to sleep, they had loitered at the table drinking cups of coffee, some chasing it with even more booze. But they were excited too for their last day, the boat picking them up that afternoon.

"It feels like we've been here forever," Jasmin said, looking exhausted, no makeup to cover the bags under her eyes.

"What matters is that we're getting out of here today." Frank looked older with his salt-and-pepper stubble, the gray roots of his hair more obvious, less a movie star than ever.

"Amen to that." Lauren raised a glass of brandy, her hair an uncombed rat's nest.

"There are going to be questions," Nicky said. "You know, about what happened—to Bagdasarian and Rachel and Echo."

"Questions from *who*?" Schwegler asked.

"The authorities, who else?" Nicky's stubble had filled in, practically a beard. "So, you might want to think about your answers."

"I have nothing to hide," Schwegler said.

Nicky snorted.

"We should get ready," Sabrina said.

Casting suspicious glances at one another, they began to leave the table, some more easily than others, depending on how much alcohol they had drunk.

Lauren was halfway to the elevator when her heel caught on the edge of a rug.

Ian, drunk and stoned and still in shock, made a halfhearted attempt to catch her but missed, and she went down hard.

"My ankle!" she shrieked, then tried and failed to get up.

Ian and Nicky carried her to the elevator and up to the room. Sabrina got ice, wrapped in a towel. "This will help," she said. "Just rest a while and you'll be fine. See you in a bit." She gave Lauren a pat, then headed off to her room.

Lauren, foot wrapped in the towel with ice, sat up in bed barking orders about what to pack.

Ian stumbled around not really caring, thinking about what lay ahead for him once they were home. Would she really cast him out? And if so, where would he go? What would he do? And worse, would she set the Manchester coppers on him? He stuffed Lauren's clothes into her Louis Vuitton suitcase without looking.

"Ian! That blouse is Chanel!"

"Oi, does it really matter, love, after all this?"

She saw his point though she took it as a personal affront he was balling up her designer clothes like they were from Target.

Ian made a show of folding the blouse, then the gold bathing suit she'd been wearing when he had tried to push her overboard and failed. *Too bad*, he thought. The idea of falling into the water brought another flash of the lagoon, the severed leg, the head bobbing, and he shuddered.

"What's with you? *I'm* one with the goddamn sprained ankle!"

"You'll live, for Christ's sake!" He was too tired and shook up to sugarcoat it.

Lauren sat up and let out a breath so fierce Ian would not have been surprised if it had been flames. "Yes, I will. But maybe *you* won't. Kind of depends on the statute of limitations, doesn't it?"

He didn't answer. What was the point? But a picture of the local chip shop, the smells and sounds—fried fish and Britney Spears on the radio—were on his mind, the stick-up, a dare, part of the Fallowfield Mad Dogs initiation, and Ian Lumley, fifteen years old, angry at the world but scared shitless.

"I ain't doin' it," he said. But his mate Teddy had said, "Why not?" And so, drunk and stoned, bandannas over their faces, they waited till the shop was empty except for the counterman, a pimply-faced kid, then burst in, shouting, "Hand over yer cash!" waving the illegal untraceable pistols they'd gotten from the gang leaders, Ian so nervous he thought he'd piss himself. But it was over fast, they were outside and free, laughing like hyenas until the pimply-faced kid came after them, hollering, "I know you, Teddy and Ian from fuckin' Fallowfield! I know you!"

Fatal error. Teddy waved his gun, "Shut up, shut up, you don't know me from shite!"

The kid so stupid he kept coming, kept shouting, "I know you, I know you!"

Teddy aimed his pistol, but Ian knocked it from his hand. Teddy cursed, then grabbed Ian's hand, aimed his gun and squeezed his fingers. Ian could still feel the pistol jerk in his hand, hear the *pop-pop*, then both of them running, lungs aching. Ian looked back only once, saw the kid on the ground, blood puddling.

"Jesus Christ, Teddy!" was the only thing he said.

For a while it was a story in the local paper, the coppers looking at gang members in Gooch Close and Cheetham Hill, but no one was arrested. The story eventually faded away for everyone except Ian, who saw it in his mind three, four times a day and every night, that stupid pimply-faced kid shouting, *I know you, I know you*, and falling.

He and Teddy didn't talk about it, ever, not till after the Bleedin' Drunks had broken up and Teddy was arrested for grand theft. "I won't rat you out, mate." Teddy's last words before he was sent to Hindley, where he died in a gang fight. Ian, the only one left who knew what had happened and only admitted it once. To Lauren, one drunken night when they were young and in love. "Oh my God, Ian, *really*? I'm...shocked." Though the look on her face said something else, that she was turned on.

84

A half hour later, Nicky and Sabrina asked if Lauren and Ian were ready to go.

Lauren struggled to get out of bed. "Ian, help me!"

Ian got an arm around her waist and hoisted her up, but when she tried to stand on her own, she couldn't. And her ankle looked bad, swollen and turning blue.

"Fuck," she said, hobbling on one foot until she gave up and collapsed back on the bed. "I'm not going to make it," she said, choking back tears.

"You'll be okay, honey." Sabrina took in the vials of drugs lined up on Lauren's night table. "Take a pill and relax."

"They'll come back for you," Nicky said.

"*Who?*" Lauren cried.

"The captain and his first mate. They have to come back for the luggage and..." He stopped, didn't want to say it, *the dead bodies*.

Lauren let her head sink back against the pillow.

"You can ride in the wheelbarrow, love," Ian said with a grin.

"I'm sure they've got a stretcher on the boat," Nicky said.

"At least *one* of you cares," Lauren said, glaring at Ian. "You'll make sure they come back for me, that I'll be okay?"

"Of course," Sabrina said. "How could we forget to do that?"

"You promise?"

"Don't be silly, Lauren. Of course we'll be back and you'll be fine."

"Say it, that you promise." Lauren gripped Sabrina's hand.

"I promise," Sabrina said, and leaned down for a quick hug. "Now rest that ankle. We'll be back soon and with a stretcher. Because I'm not going to carry you, bitch!" She laughed and Lauren managed one too.

"Come on," Nicky said. "We need to get going."

Lauren tried getting comfortable in bed while the rest of the group arranged their luggage downstairs and prepared to leave. She could hear them chattering as they put on slickers and sprayed themselves with DEET, thinking maybe this was it, God's punishment for what she had done. She didn't believe in God, but she believed in karma.

"That damn board meeting," she mumbled to herself, all that was needed to put her back there, the company's in-house pharmacist alerting them to their wonder drug's highly addictive nature and the potential for death.

"Is that our problem?" she'd said. "If a patient can't control themself?" A point she argued until almost everyone voted with her to keep the information quiet. It had been early enough in the process to make changes or at least warn the doctors they were telling it was perfectly safe, but the drug was already a success and showing signs of becoming their biggest moneymaker ever, and Lauren believed what she'd said, that people could make their own choices, something she continued to tell herself for years, even when she knew it was a lie.

Ian's peck on her cheek startled Lauren back to the moment.

"See you, love."

"Where do you think you're going?"

"To the boat."

"Are you kidding? No way you're leaving me here alone."

"You don't need me, love. You're dumpin' me the minute we're back home, remember?"

Lauren sat up, her body rigid with fury and desperation. "You can't leave me, Ian. I forbid it! What if an animal breaks in or…there *is* a killer here!"

"Oh, come now, Petal, you'll be just hunky-dory." He turned to go, Lauren shouting after him.

"Don't you dare leave me, Ian. You hear me?"

He glanced over his shoulder, "Yes, love?"

Serious now: "What will it take for you to stay?"

Nicky shouted from downstairs. "Ian, you coming?"

"Just a minute!" Ian shouted back. Then to Lauren, repeating her question back to her, "What will it take? Let me think." He tapped a finger against his chin. "First off, a promise, in writing, that you ain't ever callin' them Manchester coppers."

"You know I wasn't going to do that," she said.

"*In writing*, love."

"Fine. What else?"

"I reckon a million for every bloody year we been together."

"That's twenty million dollars. Are you insane?"

"I don't think so, Petal. Oh, and I'll need a bit more to get me bandmates over here and that club, the Wilson, back on its feet. Better make that twenty-five, hidden costs and all."

"You're out of your mind!"

"I don't think so, love." Ian grinned. "Twenty-five mil is not going to make a dent in your six, or is it seven, billion."

"We have a prenup, remember?" Lauren folded her arms across her chest. "You get what you were wearing on your back when we got married, and nothing more."

"Okay, love, have it your way. Stay here. *Alone.* Ta." He waved and started out of the room again.

"*Ian! Get back here!*"

He peeked back in. "Yes, love?"

"*Fine*," she said, seething but resigned. "I'll give you what you want."

"And the guarantee, no call to the coppers?"

"Yes, yes, I already said that."

"Mint. Let's make it official." He found a sheet of hotel stationery, handed it to her along with a pen, then dictated, "I, Lauren Ziff...promise I will not tell nothin' to the Manchester coppers."

"I already said I wouldn't do that."

"Just write it down, love, in your own words. Your English is better than mine. Okay, again, I, Lauren Ziff, bequeath... no, *gift*, that's better for tax purposes, twenty-five million U.S. dollars to my loving husband, Ian Lumley, even if we separate, divorce, or I die." He paused. "You gettin' all that, love?"

"*Yess*," she hissed.

"This contract negates any former prenuptial agreement," he went on. "Now, sign and date it."

Lauren scribbled her signature so hard the paper almost tore. "That it?"

"Actually, no, love. Add that you'll pay any taxes I may incur. The IRS can get a little greedy. You got that?"

Another hissed "Yess."

Ian took the paper, went to the doorway, and called for Nicky.

A minute later, Nicky appeared. "You ready to go?"

"I need you to be a witness." Ian handed him the paper. "Sign and date this, will you, lad?"

"What is it?"

"Just a little agreement between me and the trouble and strife. Have a look."

Nicky skimmed it, his face lighting up, his dream reawakened, but he could see Lauren was steaming so he said nothing, just signed.

"Okay, mate, now you and the others go on." Ian folded the

agreement into his pants pocket. "I'll be staying with me beloved wife. After all, it's a husband's duty." He patted Lauren's shoulder. "And, lad, don't let the first mate forget that wheelbarrow when he comes back for poor ol' Lauren here."

"Fuck you," she said.

"What's going on up there?" Jasmin asked when Nicky rejoined the group.

"They're fighting," he said.

"Such a fun couple," Jasmin said.

"She's…disappointed is all," Sabrina said.

"Aren't we all," Jasmin said, then turned to Nicky. "I hope we can be just like them when we grow up, don't you?"

Sabrina shot her son a look, but it was Jasmin who gave her a tight-lipped smile.

"We'd better get going," Nicky said.

85

The rain was heavy. The pond had spilled over its natural stone border, a few koi flopping on the ground, gills pulsing, gasping for breath. The lagoon had risen too, no visible body parts, thank God, but it made the house look postapocalyptic, its foundation half underwater.

"Another day of this, and the boat could have sailed right to our front door!" Sabrina said and forced a laugh.

The path was difficult to find, its entrance overgrown, but they found it, propelled by the singular thought of meeting the boat and getting off the island.

Only a few feet in, huge palm trees hid the sky, making the path hard to navigate. Another couple of yards, the once narrow stream had flooded, sending brackish water up to their ankles.

Jasmin grasped Nicky's arm as they trudged forward, pushing aside pods of poison berries and bloated frogs floating on the surface. "It's like one of the plagues!"

"More than *one*!" Sabrina said. She noticed Frank was struggling, his breath labored, and she asked if he was okay.

"Sure!" he said, trying to imagine he was playing a role in a disaster film, though he could feel his heart straining.

"Aren't we there yet?" Jasmin asked, a quick look over her shoulder to see if anyone was following them: *the phantom killer*? She shivered though it was so hot she could hardly breathe.

"It's not far," Nicky said though he'd lost all sense of time and distance. He looped his arm around Jasmin's waist as they made their way through the swampy water, all of them trying to ignore the heat and dead frogs and iguanas perched on upturned tree trunks and the rotten, sulfurous smell of decaying animal carcasses that hung in the air.

Sabrina slogged through. *Pure torture*, she thought, reminded of that list she had been making of people who would possibly want to hurt her and the only name she had come up with, *Victor.* But it wasn't possible; the man was dead. Still, she looked back and up into the trees, half expecting to see him watching over them, laughing. No, she was going crazy, that was all.

"We're almost there," Nicky said, though he wasn't sure. His head felt on fire, images of people overdosing mixed with dive-bombing sharks and his father telling him he had no talent. His father, who was dead yet still manipulating him.

The minutes dragged on until they finally caught a glimpse of light through the trees.

86

The beach felt like an entirely different ecosystem, cold and damp, salt spraying from the waves crashing onto the shore. The small group stared out to sea for signs of the yacht, though seeing past the thick fog was almost impossible.

"It will be here soon," Nicky said, still playing the hopeful leader.

Weary from their trek, they hunkered down on the sand, shivering in their slickers. It was ten, fifteen minutes before anyone spoke. Then Frank looked around and said, "Where's Schwegler?"

Nicky glanced back toward the path. "Shit, did we lose him along the way?"

"I don't remember seeing him at all," Sabrina said. None of them did.

Nicky got up, was about to recheck the path, but Jasmin grabbed hold of his arm and tugged him down. "No way you're going back there."

"He'll miss the boat," Nicky said.

"No, he won't," Frank said. "If he's at the hotel, the first mate can get him when he goes back for Lauren and Ian."

"I was sort of hoping never to see him again," Jasmin said and shivered.

Nicky put his arm around her. He could feel his mother watching them. He wanted to say, *Don't worry, it's nothing*. He'd made up his mind: Once he got home, he and Jasmin were finished. He didn't care if she got most of the inheritance. He never believed she would share it with him anyway, not that he'd have shared anything with her.

The wind picked up, blowing sand and pebbles and bits of shell, the fog thickening.

"Jesus," Sabrina said. "What next? We've already had frogs. Locusts? Boils?"

"I think it's killing the firstborn," Nicky said and wondered if his father would actually try to kill him, his firstborn and only son.

"How will we see the boat?" Jasmin asked.

"Don't worry," Frank said. "We'll *hear* it."

But all they heard were the wind and the waves, the seagulls and the eerie rattling call of kingfishers.

Then someone was shouting.

A moment of excitement until they realized it was not coming from the direction of the sea.

"You left me behind!" Schwegler emerged from the path, muddy, sweating, and breathless.

"Where the hell were you?" Nicky asked.

"Asleep. In my room. You might have had the decency to wake me."

"It's not my job to be decent," Nicky said.

"And you are not!" Schwegler said. "But I thought that you were in charge." He sagged heavily onto the sand and let out a grunt. "So, the boat, it is late?"

No one answered, all of them holding their breath.

A half hour passed, the sun, a pale ghost behind the clouds, sinking lower in the sky.

Another twenty minutes. Then thirty. No one dared to say anything until Jasmin blurted it out: "*It's not coming!*"

"Don't say that!" Sabrina shouted, her words almost lost under the howling wind and surf.

Nicky stood and gazed out to sea, a misty gray mass merging with the sky. "It's this damn fog."

"Right. It's delayed, that's all," Frank said with actorish optimism.

They were all standing now, facing the sea, trying to see beyond the fog by sheer will and blind faith.

When another twenty minutes passed, Sabrina said, "It's not going to make it, is it?"

"You're *wrong*!" This time it was Jasmin who was shouting, almost crying, "It *is* coming! *It has to*!"

But when more time dragged by and the fog thickened and the tide rolled in and they had to back up several feet or get soaked, and when that pale ghostly sun was practically sleeping on the murky horizon, whatever rays of hope they had, shattered into shards of despair.

Had Victor brought them all here to abandon them? The unspoken thought in almost everyone's mind.

"We've got to go back," Nicky said, resigned. "Before it's too dark to see."

"No!" Jasmin dug her feet into the sand. "I won't go back there! I'm staying here."

"I will stay with you," Schwegler said.

Jasmin looked at him and moaned, "God, no!" Then, she tore away from the group and started running down the beach.

Nicky raced after her, caught her, and held her. "We can't stay here, Jas." She was shivering in his arms, and her rare vulnerability touched something in him. "In another hour the tide will be high, the beach will be gone, and it will be dark."

"Then I'll wait that hour!" she said. But when the waves lapped at her toes, her eyes filled with tears and she fell against Nicky with a sob and let him lead her back to the group.

The path was so dark they had to hold on to each other as they plodded forward, practically blind, the hot air electrified by the buzz of insects and birdcalls, the steady patter of rain as they splashed through puddles and sloshed through mud. Mosquitoes nipped at their flesh, shadowy trees swayed like Halloween witches, and the loamy, sulfurous smell made it hard to breathe. But if anyone noticed, they didn't say, only cursed under their breath and swatted at bugs as they marched on, their spirits dampened and nearly broken.

87

The hotel finally put in an appearance shimmering like a mirage, there and not there, windows casting beams of light across the lagoon, which had risen even higher, its waters lapping up to the front door.

Inside, shoes and slickers were discarded in a heap.

"I need a drink!" Jasmin's first words.

"Me too!" Sabrina said.

The table was a mess of crumbs and dirty dishes. They pushed everything aside while they got the last of the clean glasses and poured wine, whiskey, vodka, and port, the air heavy with the scent of alcohol and frustration.

"Lauren and Ian must be asleep," Nicky said. "I'll wake them."

"Why bother?" Jasmin said. "Just to give them the bad news?"

Rain streaked the windows and lightning lit up the room, highlighting the mess, stark and fast, then quickly faded.

By the second round of drinks, Nicky announced he was going to sleep, temptation gnawing away at his AA resolve.

Jasmin said she would join him in a minute, and Sabrina gave her another look though at this point she hardly cared.

Schwegler sat wearily at one end of the table, drinking and smoking one of his elegant cigarettes. Frank grubbed one and puffed on it though he was coughing.

The minutes crawled by, the time blurred by alcohol and gloom.

"Can't we charter a boat or something?" Jasmin asked, more than a little desperation in her voice.

"Oh, *sure*," Sabrina said. "Why didn't *I* think of that?"

"Look, we'll be getting out of here tomorrow," Frank said.

"We said that yesterday!" Jasmin said, almost a sob, and looked over her shoulder for the umpteenth time.

"What are you looking for?" Sabrina asked her.

"I don't know, the boogeyman?"

No one laughed; everyone looking over their shoulders as well.

"The boat has to get through eventually," Frank said. "Or they'll send a helicopter—or something."

"A *helicopter*?" Jasmin gave him a pathetic look. "This isn't one of your dumb movies, Frank!"

"Don't take it out on me!" he snarled at her.

"Fuck it," she said. "I'm going to bed. Where's Nicky?"

"He went upstairs an hour ago," Sabrina said. "Didn't you notice?" Even now she couldn't help being snarky.

Jasmin was too tired and miserable to answer. She pushed away from the table and the others did too.

The elevator was making its slow ascent, each of them tucked into a corner, when the house was rocked by more thunder and lighting, and the elevator jerked to a stop. Its interior light dimmed, then died.

"*No! Fuck, no!*" Jasmin said, hitting all the elevators buttons.

"Fuck is right," Frank said, trying to catch his breath, but he grabbed her hand. "You're going to break it."

She swatted him away. "It *is* broken, you moron!"

The view through the metal gate showed they were stuck a couple of feet below the landing.

"You Americans are always so impatient," Schwegler said. "Give it a minute and it will come back on."

But several minutes passed and it didn't. Then Jasmin was hitting the buttons again and shouting for help.

"Stop!" This time it was Schwegler who grabbed her hand.

"Don't touch me!" Jasmin tugged her hand away, practically slapped him. Her anxiety felt like bugs were crawling inside her body, into her mind.

"Fine," he said. "Break it so we will be stuck here forever."

"Please, everyone, relax!" Sabrina was trying hard to do that herself.

"We're marooned on this fucking island in a broken elevator, and you want me to relax! *Fuck, fuck, fuck!*" Jasmin was shrieking.

Sabrina put her arm around her, the two of them trembling together. "I know, honey, I know. But the power will come back. You'll see."

"Right." Frank said, trying to still his nerves and his heart. "Just give it a minute."

And they did, everyone holding their breath, the crowded space charged with anxiety.

"Fuck!" Jasmin said again.

A minute later Nicky was leaning over, peering into the cab. "Hang on," he said, and disappeared, Jasmin frantically shouting after him to come back.

"I just needed this." He was back at the grate, Swiss Army knife in hand, using the heaviest blade to wedge the gate open just enough to tug it back. Then, one by one he helped them out and into the hotel's dark hallway.

"I can't see a thing," Jasmin said.

"The hurricane lamps!" Sabrina said.

88

Sabrina led the way, the hurricane lamp in her hand casting shadows along the dark corridor.

"This just gets better and better," Jasmin said. "Where were you?" she asked Nicky.

"Getting your ass out of the elevator, remember?"

"I meant before that."

"In my room staring at the ceiling. That okay with you?"

Everyone was tired and touchy, frustrated, on edge, scared.

They waited at Schwegler's door until he found the hurricane lamp in his room and got it lit. There was another lamp in Jasmin's room.

"Aren't you coming in?" she asked Nicky, way beyond caring what Sabrina thought.

"In a bit."

"Why? You need more time to stare at your ceiling?" She was practically vibrating in place; her nerves ending felt electrified.

"I want to see my mother to her room first."

"I can do that," Frank said. All pretenses clearly off.

Nicky controlled his comments, if not his emotions. He knew his mother had had a series of short-lived affairs since she'd left his father. He didn't see Frank lasting beyond the weekend, though he was still getting his head around the fact that his mother had slept with his father's brother and was doing it again.

"I'll walk you back to your room," Sabrina said to Nicky. "You haven't got a lamp." She didn't wait for his answer, leading the way again. With the electricity off and the AC shut down, the hallway was already hot and close. "Your room? Or *Jasmin's*?" she asked.

Her words were punctuated by a loud clap of thunder. A second later, lightning lit up the hallway, the large gold room numbers glittering for a few seconds, one door ajar.

Nicky told his mother to wait, but she followed with the lamp as he went to the open door and peeked in.

The room reeked of weed and it was dark, just enough light from the lamp, the shadows starting to fill in.

89

"Oh, sorry." Sabrina stepped back, embarrassed. "Let's go," she said to Nicky.

He took the lamp from her hand and held it up. "Wait," he said, a swath of amber light illuminated the couple in bed along with the side tables, vials of pills, an ashtray overflowing with roach butts.

"Let them sleep it off," Sabrina said.

Nicky raised the lamp higher, caught the light reflecting off something slick and shiny, then took a few steps in.

"What are you doing?" Sabrina whispered. "*Come on*."

But Nicky moved closer because he saw it now, something over their heads, something translucent, their faces beneath like a blurry watercolor, their lips almost touching in a veiled kiss.

Sabrina saw it too. A second later, Jasmin was there. And behind her, Schwegler. Then Frank, who was immediately shouting, "Jesus Christ! Get those bags off their heads!"

He lunged past Nicky and the others, grabbed hold of one bag, then the other and tore them off. Lauren and Ian's heads lolled back and forth, the torn plastic hanging below their blue-white faces like a layer of ragged skin. Frank slapped their cheeks and pounded their chests. Then he leaned over, opened Lauren's mouth, and pressed his lips against hers, pinching her nostrils and breathing into her mouth. When he came up for air, he tugged Nicky down with him: "Do for the same—*for him!*"

Nicky took a deep breath and forced Ian's mouth open. Then he laid his lips on Ian's and let the breath out. Over and over, breaths were inhaled and exhaled while the rest of the group stood back, watching in shock as the two men tried to breathe life into two lifeless bodies.

90

"Let it be," Schwegler finally said. "They are gone."

Nicky gazed down at Ian's ashen face, his inky hair crushed and flattened.

For a moment no one said anything, gripped by shock and fear, the room filled with the sounds of Frank and Nicky trying to catch their breath, and the wind and rain spattering against windows.

Then Jasmin was muttering, her body shivering uncontrollably. "Oh my God, Oh my God, Oh my God…"

Sabrina stared at the bodies, the torn plastic. "I promised her we would come back for her, that she would be okay! I *promised*!"

"There's nothing we can do." Nicky stroked his mother's back, trying to calm her, trying to calm himself.

Frank put his arm around Sabrina, but she pulled away, an image blinking in her mind. "*The Lovers*," she said, her voice a hoarse whisper.

"What are you talking about?" Jasmin said.

"It's…a painting…by René Magritte…a famous one…" The words tumbling out as she described it. "A man—and a woman—their heads sheathed in cloth, exchanging a blind kiss."

Everyone stared from Sabrina to the dead bodies, the air in the room tingling with electricity and dread.

"That's *crazy*!" Jasmin said, panic rising while she tried to take in what Sabrina was suggesting, that the bodies had been posed. "Why,

why would anyone…? It makes no sense!" But nothing about the weekend made sense.

"It's a coincidence," Frank said. "It has to be. That's all."

"Maybe," Sabrina said. "But someone took the time to wrap their heads."

Frank nodded. "*They* did. I mean, *he* did, or *she* did, you know, took turns and…" He was trying hard to make sense of it.

Nicky was straining to sort out his feelings, the mix of shock and sadness, of losing someone he thought would become a friend, and the loss of his club dream, a thought that filled him with shame. "You're saying that Ian killed Lauren, then himself?"

"Or maybe she killed him and then—" Frank wasn't sure what to think, his mind scrambling, the room so hot he could hardly breathe.

"*Why* would they do that?" Sabrina asked, the idea of it incomprehensible, *crazy.* She stared at Lauren's face, then Ian's, still not believing it, that they were gone.

"A suicide pact," Schwegler suggested, sounding cool, dispassionate.

"No, no way." Nicky hadn't bought the idea of suicide before and wasn't buying it now. Then he remembered his last conversation with Ian, the contract he had witnessed, pictured Ian slipping it into his pocket. *Where was it?*

Jasmin was wringing her hands, unable to stand still. "You know what I think, there's an evil spirit on this island, a demon or a, a curse!" She spun around, the lamps casting shadows across the walls and the primitive masks, palm leaves batting against the windows. For a moment she was four years old at her grandmother's feet, hearing the old woman go on about curses and ghosts and *yaoguai,* supernatural creatures and spiteful animal spirits and fallen celestial beings. "Villain hitting! That's what it is!" she shouted, then whispered, "*Da siu yan*," the term her grandmother had used when speaking of black magic and cursing her enemies.

Nicky touched her shoulder, told her to calm her down, but she slapped his hand away.

"I will *not* calm down!"

Sabrina kept staring at the bodies, looking from Lauren to Ian, still seeing the Magritte painting, shaking now, her nerves like exposed wires. "We have to get out of here!"

"It'll be okay, baby," Frank said, getting his arm around her.

"What about this is *okay*, Frank? Tell me!" She pulled away from him.

"It's a curse! A demon! It has to be!" Jasmin cried. "There was no one else on the island. We searched, and we were all on the beach when this happened."

"Not all of us," Frank said, slowly raising his eyes toward Schwegler.

The others' followed his glance.

"That's right!" Jasmin said, the accusation bringing her back to reality. "You were late to the beach, very late. It had to be you!"

"I–I was asleep," Schwegler said, fumbling the words. "In my room."

"So you say." Jasmin pointed at him, her hand shaking.

"*Bitte, das ist lächerlich.* Ridiculous."

"You were the only one here in the hotel with them." Frank said, his voice low now and threatening.

"What about *him*?" Schwegler turned and aimed a finger at Nicky. "Where were *you* all that time we were downstairs drinking?"

Nicky took a step closer to Schwegler, face-to-face, his hand raised in a fist ready to strike.

"Stop it!" Sabrina cried. "Everyone, just stop!"

Frank reached down and touched Lauren's wrist. "She's ice-cold, Schwegler, clearly dead for a while now, and *you're* the only one who had time to do it."

"Frank is right!" Jasmin said. "There was no one else!"

"What about it, Schwegler?" Nicky stood his ground, demanding.

"Why would I do such a thing?" Schwegler managed to keep his tone cool, but he'd stabbed a cigarette into his mouth and his hand was shaking so badly he could not get it lit.

"Stop," Sabrina said again. "We're all exhausted, going crazy from this place and the deaths. It's all too much. But Mr. Schwegler is right, it *is* ridiculous! He had no reason to do such a thing." She wasn't sure if what she said was true, but she hoped it was because when this nightmare was over, she wanted Schwegler to remember she had been on his side.

Schwegler smiled at her, lips parting to reveal his small discolored teeth and Sabrina returned it, hoping she was not defending a killer.

"*Really*, Mother?" Nicky could see what she was doing, why she was defending Schwegler.

"'Really, Mother,' *what*?" Sabrina turned toward her son and hissed: "Just remember I know everything you've done, *everything.* So don't you *dare* judge me!"

Her words more than stung; they sent Nicky reeling back in time to a dimly lit basement, moving among the crackheads and addicts, the magnanimous rich boy distributing dope, his fingers tapping his girlfriend's arm, the look of terror and blind faith in her eyes. *You love me, right, Nicky?* while he found a vein and slipped the needle in. *You'll be fine, I promise, trust me, you're going to love it*. Then her lids fluttered, and her body went limp in his arms, and he was shouting her name over and over, but too late. He'd never even gotten to try the smack. But the worst part? He left her there. Along with the others, not knowing how many of them had tried it. Flashing red lights and ambulance sirens streaking past him only blocks from the scene, his head down and collar up, a scared young man on a dark street not looking back.

He unconsciously touched his chin, feeling the scar beneath his heavy stubble, a memento of that night, falling on his way out of that basement, a deep gash that was never treated. *Better not see a doctor, who knows what they will ask.* His father's words. The scar a constant reminder of what had happened, not that he needed any physical proof to remember, the wound a lot deeper than his flesh.

"Klonopin and tramadol," Jasmin said.

"What?" Nicky looked around, getting his bearings.

"Tranquilizers and painkillers," Jasmin said. She was going through the vials on Lauren's bedside table and holding them up.

"Are you saying they took them?" Frank asked, looking down at the bodies.

"Maybe," she said. "But it doesn't matter. *I'm* taking them!" She needed something, anything to calm her jangled nerves.

Nicky had tugged himself out of the past, but needed an answer, unable to stop himself from going through Ian's pockets.

"What are you *doing*?" Sabrina cried.

"There was a paper, a contract Ian had." He felt crazy, a hand in Ian's pocket as he stared up at Schwegler. "Did you take it?"

Schwegler returned his stare, sweat beading up on the back of his neck. *The contract with Bagdasarian? How does he know?* "I have no idea what you are talking about."

Nicky looked at him, saw the lie in his eyes. "You *did* take it! Give it to me!"

Sabrina glared at her son. "What are you talking about? Have you lost your mind?"

"He stole something from Ian—a contract that concerns me."

"Concerns *you*?" Sabina stared at him. "*How?*"

Jasmin stared too. Had Nicky made some sort of contract with Ian about his inheritance? Her mind was scrambled, the arrangement she'd made with Nicky, her grandmother's incantations, the bar, the man, tossing a blond wig into a trash can, horns blaring.

Nicky was trying to control himself but couldn't. He wanted that contract, the money for the club. "What did you do with it?" he shouted at Schwegler.

Now Schwegler realized Nicky was talking about something else entirely, that this contract had nothing to do with him or Bagdasarian. "You are mistaken," he said coolly.

Nicky had his hands under Ian, searching for the contract, Ian's body undulating.

"Nicky!" his mother shrieked. "*Stop!*"

That's when he saw what he was doing and took a step back, feeling as if he might be ill, a realization washing over him that the contract meant nothing, that Lauren and Ian were dead, and the contract had been between *them*, not *him*. Though it didn't matter. None of this mattered. "Oh God." He took in the faces staring at him. "I'm sorry," he said, then looked down at Ian and said it again, "I'm sorry, my friend, so sorry." Tears gathered behind his lids while he tried to catch his breath and regain what little was left of his dignity and decency.

Sabrina laid her hand on his back. "Forgive me," she said to him, her voice trembling. "I didn't mean to…"

They were all losing it.

Jasmin was shaking Lauren's pills into her palm, some from each vial. "I'm taking these. I *need* them!"

"Give me some," Sabrina said and took a handful, then offered them to Schwegler.

He waved them away. "I do not take drugs." A picture of his

mother laid out in her black dress shuddered through his mind, her face as blue-white as the corpses on the bed.

Frank plucked a half-smoked reefer from the ashtray on Ian's side of the bed, along with several fresh ones.

Nicky watched them all, feeling sick and sobered—sick of them, sick of himself, chastened and humiliated. "I'm going to my room." He was desperate to get away from them and the drugs, but mostly he wanted to get away from himself.

"We all should go to our rooms," Schwegler said.

"And lock your doors," Frank added, watching them all leave, clutching Ian's stash of weed in his hand.

91

Light from the hurricane lamp picked out the mess Sabrina had left behind in her rush to leave—a pair of shoes on the floor, a blouse draped over a chair—she'd had no intention of ever coming back. She had brought a bottle of port from the kitchen and poured them each a glass. They needed something, anything, to steady their nerves.

The room was stifling, and Sabrina asked Frank to open the window.

"You mind if the floor gets wet?" he asked.

"People are dying all around us and you care if the floor gets wet?" she snapped, then took a breath, knew she was taking out her anxiety on Frank, but she was tired of his questions, tired of him too. How quickly that had happened. If she were not afraid to be alone, she would tell him to leave.

"What's gotten into you?"

"Are you *kidding*? Do I have to say it *again*, that people are *dying*? Jesus, Frank." She heard Lauren telling her to take care of her dreams and her eyes filled with tears.

"I'm sorry," he said, and he was, but annoyed too, that she was taking out her frustration on him. He opened the window, listened to thunder rumbling in the distance, and wondered if the storm was retreating, or a new one was brewing.

Sabrina went through the pills she'd taken from Lauren, no longer sure which was which.

Frank took one and held it up to the lamp. "Klonopin," he said. "I used to take them." He popped the pill into his mouth, then lit one of Ian's joints and took a toke.

"Isn't that a bit much, Frank?"

Frank held the smoke in his lungs, his voice coming out in a squeak. "Why not?"

He had a point. After all they'd been through, Sabrina couldn't think of a single reason not to get thoroughly wasted. She washed a pill down with her coconut water, chased it with port, even took a hit off Frank's joint.

"Look who's talking!" Frank said and dared a laugh, and she had to laugh too, both giddy with sadness and fear.

Sabrina stripped off her clothes and sank onto the bed, the glass of port balanced in her hand. Frank joined her, took a hit off the joint, set it aside, then lit a cigarette, inhaled, and coughed.

"You should ease up on those."

"Which one?"

"*Both*."

He took a few more puffs, put the cigarette out, and kissed her cheek. "I'll stop once we get home."

We? Sabrina didn't think so. She lay back, already feeling the drug and booze loosen her muscles and her mind, but with it, a nagging thought rose to the surface. "Do you think we're being punished?"

"For what?"

"What we did to Sarah."

"Oh, that."

"Yes, *that*."

"Sarah." He said her name on an exhale, sounding weary. Sarah, his long-suffering, prone-to-depression wife, who had put up with his philandering, all the starlets and wannabes eager to fuck the latest Hollywood hunk. Until his affair with Sabrina. *She's your brother's wife, for Christ's sake!* Followed by fights and tears and threats of suicide. What Frank liked to call *the usual Sarah drama*.

He reached for the joint and took another toke but rather than blur the past, it brought it back in high definition—the police station's beige walls, the detective's dour face as he described the accident: *Her car went off the cliff but there were no skid marks. It looked almost...intentional. Was your wife depressed?* A mix of sympathy and suspicion in his tone, though he'd asked for Frank's autograph.

After he was cleared of any wrongdoing, Frank was deluged with interviews and publicity, the story in every tabloid: *Movie Star's Wife: Accident or Suicide?* Not the worst PR as he had a film coming out, one everyone knew was a dud. He told all the reporters the same thing, *I'm devastated*, when in fact what he'd felt was relief. He was free.

"We knew she was unstable," Sabrina said. "She'd had shock treatments more than once."

"Can we not talk about this?" he said, sounding annoyed.

The truth was that Sabrina hadn't cared about Sarah back then, hadn't even thought about her. Now she had to wonder if this was all some kind of karma, her selfish disregard coming back to haunt her. "It was a mistake, and here we are making the same mistake all over again."

"Is that what this is, what *I* am, a *mistake*?"

Sabrina managed a halfhearted no, though she knew it *was* a mistake. She didn't want to be with Frank, didn't want to be with any man. She'd had enough of the narcissistic D'Arcangelo brothers! What she wanted was to take care of herself, her dreams and her career. She took a sip of port, her hand unsteady, and it spilled, dark ruby splotches staining the sheets. "Damn!"

"Forget it." Frank pushed the sheets aside, then touched her shoulder, his hand moving over her breast.

Sabrina pulled away. "Are you kidding?"

"Why? Are you mad at me?"

"It's not about *you*, Frank! People have *died*! I'm upset and *scared*. Aren't you?"

"*Sure*," he said, anger and frustration bubbling up in him, her rejection palpable and intolerable, the idea of going back to his empty life unbearable. Was she breaking up with him? He thought he would rather kill her than lose her.

Sabrina could feel him seething beside her, the heat radiating off his body. She shifted away, reached for her bottle of coconut water and polished it off. "I'm tense, on edge from everything that's happened. Can't you understand that?" She felt drained, exhausted from the past three days, and from Frank, but so drowsy she could barely keep her eyes open.

"Of course," Frank said, trying hard to sound patient though he was still bristling, his mind replaying the nonstop rejections of his career, his life, now Sabrina. He wanted to confront her, demand to know why she had led him on if she thought he was nothing more than a *mistake*. But the weed and the pill had made his brain fuzzy, and by the time he'd found the words, Sabrina was asleep.

92

"I feel like I'm unraveling!" Jasmin popped one of Lauren's pills.

"You'll be okay," Nicky said, hollow words but he was not sure if her panicked little girl act was real or not. It was so totally out of character. Though he felt it too, saw himself going through Ian's pockets, out of control, this hellish weekend enough to unravel anyone. He wanted one of those pills so badly it scared him.

"Will I be okay, *really*?" Her voice was so plaintive that it touched something in him.

"I promise you will," he said, a promise he couldn't possibly keep, that old memory slipping into his mind again the way he had slipped the needle into his girlfriend's arm saying the same words: *I promise you'll be okay.*

They undressed and lay naked on top of the covers, sweating, Nicky fighting his cravings, clenching and unclenching his fists.

"You should take something," she said.

"You know I can't."

"How about some distraction then?" She rolled toward him, her hand on his chest.

"Really? *Now?*" Only minutes ago, she had been scared, falling apart.

"I need it," she said, then tapped the Swiss Army knife on his bedside table and laughed nervously. "Unless you're planning to kill me and keep all the inheritance."

So, she wasn't *that* unraveled. "I just might."

She carefully placed another pill on the tip of her tongue, displayed it for him before she rolled her tongue back and swallowed. "You *sure* you don't want one?"

He sat up irritated, his hunger for the pill, his resolve close to crumbling. "I'm leaving."

"*No, you can't!*" She grabbed his arm. "I'm sorry, I was teasing. *Please* don't leave me alone!"

He lay back and reached for his knife. "I *should* kill you."

Jasmin plucked it from his hand, held it a moment. "Suppose I kill *you*," she said, then shuddered, seeing an image of her father, who had left when she was still a child but not before leaving his mark, something you could not see but always there, a scar, her secret shame that she would never forget or forgive.

"You okay?"

Jasmin barely nodded, trapped in the memory now, reliving it, tracking him down, the father she hardly knew, finding him and following him, observing him from a distance with his new wife and family, no idea what she would do until that afternoon when she'd stood at the edge of a playground and watched him pushing his daughter on a swing, five or six years old and the only kid in the playground not laughing. And she knew. For weeks after, she charted his movements—when he left for work and when he came home, the bar where he stopped for drinks—noting it all down until she was ready. Then she waited outside his office for him to come out in his expensive topcoat, an added insult; he had not given her mother anything.

Jasmin stirred, a flicker from the hurricane lamp tugging her into the present but only for a second before she was back on that dark street, high on cocaine, headlights like shooting stars as she trailed her father into the bar and took the stool beside his, offered him a smile when he looked her way. He didn't recognize her, she was no longer a little girl, seventeen now but looking older with heavy makeup and a blond wig. For a moment she worried she was too old for his taste. Then he smiled back, offered to buy her a drink, his hand on her thigh, all of it still so vivid in her mind, the bar dark and smoky, the music's thumping beat pulsing through her, the television over the bar blaring, a cacophony of distractions, so when the drinks came, she just leaned in and let him kiss her neck while she slipped the roofie into his cocktail.

She had come prepared, waiting until he finished his drink, then cooing, "My place is nearby," and leading him outside. He was already a little wobbly, and she gripped his arm and laughed as they crossed the street, dodging cars and buses, horns blaring, all the time watching and waiting until she saw it, the taxi barreling down the street. A picture of herself as a little girl in a dark bedroom, his shadow looming over her and the smell of him as she shoved him, saw him lurch and fall, the taxi careening, horn blaring, brakes screeching, the sound of metal hitting bone and flesh as she hurried away, dropped her wig into a trash can, and never once looked back, never once felt sorry.

She was shivering beside Nicky though the room was stifling, and he asked again if she was okay. She turned and kissed him hard.

"*Please*," she said, a rare urgency in her voice. "I *need* to get lost."

"You're already lost," he said, kidding, but he was hard, and for a few minutes they did get lost, though Jasmin seemed far away, practically asleep before they had finished.

Nicky lay there listening to the rain, his mind still reeling, the shock and horror of the day, of everything, catching up with him until exhaustion took over and he fell into a jagged sleep.

Was it the thunder and lightning that awakened him? Nicky sat up, surprised he had been sleeping at all. The room was sweltering, his body slick with sweat.

Jasmin was up too. "I heard something."

"Thunder, I think. Go back to sleep."

"Where are those pills?" Her hand groped the side table in the dark.

"You've already taken too many."

"Oh, please," she said. "One more won't kill me."

93

Frank stirred, his brain still foggy from weed and pills and booze. The room felt even hotter than last night, the sky outside the windows dark. He glanced over, surprised to see Sabrina sitting up.

"Oh, you're awake," he said. Her arm was raised as if she were about to speak, but she didn't. "You're still mad at me, is that it?"

When she said nothing, he pulled himself out of bed, annoyed, his body sluggish and sore from yesterday's trek, legs itchy with mosquito bites. He noted the puddle beneath the window, his feet getting wet as he closed it. But a second later he opened it; it was too hot to keep it closed, and Sabrina was right, who cared about a puddle.

In the bathroom, he splashed his face with water and took stock of the gray in his stubble, his puffy eyes. He would need a blepharoplasty, upper *and* lower lids, if he was going to revive his career. He felt awful, headachy and hungover, and irritated with Sabrina, the way she was still punishing him or, worse, dismissing him. But he had to make it okay, had to salvage what they had or what he hoped they had.

His clothes were on the bathroom floor in a heap. He pulled on his pants, slipped into his shoes, sniffed the armpits of yesterday's polo shirt. Not great, but out of clean clothes, he tugged it over his head.

He used Sabrina's toothbrush, raked his fingers through his hair, noting the roots were worse. He would have it touched up once he was home and had his inheritance, at a salon this time, like in the old days when he had money, and he would again.

A few steps back into bedroom, the rain was still fanning in from the window, the wind strong, but a few clouds had lifted, the room a bit lighter.

Sabrina was still sitting up. The sheets were draped over her arm and covering one leg, a Rorschach test of last night's wine stains, which looked worse in the daylight.

"I'm going downstairs for a coffee, happy to bring you one," he said, trying to be nice. "We should kiss and make up."

94

Sabrina didn't answer.

"Oh, come on, you can't still be mad at me," Frank said, noticing that she hadn't moved, still sitting upright in the same position, one arm raised. And when he got closer, he saw that her eyes were open, fixed and unblinking.

"Sabrina?" he said, holding his breath as he reached out to touch her. When there was no response, he tapped her again. Then harder, a slight push.

Arm still raised, she tumbled to the side, then fell off the bed, Frank catching her mid-fall, shouting her name, "Sabrina! Sabrina!" his mind filled with panic, unable to think, too frantic to notice the sprig of what might have been Queen Anne's lace that tumbled to the floor along with her, trying to shake her awake, now taking in the bruises around her neck, her beautiful mouth gone slack. "Sabrina! Sabrina!" shouting, then hugging her to him, howling "No!" and cursing, unaware that the bedroom door had been thrown open and Nicky was standing there, army knife in his hand, trying to make sense of the scene.

"What's going on?" Nicky said. Then he was moving toward them, pushing Frank aside and watching, paralyzed, as Sabrina's body fell to the floor.

"N-n-no…no!" Nicky stuttered as he tried to revive her, slapping her cheeks, feeling her cold, naked flesh, his lips on hers trying to breathe life into a lifeless body *again*, this one his mother! Knowing she was gone but refusing to believe it, he searched for a pulse, a breath where there was none. He scooped her into his arms, then fell to his knees and wailed, "Oh God, *no*!"

He saw the blue-purple bruises on her neck and looked up, his eyes wild, and shouted at Frank, "What have you *done*?"

Jasmin, disheveled and disoriented, stood frozen in the doorway, a hand to her mouth that failed to hold back her scream.

95

Nicky was on the floor, his mother's body in his arms, holding her tight, rocking back and forth, and weeping, tears streaking his face as he choked on sobs. After a minute, he set her body down and rose slowly.

"You—" He lurched toward Frank, his mind reeling, explosions behind his eye like sunspots, his army knife out.

Frank faltered. "No, no, I found her like that. I didn't—I could never—" His hands were out in defense as Nicky advanced. "You have to believe me—" He reached out, knocked the knife from Nicky's hand, but not before it sliced his palm.

Nicky kept coming, throwing punches now and kicking until Frank fell. Then he was on him, grunting and swearing, his hands around Frank's neck.

"Nicky! Stop! *Stop!*" Jasmin tugged at Nicky's arms, dug her nails into his hands "You're *killing* him!"

Frank was gasping for breath, his face going blue, but Nicky did not let go.

Then a blur, someone charging into the room, wrenching Nicky's hands from Frank's neck and tugging him away.

Schwegler stood between the two men, breathing hard, Frank on the floor rubbing his throat, gasping for air, Nicky, a few feet away, beside his mother's body, trembling with emotion.

Jasmin laid a hand on Nicky's shoulder, felt the heat and grief coming off him. "We're all going to die," she said in a hushed whisper, her face drained of color, her whole body shaking.

Schwegler attempted to comfort her, an arm around her shoulder, but she shook him off. "Get away from me! You, you could be the killer!"

"*Nein, nein.* It is…" Schwegler aimed a finger at Frank, then at Nicky, his hand shuddering back and forth between them.

Nicky rose, grabbed Frank by the shoulders, and held him. "*Why?*" he asked, his voice fracturing with grief.

"I didn't do *anything! I swear.* We drank wine, we smoked weed, we fell asleep. After that…I don't know what happened… I…"

Schwegler knelt beside Sabrina's body, touched her neck, the bruises. He looked up at Frank. "You expect us to believe you slept through *this*?"

"I don't care what you believe!" Frank gripped his palm, suddenly aware of the knife wound, blood seeping through his fingers. "But, Nicky, *please*, you must *believe* me! I couldn't…" There were tears in his eyes, on his cheeks, and for once he was not playing a part. He came toward Nicky, beseeching, but Nicky shoved him away.

"I need to bury her," was all he said.

"No," Schwegler said. "The grounds, everywhere, are flooded. She could be washed away…lost."

Nicky was numb, but he heard what Schwegler had said and knew he was right. He lifted his mother's body and laid her back on the bed. He closed her eyes and kissed her forehead and wrapped the sheet around her gently.

96

Jasmin made an effort to bandage Frank's hand, her own hands trembling badly, the whole time Frank declaring his innocence, though more softly now, as if something inside him had broken.

Eyes blurred by tears, Nicky looked at Frank, then Jasmin, and finally Schwegler, all that was left of the group, "Go," he said to them. "Get out." Then, he rose and stood beside his mother's body like a sentry.

Jasmin noticed the odd sprig of Queen Anne's lace on the floor. Without thinking, she picked it up and held it but only for a moment, her hands shaking too badly. "I'll stay with you," she said.

"No," Nicky said. "I need to be alone with her. Go to your room. Lock the door. And don't let anyone in but me."

97

Back in his room, Schwegler was trying hard to dispel a memory that had been brought to the surface by Nicky's display of grief: himself at nine years old beside his father at his mother's grave site, his aunt Gertrude, his mother's sister, keening and collapsing in tears, hearing his father's snort of disgust and trying but failing to control his own tears until his father slapped him hard across the face. From that day on, he never shed a public tear.

He waited until his hands stopped shaking and he felt in control again. Then he checked and rechecked his hummingbird pistol.

One thing for certain: He was going to get out of here alive.

98

Nicky sat beside his mother's body, the time impossible to gauge, like the loss itself, like the past few days of murder and madness. His eyes were burning, his throat hot and raw. He had been crying for a long time and felt cried out though the tears kept coming. He ran his hand over the body he had wrapped in a sheet, a palpable throb in his chest.

Was this what heartbreak felt like? He wasn't sure. He'd never felt it before. Never cared for anyone that much. Except himself. And his mother, who he knew always loved him despite his faults and hers. A montage of maternal memories skittered through his brain, impossible to hold on to, and he wondered how long before he forgot them.

He tried hard to think, to be rational. Had Frank done this? But why? And who else would want to do this to her?

How have you helped me or hurt me? His father's question. His father's game.

An idea gnawed at the edge of his subconscious, something he could not see but felt, of something, someone pulling the strings. It was the same inchoate feeling he'd had when they had searched the hotel and grounds.

It was a moment before the thought, like some parasitic worm, worked its way through him, the pieces falling into place—his mother's affair with Frank, the two brothers' estrangement that now made perfect sense: Frank and Sabrina had definitely *hurt* him. Had his father brought them here, brought them all here to play them like pawns in a chess game, to exact revenge? Was he still here? Was he watching?

Nicky felt a chill.

But how? His father was dead. There'd been a *New York Times* obit: "Acclaimed New York Artist Dead at Sixty." Though he had never seen the body. There had been no funeral.

Only this hideous memorial.

Was it possible his father had staged his own death? Or was he going crazy from the insanity and paranoia of the past few days, all of it now fueled by grief?

The image of his father at his first and only art exhibition was back in his mind, the big man, the famous artist holding court, stealing Nicky's thunder, declaring his son's artwork no good, amateurish, and telling him to quit.

No question his father could be cruel. *But could he kill?*

Nicky considered the question.

Maybe. Maybe not.

But he could pay others to do it for him, the way he did so many things, like hire lawyers to shield his son's crime and pay people to paint his paintings.

Images swept across Nicky's brain, assistants and assassins, men in black hiding in the bush, watching and waiting to emerge and strike, taking them out one by one.

99

Jasmin felt like a jack-in-the-box about to pop, images of the murder scenes shuffling through her mind like a tarot deck of horror, an alarm sounding in her brain that would not stop. She had to get out, away from this insanity, away from the killer before *she* was killed!

I can do this!

She had been brought up to see life as a series of goals, challenges, prizes to be won, though she had failed to commit to almost anything—her modeling career, her marriage—always looking for the next best thing, something to give her life *meaning*. She was like a leaky pot that could never be filled. No matter what she got, it was never enough, the pot always draining, leaving her feeling empty again.

She downed another one of Lauren's tranquilizers—*Thank God I have them!*—and rummaged through her things, deciding what to take, what to leave, tossing aside soiled Chanel blouses, torn Dolce & Gabbana slacks, her mud-splattered Jimmy Choo sandals.

She chose a few pairs of clean underwear, a couple of T-shirts, a pair of shorts, stuffed them all into her Prada tote, then slipped into a vintage Alexander McQueen dress, his signature skulls on a bright-red background. Red, the Chinese color for good luck. Then she stepped into her only pair of clean shoes, an impractical pair of stilettos.

Her grandmother was in her head, her mind alive with ghosts, fallen celestial beings, and supernatural creatures. *Yaoguai!*

Makeup out, she darkened her brows, mascaraed her lashes, swept blush across her cheeks, and added bright-red lipstick. She had to look good. No doubt, there would be reporters and photographers waiting for the famous one-named model when she got off the boat. She pictured her face in *Entertainment Weekly*, *USA Today*, blotted her lips and noticed that damn broken fingernail. Something to hide when they took her picture, or was it better to show it off? *See how I suffered!*

A tap of perfume behind her ears, at the base of her throat, the deep burgundy color of the bottle reminding her of blood, of death, of all that had happened: Bagdasarian in the tub, Echo floating in the lagoon, Lauren and Ian, Sabrina in Nicky's arms. She felt a lump in her throat, sadness coupled with terror. But then, unbidden, that thought again: fewer heirs to deal with. Awful to think such a thing, she knew that, but a fact.

More perfume across her wrists, her mind sorting through the remaining guests, who to trust, who to fear.

Frank, conniving, though weak. But had he killed Sabrina? It was possible. She had smelled the desperation on him immediately.

Schwegler, still her number one suspect, the outsider with a clear motive: control of the D'Arcangelo art estate, something she could not allow to happen.

She ran a brush through her hair, then stopped, the thought coming to her: *What about Nicky?*

She pictured him keening over his mother's body, a bit too much drama and emotion for the Nicky she knew, the spoiled, self-centered brat. *Was it an act?*

They were all suspicious but only one of them a killer, and no way she was waiting around to find out who. She was getting out, the one who survived, the one who got Victor's money, all of it. A way to finally fill that leaky pot, make something meaningful of her life, to do good, to help women and needy children. *Yes!* The idea filled her with hope but only for a moment because she knew she wouldn't do it; then the hope leaked out and she wanted to cry.

No! There isn't time for that!

A deep breath, shoulders back.

Yǒu zhì zhě, shì jìng chéng.

Eye on the prize.

About to leave, an impulsive act: Lipstick uncapped, she scrawled a message on the bathroom mirror.

Then she tossed the vial of Klonopin into her handbag, clasped the feng shui charm in her hand, and headed out.

100

Frank lay on his bed, a joint in his hand, an empty glass of whiskey sweating on the bedside table.

Sabrina, dead.

Had he done it in his sleep? In some crazed dream? He'd read about such things happening, but was it possible? All he could remember was smoking weed and drinking port, the few angry words they had exchanged, then nothing.

He squeezed his eyes shut against the picture of Sabrina, her blank stare, the bruises on her neck.

The movie he'd been shooting in his mind—star-crossed lovers reunited after twenty years—was over, the heroine dead, a tragic ending. He took another toke, an idea wafting over him like the weed: *Write the screenplay, play the lead! Why not?* It was a good story and his to tell.

Jesus. What was he thinking?

Maybe Sabrina was right: They were being punished; it was karma, payback.

He tried counting the cracks in the plaster ceiling, his brain fuzzy, that phrase on repeat in his brain: *How have you helped me or hurt me?*

It was true; he had hurt Victor. *They* had hurt Victor. But the guy deserved it, the way he had mistreated his wife. The big brother he had once adored, in the end, a cad. As for his wife, Sarah, they'd hurt her too. But it wasn't like they had forced her to get drunk or pushed her goddamn car over the cliff!

Another toke. Another sigh. None of it matted. Not now.

A picture of Sabrina's body tumbling off the bed, and he shuddered.

It couldn't have been me.

But a moment later he thought maybe he *had* done it, drunk and stoned on weed and pills. And he'd been so angry, so distraught at being cast aside, rejected. Either way, the dream, his future, were over.

Unless his brother had left him money.

Why he had come here in the first place? He should never have allowed himself to be distracted, to distort reality, to fall into a role the way he always did.

The past washed over him in waves—his parents fighting, his mean-as-fuck father, his punching-bag mother. As far back as he could remember he had disappeared into roles, donning costumes, assuming other personas, anything not to be himself. And it had paid off when he became an actor. He had to laugh, thought he should thank his parents for his career, for teaching him how to disappear. But now what, with his career behind him? He'd never taken the time to find out who he was, afraid to find the sad, scared little boy inside him.

But that no longer mattered. Right now, he had to get off this goddamn island, get his money, rehabilitate himself and his career, and move on. People got over a lot worse, and he would.

A picture of Sabrina's lovely face in close-up, her iridescent eyes and beguiling smile. No, he would never get over her.

A deep breath, followed by that familiar pain in his chest, the sharp stabs, his heart racing. But he knew what to do, nitroglycerin under the tongue.

Up quickly, into the bathroom, he searched for the tiny bottle, then remembered it had been gone for days, along with his other meds.

Fuck.

He found the blue plastic pill container in his Dopp kit and popped open the compartments, could not help himself, though he had done it before and knew it was empty. He went through his suitcase again too, underwear and T-shirts, balled-up socks falling to the floor. But there were no pills. And now, after all that had happened, he had to wonder, *Had they been stolen? And by who?*

Another stabbing pain in his chest. He told himself to be calm, to breathe, though his cardiologist had warned him about the danger of missing his medication. *Particularly the Plavix, which keeps those nasty platelets from attaching to the new stents in your heart. You don't want a stent thrombosis, do you?*

No, he did not!

He fell back onto the bed, relit the joint, and took a deep drag. Surely, he could survive without medication for a few days.

101

"Jas?" Nicky surveyed the room, her clothes and shoes strewn about, called her name again, then checked the bathroom. The medicine cabinet was open wide and empty, the scent of her perfume in the air, the bloodred bottle of Hypnotic Poison on the counter beside cotton balls, mascara, an eyelash curler. He closed the medicine cabinet and that's when he saw it, the message scrawled in lipstick:

See you around, Mama's Boy!

It was followed by a heart emoji and her signature *J*, scribbled with a flourish.

But where was she? Had she been foolish enough to make a run for it? No, she wouldn't. She couldn't. He searched for her Prada tote bag, but it was gone. A bad sign.

Down the stairs fast, he checked the living and dining rooms, noted the table a mess of dirty dishes, open bottles of wine, ants and insects feasting on scraps of food.

"Jasmin!" he called. "Jasmin!" but there was no answer.

Outside, the rain had stopped, the air hot and soupy.

He glanced at the flooded lagoon, thought of Echo, or what was left of her, and shuddered. No way to cross, even it if it were not infested with sharks. In the other direction, the path was overgrown, but the only means of escape. *Had she dared?*

Only a few steps before he saw it on the ground, just at the entrance to the path, her feng shui charm, red tassels and gold coins glittering against the mud.

He thought, *Oh, Jasmin, no;* then he gripped the charm in his hand and took off down the path.

102

Frank raised the window, stuck his head out, felt the dampness on his face, tried to clear his mind, to relax. The tightness in his chest had gotten worse. He needed to breathe the way his yoga instructor had taught him: *Eyes closed, inhale through the nose, exhale through the mouth.*

One…two…three…inhale. Four…five…six, exhale. Again. And again.

And it worked. After a few minutes of deep breathing, the pain had started to ease. Another deep breath, then another. He was going to be all right.

103

Everything was soaked, steam rising off the ground in a thick vapor, the path overgrown, but that did not stop her.

Prada bag on her shoulder, high heels sinking into mud, Jasmin made her way over rocks and branches, forging ahead, propelled by the idea of getting to the beach and the boat, her only chance of survival.

A short way in, trees blocked the sky, everything lost in shadows, the hot, moist air electrified by chirps and trills, wheezing iguanas, the piercing shriek of piha birds, but she ignored them all. *You can do this!*

After a few yards, she shed her heels and plodded forward, ignoring the bug bites and leeches attaching themselves to her bare feet and ankles. She had forgotten to bring water and her mouth was dry, but there would be water on the boat, and she would be there soon.

Perspiring, mascara running down her cheeks, she repeated the phrase, *Yǒu zhì zhě, shì jìng chéng, Yǒu zhì zhě, shì jìng chéng,* her mantra, *Eye on the prize,* as she fixated on getting to the boat and going home to claim her inheritance.

I have done what was asked, stayed the weekend, and I have survived!

She was nearing the end of the path, had just caught a glimpse of the beach and felt relieved, when something slammed into her from behind and she toppled.

104

Suddenly nauseated, Frank hauled himself out of bed, raced to the bathroom and collapsed over the toilet just in time. Throat burning, eyes watering, he stayed there a few minutes, trying to collect himself, spent and trembling, his skin gone cold and clammy.

Hands on the toilet, then the towel bar, he hoisted himself up, turned the sink faucet on, leaned over and gulped water, then splashed more on his face.

A deep breath, then another and he felt better.

But only for a minute.

Then the aching in his chest was back, the sharp, stabbing sensation getting worse, like the pain he had ignored for almost a year until that night only three months ago when he could no longer ignore it, so bad he knew he had to get to a hospital, where doctors confirmed he was having a serious heart attack, hooked him to IVs, and told him he was foolish and lucky. Foolish he had waited so long. Lucky he was alive. *Another hour, and you would have been dead.*

Frank stuttered for breath and leaned back against the bathroom wall, the pain suddenly so acute he grabbed his chest and let out a high-pitched squeak, an image flaring in his mind, his face on the cover of *People magazine: "Sexiest Man Alive."* He took a deep breath, managed a few steps, and made it into the bedroom before he went down.

105

Back at the hotel, Schwegler headed down the hallway, the air heavy and putrid smelling. He could hardly breathe, trying to think, to go over it, how to tell his father he had succeeded without telling him the rest.

Time-lapse pictures bloomed and died: Victor's beautiful ex-wife, the girl's head floating in the lagoon, Bagdasarian in the bath—the last one the only one that really mattered.

The hotel was hot and eerily quiet, just a low, mournful howl of wind that brought no relief, insects nipping at his face, his arms, his fleshy neck. He swatted at them again and again until his palm came away red with blood, the sight bringing with it the old memory: the schoolyard, the threats exchanged, throwing the punch, the sickening sound of the boy's skull hitting concrete, blood fanning out behind his head, the look of terror on the boy's face, kneeling down to help him, and his hand coming away coated in blood.

He closed his eyes, but the memory continued, his father saying, *Gut für dich, dass du dich verteidigt! Good for you, defending yourself!* The only time he could remember his father being proud of him—for killing a boy!

"*Vater, hilf mir!*" *Father, help me!*

What he'd said then and said now, his words echoing in hallway, dying in the shadows.

And still the memory played on, his father's lawyer telling him not to worry, that he was too young to go to prison, and he didn't, not even a juvenile facility. Nothing at all, as if it had never happened, and understanding for the first time the power of being from a rich and powerful family and feeling good about it.

He was almost at his room when the memory faded, and he saw it: the flickering light of a hurricane lamp through a half-open door, which drew him like a moth to a flame.

106

The path was an obstacle course of fallen branches and rocks, tree-tops blotting out the sky, everything difficult to see, but Nicky pressed on. He had to find her. He had failed to protect his mother and his girlfriend before that, but he would not fail again. He would find Jasmin and bring her back to safety.

But where was that? Back at the hotel with a possible murderer lurking? His mind was a jumble of images and thoughts, murders, suicides, paranoia, and grief.

Sweat dripped into his eyes, leeches attached themselves to his shins, but he kept going. He was no longer playing at being a hero. He would be one. A way to make up for his past, his transgressions, the tragic losses he had caused.

A break in the trees, a glimpse of ocean in the distance. He would soon be on the beach. A sigh of relief. He was only a few yards away when he saw something lying across the path—a *snake, a zebra?* Was that even possible or was he hallucinating? A few more feet and he made out arms and legs—human ones—the black and white stripes, the skull design of a dress, and one he recognized.

He dashed, leaned down, and said her name, "Jasmin?" assuming she had collapsed from heat and dehydration. But then he turned her over, saw the blood on her lips and the blank stare. *Oh no!* He swiped the blood away and held his canteen to her lips. When the water dribbled over her cheek, he placed his lips on hers, attempted mouth-to-mouth. *My God, how is this happening again?* Over and over, he breathed into her mouth but there was no response, nothing.

Finally spent, his own breath giving out, he lifted Jasmin off the ground, an image of lifting his mother's body from the bed flickering in his mind as he did. Then he carried her from the path to the beach where he laid her on the sand and sat beside her, feeling numb as the fog began to lift and a sliver of blue sky appeared.

After a while, he made his way back to the hotel, Jasmin in his arms. He barely felt the heat or her weight or any sense of struggle, the whole time trying to make sense of what had happened, of what was still happening. *Only two people left and one of them is a murderer, unless there is someone else!* The persistent thought repeated in his mind as the path ended and the hotel came into view, the shimmering white building now a mausoleum to which he was adding another body.

Arms aching, legs straining, Nicky made it up the grand staircase and into Jasmin's room, where he rested her body onto the bed, wiped the mud off her face, and swept the hair from her forehead. He thought he should say something about what she had meant to him, but when he tried to come up with the words, he realized she had not meant much to him at all. Just one more person he could not protect and had not saved.

So, all he said was "Goodbye." Then he placed the feng shui charm on her breast, drew the sheet over her head, and went looking for a murderer.

107

With the windows open, the wind swept through the hotel, jangling the masks and rattling the chandeliers. The hotel was almost dark now, light from the remaining hurricane lamps casting low flickering shadows.

Ignoring his bug bites and bleeding ankles, but fueled by anger, Nicky made his way down the hall, the Swiss Army knife in his hand.

At Schwegler's room, he paused, then pushed the door open in one fast move. A quick scan left, then right. Knife out in front of him, he took a few steps in, saw the unmade bed, the wrinkled linen suit hanging on the back of the closet door. On the bathroom counter, a straight razor, shaving cream, a bottle of Vetiver cologne. But no sign of Schwegler.

Back in the hall, he headed toward Frank's room, the wind howling behind him.

The door was open halfway.

Gripping his knife tighter, he peered in.

At first, all he could see was darkness.

Then, a silhouette that morphed into a man standing over a body.

108

It was Schwegler, his back to the door.

Below him, Frank, curled into a fetal position and not moving.

Nicky froze, hardly breathing, watching as Schwegler removed his hands from Frank's neck and slowly began to rise. Then, heart beating fast, Nicky turned and retraced his steps, hugging the hall until he reached the grand staircase and raced down. He had no idea if Schwegler had seen him.

At the bottom of the stairs, he cast a look over his shoulder before he sprinted from the foyer to the dining room, then into the pantry.

His eyes scanned the shelves, the boxes of cereal, tins of freeze-dried food, packages of coffee and tea. Below them, bottles of liquor: Jack Daniel's, Johnnie Walker, Jim Beam, Jose Cuervo. *Old friends. Old enemies.* Nicky jammed a half pint of Jim Beam into his belt, then rustled through the cabinets and drawers until he found something that looked like a two-headed hammer—an old-fashioned meat tenderizer, one end flat, the other with spikes. He added it to his belt. Another minute to strap steak knives to the fingers of one hand, winding plastic wrap round and round until the knives were secure and he had created a Wolverine-like claw.

Then, crouched in a corner but with a clear view of the dining room, he waited, taking slugs of whiskey. The liquor burned his throat and hit his gut like acid, harsh and hot. It tasted of failure but right now he needed the faux courage it provided. If he lived, he would go back to rehab. If he didn't, what the hell.

Mind and body on high alert, he waited, heart pounding and as ready as he ever would be.

109

Had someone been watching him?

Schwegler was not sure, but paranoia was the name of the game, and it was a game he intended to win.

A last look at Frank's body before he gave up searching for a pulse. Then he crossed himself, got a grip on his small pistol, and headed out of the room.

The hallway was empty, but he stood there a minute, his eyes adjusting to the dark, looking, waiting.

Wind whistled through the hotel as he made his way forward.

At the top of the staircase he hesitated, an alarm rippling through him. This was it, he could feel it, the moment he had been waiting for, and he was prepared: If life had taught him anything, it was how to survive.

He inched his way down the stairs, the hummingbird pistol in his hand, cocked and loaded.

110

Were those footsteps or just the wind?

Nicky dared a peek and saw it: the elongated shadow of a man creeping across the floor from the dining room to the pantry's entrance.

Eyes focused, every muscle constricted, he took a deep breath and vaulted from the pantry feet first, landing a solid kick that sent Schwegler careening into the wall, the pistol flying from his hand. Then he was on him, knife slashing, blood spurting, but Schwegler wrestled the weapon away and was up, roaring, an injured animal barreling forward and knocking him off his feet. The two men went down, colliding into the dining room table, dishes crashing, shards of glass raining down on them.

Schwegler was up fast, hoisting a chair above his head which he brought down, hard, Nicky scrambling sideways at the last minute, wood splintering beside him. But Schwegler kept coming. Upending the table, he snatched a knife and swung it at Nicky, who stumbled backward, dodging and weaving; then he tore out of the room. Schwegler was fast, catching him by his hair at the front door and dragging him back as they fell together, Nicky swiping at him with his Wolverine-like claw, the knife points nicking Schwegler's flesh, but he twisted Nicky's hand back, wrist bones at the breaking point before Nicky managed to thrust a knee into his groin and broke free, up again and racing toward the front door.

Outside, it was dark, birdcalls and cicadas, zigzags of lightning electrifying the night air as Nicky ran and Schwegler came charging through the door, his gun firing.

A hot stinging in his leg and Nicky went down, his chin hitting rock, a cracking sensation deep inside his skull. He pulled himself up, was running again but didn't get far before Schwegler tackled him and the two of them tumbled into the pond, water spewing, koi spilling out. Schwegler was on top, holding Nicky under, murky water flooding his nose and mouth, his lungs starting to ache.

Arms flapping, punching, he got his head above water, gulped air before he was dragged under again, but this time his Wolverine claw found Schwegler's back, the knives plunged deep between the man's shoulder blades. Arms twisted back, Schwegler whacked Nicky's claw away, but one of the knives had broken loose and lodged itself deep in his flesh. Schwegler reeled up and out of the water, howling, fumbling to get a grip on the knife in his back while Nicky dragged himself from the pond, gasping for breath, eyes darting one way, then the other, trying to see in the dark, before he was running, dragging his injured leg.

Schwegler yanked the knife from his back with a strangled scream, the knife in his hand now as he caught Nicky at the edge of the path and knocked him to the ground, Nicky on his back, Schwegler crawling on top again, their faces inches apart, both men grunting and spitting, the knife in Schwegler's hand just inches above Nicky's throat.

Nicky had a grip on Schwegler's wrist with one hand and reached back with the other, searching the ground until he found something—a large, jagged rock which he raised above Schwegler's head.

He was bringing it down just as Schwegler was lowering the knife to his throat.

Two Days Later

When the skies had finally cleared and the seas had calmed, Captain Thomas made his way back to the island. He was certain the guests would be happy to see him after the delay.

He anchored the Pershing 140, and with First Mate William took one of the inflatable rafts to shore. It was a sultry day, the ocean water warm, steam rising off the beach.

The men made their way along the path, occasionally stopping to clear fallen trees and branches, noting how overgrown it had become.

"This gets any worse, no one will be able to reach that damn hotel!" the captain said, already clammy with sweat.

The first mate said nothing; he didn't have to. After working several jobs together, they communicated through nods and winks and understood each other perfectly.

The path ended and the hotel came into view.

"Will you look at that," the captain said. "Half the windows are open."

It was well over ninety, and he had never known rich people to forgo the air-conditioning. Perhaps, he thought, this group was less spoiled than most.

A dozen koi were lying dead around the pond, mouths open and glassy-eyed. "Poor devils," he said. "I guess it overflowed from the rain."

William nodded.

Inside, the hotel was quiet with a sweet flowery scent gone rotten.

Captain Thomas exchanged an anxious look with William, who was already holding a rag over his nose. The captain called out, "Hello, hello," noting a few primitive masks on the floor and a general sense of disorder, though it was not until they were in the dining room and saw the upended table, the floor littered with broken dishes, bits of food and spilled wine, insects feasting, that his inner alarm sounded full force. "What the hell...?" He called again, "Hello, *hello*!" louder this time and several more times as they headed up the staircase.

At the top, the smell was stronger. Worse as they headed down the hallway.

William wrapped the rag tighter around his nose, the captain breathing through his mouth, adrenaline kicking in along with his fear. He stopped a moment, went through his worn canvas tote bag, and came up with a bandanna, which he fixed over his nose and mouth and tied behind his head.

Bagdasarian's room was first, a random choice and a bad one, the room sweltering, the air thick and rank. They saw the blowflies buzzing before they found the body on the bathroom floor, that sweet rotten smell so strong it grabbed them both in the back of their throats. Captain Thomas fought his rising nausea as he took it in, the small oozing blisters, the green-tinged flesh that looked as if it had loosened and might slip off the bone. The former naval captain had seen plenty of ugly things in his day, as had William, a former guest of the state, but for both of them, the scene ranked high.

"I've got to call the coast guard," the captain said. His words, muffled beneath the bandanna brought to mind his anonymous employer. Did he, or she, know about this? He had no idea and yet he was somehow certain he would never hear from that employer again.

"There's no service," William said.

"Right." The captain nodded, then said, "Let's go," though their search was far from over.

He and First Mate William went room to room, each new body a new horror.

They found Rachel Ronan in bed, flowers on her chest shriveled and rotting. She might have been sleeping except for the fact that a part of her chin had been nibbled away, flies and moths fluttering around the wound in ecstasy.

The captain let out a groan of disgust before they moved on.

They discovered Lauren and Ian in bed, side by side, their waxy green faces almost touching, the plastic bunched at their necks making their heads look like unwrapped deli meat.

In the next room, he slid the sheet off Sabrina Fleming and recoiled, her once beautiful body crawling with large black and orange-spotted bugs.

"Damn carrion beetles!" he said, trying hard not to gag.

Frank D'Arcangelo was on the floor in his room, hands clutching his chest, face frozen in a grimace of pain.

First Mate William did the honors in the next room, sheet pulled back to expose former model Jasmin Li, well beyond anything hair or makeup could salvage, the bloody foam from her mouth blurring her lips into a hideous Joker-like grin.

"That's seven," the captain said, going through the guest list in his head.

They went up and down the hallways, checking the rest of the rooms, examining bathrooms and opening closets, but found nothing. They did the same downstairs.

Outside, they took much-needed breaths before they searched the grounds.

Among the dead koi, they found a couple of sharp bent steak knives coated with what looked like dried blood. The captain slipped them into his canvas tote as they headed toward the lagoon.

"What's that?" he asked indicating something white floating on the surface.

William got hold of a long bamboo rod, half in, half out of the water, and tried using it to snare the object.

"Shit! William! Drop it, drop it!" the captain shouted as the blunt nose of a shark broke the water's surface, snapping at the bamboo rod.

William stumbled back, practically fell over.

"Fucking tiger sharks!" the captain said, helping the first mate up. "I should have known better."

On his feet again, William pointed again to the white object, stirred by the shark's movement, floating toward them.

They waited till it was only a few inches away before getting hold of an edge and plucking it out of the water fast.

"What is it?" the captain asked, nervous until he saw it was just a shirt or blouse. They flattened it onto the ground, could make out the faded floral pattern and embroidered stitching along an edge.

William pointed to something caught in the stitching that looked like a piece of cork until he got closer and jerked back.

"What?" the captain asked, leaning closer, just enough to see it was a finger, wrinkled and bleached white, the fingernail loose and polished bright blue.

"Holy shit!" he said, letting out a breath. "Looks like someone went for a deadly swim!"

They used a couple of sticks to fold the blouse, making sure the severed finger was wrapped tightly in the fabric before the captain gingerly picked it up and put it into his canvas bag. "Jesus Christ," he said, shaking his head.

Behind the hotel, they checked the swimming pool but found only leaves and dirt and dead frogs. A relief. But when they followed a double line of etched grooves in the mud, they found another body, a man's, his face so bruised and bloody the captain could not identify him. He checked for a pulse, expected none, and he was right.

"Looks like he was dragged here in an attempt to hide the body." He indicated the ruts in the dirt and William nodded.

"That makes eight," the captain said.

They continued to search the grounds, behind thickets of bushes and fallen trees, but found nothing, Captain Thomas wondering aloud if they had somehow missed another body. That's when the alternate reality hit him: that the missing body was the killer. He stopped, slowly revolving in place, eyes scanning the land and foliage. *Was the killer hiding, watching them, waiting to make a move?*

"Let's go!" he said to William. This time his tone was urgent.

They started down the path, darting glances behind them, moving fast, the thought of a killer, desperate and with nothing to lose, somewhere in the shadows, and following.

The Next Day

The coast guard and FBI arrived with a legion of photographers, medics, and forensic specialists. Moving like highly directed ghosts, they bagged the bodies, swabbed for prints, and inspected every inch of the hotel.

Scuba divers in shark tanks explored the lagoon, where they discovered a few more body parts, all collected and bagged for later testing.

Several soldiers spread out to comb the path and the surrounding jungle.

It was there they found the missing guest. Hiding in the bush. Beat-up, dehydrated and exhausted, he did not put up a fight.

His rights were read, handcuffs secured, then a phalanx of soldiers led him back to the beach and onto a large coast guard patrol boat where he was stripped, searched, and photographed before they locked him in the brig for the voyage back to civilization.

PART III
11 MONTHS LATER

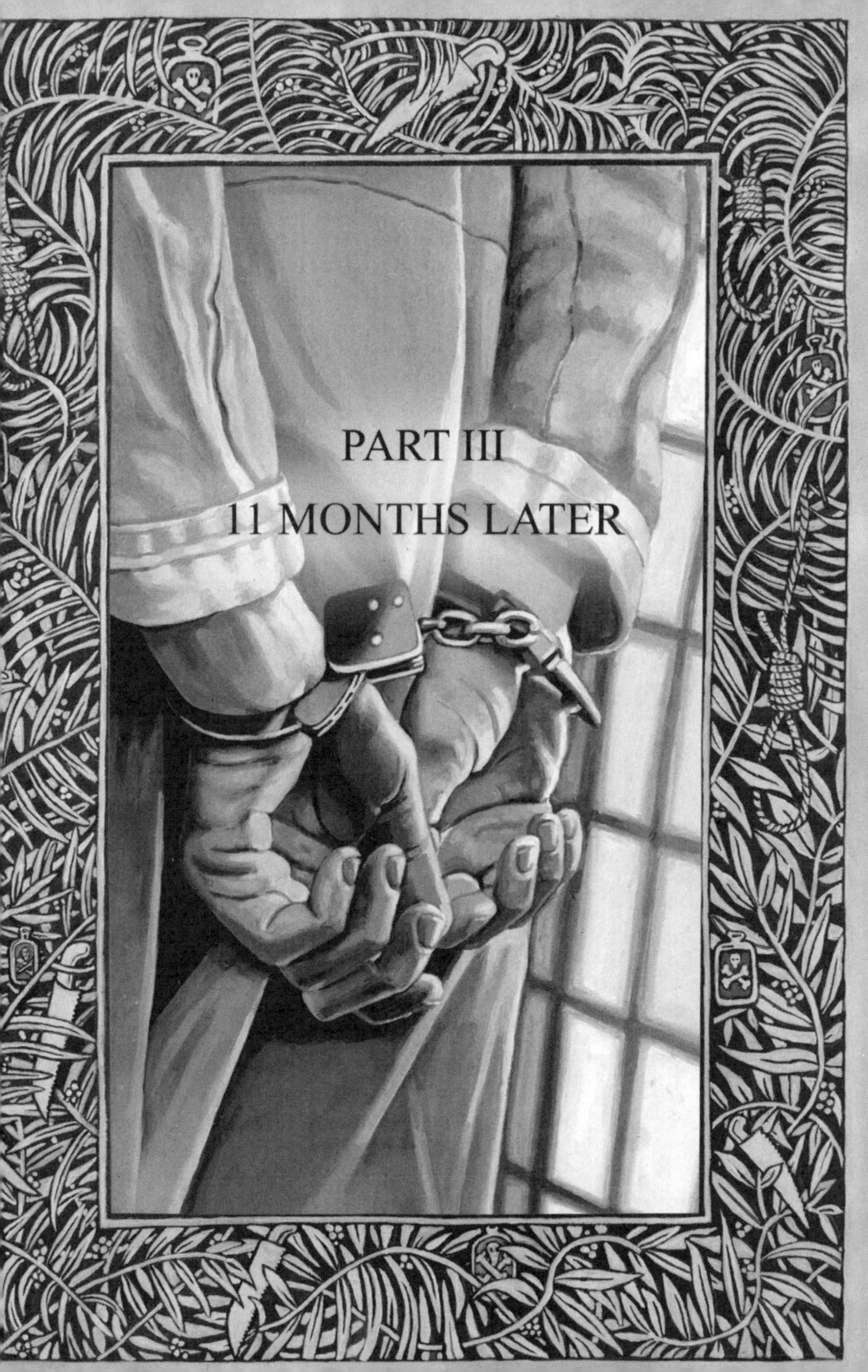

Eleven Months Later

The decision to hold the trial in Florida was determined by the fact that all the guests had originally arrived in Fort Lauderdale. With nine first-degree murder charges, the case made headlines in the press, went viral on social media, and was televised and watched by more than thirty million viewers, the largest audience for a trial since OJ stabbed his wife, the Menendez brothers shot their parents, and Gywneth Paltrow had a collision on the ski slopes of Park City, Utah.

Even before the trial began, most saw the outcome as a foregone conclusion, several high-profile producer/directors vying for the film and television rights.

The major players in the real-life trial included the prosecutor, a graduate of the Florida State University at Tallahassee, a slick, young hotshot with a winning streak of convictions that he had no intention of breaking.

The defense attorney, a well-known advocate for the underdog, was a good lawyer but with a problem: Like everyone else, she believed her client was guilty.

The judge, a lifelong Florida resident with more than forty years on the bench, who was planning to retire after the trial and impatient to get home to his BarcaLounger, wide-screen TV, and ESPN.

After opening remarks, Captain Thomas took the stand for the prosecution to describe the search he had conducted with First Mate William and their discovery of the victims. His tough, no-nonsense manner played well and was particularly effective when he was overcome by emotion, mainly due to the fact that his lucrative career was over. With his anonymity blown, he would need to find a new line of work.

He was followed by a member of the FBI's forensic team who detailed the condition of the bodies, distributing crime scene photos to the jury over the defense attorney's objection, which was overruled. Several jurors requested a recess after viewing the horrifying full-color images.

The soldiers who arrested the prisoner testified he had offered no resistance, an observation the prosecuting attorney seized upon as an indication of guilt.

Victor's one-time studio assistant, the only witness other than the defendant who had been on the island and survived, was not called to the stand. Since he had left the island prior to the murders, he could offer little, and the district attorney did not need his testimony to pursue a conviction. The defense also decided to exclude him. Though he had nothing damning to say, he had nothing positive either, and the lawyer sensed he did not like the prisoner and could only hurt the case. That left her with little choice: Though she knew it was a risk to put her client on the stand, there was no one else.

She brought him through a series of questions about the murders, all of which he denied, leading up to the last day and that fateful fight, which she had him describe, though he said much of it was "a blur."

TRIAL TRANSCRIPT. PAGE 43:

Attorney: Please explain how the fight ended.

The Witness: We were going to kill each other. It was him or me. I had to defend myself.

Attorney: So, you killed him in self-defense.
The Witness: Yes.

It was here that photographs of the defendant's injuries, his self-defensive wounds, taken at the time of his arrest, were offered into evidence and shown to the jury.

The attorney asked the defendant to point out what remained of those wounds, and he did, despite the DA's objection, which was overruled, by removing his jacket and shirt to display an assortment of scars on his chest, arms, and neck, the worst on his back. He then took off his pants, again over the DA's objections, to indicate a lengthy scar on his upper thigh. It was a dramatic moment, everyone hushed as the defendant stood in front of the courtroom nearly naked.

The attorney used the term *self-defense* several more times before the defendant got dressed and the district attorney cross-examined.

TRIAL TRANSCRIPT. PAGE 57:

District Attorney: So, you have admitted that you killed him.
The Witness: You would have done the same, had you been in my position.
District Attorney: This is not about me or what I would have done. It is about YOU and what you did. You have stated that you and the man you killed were the last two people on the island. Meaning everyone else was dead, is that correct?
The Witness: Yes. So, you see, it had to be him.
District Attorney: Are you suggesting that the man you killed murdered the others?

The Witness: Yes. There was no one else.

District Attorney: Other than you. So, after you murdered him, you attempted to hide his body. Why?

The Witness: It was…an impulse.

District Attorney: And after your IMPULSE to hide the body of the man you had just murdered, you had an impulse to hide yourself. Why was that?

The Witness: I was…frightened.

District Attorney: Of what? You had just killed the man you say was the murderer and by your own statement there was no one else on the island. Who was left to be frightened of?

The Witness: I don't know. It was…a feeling.

District Attorney: A feeling as opposed to an impulse?

The defense attorney objected.
The court sustained the objection.

District Attorney: I see. And then you hid.

The Witness: I needed time to think.

District Attorney: But you hid. Yes or no? Please answer the question.

The Witness: Yes. As I said, I needed time to think.

District Attorney: You mean time to come up with an alibi.

Another objection sustained by the court.

The Witness: I was not thinking rationally.

District Attorney: But rationally enough to hide the body of the man you had just murdered and then to hide yourself.

No objection this time as it was fact.

In his closing statement, the DA stressed that the defendant had hidden from Captain Thomas and later from the coast guard and the FBI. That he would have escaped if he had not been apprehended, and by his own admission, there was no one else on the island, ergo no one else who could have committed the crimes. As for motive, the DA cited inheritance of the D'Arcangelo estate, worth multimillions and only possible with the elimination of the other heirs, whose murders he reiterated to the jury in detail.

It was during the recap of these gruesome crimes that one of the victim's relatives who was in the courtroom, a flawlessly dressed Chinese woman, stood, aimed a red-lacquered fingernail at the defendant and shouted, "You killed my baby! You killed her! You killed her!" three times before the judge had her removed from the court. A reporter who witnessed the accusation later wrote that Mrs. Li's fingernail was the "proverbial nail in the defendant's coffin."

In closing, the defense attorney did her best, restating there were no witnesses to any of the murders, that the charges were based on supposition and not evidence. And that, in the end, her client had been defending himself against the actual murderer in a fight to the death, once more pointing out his defensive wounds. She summed up that he had been unjustly accused simply because he had survived.

It was a decent argument for his possible, though not particularly compelling, innocence.

The defendant had already been tried in the press and on social media, where everyone's opinion was that he was guilty.

The jury of eight men and four women deliberated for less than an hour and agreed.

The trial, with its outcome a predictable conclusion to most, was over in just two weeks, a disappointment to reporters, the producers and advertisers of Court TV, social media pundits, YouTube, and tabloid newspapers everywhere.

Raiford Prison

The town of Starke, heavily populated by the staff of the nearby Florida State Prison, a.k.a. Raiford Prison, housed approximately 1,500 prisoners. For some, their final destination. Since the 1976 resumption of capital punishment, Florida had executed 106 people, forty-four by electrocution, sixty-two by lethal injection, the method of *how* to be killed a (sometimes) courtesy the state extended to the condemned. Currently, 276 offenders were awaiting execution in Florida and would choose how they preferred to die.

The prisoner, convicted of what was now commonly referred to as the "Paradise Lost Massacre," and who had arrived three weeks earlier, had chosen lethal injection. Placed in a special security cell, he was now on "death watch," with guards checking hourly and taking notes, such as *the inmate has moved from bed to chair, did not eat dinner, is reading a newspaper*.

His attorney had fought for a stay of execution but had lost as there was no new evidence and public opinion was strong that someone had to pay for the crimes.

Today was the guard's final check as it was the prisoner's last day.

Hans Schwegler had slept little in the past eleven months, eaten less, and had lost over thirty pounds. Every day, he did push-ups and crunches in his seven-by-twelve-foot cell and, when possible, lifted weights in the prison gym. His body, though diminished, was ropy and so attenuated that he resembled a concentration camp internee.

That morning, he had showered and used an electric razor, always with a guard standing nearby. Now, he sat poised on the edge of his cot in the small windowless cell and played with a loose thread at the cuff of his baggy jumpsuit. Unable to sit still for long, he paced the length of his cell and back, counting the laps until he lost count. Then, he pressed his cheek against the cell's steel bars and squinted to read the clock at the far end of the hall. He had two hours and eleven minutes left to live. No time. An eternity.

From the prison library, he had gotten a tattered paperback copy of *Beyond Good and Evil*, by German philosopher Friedrich Nietzsche, who had suffered a complete collapse and lost all mental faculties at the age of forty-four and never recovered. The idea of this brilliant and influential man whose life had been cut short gave him an odd kind of solace. He tried to reread a few favorite passages, but the words began to float off the page and his mind flooded with scattershot imagery: the hotel and swampy overgrown path, the guests and their murder scenes, that last fight, his arrest and trial, all mixed with bits of free-floating conversation flickering through his brain like an odd jumble of someone else's memories.

When his last meal arrived—steak, mashed potatoes with gravy, green peas—he pushed it away, sampling only a couple of teaspoons of faux whipped cream off the top of his dessert, a hot fudge sundae, the chocolate sauce as cold and coagulated as blood. An hour later, when the uneaten steak sat in a pool of grease and the ice cream had melted, he asked that it be taken away.

For the next hour he paced.

When he looked up, the warden, three guards, and the prison chaplain stood outside his cell. The warden gripped a cell phone, the priest a well-worn Bible.

"Ready?" the warden asked.

His first thought: *What if I say no? What then?* He saw himself tearing down the hall, guards chasing him, inmates cheering him on. But he said, "Yes."

The prison chaplain, an elderly white man who had visited a few times and read him passages from the Bible, said, "Is there anything you wish to say, anyone you would like to ask for forgiveness?" The man had asked this question several times before, and Schwegler had not come up with an answer. *Meine Mutter* was his only thought but he did not say it. He wished he believed in an afterlife so he could be reunited with his long-dead mother but wondered if she would recognize him after so long. And shouldn't the mother who had never protected him in life be asking *his* forgiveness? He shook his head no, as he played with a cheap-looking silver crucifix, a gift from the priest, which he wore despite the blue ring it left around his neck and the fact that he did not believe in God. *Or perhaps*, he thought, *God does not believe in me.*

One of the guards, a heavyset Black man with a kind face, the one who had delivered his meals every day and always asked how he was doing, laid a consoling hand on his shoulder and asked him to stand.

"Is there anyone you want to call?" the warden asked, offering the cell phone.

Schwegler shook his head again. He'd made only one personal phone call in all his time behind bars—to his father, who had expressed disdain, not for his crimes, but for losing the D'Arcangelo estate. When he proclaimed his innocence, his father said he had missed the point and informed him he would be changing the family name. "No one wants to do business with the father of a *Mörder*, a murderer." His last words were, "*Du warst immer eine Enttäuschung*." *You were always a disappointment.*

There was no one else to call. No wife, no girlfriend, no boyfriend, no friends at all. The person he felt closest to right now was the kind-faced death-row guard.

The warden led the way down a hall, a wide corridor of cold fluorescent light. There were no handcuffs or leg chains, just guards on either side of him and the chaplain reading from his Bible. He moved through a barred door down another hallway and through an oval-shaped door that opened into an octagonal-shaped room, all the time as if he were floating, as if his body had already left him. But when he saw the gurney in the center of the room and the table beside it laid out with tourniquets and needles, his mind was shocked into reality, and he backed up with a gasp.

The kind-faced guard gripped his arm gently but firmly. "It's okay, son," he said, and when Schwegler looked, he saw there were tears in the man's eyes. He wanted to ask him, *How can you do such a job?* but could not speak.

A night on the island when the guests had been discussing how they would like to die came to him, and he heard himself say, *I like the idea of closing my eyes and going to sleep*, and he thought, *I chose this. Twice.* He hoped he was right, that the lethal injection would be quick and easy, a less painful way to die than a jolt of electricity or poison gas, though right now, looking at the metal gurney with its plastic sheets, restraints, and stirrups, he was not so sure.

He forced himself to look elsewhere, noting the curtains at even intervals around the room, one half-open exposing a small window, and realized his death would be witnessed. He shuddered at the thought, felt his legs go weak, and might have fallen if the guard had not once again tightened his grip.

The tie-down team strapped him to the gurney, one man at his head, one at each arm and leg, the zipping sound of Velcro restraints opening and closing as the straps were tightened across his chest and waist, around his wrists and ankles.

"Rest your head on the pillow," one said, pressing his head back with a calloused hand.

Schwegler lay back and counted ceiling tiles until he spotted the camera that would record his death. He hoped he would be dignified, not cry or scream or lose control of his bodily functions, the thought of that unbearable.

"All good," said the man at his head. Another, at his feet, gently touched his ankle before leaving.

The tie-down team was replaced by a medical crew, technicians wrapping tubes around his arm, flicking fingers at his veins.

"Make a fist," one said.

"There, that's a good one," said another.

But when they jabbed the needle into his arm, the vein rolled away.

A technician said, "Damn," and stabbed him with a second needle, this one fourteen-gauge, the largest commercially available, the pain so sharp Schwegler thought he might faint and hoped he would. *If I do, will they revive me only to kill me?*

The technician said, "I got a vein and it's a good one," then left as the chaplain came back, people appearing and disappearing like ghosts. *Am I already dead?* Schwegler wondered. He strained to raise his head, saw the curtains part, faces appearing behind the glass—the familiar DA, the Florida state attorney general, an aide from the governor's office, a reporter who he knew had followed the case, and Jasmin Li's mother.

He closed his eyes.

The warden took up a position at his head. The chaplain, at his side, repeated his question, "Do you wish to apologize to those you have hurt?" But what Schwegler heard was Victor D'Arcangelo's question—*How have you hurt me or helped me?*—and so he nodded though he hadn't meant to, and when he opened his eyes, he saw a microphone descending from the ceiling and though he had nothing to say, words rushed out of him, "*Vater unser im Himmel, geheiligt werde dein Name, dein Reich komme.*"

"What are you saying?" the chaplain asked.

He wondered how a man of God did not recognize the Lord's Prayer, even more surprised that he was reciting it, his mind a mash-up of languages and half thoughts, so amplified and echoing through the microphone, it sounded to him like someone else was speaking, possibly God.

A hand touched his arm, and when he managed to shift his vision, he saw it was the chaplain who asked if he was finished speaking and he said yes, then saw the man make the sign of the cross and the warden nod at the mirrored wall where the executioner must have started the process of releasing the drugs, sodium thiopental, Pavulom, potassium chloride, one after another, because he felt something cold rush into his arm, then a bitter taste on the back of his tongue as the cool in his veins turned hot and he wanted to shout, *I am innocent!* but he could not speak and was no longer sure if he was. *Perhaps I did kill them!*

That thought was interrupted as he realized this was not at all like he had imagined, a drug-induced stupor followed by a peaceful sleep. Instead, he was hyperaware of his body—the air going in and out of his lungs, oxygen traveling along his veins and arteries, his heart pumping blood—and of his surroundings, the chaplain and warden and the faces at the windows—Alex Bagdasarian and Rachel Ronan, people he had wronged. He wanted to say, *I am sorry!* but then it was Nicky D'Arcangelo's face, his mouth stretched wide and shouting, *It was me who killed them!*

Then he saw his own hand coming down and the knife piercing the young man's throat but the sounds he heard were his own guttural groans, and he realized it was not any of those faces but his lawyer's face and the district attorney's, and the reporter's, while a voice somewhere beside him said very quietly, "The drugs are working," and his breath faltered and his lungs ached and a frost surrounded his heart and there was a hissing sound like air going out of a balloon, which he recognized was his last breath as his heart turned to ice and cracked apart and the world went bright white and he was flying.

PART IV
THE TRUTH

You have to understand, I was going to get caught unless I killed them.

Let me explain.

I want you to know, to understand the genius of my plan, to hear the truth about what happened. I am not going to write it down and I'm only going to say it once, so listen carefully and pay attention.

There were many factors I had to consider: my survival of course, and my moral conviction, my *obligation* to right wrongs. Some might say I had a choice, and that's true, but it was a choice made from necessity.

Life is full of choices: You do something; then you do something else. One thing leads to another. Cause and effect, right? But you've got to cover your tracks, cover your ass. Survival of the fittest. What it's always been about and something I learned young. Which is why I'm here, and they're not. Why I succeeded and they failed.

It wasn't easy, but I was up to the challenge. And I took my time. I planned. I researched. I had dedication and faith.

Still, life is full of surprises. You can plan and plan and plan, think you have prepared for anything, and something goes wrong. But that's the trick, being able to roll with the punches, to adapt, to seize the opportunity. When something didn't go as planned, I improvised, made the best of it, the *most* of it.

What's that saying? *Man plans, and God laughs.* Well, God is not laughing now.

I should be the one who's laughing. But I'm not. That's not who I am. Ten people died, and it was not something I did for laughs. There was a *reason*.

It started with the job. Almost five years ago. Something I did not go into with a plan. That was later. It was an idea that came to me, a seed that grew over time. Small at first, and just barely acknowledged, but something I nurtured, encouraged, allowed to morph and change until it became *big*, filling my mind and permeating every part of my body until I could think of nothing else.

I will admit there were times I had my doubts. *You can't do this! You'll never get away with it! You'll get caught!* But then I'd stop, rethink, examine the problem, and come up with a solution. I'm good like that because underneath my doubts and insecurities, I'm strong, with a will of steel, something I built *all by myself*!

I had been working for Victor D'Arcangelo for almost a year when I had the idea. I'd become his number one studio assistant, the one who ran his studio and made it hum. Before I got there, his records were a mess, in shambles, practically nonexistent. He was lost. Like so many artists, he was terrible at business and refused to learn. He left that to the galleries that represented him—a bad idea—but even they came to appreciate me and my organizational skills. Up to a point. But Victor, he loved it. "You are so fucking anal-retentive," he'd say and give me a pat on the back or tussle my hair like I was a kid.

He had no head for business, but now he didn't need one, because he had me.

Like anything I do, I was methodical about my plan. I wrote everything down in the same pads I used for my work, four-by-six vertical notepads, spiral-bound, each with 120 pages, the perfect list-making pad, and easy to carry in my pocket. Some people might say I'm obsessive about things like that—the perfect pad, the right pencil—but it's *important*. And no way I was writing it on a computer where anyone might get access to it.

I used those same pads to keep the studio logs. One pad to cover a three-month period, four notebooks per year, each detailing the day-to-day studio operations—the artwork going out to galleries and museums or collectors, if they were loans or sales, and if sold, for how much. I would date the pads on the last page and initial them, then hand them over to Mr. D at the end of each month. He would give them a cursory look, skimming the pages like a flip-book. He didn't care. Over the next four years, there were sixteen of them, all neat and detailed. There was talk about one day donating them to the Library of Congress, but we never got around to it.

For my personal plan, I filled several pads before I grasped the scope of what I was doing, what I was after, the enormity of it, and how I was going to pull it off. I wrote down everything, all my thoughts, all the guesswork—*try this, try that, what about, what if*—and of course there were times I got specific, pages where I made lists of what I needed, and perfected my strategies, clarifying and following each idea to its logical, even *illogical* conclusion. I knew I could not leave anything to chance, that I had to consider and analyze every possible misstep. *If this happens, then try... If that happens, then try...* It was the only way I could see what I might be missing, how I might screw up and get caught, a possibility I could not allow.

The plan became my art! I had stopped making my own paintings a few months after I got the job because I was too busy running the studio. Don't get me wrong; I was happy to do it. Early in life, I learned how to see what people wanted, what they *needed*, and I would become that person. I created a grab bag of personality traits I could reach into when I needed them. I've had dozens of personalities, been dozens of other people, some for weeks or months or even years, some for just an hour or even a few minutes, personas I abandoned when they were no longer necessary, as easily discarded as people. Why hold on to them? For what?

In the case of Mr. D, it was easy to become who he needed. I was Friday to his Robinson Crusoe. Alice B. Toklas to his Gertrude Stein. I liked serving him and at the same time pulling the strings from behind the curtain. So much better than being center stage where everyone can see you. And hiding came naturally to me. For so long I had wanted to disappear, to hide my acne-pitted face, and did, as soon as I was able to grow a beard.

I can't say Mr. D was a saint. He loved playing the bad-boy artist, the *genius* who could do whatever he wanted, whenever he wanted, take without asking. He treated people like extensions of himself, there to make him feel good, to wait on him and worship him, especially the wives and girlfriends, and there were plenty of the latter. It's hard to blame them for wanting to pay him back, something I learned from him. But even when he was cruel or insensitive to me, which he could be, my first allegiance was always to him.

I made it possible for him to do nothing but make art, be the best possible artist, to be the famous artist he was and more, which was no small thing. I did everything for him: managed his studio, bought his art supplies, made appointments and canceled them, liaised with his art dealers and curators and collectors, hired and fired the other studio assistants, which was crucial—not just to him, but to me. I did his shopping and ran his errands, brought his custom-made shirts to the cleaners, made sure his shoes were shined, his sneakers and running shoes spotless. I arrived early while he was still sleeping and made his breakfast, poached organic egg whites, fresh squeezed orange juice, black coffee. I became more important to him than any of the wives or girlfriends. They were disposable, dispensable. But not me, I was *in*dispensable. The more I did, the more he needed me, depended on me, trusted me. I made sure of that. You could say I was self-sacrificing, and I was, but I did not give up my goals.

The most important thing I did (which you already know if you were paying attention) was to help paint his paintings. Other assistants did as well, but I was the one in charge, the one who organized the painting crew, who had them sign NDAs. It was only later that I did *all* the work, painted the entire paintings and forged Mr. D's signature perfectly. But I'm getting ahead of myself as I tend to do when I'm excited. I'll get back to this because it's important.

I was the one who paid the other assistants, who paid everyone who worked in Mr. D's studio, off the books, in cash, no health benefits, no workers' comp, and no one complained because they liked getting cash, earnings they did not have to report. It worked well for them, and for me.

Every week I got the money out of Mr. D's checking account, taking a little extra for myself, first a few hundred, then a few thousand. It was never missed. Like I said, Mr. D had no head for business, and truthfully, he didn't care, because his paintings were selling for hundreds of thousands to well over a million each, so he always had plenty of money. He was secretive about it too, which worked well for me when I took over his finances because I was the only one who really knew what he had. He kept a ridiculous amount in his checking and savings accounts, and after his first divorce, he started keeping a large percentage of his earnings in cash so his wives, past and present, wouldn't know how much he had and try to go after it.

It was around that time I decided I deserved more. And eventually, that I deserved it all. And why not? I was doing everything.

They say knowledge is power, and that's a fact. You have to do your homework, and I always did.

Socrates said, *I know that I know nothing*, and I understood what he was saying: that you need to feel humble as well as confident, so you don't get cocky and screw up.

I discovered Socrates back in junior high when I was diagnosed with ADD or ADHD, maybe both. And it was true, I couldn't sit still and had a really hard time concentrating and was constantly getting in trouble because I couldn't control myself and, the worst part, I felt stupid.

They sent me to the school social worker, who gave me a series of tests. Later, I stole the report where she described me as *severely damaged*, which made me think of ancient crockery that's been broken and glued back together. To be honest, there have been times when I've felt like that, as if I am holding the pieces of my splintered self together through sheer will.

She prescribed medication, which I took for a while, but it killed my appetite, and I couldn't sleep and was jumpier than ever. Plus, I developed an eye tic, and the kids started calling me "Blinky," not that they were ever nice to me. So, I stopped taking the meds, just flushed them down the toilet. I sometimes wonder if the alligators who supposedly live in the city sewers got all jittery and started having eye tics! It's a funny thought, right?

I made the decision to manage the ADD on my own and make it work for me. I started writing out what I would do every day, every hour. Started going to the library too, where I discovered I could read as long as I was interested in a subject. That's when I realized that I was smart, maybe even a genius. Most people thought I was dumb, which was fine because it allowed me to stay under the radar.

The library became my home away home. I not only read but looked at a lot of art books and got really good at duplicating almost anything. I could sit and copy a painting or a drawing for hours. I'd say that helped me the most. A way to channel my energy, which gave me discipline and focus. In the end, it's what helped me conquer my ADD, and why I decided to become an artist.

Socrates wrote that wisdom was a journey of self-discovery, of constantly seeking to expand your understanding, and that's what I did, reading anything I could get my hands on to learn more.

Aristotle, another Greek philosopher, said it's not just about being smart, but about making morally sound decisions. That got me thinking about my plan, how it should have a moral component, and I found one: *Justice!*

I also discovered Friedrich Nietzsche, a German philosopher who really spoke to me and gave me lessons to live by. He basically said that all knowledge comes from your own needs, that everything you do is about your own growth, self-assertion, and dominance. Everyone talks about Nietzsche's nihilism—basically the belief that life is inherently meaningless—and I get that because I have felt like that plenty of times. But Nietzsche saw it as a starting point, something you had to get past and evolve beyond to reach new heights of creativity and control, all of it exemplified by what he called the *Übermensch*! A German word which roughly translates as *beyond man*, like a superman, someone not bound by traditional morality or society's rules, and something I took to heart.

If you have never read *Crime and Punishment*, by Fyodor Dostoevsky, a Russian writer, you really must. Especially the first part about the crime. (You can skip the second part, the punishment part, which is long and preachy.) I think Mr. D believed he was an *Übermensch*, though I'm sure he did not read Nietzsche because I never saw him pick up a book! The only thing he was interested in was making art. That, and women. He was dedicated to both, though he was only loyal to art.

But reading changed me. It taught me how to focus on my plan while remaining open to other possibilities. It made me see *beyond* my goal and to give it *meaning*.

It wasn't just philosophers who influenced me. There were other writers, other books, like *The Talented Mr. Ripley*, in fact all the *Ripley* books. I identified with Tom Ripley, the poor boy, the outsider able to take on other personas to be a convincing impostor! I'd say Tom and I were true brothers under the skin. And like me, he only did what he did out of *necessity*.

And now, I needed to focus my research on the guests. Once they had been selected, I got to know everything there was to know about them. You could say I researched them to death!

Some of the things Mr. D had told me himself, often grumbling about insults and injuries those near and dear had done to him: how Rachel Ronan had stopped writing about his art and Lauren Ziff had practically destroyed his art market, and Echo Ojai had tried to blackmail him. The worst offender was his first wife, Sabrina, who had slept with his brother, Frank. And his son, Nicky, a big disappointment to him, a former junkie and a complete loser, who he had discovered in bed with his last wife, Jasmin Li!

Mr. D held grudges, which I understood. He liked having something on the people in his life that he could use against them, which became things *I* could use against them. I found out more by going through his correspondence, all his letters and emails and texts, and of course I did a lot of research on my own online and at the library, pouring over microfiche, and thank God for Google! Every time I discovered something new, it spurred me on, excited me, and gave me confidence that I was on the right track.

You know they all died, that's no secret. But how they died and *why*, that's the thing.

Alex Bagdasarian was the first, you know that too, and it was part of my plan. But who could have predicted he would have too much to drink and that he would take a bath? But he did! More than luck, I would say. Like it was *supposed* to happen. Like he *wanted* to die. And maybe he did. With all his debts and the bookies coming after him and the way he was stealing from his artists, he deserved to die. I'm sure you agree. Maybe he *should* have killed himself, and who knows, he might have. But I couldn't wait or leave it to chance.

Mr. D suspected Bagdasarian might be cheating him, so I took it upon myself to do some investigating by dating one of Bagdasarian's assistants who I got to know through my work with the gallery, a pretty girl. Don't be surprised, I'm not a bad-looking guy (once I grew the beard that covered my pockmarks). She was an artist like me and hated her job at Bagdasarian's gallery, something she mentioned to me more than once in conversation, assistant to assistant, you know. And I made a note of it. I was always on the lookout for things I could use. I dated her for a few months until I got what I needed in bed. I'm not talking about the sex, which was okay, but what she told me, the fact that she knew Bagdasarian was making under-the-table sales, according to her something that almost everyone in the gallery knew, but didn't dare say if they wanted to keep their jobs. Once I got that information, I ghosted her.

I didn't tell Mr. D what I had learned. It was just, for me, another part of my moral objective.

Mr. D stayed with his art dealers, Bagdasarian and Schwegler, knowing they were sharks, but in the art world you need a shark. Plus, the two gallerists had made him a star in the United States and in Europe, made him a lot of money too. He'd thought about leaving them, mentioned it to me on more than one occasion, but he didn't want to start over again with new art dealers. He rationalized that the devil he knew was better than a new devil he could not predict.

As for the *way* Bagdasarian died, you know that too. In the bath, like a sitting duck. He was old and out of shape and at a disadvantage being naked. He was shocked to see me, to say the least, and became angry and belligerent, but how could he stop me? I held him underwater, watching the little air bubbles come out of his mouth until they stopped. When I thought he was dead, I sat back to catch my breath but a second later he was exploding out of the water like Glenn Close in *Fatal Attraction*, spitting and gasping and lunging at me. *Jesus!* I had to punch him and hold him under again. This time, even when those bubbles stopped and he was motionless, I didn't let him up. I had to be sure he was dead.

Afterward, I remember thinking, *You've done it, killed the first one, and there's no turning back*. But of course, I could have. Not gone back. But I could have stopped. Nothing said I had to keep going, except that killing one of them accomplished nothing. For my plan to work, I had to kill them all.

I didn't think anyone would come looking for Bagdasarian right away. Why would they? There was no reason to think anything was wrong with him and they were a selfish group, only concerned with themselves. Of course they would find him eventually, and I wanted them to, wanted them to get paranoid and start suspecting each other. And knowing what I did about them, the things they had done, I was pretty sure I could count on their bad behavior, and I was right.

I was about to leave the bathroom when I got inspired and thought of a way to make the scene interesting, *artful*. All I had to do was pose him a little, lift his arm out of the water and let it hang over the rim of the tub, enough to ape the painting that had come into my mind, *The Death of Marat* by Jacques-Louis David. It's a famous one about a French revolutionary murdered in his bath. For years I had a print of it on my wall.

After that, I hid and waited, which was harder than I imagined because all sorts of things came into my mind, my childhood, the foster parents, all they had done that was hurtful to me. By the way, it was me who came up with the question: *How did you help me or hurt me?* It was not Mr. D's idea. None of it was. I knew from my research and what he'd told me that they had all hurt him, so I knew the question would get them going and stir up their guilt.

After Bagdasarian, I went on to the next, and again circumstance and opportunity were in my favor. I was moving from one hiding place to another when I saw Rachel Ronan come out of Bagdasarian's room, which was a surprise. She saw me too, but I took advantage of her shock. I got a chloroform-soaked rag over her nose and dragged her back to her room. I was always prepared and I had done my research, knew that in lower doses chloroform would knock you out, and in higher doses it caused cardiac arrest, which is what I was after.

Fun fact: Chloroform is sometimes called "Sudden Sniffer's death." Funny, right?

I should say I had nothing to do with Rachel falling overboard. I still don't know if one of the other guests pushed her (Lauren Ziff? Alex Bagdasarian?) or it was a suicide attempt, and I guess I never will. I only learned about it because I'd made a deal with the captain to report everything, and he did. I knew all about the captain too, his past jobs and the shameful military incident he was hiding. I knew about his first mate too, William, the jailbird. Knowing about them was my insurance, in case I had to use it to put pressure on them for one reason or another or if they discovered anything about me. But neither of those things happened. In the end they performed well. I have no complaints.

As for Rachel, she never knew what hit her, and I was glad about that. I had no reason to make her suffer except for her betrayal of Mr. D and that nasty business with her mother, which some might call fatal neglect, but it was still murder—so easy to hack into hospital records, it's a joke! Rachel knew what she was doing and had to pay for it.

I arranged her on the bed and folded her hands over her chest, all dainty and ladylike, which I thought she would like. She had a vial of Ambien, another stroke of luck. All I did was empty it and put it on the floor so it looked like she had taken all the pills. I wanted them to think it was suicide. For a while. I knew it would not be long before they got suspicious and started accusing each other, which they did.

The rest of the group was downstairs drinking and talking about how awful it was to be trapped on the island, and in the rain. Boo-hoo, right? What a bunch of spoiled brats! The rain was the least of their problems, but for me an unforeseen and helpful coincidence. I was planning to stall the boat from returning, but then the rain and fog did it for me. Sometimes I can (almost) believe there is a force mightier than myself, though I wonder what Nietzsche would have said about that.

The flowers were a last-minute improvisation. I just used what was there, overturning the vase, soaking Rachel's blouse, scattering the flowers on her breast and on the floor. It was an attempt to suggest a painting I had seen years ago in a library book, one from the 1800s that I loved, *Ophelia* by the artist John Everett Millais, part of a group of English painters and poets who were fascinated by early Renaissance Italian art. I read an entire book about them, and that painting stayed with me because it was kind of hot, with something unearthly about it, this beautiful dead girl floating in the water. Don't get me wrong; I'm not some kind of kinky necrophiliac. I'm just a normal guy.

I wasn't sure if anyone would get the connection to the painting because it was so subtle, even though most of them were (supposedly) interested in art. I was glad that Sabrina got it. But it wasn't about them; it was about making the scene more interesting for *me*, something beyond the practical part, that being the elimination of another heir.

I was aware of the exposé Rachel was trying to write, the one that included Lauren Ziff, something I was sure would infuriate Lauren and cause trouble, another reason for having them at the memorial together. I also knew that Rachel was going to inherit money. I knew all of Mr. D's plans—who was getting what and how much—and that money would have changed her life. (If there had been any left for her to inherit.)

Ironic, isn't it? They were all there ready to do anything to get an inheritance that no longer existed because I had taken it! Of course there were the future sales of Mr. D's paintings, which would be significant, but no cash prizes for the heirs!

I was sort of surprised that Mr. D had left Rachel anything, but he had decided to forgive her for the loss of interest in his work and was thankful she had been there at the beginning. I also knew she was down and out and might come sniffing around for the money she had inherited. So, like the others, she had to go.

As for Echo Ojai, I invited her because I knew Mr. D's family, his wives and son, would be shocked to discover she existed, one more rival for Mr. D's money. Like I said, I knew about her attempts to blackmail Mr. D because I had read her letter to him and was pretty certain he would have wanted me to get even on his behalf. Plus, I was sure she would start trouble with the other guests, which she did. I guess you could say she had a hard life, something I can relate to, but to be honest, I just didn't like her.

I also knew she sleepwalked but again it was some sort of divine intervention that I caught her in the act, downstairs in the living room while the rest of them slept. I mean, come on, that's more than good luck! I held the front door open for her and led her right into the lagoon. She was up to her knees before she woke up, looked around, saw the sharks, and started screaming her head off. No pun intended. I saw them coming at her but didn't watch the carnage.

I'm a little squeamish when it comes to violence. But I did hear the screams and some truly awful sounds of jaws snapping and crunching and frantic splashing around. Pretty awful stuff.

Her screams are what woke the others, so I had very little time to make art. I improvised the first thing that came into my mind, John Singleton Copley's painting, *Watson and the Shark*. It was pure coincidence, the cluster of bamboo beside the lagoon. All I did was break one off, turn back, and ram it into one of the sharks. It was then I caught a glimpse of what they had done to Echo. The Copley painting is pretty violent too, one of those "true story" paintings about a guy losing his leg in a shark attack, so I was actually pretty accurate. And I risked my life with that harpoon all in the name of art!

After that, I spent a lot of time in hiding. Which is what I did when they searched the hotel. There were several empty rooms, and I moved among them, sometimes just minutes ahead of the group, which was exciting. When I got away with it, I began to think of myself as invisible, able to move around like a ghost or the angel of death, invincible and untouchable. It was then I also knew that I would get away with it all, the whole plan.

And I had more good luck. Lauren Ziff's twisted ankle and the fact that she and Ian were left behind. You can't say God was not on my side, or fate, or Nietzsche's spirit, and it reinforced my moral imperative: that every one of those people *deserved* to die.

When the group got back from the beach and started drinking, everyone but Nicky—Mr. D's spoiled son—it was more good luck.

As for the electricity going out, it had nothing to do with the lightning. I cut the power because I wanted them to sweat.

Lauren and Ian were dozing. Ian stoned on weed. The room reeked of it. And Lauren had taken pills, Klonopin or tramadol or both, the vials sitting on her bedside table. I dealt with Ian first, getting the bag over his head, which wasn't hard, him being stoned and a weakling.

According to the Greeks, a fit body is just as important as a fit mind, and I have always kept myself in shape. But I had been working out triple time in preparation for the weekend and was in the best physical shape of my life. I could have taken Ian even if he hadn't been so stoned. It's sort of sad really. In a way the poor guy was collateral damage because he never did anything to Mr. D though he did have his own history of crime, which he needed to pay for.

Lauren woke up while I was suffocating Ian and started screaming, but there was no one to hear her. She tried to get away, stumbling around with her bum ankle, which was pretty pathetic to watch. I almost felt bad, but you should have heard the names she called me before I finally shut her up. I don't think she felt much because of the drugs she had taken, which was good. I am not a sadistic monster out to make anyone suffer, though she was, in fact, one of the biggest "hurters" among them, having almost destroyed Mr. D's auction market and practically ruining his career. And let's not forget the hundreds of thousands of innocent people who were killed by Ziff Pharmaceuticals by using a drug she'd argued in favor of despite knowing its addictive nature. I kind of did her a favor because it's likely she would have ended up in prison where no doubt she'd have taken her own life (probably with opioids!).

The idea for the Magritte painting, *The Lovers*—one of my all-time favorite works of art—came after they were dead. And it was easy. I just pushed their bodies together and their heads close as if they were kissing. It was funny considering how they pretty much hated each other. But you know, Lauren might have liked becoming a character in a famous painting, being an art collector and all, even if she bought art for the wrong reasons, status and resale value.

I left her pills prominently displayed right there on her bedside table, so they couldn't be missed, and did the same with Ian's weed. I figured most of the group would have a hard time resisting, and they did not let me down. They never did. The fact of them all being stoned and drinking and popping pills made it a lot easier for me too. You see, these are the kind of things you can't plan. You just have to be aware of the opportunities that come your way and make the most of them.

It was a little shocking that Mr. D's ex, Sabrina, and his has-been actor brother, were sleeping together *again*, considering their infidelity had caused her divorce and his wife's probable suicide, but clearly, they didn't care. They were selfish people who betrayed Mr. D and way up there in the *hurt him* category.

I know for a fact that Mr. D had never forgiven his brother for sleeping with his wife. *Who would?* And there he was, reigniting the affair at Mr. D's memorial of all places! That shows you the kind of person Frank was. I was disgusted by them both, though it was exactly what I'd hoped would happen, and again, it worked in my favor.

They were sleeping like the dead when I broke into their room. Frank had been smoking weed and drinking heavily, not a good idea for a guy with a bad heart, but good for me. He was one of those really indulgent people, unable to resist his vices. If he had read the Greeks or Nietzsche, rather than his silly Hollywood scripts, he'd have been a lot better off.

As for Sabrina, I had spiked her coconut water and the port with some of Lauren's pills plus a few hemlock seeds. I couldn't resist the irony of her being poisoned by a deadly plant, and hemlock was growing everywhere on the island. She'd even pointed it out herself! All I did was raise her arm, already stiff from the hemlock and maybe the onset of rigor mortis and arrange her pose with the sheets just so to replicate another great Jacques-Louis David painting, *The Death of Socrates*. I hated to repeat myself with the same artist but it's a really great painting, and even more ironic because it depicts Socrates's final moments after being sentenced to death and he is drinking poison hemlock! You don't get that many chances to have art imitate life so perfectly! I left a sprig of hemlock on her chest as a hint, but I think Frank must have knocked it off without even noticing.

I want to be clear that Sabrina was unconscious and felt no pain (that I know of). I'm not a monster; I was simply doing my job.

I'd only met her once or twice, at the studio, though she never noticed me, and I resented the fact that Mr. D had left her money, maybe out of guilt or the fact that she (supposedly) cared about him when he got sick. I knew she was the type who would come looking for her money once he was dead, being hard up and mercenary, so I couldn't take any chances. In the end, I did her a favor because her death made her famous. Those poisonous plant paintings of hers became sought after, though she wasn't around to benefit from the success. A shame.

Frank slept through it all. Amazing. I figured I would take care of him later, or that Nicky might do it for me, believing Frank had killed his mother, and he almost did. But in the end, no one had to kill Frank. He was pretty much killing himself. Though it's true I helped by taking his pills away. Again, I had done my research and knew how vital Plavix was to prevent his stents from giving him a second heart attack. Though I'm guessing he would have eventually had one all by himself, the way he was carrying on with booze and weed, even smoking. I mean, everyone knows cigarettes will kill you!

In the same way Sabrina's artwork took off, Frank's death sparked a renewed interest in his films. Netflix and Hulu both had Frank D'Arcangelo retrospectives and a whole new generation started streaming his movies. It's funny how life works, isn't it? I don't know if he would have made any residuals from the streaming, but I'm sure he would have been happy to get the attention.

For me, it was always about the plan, so I was annoyed when Jasmin made a run for it, something I didn't expect, and I sure as hell did not need an extra trek down that godforsaken path. But I had to stop her.

She would have been furious to know that Mr. D had *not* left her any money. From what he'd said about her, I'm pretty sure he'd grown to detest her and regretted marrying her in the first place. But under New York State law she was entitled to half of whatever money existed and half of Mr. D's future art sales. If she had lived, you can be sure she would have pursued the missing money, probably even hired a private detective, and I couldn't have that. I had to cover my crime, my embezzling. But I have to be honest and admit that at a certain point the game itself took over, almost overwhelmed my motives because I had started to enjoy it! Some might call that madness. I call it *creativity!*

Jasmin and I had met before the weekend, at the studio several times and when I delivered things to the lavish Tribeca loft where she and Mr. D lived, and again, at the end when he was sick, but she barely acknowledged me and always treated me like the help. In her eyes, I wasn't important enough to remember, so I made a point of letting her get a good look at me before I pushed her face into the mud and held it there. Too bad there was no way to make anything artful out of that, but I had to act fast. I knew Nicky, in his newly acquired heroic role, would come after her and I didn't want him to catch me in the act because I had other plans for him, the same way I had planned everything.

Like the memorial, which was planned before Mr. D was dead. I did it all, rented the hotel, the yacht, found the captain, got my own small boat, and paid for it all through Mr. D's accounts. I wanted it to look like *he* had done it, knowing he was going to die. He had been sick the year before though he'd made a full recovery and was doing fine. It was unfortunate that the credit card company called Mr. D about the yacht because it was so expensive, which got him checking into other bills, then looking at his bank accounts, something he had never done before. It's ironic that he got sick again, just then. You just never know, do you?

I remember when I gave him the last studio logs—of course I was still keeping them, it was my job, and I wanted the studio to run smoothly until the end—but he was too sick to look at them. So, I just put the same kind of rubber band around them and dumped them into a file cabinet.

When he got sick, naturally I was the one who took care of him, bathed him and prepared his meals, though he wasn't eating by the end. It was sad, and a puzzle to the doctors who couldn't figure it out. At first, they thought it was just a bad flu, maybe even a new strain of COVID-19, which was a good enough reason to keep everyone away, for a while. By the time his wife and son and ex came to see him—all just protecting their interests, I am sure—it was too late.

Jasmin was the only one who noticed the discoloration of his fingernails, which she attributed to him painting, though he hadn't been doing any for months. They were separated by then, so she wasn't around that much. Those white spots on his nails were the only sign of thallium poisoning, which (I've heard) comes in crystals that can be mixed into food and drinks because it's colorless, tasteless, and odorless and is often confused with viral encephalitis leading to heart failure, which was the official diagnosis of Mr. D's death.

There was no autopsy, and he was cremated right away, something he wanted and I carried out. I had a copy of the paper he signed during those last terrible days saying it was his wish, though I'm not sure he knew what he was signing, like so many other papers I had him sign during that awful time.

I wrote the evite from his email account before he died, as if he had written it. I even showed it to him for his approval, though by then he was in a coma. Which was sad because I would have liked him to know what was being planned in his honor. Later, when I sent it out, I personalized each of the guest's evites but made them all the same offer, one they could not refuse: *Be at the memorial or forfeit your inheritance*. I knew they would all come to protect that.

I have to say, Mr. D's death hit me hard. Even harder than I had imagined. He was the father I never really had, my art father and spiritual father, the father who taught me through example how to be demanding and ruthless, how to always put my own feelings first, no matter who got hurt. I'm sure he would have understood what I did, even to him. Like all fathers and sons, the son eventually has to surpass the father or he can't grow, can't become *himself*. It was the hardest thing I ever did, but I had to get rid of him—the person I loved most in the world—to become myself. It's like Oedipus in that ancient Greek play, where the oracle tells him he is destined to kill his father.

When it came down to the last two, Nicky and Schwegler, which is what I had planned, I just let them battle it out on their own. I hoped they would kill each other, but if not, I didn't care because I knew that whoever won the battle would be the last man standing and, therefore, held responsible for the other murders. I sort of hoped it would be Nicky because I liked the idea of him finally being held responsible for *something*.

He was such an entitled little brat, ungrateful for all he had gotten for no other reason than his privilege and good looks. And don't forget, he was a murderer, his teenage girlfriend for one, and probably others. Mr. D told me all about it, how his son had come to him and told him what he'd done, all distraught, but mostly scared of being caught. Mr. D lawyered up just in case, though nothing ever happened. Nicky got away with it. He always got away with everything. But not this time. Ultimately, life is a kind of balance sheet, and Nicky needed to pay up.

In the end, it turned out better that Schwegler won the fight because Nicky would have been a more sympathetic witness. I'm sure all the women and half the men on the jury would have fallen in love with him, so he could have been exonerated and gone free and the case would have remained open and be pursued, and I needed it to be closed. For good.

The fact is, Mr. D had left Nicky a lot of money, which was irritating because unlike me, he was a terrible son, and he didn't deserve it. I'm sure Nicky would have pursued his inheritance, where it had gone and what happened to it, if he had lived. So, he had to die.

You might say I had it all figured out, all sewn up, had covered my tracks perfectly. And I had. But the fact is, most criminals get caught, no matter how good they are, and I couldn't take that chance. I didn't want anyone coming after me. Plus, there were those D'Arcangelo paintings I had made during the last months of his life, the ones I had in storage and planned to auction in a couple of years. So, I had to be sure there was no one around who might recognize a forged D'Arcangelo, like his art dealers or Sabrina Fleming, not only his ex-wife but an artist, or even his son. After that conversation on the island where he accused me of painting his father's paintings and suggesting I might make copies to sell, I knew for sure he had to go. They all did.

I left before Nicky and Schwegler fought it out. Like I said, I didn't care who won. My work was done, and it was time to go. I retrieved the speedboat from the small cove where I'd hidden it from the beginning, took off, and never looked back.

PART V

2 YEARS LATER

The archivist hired for the recently formed Victor D'Arcangelo trust was a graduate of New York University's prestigious Institute of Fine Arts, a young woman who had written her PhD thesis on the artist and had devoted several years of research to his life and work. She had interviewed D'Arcangelo twice in what turned out to be the last year of his life and though she found him smart, attractive, and extremely knowledgeable about painting, she sensed something predatory below his suave and cultured appearance and was careful to keep a professional distance.

As there had been no immediate or even extended family members to spearhead the project, it had taken the estate almost two years to create the trust. Adding to the problem was the demise of the Bagdasarian Gallery, which had represented the artist, and the fact that many of their files were lost or missing, which made the archivist's work difficult. This was only her third week on the job, but it was the kind of quiet, studious work that she loved, and she felt as if she were doing something important for the future of art and art history.

This morning, she had arrived at Victor D'Arcangelo's former studio at nine sharp, as she had for the past three weeks, and had already been at her desk for an hour when she took her usual break: a walk through the empty studio, something she did every day as a kind of ritual.

As she strolled through the four-thousand-square-foot Tribeca loft, now little more than a storage facility, late winter sunlight streamed in from a wall of floor-to-ceiling windows. Plastic-wrapped paintings were stacked against the other walls or in racks, many waiting to be labeled.

She stopped to admire Victor D'Arcangelo's paint table tucked into a corner, a somewhat petrified relic of the artist's glory days, its open bottles of mineral spirits and linseed oil calcified, the large glass palette clotted with mounds of dried oil paint, brushes in coffee cans where the turpentine had evaporated, the bristles gone stiff and brittle. The archivist had been surprised that D'Arcangelo's studio assistants had not cleaned it up or thrown it out, though she was glad. She was currently looking for a museum that might want to acquire it as an artifact, though she secretly hoped none would as she intended to take it home and keep it herself.

Other than the occasional hiss and clang from the old radiators, the studio was quiet and still, and gave off a feeling of time stopped.

After the walk, the archivist returned to her desk and took stock of the various loan forms and bills of sale that she had yet to go through, along with the small notepads she had found only yesterday at the bottom of a file cabinet. From a cursory look, they appeared to be a studio assistant's log, and she hoped they might contain information about several missing artworks and help her to locate them, not only for the archive, but for the monograph she was writing and planning to publish, the first catalogue raisonné with an annotated list of every known artwork made by Victor D'Arcangelo.

More interested in going through the studio logs, she laid the loan forms and bills of sale aside for another day.

The small pads were in groups of four, fastened with a rubber band, the handwriting in each small and obsessively neat. It took her almost an hour to get through one pad, which she realized from the dates and daily entries added up to three months. The information was mechanical but detailed, giving her a clear idea of the day-to-day workings of the studio. Like any good researcher, she was pleased to have it, a picture of the once busy artist's studio taking shape in her mind. She underlined anything related to artworks that had traveled so she could follow up and make sure they had been returned, also noting any art collectors whose names were unfamiliar to her and the artworks they owned.

When she had gone through the first three pads, she took another break, this time to the bathroom, where she splashed her face with cold water, her eyes stinging from squinting at the small writing. Then, she ordered a chopped salad, which she ate at her desk and began to read the fourth pad. By the time she had finished the last pad in the second set of four, the winter sun had faded, the windows almost dark.

Though tired, she tugged the rubber band off another group of pads and spread them across her desk like a deck of cards, noticing right away that one was bulkier than the others. It turned out to be two pads, one stuck inside the other, making it a group of five pads, not four. The notations in this extra pad had seemingly nothing to do with the running of the studio and made little sense to her but she kept reading, fascinated by what appeared to be some sort of plan, with notes like, *Try this… Try that… If that doesn't work think about…* There was a page listing high-end yacht rental agencies and their fees—$30,000 to $40,000 for a weekend—which made her sit up and take notice. Another page with information about first-class airline tickets from locations like New York and Los Angeles to Fort Lauderdale, followed by several names of limousine and town car rentals. Even more puzzling were the quotes from Socrates and Aristotle and more from Nietzsche. She wondered if perhaps she had stumbled upon some student's coursework notepad. She was baffled.

But when she compared this pad to the others, the handwriting was identical. Only the content was different, this one clearly a more personal journal. She still wasn't sure about what but kept reading, interested in finding out.

She was surprised by a page that itemized various poisons—arsenic, strychnine, cyanide, rat poison (thallium)—the last one circled with a note beside it that said, *Not available in the United States*, along with a company name and an email in England. It gave her an odd, somewhat creepy feeling in the pit of her stomach. And when she flipped a page and found the list of names—Alex Bagdasarian, Sabrina Fleming, Jasmin Li, Nicky D'Arcangelo, Frank D'Arcangelo, Rachel Ronan, Lauren Ziff, Hans Schwegler, Echo Ojai—she stopped short, then read them again.

She immediately recognized Alex Bagdasarian as Victor D'Arcangelo's New York gallerist and Hans Schwegler as his European counterpart, and Jasmin Li as the woman married to the artist at the time of his death. The name Rachel Ronan was familiar, and it took her only a moment to remember why—the former *New York Times* art critic who had championed Victor D'Arcangelo's early work, someone the archivist knew of and had quoted in her thesis.

For several minutes she studied the list as if it were a kind of Rosetta stone. The names, she thought, must have some deeper meaning. She made a note of the unfamiliar ones: Lauren Ziff and Echo Ojai. Only a moment before the first name came to her without looking it up—one of Victor D'Arcangelo's art collectors. Then she googled Echo Ojai. Within seconds her screen was filled with links to various articles, the first of which identified Echo Ojai as Victor D'Arcangelo's illegitimate daughter with another link to her death, which she clicked on, an alarm bell already beginning to sound in her subconscious.

Nine People Dead on Tropical Isle

Her eyes flicked between the article and the list of names in the notepad as reality hit her so hard she rocked back in her seat and gasped, "*Oh my God.*"

It was not necessary to google the rest of the names or read any further to know these were the people who had died at Victor D'Arcangelo's memorial. The trial might have been almost three years ago, but it was something she would never forget, a story she had followed with horror and a personal investment—*her* artist, his family and business associates all murdered by one man, *Hans Schwegler*.

The archivist did not need to look back at the list to remember that his name was on it, but she did.

Then she googled a few more articles, needing to see the proof in black and white, and there were many, all with the same names, all of them the people murdered on the island.

Fingers shaking, she went back to the pad and riffled through it, stopping at the last page where she noted the date followed by an initial, *M.* Then she checked the studio logs, each of the pads dated at the end and with the same initial.

A moment to let it wash over, then she went into her own email, typing in a search for Victor D'Arcangelo. There were dozens of messages, all going back several years, the earliest ones to set up her studio visits, then ones with follow-up questions she'd had for the artist.

She went through the emails, her eyes skimming them for a name.

And there it was: MY ASSISTANT MARCUS WILL TAKE CARE OF THAT. HE TAKES CARE OF EVERYTHING.

My assistant Marcus.

M.

The archivist closed her eyes and thought back. She remembered meeting him at Victor D'Arcangelo's studio, a young man in his early thirties, his hair in a careless topknot, with a scraggly beard that didn't quite hide some old pockmarks, but he was nice-looking, even handsome. She recalled how he had greeted her at the door and showed her into the studio and had introduced himself, his soft voice like a purr. He had brought her a sparkling water during the interview and was courteous and shy, often looking down or away, though he'd hovered nearby throughout the interview, at Victor's beck and call.

And she remembered something else, that when he showed her out and she thanked him, he smiled and she noticed his ice-blue eyes, and the way they seemed to burrow into her had made her feel so uncomfortable that she had to look away.

Fighting a chill, she went back to her laptop, skimming articles, not sure what she was looking for until she found it, a name that appeared in three separate pieces.

> "The jury was unanimous, but something about it didn't feel right. I was never convinced," said Detective David J. Cross of the Miami-Dade Police Department, a career officer with a long list of citations. Detective Cross, who heads up the Criminal Investigation Division, followed the case closely, had even attended the execution, something he lobbied against. "I just didn't see the evidence," he said.

The archivist wrote the detective's name on a piece of paper, the pen shaking in her hand. A moment to google the Miami-Dade Police Department, noting there were more than a dozen stations. Cell phone out, she decided to go with the first on the list, surprised when an actual person answered.

"City of Miami PD," the woman said.

The archivist cleared her throat. "Is there a way to reach Detective David J. Cross?"

"Is this a personal call?"

"No," she said, taking a breath. "I'm calling with information."

"About?" Behind the operator's terse voice the phone beeped, an indication that the call was being taped.

"It's about the Paradise Lost Massacre."

READING GROUP GUIDE

1. From failing art galleries to dormant acting careers, each guest has their own reasons for needing D'Arcangelo's inheritance. Who do you think needs it most and why?

2. European art dealer Hans Schwegler says he is often compared to Goldfinger from the James Bond movies. If you were casting a movie, who would you choose to play these characters and why?

3. All the guests have their own hidden agendas. Who among them do you find the shrewdest and most cunning? Who appears to be the most innocent or a victim of circumstance?

4. Does anyone raise more red flags than the others?

5. Throughout the book, the way the characters are related is revealed in bits and pieces. Were there any connections you guessed at? Some that shocked you completely? Discuss.

6. As tragedies occur, the guests try to make sense of what's happening with their own theories. What are some of the different ways they each respond? How do you think you would react if you were on the island?

7. Artwork, and the realities of the art world, permeate the storyline. Did you learn anything new about the art world that you did not know before reading?

8. As the book progresses, we get different glimpses into each character's backgrounds and their own secrets. Did learning more about them change your perspective on any of them? Whose story surprised you the most?

9. Do you think the inheritance is the only motivation at play here, or might there be something else? Share some possible other motives.

10. Several artworks are mentioned or referenced in the book. Share your own favorite painting, sculpture, or work of art.

11. What about the story surprised you the most? Did you have a favorite twist? Discuss.

A CONVERSATION WITH THE AUTHOR

This novel includes so many different perspectives and character motivations. What inspired you to format it this way? How did you balance everyone's viewpoints?

That's what made writing this book fun and difficult: keeping track of the characters! I had a chart with each character's name and vital statistics pinned to the wall in front of me, but the more I wrote, the more I got to know them until each character stood out as a clear individual in my mind. I was inspired by classic whodunits where there are multiple characters, each with a motive or something to hide. As for point of view, the first three-quarters of the book is written in close third-person, a way to make it seem as if you are seeing it through each character's POV, but it's really an omniscient voice that reveals each character, what they see, hear, and say.

Artwork, and the ins and outs of the art world, are an underlying thread in your novels. Is there something in particular that fascinates you about the art world? What do you think art can tell us about human behavior?

I was a serious artist for half my life and know the contemporary art world well. It's a place where people collect and compete for unique objects and spend absurd amounts of money to do so. A world where everyone is competing—artists, gallerists, collectors—which intensifies jealousies and backstabbing, so it's a great setting for crime writing.

On the other hand, being an artist is a wonderful thing. Often a difficult life choice with little reward other than making the work, but that's what it's about and why people choose to do it. Art is special because it's one person, the artist, making objects that reflect a unique vision, and that's why it's valued.

Looking at art gives us insight into the artist and tells us about ourselves because each of us interprets the artwork through our own eyes: The viewer completes the artwork. I often tell people if you simply stand in front of a painting, it will slowly reveal itself and you will see what *you* bring to it.

This novel marks a new direction from your previous novels. Was there anything new or exciting about drafting this story? Did your writing process change at all?

It's true that this is different from most of my previous novels, but every book is new and exciting and comes with its own set of challenges. My writing is always my writing, but for *Ten Perfect Guests*, it was necessary that I know the entire story—the setup, the framework, the ending—all beforehand. I had dozens of pages of plot notes and an outline that I constantly amended before I began the actual writing, which is something I never do. In some ways, it made the book easier to write, but having ten characters and trying to make the elaborate plot appear effortless was difficult. But it was the challenge I had set for myself, and I learned a lot by writing it.

What is it like to create characters who are at times unlikeable, even to, and sometimes especially to, each other?

I see this differently. To me, the characters are human and, like all humans, flawed. Some have done something truly awful, but what separates them is if they committed the act accidentally or intentionally. Every one of these characters has something in their backstory that deeply affected who they became and what they did. I have empathy for all of my characters, good and bad (and the "bad" ones are much more fun to write). I love creating them and seeing how they conduct themselves in the world and, in this case, under extreme conditions. How peoples' strengths or insecurities make them act is always fascinating to me.

You yourself are an artist, and you paint and create your own artwork. If you were to paint one piece of art to depict this story, what do you think the piece might look like? Are there certain media you would use?

I would make my own version of Leonardo da Vinci's *The Last Supper*, all the characters at one long table, eating and drinking and casting suspicious looks at one another. And I'd use oil paint because it's the most pliable medium. The illustrations I made for the book are painted in gouache, which is extremely difficult because it dries in seconds and you can't manipulate it. It was a challenge, like the complex plot, but I like setting up challenges for myself. The illustrations separate and introduce the five sections of the novel, all framed with the same design. I wanted them to be reminiscent of classic illustrated manuscripts because the book deals with classic crime fiction.

Since you do both art and writing, which do you like better?

I love them both. Making a drawing or painting is physical and immediate. You can see the whole thing as you make it and react to it, so it's more direct. Writing is slow and internal. It's impossible to see the whole story or book at once. And it's not at all physical. But what I love about writing is inhabiting the world, getting lost and living inside it, creating the characters and setting and dialogue. In writing, you have to be completely *in* it, with no distractions. When you draw or paint, your mind is free to wander, to listen to a book or music while you work, which I cannot do when I write. It's what I missed most about writing: music!

ACKNOWLEDGMENTS

My thanks, as always, to the following people for their help and guidance:

Shana Drehs, whose smart, insightful, and sensitive editing brought this book to a higher level and made it so much better. I am deeply appreciative.

Jane von Mehren, my extraordinary agent, who not only sells books but is my first reader, and indispensable. I could not do this without her.

More thanks to the terrific team at Aevitas Creative Management: Todd Shuster, Erin Files, Mags Chmielarczyk, Allison Warren, and Kayla Grogan.

At Sourcebooks, Cristina Arreola, Aubrey Clemans, Molly Waxman, and the rest of the team, all of whom obviously take their cue of excellence from the top, the amazing Dominique Raccah.

My generous friends who lent their beautiful homes so I could escape and write parts of this book in seclusion: Judd Tully, Rea David, Susan Crile, Jane Rivkin, Dave Cross, and Margo Alexander.

Ben Bunch for his continued technical support and friendship.

Dr. Lauren Rosenberg, cardiologist, for her expertise in physical matters of the heart, and Dr. Daniel Silvershein for all the rest. But any and all medical misinterpretations or mistakes are mine.

To the writers who, over the years, have supplied me with wonderful blurbs. I can't begin to say how much I appreciate your kind words.

Douglas Lyle Thompson for his help with all things photographic and more. And to the rest of my family, Doria Santlofer and Nico Joy Thompson, who give my life meaning.

With more thanks and a sly nod to Agatha Christie.

My heartfelt thanks and appreciation to the booksellers and critics who have supported my work for years. And to the readers. Where would I be without you?

ABOUT THE AUTHOR

© Douglas Lyle Thompson

Jonathan Santlofer is an artist and author of seven novels, including the national bestsellers *The Lost Van Gogh* and *The Last Mona Lisa*, the Nero Award–winning *Anatomy of Fear*, and the highly acclaimed memoir *The Widower's Notebook*, a featured segment on *Fresh Air with Terry Gross*. He is the editor of several anthologies, including the *New York Times* notable book *It Occurs to Me That I Am America* and the bestselling serial novel *Inherit the Dead*. His short stories have appeared in *The Strand*, *Ellery Queen*, and numerous story collections. As an artist, Santlofer's artwork is in such collections as the Metropolitan Museum of Art, Art Institute of Chicago, and Tokyo's Institute of Contemporary Art. He is the recipient of two National Endowment for Arts grants, has been a Visiting Artist at the American Academy in Rome, the Vermont Studio Center, and serves on the board of Yaddo, the oldest arts community in the U.S. He lives in NYC, where he is at work on a new novel.

Interior artwork created by the author, Jonathan Santlofer.